**Two brand-new stories in every volume...
twice a month!**

Duets Vol. #33

Featured authors are Liz Ireland, who creates
"sassy characters, snappy dialogue and
rip-roaring adventures..." says *Romantic Times*,
and talented new author and
Golden Heart finalist, Jane Sullivan.

Duets Vol. #34

Popular writer Tina Wainscott "is back and in a big
way," says *Romantic Times*, making her Duets debut.
Sharing the spotlight is Barbara Daly,
well-known for her wonderfully wacky tales.

Be sure to pick up both Duets volumes today!

The Wrong Mr. Right

"I have the oddest urge to kiss you."

Marisa's heart jumped. "Let's not go there," she said. "I'm not your type. And you're not mine, either."

"Very true," Barrie conceded.

"And...I wouldn't kiss you back," she continued.

"You sure about that?" Barrie asked.

"Very. Well, mostly." Marisa swallowed hard. Her stomach was quivering, her hands were trembling. This was not good.

Suddenly, his lips were on hers, and she felt giddy and flushed, all at the same time. She wasn't responding, was she? Her eyes weren't closed—it had just become dark all of a sudden. And her mouth wasn't moving in sync with his, right? That was just the earth shifting.

The earth shifting? Marisa opened her eyes. How had her arms gotten around Barrie's neck? "Did we just have an earthquake?"

For more, turn to page 9

Never Say Never!

"Zeke?"

Zeke closed his eyes and held his breath. Then he realized he wanted to feign sleep, not death. Tish was staring at him. He could feel it. With a disgusting show of snorts and honks, he turned over on his side, away from her.

Next thing he knew, he felt the bed sag as she sat down beside him. "Good, you're awake," she said. "Zeke, I've been thinking about you."

He opened one eye, then the other. "Wha-what?" he said drowsily.

"About why you're afraid of women."

That was too much. He rolled over. "I am not afraid of women." He was just afraid of her. He loved women. In their place.

And their place was not in his bed uninvited with their curly blond hair flying all around their faces, their blue eyes gleaming in the darkness and wearing...

Oh, my God, what is she wearing?

For more, turn to page 197

HARLEQUIN DUETS

ISBN 0-373-44100-2

THE WRONG MR. RIGHT
Copyright © 2000 by Tina Wainscott

NEVER SAY NEVER!
Copyright © 2000 by Barbara Daly

This edition published by arrangement with Harlequin Books S.A.

® and TM are trademarks of the publisher. Trademarks indicated with ® are registered in the United States Patent and Trademark Office, the Canadian Trade Marks Office and in other countries.

Visit us at www.eHarlequin.com

Printed in U.S.A.

The Wrong
Mr. Right

TINA WAINSCOTT

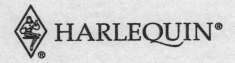

HARLEQUIN®

TORONTO • NEW YORK • LONDON
AMSTERDAM • PARIS • SYDNEY • HAMBURG
STOCKHOLM • ATHENS • TOKYO • MILAN • MADRID
PRAGUE • WARSAW • BUDAPEST • AUCKLAND

Dear Reader,

Have you ever wanted something so badly, only to find out you didn't want it at all? How about the other way around? We all have certain ideals we want to live up to, especially where family is concerned. We want to make them proud of our accomplishments. But sometimes their dreams and ours don't coincide. That's the problem my heroine, Marisa, faces in my first book for Duets. What she wants out of life would make most parents proud: a college education and a career. But when you come from a family that believes finding true love and fulfilling old family traditions should come first—it, um, gets a little complicated.

When I finished this book, I wanted to be a part of this close, wacky family. (Don't get me wrong—I'm very happy with my slightly-more-normal version!) But I had so much fun hanging out with the Cerinis, and watching my tall Scottish hero, Barrie, try to figure them out, I didn't want to leave. I hope you feel the same.

Because it could happen to you...

Best Wishes!

Tina Wainscott

To my cousin Barrie James, in Scotland.
Here's wishing you a happy ending.

Special thanks to:

My long-time friend, Michael (Miguel) Lawton
for all his help on researching Southern California.

My Romex friends on Genie for their help:
Hannah Rowen, Karen Harbaugh, Sharyn Cerniglia
and Sonia.

John Sciarrino of Giovanni Photography,
whose help was invaluable
(though I take full credit for any mistakes).

1

"YOU KNOW WHAT they say: Sixth time's a charm. Or you can break Mama's heart, and become the family failure."

Marisa Cerini rolled her eyes at her sister, Gina, who was chopping garlic at the kitchen table. "Your help I don't need."

She shrugged. "Just trying to be encouraging."

Mama crushed Marisa in a bear hug that was so fierce, Marisa barely had the strength to return it. "You're gonna meet him this year, I can feel it."

Poor Mama, she said that every year. For five years Marisa had let her down, along with the rest of the family. Unfortunately, that was nothing new. That was the problem with growing up in a family of Italian traditionalists when you wanted a career. And living in the most romantic town in America when being romantic didn't come naturally.

"You're gonna make us proud." Mama plucked a square of cooking chocolate from a dish on the counter. "I think I'm gonna cry."

Marisa leaned against the wooden counter that bore the scars of three generations of cooking. "Don't cry, Mama. You'll get us all bawling."

"Can you fault me for crying on such a momentous occasion?" Mama said with her usual dramatic inflection, placing a hand to her bosom.

"Mama, you cry when Nonna takes her lasagna out of the oven."

"Nonna's lasagna *is* a beautiful thing." Gina twirled a strand of her long, dark hair. "Remember that time Nonna nodded off, and the lasagna came out a smoking black brick, and we all cried?"

"Even Pop," Marisa agreed.

"Crying easy is a family trait. There's no shame in it." Mama pushed back her thick, salt-and-pepper hair and started fussing with the hem on Marisa's dress.

Nonna, her precious grandmama, was a spry woman with waist-length gray hair, which she always wore coiled on her head. The weight of it tilted her like the Leaning Tower of Pisa. "You will finally take your place among the women in our family, meeting your husband in the town square during the festival. Wine, full moon and *amore*." She clasped her hands in front of her. "So sweet, so sweet."

The tradition. It had started generations ago in Cortina, Italy, when a girl in Mama's family had met her true love at the original Vino and Amore Festival. And so it went that every woman in the family met her true love at the festival when she was twenty. It continued when the family moved to the small Southern California town of Cortina, founded by immigrants from Cortina. The tradition was as much a part of their lives as Christmas was to the rest of the world. At the age of twenty, Marisa, too, had gone through the ceremony of donning the dress and taking that momentous step.

Only she'd stumbled. Maybe she hadn't been looking all that hard the first time. After all, she'd had other things on her mind besides romance, though she would never admit it. She had been taking community-college courses on the sly and getting her business degree. The third time she'd been kind of looking for him, but he'd obviously slipped by. The fifth year she'd looked a little harder, but no luck. It hadn't helped that Little-Miss-Perfect Gina had met her true love the first time out and was now pregnant. A high chair already sat in the kitchen, and enough baby toys were piled in a bin in the family room to last the kid into high school.

Nor did it help that the Cerini family newsletter from Italy was sitting on the table open to the wedding and baby announcements...and engagement notices from the women who had met their true loves at the most recent festival over there. The parchment newsletter would have a place of honor on the refrigerator until the next one arrived. Similarly, the Cerinis in America sent a newsletter every season to Italy. Marisa's name hadn't appeared in the "good news" section since her birth.

Nonna made last-minute adjustments to Marisa's lace collar. "Salvatore and I always say tradition has gone the way of the past. Young people don't go to church, and they blend our Italian blood by marrying outside our culture. You remember the Pontinis' shame when their daughter married an Irish man."

Oh, brother, here it comes, Mirasa thought as Gina got her pious look. "I did good, huh, Nonna? Nice Italian husband, baby on the way."

Nonna pressed a work-worn finger to her mouth, then to Gina's belly. "Salvatore and I are so proud, so proud."

Marisa could hardly swallow the lump in her throat. Now that she had completed her degree, she was ready to fit back into the "traditional" role and try to find a husband. She wasn't the most romantic woman in the world, but she truly wanted to try. She just wanted to squeeze in a career too, without her family noticing.

When Cousin Giorgio announced he was retiring from managing the sales department of the family's cookie company, Marisa was ready. She'd asked her father to consider her for the position while pretending it wasn't monumentally important. If the family thought that being Pop's secretary was supposed to fulfill her, she'd failed again. Pop had tapped her cheek and said he'd think about it.

Sure he would.

Nonna kissed Marisa on the nose. "You will make us proud, too. Just make sure he's not too big." She wagged her gnarled finger. "Too big is no good."

Marisa's mouth dropped open. *"What?"*

Nonna had already walked over to the sewing basket, a bin large enough to house a small family. Mama said, "She didn't mean too big...like that."

Good grief, she hoped not. Discussing male anatomy with your *nonna* was as weird as...well, as the way Nonna talked regularly to her husband, who had died five years ago.

Marisa held up her shoulder-length dark hair. "Should I wear my hair up or down?"

All three women answered simultaneously.

"Up."

"Down."

"Up."

She looked at her reflection in the full-length mirror, pursed her lips, then released her hair. "Down. Definitely." She tilted her head. "Maybe."

"What's this?" Mama said, peering at her face. "You plucking eyebrows? Cerini women don't pluck."

But everybody else does! she wanted to yell. "Only a few strays."

"Your eyebrows are beautiful the way they are. Natural beauty, like your *nonna*." Nonna had skin the envy of most of the women in town, even much younger ones.

Marisa sighed and shifted in the lacy dress. If only she could wear something less...frilly. But frilly was romantic, and she was romantic, darn it. But why did the traditional dress have to be white? Could her hips *look* any bigger? She eyed the burgundy and gold drapes in the living room. Something like that would camouflage. "What if I don't meet him again this year?"

Nonna raised her hand, tips of her fingers pressed together. "It is *destino!* My granddaughter will not let her family down, this I know."

"I didn't," Gina said.

"I know," Marisa muttered.

"It wasn't easy, knowing the mantle of tradition was on my shoulders, especially since you hadn't come through."

"*I know.*"

"You'll do fine. He only needs to be Italian, single and heterosexual." Nonna waved aside Marisa's concern. "Three thousand people from all over the country are coming to the festival. He will be there somewhere."

Gina said, "Just don't do that thing you do when you get nervous."

"What thing?"

"Oh, I shouldn't have mentioned it."

Marisa threw up her hands. "Well, you've already started, so you can't back out now."

Gina rubbed her humongous belly. "All right, your mouth hangs open and you stop talking."

She knew about the not-talking part. That was an annoying habit, too many things crowding into her head at once. "My mouth doesn't hang open!" All three women nodded. "My mouth hangs open? Why didn't you tell me this before?"

"Like when you were talking to Nino at the dry cleaners last week. He said you looked cute, and you did the zombie thing." Naturally, Gina had to demonstrate.

Marisa glanced out the window. The skies were starting to look like wads of cookie dough with big moldy spots. They hung so low, the mountains to the east were obliterated. "What if it rains? What if the airline lost his luggage or he's delayed until after sunset? What if—"

"Stop worrying!" Mama said. "You think all the women in our family worried about delayed planes and luggage?"

"They didn't have planes back then."

"Details!"

Marisa took another look in the mirror. "Maybe I should wear my hair up."

"Up, down, up, down. You're gonna drive your husband-to-be crazy with all your indecision." Mama spritzed her with rose water. "Go find your *amore*, my worrywart daughter."

Marisa walked into the foyer where her father was getting ready to head out. The festival inspired him to wear hideously bright clothes that, thankfully, stayed hidden the rest of the year. His hair was slicked back with gel but two tufts always managed to stick out over his ears.

"*Ciao,* Pop." She squinted at his violet shirt and gold pants.

"*Bella!*" he said, turning her around.

"Pop, have you had a chance to think about my taking Giorgio's position?"

"You don't really want that job, do you? Lots of hours, stress."

Her mind screamed *Yes, oh, yes!* but she said, "I can handle it."

"You're not gonna break your mama's heart and become one of those career girls like Mrs. Perrini's daughter, are you?"

"No," she said carefully. "I just want a little more challenge, that's all."

He studied her for a moment. "Okay, I'm going to give you that job…"

"You are?" She waited for the "if."

"If you meet your *amore* today." He kissed her on each cheek.

She walked down the hall to stick a blob of tooth-paste in her mouth. She heard her brother, Carlo, in his room conducting the business he ran on the side: bet-ting. His words halted her. "Ten-to-one she doesn't find the guy this time. You in?"

Mouth open in outrage, she stepped into his room. Sports paraphernalia cluttered every wall, shelf and horizontal surface, except for the space on the far wall reserved for his blackboard betting chart. Along the top were baseball teams and their odds. Then a column titled: Gina—Boy/Girl. And in the last column: Marisa.

Carlo jotted something down, then turned to see her. "Okay, got it. And what about the fight Saturday?"

She wiped off the numbers in her column and

stomped into the foyer. "Did you know Carlo is taking odds on me finding my *amore*?"

Gina waved her hand. "He's done that for the past two years."

"Did he take bets on you?"

"Nah, he knew I'd live up to the tradition, but I do everything right. Right, Mama?"

"You go in there," Mama said, nudging Gina into the living room when Marisa narrowed her eyes.

After Marisa accepted their good-luck kisses, Mama and Nonna promptly shoved her out the door. She could barely keep her balance on the darned high heels Gina insisted made her look sleek, and she lurched precariously.

"Be careful on those loose bricks by the fountain!" Gina hollered. "Not that *I* tripped or anything."

Marisa said, "But what if—"

Mama closed the blue door, and Marisa knew how little birds felt when they were booted from their nest— distraught and abandoned. But birds only had to make their way in the world, find food and try not to get eaten.

Marisa had to find her true love.

BARRIE MACKENZIE STOOD in the ornate town square of Cortina, California, surrounded by hundreds of friendly, laughing, hugging-each-other, celebrating-love-and-wine people.

Wasn't this just a rotten bit of luck?

First his flight had been delayed, then they'd misplaced his luggage. He'd had to spend an hour listening to the poor, married sods having to call their families. Now it looked as though it was going to rain in the town *USA Today* dubbed "the most romantic town in America."

The square was actually round, and buildings encircled it like puzzle pieces. The restaurants, cafés, apartments and hotel all maintained the Renaissance charm of the city, and the massive steps leading up to the courthouse reminded him of Rome. Because of the Vino and Amore Festival, the square was crammed with food carts touting everything from full-course dinners to Italian ices. A barbershop quartet, jugglers and an organ grinder and his monkey vied for attention.

He wasn't even supposed to be there. That damned Porter. He'd been the first photojournalist Barrie hired for the travel and food magazine he worked for, and the man had to go and fall in love on his last assignment. Didn't he know the meaning of responsibility? Porter had sounded like a lovesick schoolboy when he'd called a few days ago.

"Barrie, I need you to cover the festival for me. I have met *the* woman, and I can't leave Paris until I convince her to come back with me. She's incredible, beautiful...." He giggled. "It would take me an hour to tell you about her, and that's only what I know so far."

"Porter, when you take an assignment—"

"Please, not another lecture about responsibility. I don't meet the woman of my dreams every day. You'll understand when love bowls you over."

"Sounds like it steamrolled you, man. If I ever start acting daft over a woman, shoot me."

"Does that mean I'm not fired?"

"You're not fired. But remember what I told you— don't get so involved with your subjects."

"Thanks, Barrie. Hey, she's got a sister...."

"Forget it. As it is, I need a company poster with my picture stating, 'Not Wanted: blind dates, sisters or cousins from out of town.' Bring her back and get to work."

First his boss, Stan, had been bitten by the love bug and was now expecting his first babe. The poor deluded fool expounded ceaselessly on the bliss of married life, disguising ironclad routine and restricted freedom with words like "stability" and "companionship." Now Porter was a victim. Barrie pictured the love bug as not a bug at all but something akin to a piranha, teeth bared, blood-lust in its eyes. *Chomp, chomp, chomp...*

"Salute!" A young Italian lad raised his paper cup in toast, oblivious to the fact that Barrie had no cup to toast back with. He made the gesture anyway. "Cheers." The man tossed back the contents, and Barrie had to grab his arm to keep him from stumbling into the quartet singing, "When the moon hits the sky like a big pizza pie, that's *amore.*"

He turned at the sound of cheering. A woman on one of the wrought-iron balconies tossed flower necklaces to the crowd below, Mardi-Gras style. He raised his camera, took a few shots and a mental note to research this custom.

As he focused his lens for another shot, he searched for soul. He zoomed in on the woman's cleavage. That wasn't it. Then he caught sight of a beautiful young lass trying to catch one of the necklaces. He felt an odd tightening in his middle. She wasn't his type. Streamlined blondes on the fast track with no dreams of weddings and babies, that was what he liked in a woman. Then why were they boring him lately? No soul there either, he supposed.

He made a picture of the lass in the lacy white dress,

zooming in on her triumphant smile when she caught a necklace. She slid the white blooms over her head, pulling her thick, dark hair from beneath so it flowed over the flowers. But her smile faded once she disentangled from the crowd. She had amazing brown eyes, deep and warm, tilted up at the corners. The kind a man wouldn't mind looking into first thing in the morning. He blinked. Not him, of course.

The hem of her white dress swished around delicate ankles, though she looked unsteady on her heels. She picked her way around the puddles to the fountain, whose centerpiece was a replica of Michelangelo's *David* with water cascading from the platform beneath his feet.

He felt a lightness replace the pressure he'd been feeling in his chest since his boss had taken him aside last week. Barrie could take criticism: bad composition, faulty light, he could handle. But that his photographs had no soul... Barrie wanted to be the best at what he did, so he'd work on it. As soon as he figured out what soul was.

He focused on the lass again. She twisted her fingers and searched the square. He caught himself smiling just in case her gaze met his, but it slid right past him, leaving him standing there smiling at no one.

"Have you gone daft too, MacKenzie?" he muttered, thinking of his two woman-crazy friends. He forced his attention across the square where people clamored for little cups of wine at one of the booths. In one corner a wine-making demonstration was putting on a grape-stomping contest, and the scent of smashed grapes competed with all the other aromas. These people took their wine seriously, as well as their celebrations and traditions.

Well, he had no use for traditions. He'd barely escaped his own family's tradition of being tethered to their whiskey distillery in a remote village in the Scottish Highlands. Generation after generation had lived and died on the same plot of land, never having seen the world.

As he made a photograph of a father convincing his teenage daughter to join an impromptu dance, he thought of how his own parents had used guilt and manipulation—and worse, his mother had used tears—to try to trap him into staying. Settling down meant giving up freedom, and he'd have none of that. Freedom equaled happiness.

That thought made standing there in the silliness of the festival not such a burden after all. Besides, next week he'd be on his way to Barcelona.

The dancing group had doubled in size and was making its way across the square. As it moved, it gathered people like one of those insidious congo lines. His style was to observe unobtrusively, blend into the crowd...well, as much as possible considering his six-foot-two frame.

He stole one more glance at the pretty lass at the fountain, who was looking up at David's physique. She covered her mouth, though she didn't disguise the amused twinkle in her eyes. Someone had tied colored ribbons to David's willie.

Her girlish fascination, combined with her womanly body, intrigued him. That was the opening picture for his article! As he made several pictures, he wondered if the thrumming in his chest meant he was getting close to that elusive soul.

And now to get out of the way before—

Too late. A heavyset woman grabbed his arm and

sent him spinning into the crowd of dancers. Before he could escape, another woman took hold of him. Just as he shook her off, another woman clamped on to him. The crowd moved in dizzying circles like a crazed army of ants. Some of them were singing, some clapping and shouting. Too many people, too much touching. He saw his chance and dodged for an opening, his head spinning as he wove through the dancers. A man grabbed hold of his elbow and gave him one last whirl. Barrie let his weight carry him into the open.

And right into someone.

Problem was, his back was facing that someone, and before he could regain his balance on the bricks, they both went sprawling into a muddy puddle. Conscious of his size, he twisted to the side so the unlucky victim wouldn't take the brunt of his weight.

He hoped it was a man. A big man who could handle the fall. As he scrambled to his feet, he had the awful feeling the soft body wasn't a man's. Nor was the yelp of surprise he'd heard as he'd made contact. Nor the scent of roses he smelled.

Especially not the length of creamy leg he saw beneath a once-white skirt as he slid out from beneath her. "Uh-oh." His gaze moved over the rumpled skirt, the bodice that revealed a tease of cleavage, and the mud-splattered length of neck and finally came to rest on the shocked expression of the woman he'd spotted earlier. Her cheek was streaked with mud, her hair was dripping wet and her flower necklace was crushed. "You all right? Here, let me help you up."

She waved his hand away, not even looking at him. Her mouth was open, moving soundlessly, which was probably a good thing, considering. Her wide-eyed gaze fastened on the state of her ruined dress. "Oh, no," she finally uttered.

He knelt beside her, instinctively feeling for his camera. It was still around his neck, still dry. Unlike the poor lass. He caught another whiff of the rose scent she wore. He hated rose perfume, but for some reason, on her... He shook away the thought. "You all right? Sorry about this." He nodded at the wall of people undulating around them. "It seems there's this dance where—"

"Sorry? You're *sorry?*" She turned blazing eyes on him, eyes that made him think of a tribal ceremony he'd once covered. Bonfires, screaming and...human sacrifice. Well, not really human sacrifice, not then, but possibly now. *"Do you know what you've done?"*

As he stood up, he took the opportunity to survey her again, just in case he'd missed something. "I knocked you into a puddle. Not on purpose, of course, but this dance, you see—"

"You've ruined my dress! *The* dress, the one I'm supposed to..." She broke off, panic freezing her features. She looked him over from head to toe, and he didn't much care for the disappointment he saw in her face. "You're not even the right one!"

"The right one? Only a certain sort is allowed to bump into you?"

"No. Yes! I mean— Oh, never mind! I've got to go home and change!"

His sense of responsibility kicked in. "Look, I'll pay to have it cleaned, fixed, whatever."

"It'll be too late then!" She scrambled up, ignoring his outstretched hand. The moment she got to her feet, she winced and toppled against him.

Problem was, he hadn't been expecting it. Particularly the way she placed the flat of her hand on him to brace herself, and her hand just happened to land on his...

"Holy—!" was all he could manage as his gaze flew to David's privates.

She followed his gaze first to the colored ribbons and then down to her hand. She let go with a shriek and fell on her rump. "This is not happening to me," she muttered, shaking her head.

"I believe *that* just happened to *me*," he said, shifting his pants. Her handprint had seared his flesh. And with that bit of thigh exposed again, why, she'd think he was a pervert if she glimpsed the front of his pants.

Which she did. Her face flamed a becoming plum color, and she tugged her skirt down. "*You* are a pervert!"

"If I recall correctly—and I do recall—*you* grabbed *me*." He shook his head. "But never mind about that." He knelt down beside her again, running a finger down the side of her ankle. "Your ankle's swelling. Is that why you grabbed—er, fell down again?"

She stared at his finger, making him realize that he was softly stroking her damp skin. When he removed it, she clamped her mouth shut and seemed to focus her attention back on the swelling.

"My ankle can't be broken! Not today!" She tried putting weight on it, but pulled back with a wince. "My life is ruined! I'll never meet him now!"

"I'm sure he'll understand." Whoever the lucky sod was. He shook his head. Where had that come from? *Chomp, chomp, chomp.* He could almost hear the gnashing teeth of the vicious love piranha warning him to escape its bite.

"He won't understand!"

"Then I'd say he isn't worth your time."

"You don't understand! He's the man I'm supposed to marry!"

The white dress! Her nervousness! It was all coming together. She was supposed to get married in front of the fountain. Maybe someone had tied ribbons to David's willie for the same reason Americans tied cans to the getaway car. Now he really felt bad, ruining her wedding dress and all.

He pushed his damp hair away from his face. "We can worry about the dress later. I don't think your ankle's broken. Let me take you to the hospital. I'm sure they'll have you patched up in no time." He hoped so. He didn't want to see that temper of hers flare again. Or worse, watch her burst into tears.

She'd pulled up her skirt in her panic, and even covered in muddy water, she had great legs. She caught his gaze and tugged it down again.

"Are you going to help me up or just gawk?" She covered her mouth. "I'm sorry, I'm just—"

Too late for apologies. Besides, he *had* been gawking and was none too pleased with himself for doing it. Before she could finish her apology, he pulled her up and slung her over his shoulder like a sack of potatoes. Then he leaned down and grabbed her shoe and purse.

Her shriek of indignation followed behind him as he wove through what had to be a hundred people now participating in the dance. They cheered and tossed out words like "Ah, *amore!*" on soulful sighs. What a load of pish.

"I cannot believe this is happening to me," she said, slapping his back. "Put me down, you brute!" As he started to pretend to drop her, she amended, "No, no, not down!"

He turned to find her rounded, mud-stained bum in his face. A nice bum at that. "Well, make up your mind."

"Make up my mind? Hah! You don't know me very well." She twisted around. "I mean, can't you carry me like I'm a...well, a woman instead of a...a..."

He lifted an eyebrow. "Sack of potatoes?"

"Yeah, a sack of potatoes!"

He pictured the alternative and shook his head. "I'd look like some sappy hero in one of those old-fashioned romantic movies. I rather like the sack method myself." And he continued toward the café entrance where the crowd didn't present such an obstacle course.

"Just take me to a phone. I'll call the house and see if someone can take me to the hospital."

"It'll be quicker if I take you."

"No! I don't trust you."

"Because you think I'm a pervert? Sorry, but I couldn't help noticing your—"

"No, just a clumsy oaf."

"I've a mind to be clumsy again and drop you in that puddle."

"All right, you're not clumsy."

He didn't know why, but he was having fun with this crazy lass. "What about the oaf part?"

She hesitated, and he turned toward the puddle again. "All right, all right, you're not an oaf!"

"Anyone ever tell you you've got a way of making a man feel good?"

"No."

Music wafted through the air, accompanied by the

aromas of garlic and tomato sauce. He found himself walking to the jaunty beat. Her full breasts bounced softly against his back, and her thighs felt nice beneath his hands. Why, he could walk to the hospital and not mind in the least.

The music and smells, everything came to a screeching halt in his mind. What the devil was he thinking? Making things right was his responsibility, nothing more. He willed his thoughts back to the piranhas. *Chomp, chomp, chomp.*

He listed his reasons for not being intrigued by this woman with each step. Too lush and curvy. Sassy. Melodramatic. Lush and curvy. Feisty. Trouble from the start. Lush and curvy.

Wait a minute. He didn't even like his women curvy. Must be all the wine gases in the atmosphere clouding his mind. Much better if she could get a family member to take her to the hospital. Then he could apologize again, give her money—he'd gladly give her enough to buy a new dress—and be done with the whole lush-and-curvy business.

WHEN SHE HUNG UP the phone the second time, she leaned her forehead against the hand set and said in a pitiful mewl, "No one's home."

Before he could think better of it, he reached over and rubbed the mud from her cheek. When she looked up at him in surprise, he dropped his hand. Why did he have to keep touching her? He didn't even *like* touching that much. Her mouth had parted slightly, not from indignation, but as though his touch had… mattered to her somehow. She busied herself with removing the flower necklace. She had a great nose, not dainty or prissy, but perfect for her olive skin, full mouth and mole on the edge of her upper lip.

"What about the chap you're supposed to marry?" He cleared his throat. Why did his voice sound strange? "Can't you get hold of him?"

Despair dripped from her voice. "No."

"Doesn't he have a beeper? A cell phone?"

"I don't know."

"What does he look like then? Maybe I can find him."

"I don't know what he looks like. That's the problem!"

"Wait a minute. You're going to marry the chap, and you don't know what he looks like?"

"Exactly." She brushed her hair from her face, then grimaced when she felt gritty mud.

"I didn't know they arranged marriages anymore."

"It's not an arranged marriage, exactly." She let out an exasperated sigh. "I wish it was. Maybe I should have you take me to the cookie booth. That's probably where everyone is, or somewhere around here."

"I can do that."

"But they're on the other side of the square, and everyone would see me. No, that won't work."

"All right then, I'll take you to the hospital."

"But then again, everyone's going to hear about this anyway."

He shook his head. "To the booth then?"

"Just take me to the hospital. Maybe there's still a chance of saving my career!"

"Pardon?"

She waved her hand. "Never mind, let's just go."

THIS HAD TO BE some kind of nightmare. Marisa had had nightmares in the weeks leading up to the festival.

Like the one where she slept through the whole thing. Or the one where a pimple sprang up on her nose that was so big it sent children running away screaming. Or the one where she found herself standing in the square naked. Only this nightmare was a big, chestnut-haired, Scottish *oaf* who had introduced himself as Barrie MacKenzie. So there. She mentally gave him raspberries. *Pbbbbbllllltttt!*

All right, so what if he had managed to get her an ice pack and settled her ankle on his leg as they sat in the waiting area? So what if he'd had the decency to carry her properly into the hospital instead of treating her like a sack of potatoes, even if he had looked very uncomfortable doing it?

And so what if being in his arms had made her feel kind of gushy inside? He was as far from her Mr. Right as possible, even sporting faint freckles on his forehead and cheeks, and thick, auburn hair that looked silky soft and—she shook her head. Because of him, she was probably missing her date with destiny. Gina was going to love this—her position as perfect daughter was secured with concrete.

She should have had him take her to the cookie booth, she thought, glancing at him. As it was, she could already hear everyone asking, "Who was that great-looking barbarian with the broad chest and shoulder-length hair hauling you all over? The one with the sculpted cheeks and long chin and fine nose?"

"Come on," she muttered, shifting her gaze to the clock. Talk about gawking!

Luckily he'd been watching the nurses' station. "Perhaps I ought to go over and knock some heads around, get you moved up the list."

"Let's not injure anyone else, okay? You don't understand. This has nothing to do with impatience."

"Would it have something to do with the chap you're supposed to marry? The one you don't know?"

She didn't want to talk about it. Instead she surveyed her throbbing ankle, gauging the swelling. But her gaze strayed to those muscular legs the size of tree trunks. Even in his loose-cut jeans, she could see the muscles in his thighs, and she caught herself wondering if they were hairy or lightly dusted, and if the hair was blond or reddish.

"Are all the men as big as you where you're from? I mean, overall," she added quickly.

He thickened his already enchanting accent. "Back in my wee village of New York City, there are some even bigger."

"You weren't born in New York. You sound Scottish." His words had a lyrical cadence, and he sometimes ran them together. Like when he asked, *Youallright?* in a soft, low voice that made her believe he did, indeed, care if she was all right—and made her feel all right indeed.

"Aye, I am. Came to New York when I was twenty, seven years ago."

"So you wear those plaid skirts, then."

He narrowed an eye at her. "Aye, all the time. They're at the cleaners now, so I'm stuck with these." He tapped his knee.

"You're being sarcastic."

"You drink wine every day? Have a temper? That's what I've heard about Italians." He pronounced it with a long I.

"No and no. Well, maybe when it comes to the temper... I thought Scottish men wore kilts, that's all. And played bagpipes. No bagpipes, either?''

He shook his head.

So much for trying to make ethnic conversation. She looked at the bag sitting next to him. He'd carefully checked his camera and wiped the mud off the case, though only after seeing to her ankle. He hadn't done much about the mud on his clothing, which appeared no worse for wear considering he'd let her land on him. "What do you do? For a living, I mean?"

"I'm a photojournalist for a travel magazine. *Celebrations* covers events all over the world, like the Bun Festival in Hong Kong and the Chinese New Year."

Before thinking better of it, she touched his arm. "Have you been to Italy?"

"Sure. Covered Carnival in Venice last year. You?"

She pulled her hand away and sat back in the chair. "No. Hardly been out of Cortina. Not that I need to."

"Sounds like you live a sheltered life, stuck in one place, never getting out."

"I'm not stuck here—it's where I want to be. And not sheltered, no. Well, maybe a little." She shrugged. "But there's nothing wrong with that. So tell me about Italy. I've heard it's the most romantic place in the world."

He lifted his shoulders in a shrug. "It's not really that romantic."

"How can you say that? There can't be anything more romantic than taking a gondola ride in Venice, or sharing a cappuccino at a sidewalk café in Florence or a kiss in the Colosseum." Every time she came across a picture of any place in Italy, she cut it out and hung it on her apartment walls. Seemed like a good way to try to be romantic.

"The canals of Venice are sometimes filled with sewage, and the city's sinking. The exhaust regulations are so lax, all you can smell when you walk around Rome are fumes. The Colosseum's falling down, and anyway, how romantic is a place where people were slaughtered for entertainment?"

She could only stare at him. But instead of telling him how absurd he was, she found herself saying, "I'll bet you'd think it was romantic if you'd gone there with someone you love. Or...did you?" Instead of her usual vision of herself and an Italian man who resembled Antonio Sabatino, Jr., she could see Barrie and some tall, skinny blonde. She shooed away the thought. What did she care? Besides, he'd probably knock the poor woman out of the gondola.

He grimaced. "Romance and all that fluff is designed to trick people into giving up their freedom under the guise of long-term happiness that actually lasts approximately as long as a good World Cup football match."

As her mouth dropped open, a nurse called her name. *"Fluff?"*

He hoisted her up into his arms and carried her into the examination cubicle. And bless his soul for not making any exerting noises as he did it. Despite his large size, he was gentle as he set her down on the bed. He leaned right into her face and said, "Fluff."

"The doctor will be right in to see you," the nurse said, but Marisa was lost in Barrie's eyes for a moment. They were the shade of the sky just before rain, blue with a grayish tinge.

She started to say something, but the way he was looking at her stole the words right out of her mouth. In horror she realized that her mouth was indeed hanging open, and she clamped it shut. She knew the awkward feeling, sure. But she wasn't supposed to feel it with Barrie, who was not her Mr. Right at all. She rubbed her nose, using the excuse to break eye contact. "Silly goose." She wasn't sure if she was saying it to herself or him.

"*I'm* a silly goose? I'm not the one who's marrying some chap I don't even know."

The doctor walked in. "Well, well, you must be Marisa Cerini. Let's see if we can get you straightened out."

Barrie let out a noise that sounded suspiciously like a snort. "Good luck."

COULD SHE DIE right now?

Marisa looked like some deranged bride from the movie *Road Warrior*. At least there was *some* good news in all this: her ankle wasn't broken. There was also bad news: She had a slight tear in her Achilles tendon. But she wouldn't need surgery if she wore a removable splint for four weeks. The really bad news was the splint itself, a bulky thing that went from her toe to her ankle and up to the back of her knee with six Velcro fasteners in front. The really bad news was it was almost time for the sun to set. Her family would be waiting for her either to come home with her *amore* or at least have news about meeting him.

She cringed as she imagined herself hobbling on one high heel and crutches across those darned bricks to the fountain—in her muddy dress! Though she'd washed the mud off her face, she'd also dispensed with her makeup. And her hair was so stringy, not even her brush could help. She could touch up her lips and cheeks, but what did it matter when the rest of her was a mess? No one was going to walk up to her. No one was going to go near her. The nightmare image of children running away screaming was going to come true!

"If you want to avoid surgery," the doctor was saying, "you need to keep weight off that ankle for two weeks. Then you can go around with crutches for another two weeks.'' He winked. ''Good excuse to let your boyfriend here wait on you.''

She swung her gaze to Barrie, who looked as surprised by the comment as she was. Well, did he have to look so horrified? She should be the one with that look. ''He's not my boyfriend. The man thinks romance is fluff. Anyway, I'm supposed to marry an Italian. I *have* to marry an Italian! It's family tradition. I don't want to be like Rosa Pontini, the shame of her family! All the other families will talk about me. 'Those poor Cerinis. Sure, their youngest made them proud. But look at the oldest, the embarrassment of the family.''' She gestured toward Barrie. ''He's about as far as you can get from Italian! He's…he's…Scottish! He's too tall. He's too big! This is terrible! I can't stay off my ankle. I've got to participate in the festival.''

The doctor raised his eyebrows. ''I'm afraid that's out of the question. As far as the festival is concerned, you're out of commission.''

A SHORT WHILE later, Marisa eyed the crutches with distaste. She was to stay off her feet and only use them when absolutely necessary over the next two weeks. The nurse gave her brief instructions. ''Make sure your boyfriend's nearby, in case you lose your balance. I've got to get back to the emergency room.'' She smiled. ''Good luck.''

''He's not my boyfriend!'' Marisa blurted out with exasperation. ''Does he *look* Italian to you?''

The nurse glanced at Barrie with a glint of appreciation. ''You can care with that accent?'' After an extra-long pause and a too-cute smile, she left.

The one with the accent had the nerve to chuckle.

''Give me those darned things!'' She grabbed the

crutches out of Barrie's hands. She tucked them under her armpits, and took a hop-step. Then another. "See, no problem. I've got it. You don't need to hover."

He backed away. One crutch went forward, the other went backward, and down she went.

"You all right?" he asked in that way that ran the words together and sounded so darn cute. "And you called *me* an oaf?" He pulled her to her feet—or rather, her foot. They were nearly face to face, their hands clasped together. She fell into the spell of his eyes again, and the teasing glint melted to something warmer. Yep, her mouth was definitely hanging open. She snapped it shut and started looking for her crutches.

Her pride was hurt worse than either her fanny or her ankle. And the ankle hurt. A lot. "I'm fine. Just perfect. You did ask me if I was all right, didn't you? Yes, you did." Talk about getting off track! She let out a huff of breath. "I just can't walk." Panic clutched her belly as she realized time was slipping away. "And I need to get back to the square right now!"

She didn't like the way the corner of his mouth twitched. "Well, I could take you back, but being as I'm *Scottish*," he said, performing a fair imitation of her earlier exclamation, "and an oaf, I'm sure you wouldn't want me to." And then he waited, arms crossed over his chest, making him look even larger. How could he look good wet and muddy when she looked like a sewer rat?

"I took back the oaf part."

"Aye, but you were thinking it still."

"All right. I take them all back."

"And?"

"And, well, there's nothing wrong with being Scottish. You do have a neat accent."

"And?"

A nice butt, her thoughts interjected. No, don't tell him that! She let out another breath. "Will you please take me back to the square?"

His mouth quirked. "Thought you'd never ask."

"YOU DIDN'T HAVE TO be so passionate about the matter," Barrie said, carrying Marisa back to his car a short while later.

"What matter?" She squirmed to get comfortable in his arms. Oh, great, now her breast was pressed against his shoulder. If she moved, he'd think she cared. And she didn't, not at all.

"All that fuss about me not believing in romance and not being Italian. When the doctor mentioned it, you could have just left it at, 'No, he's not my boyfriend'."

She could only stare at his profile, since he was looking ahead. "I'm surprised you weren't the one jumping up and down shouting he was mistaken. After that 'good luck' remark."

His shrug made her breast rub against him. It must be the friction making her tingle, she thought. Yeah, just the friction.

"I don't jump up and down shouting about anything. You don't need a lot of noise to get a point across." He carried her to an old, light blue Buick.

"This is your rental car?" she asked as he maneuvered to open the door.

"The fellow who was supposed to cover this festival arranged for it from some rental place. It's not so bad really. You'd be surprised what passes for a car in some countries.''

''Must be exciting,'' she was saying as he sat down with her in his lap, ''to have traveled to so many places. All those foreign countries...''

He'd shifted her off his lap and was twisting her around with his hands on her waist.

''...customs...'' she mumbled, distracted by the way her behind slid across his lap.

They were nose to nose, and his hand slid a little lower on her hip. ''How did we manage this last time?'' he asked.

She could feel his breath on her chin, and for a moment she couldn't think at all. ''I think I got in myself.''

He turned her slightly, making his elbow press against her breast. ''This is what I get for being a gentleman.''

She burst out laughing, and the action made her cheek brush against the slight stubble on his cheek. She tightened her hold on his shoulder to keep her balance.

''What's so blamed funny about me being a gentleman?'' he asked.

''Considering your hand is nearly on my tush and your arm is only a fabric's width from my bra, and you're about a millimeter away from kissing me...''

He took stock of his position and rolled his eyes. ''Sorry 'bout that.''

''You're blushing!'' she said. ''You're actually blushing.''

''I'm not blushing. I'm just...hot is all.''

He *was* hot; she could feel the heat emanating from him. And wherever he touched, she burned even hotter, despite the cool breeze blowing in through the open door. He was looking at her. Their noses bumped; their chins brushed. He smelled good, a mixture of his woodsy cologne and the scent of a man who'd been out in the sun and fresh air all day. Then she realized they'd been sitting like that for at least a minute, which was a long time to be in the arms of a man she didn't know very well. Especially when she was enjoying it so much.

"Maybe we'd better—" he started to say.

At the same time, she said, "If I move this way—"

They both stopped and laughed, but their laughter faded when they realized they *still* hadn't moved.

He cleared his throat. "I was just trying to think of the best way to extricate ourselves."

"Yeah." She cleared the throaty sound from her voice. "Me, too."

Several more seconds passed. Then he said, "So I guess we should...extricate ourselves."

"I guess. I mean, definitely. I've—" She looked into his eyes. "I've got to go...somewhere," she murmured absently.

"To meet the chap you're supposed to marry."

"Oh, yes!" She gave her head a shake. Gawd, how'd she get so distracted? "What's the holdup?"

After entirely too much contact—those large hands of his sliding across her lower back, not to mention his ear being so close to her mouth she could have nibbled on it—she was finally sitting on the passenger side of the seat.

She yelped when he reached under her skirt.

"I'm putting the seat back," he said, and did just that. She lurched backward along with the seat. "Now, let's get your foot up on the dashboard."

She was reminded again of the monstrosity her leg

had become in the blue cast. "All sorted out?" he asked before closing the door.

"Sorted?"

"All set?"

"Yeah, sure. We'd better hurry," she said, taking note of the angry sky to the south and the dying sunset to the west. The silence in the car felt awkward. She tried to think beyond all that touching and being entirely too close. "If you don't like noise and shouting, what are you doing at this festival?"

"I've been asking myself that same question. But the truth is, the guy who was supposed to cover it decided to fall head over heels in love, and now I'm stuck covering it."

"Hmph. It's a wonderful festival, full of tradition and family...and lots of shouting and noise," she had to admit.

He shook his head, maneuvering through the traffic. "Family and traditions tie you down."

"They free you. You know what's expected of you. It's the rest of the world that keeps us in suspense."

He made that snorting sound again. "They're obligations in the guise of family values. If I'd followed my own family tradition, I'd be stuck in the same village I was born in, looking forward to nothing more than being chained to some lass I've known my whole life, trying to produce a son so he can take over the whiskey distillery when I'm old and dying of the drink."

"That's terrible! Marriage isn't something you're chained to. It's spending your life with your soul mate, the one person you're destined to love forever." That was what a real romantic would say and that was what she wanted. "It's keeping family traditions alive and making your own. Don't snort!" she said just as he was about to. "Grab that space over there! Oh, no, why is everyone leaving?"

Groups of people flowed from the square, and there were a lot of empty parking spaces. She pushed her car door open before he'd even put the car in park.

"Hold it there, lassie. You're not going to try those crutches again, are you?"

"I can't have you carrying me to the fountain."

"Don't be daft. You'll kill yourself trying to rush with those things."

Well, she probably would, but he didn't have to call her… "What'd you call me?"

"Daft. Foolish. Addled. Silly."

"All right, all right, I get the picture."

He was out of the car and over to her side, lifting her again as though she weighed nothing at all, God bless him. There was that about having a big guy around. Only that, of course.

The square was half as full as it had been when she'd left. People were crowding into the cafés or leaving to find other shelter. Those moldy-cookie-dough clouds blotted out the setting sun. Papers skittered across the bricks, and flowers shuddered in their long planters. The wine cart had moved beneath an overhang along with the quartet, and the grape-stomping demonstration had closed. She searched for eligible candidates.

Just keep your cool. There are still people here, she said to herself as they reached the fountain. *He's got to be here. All I need is a little time before the rain—*

The first drop hit her nose, driven by a damp, earthy wind.

"Is that rain?" he asked.

Another drop splashed her forehead. "It can't rain yet!"

He looked up at the darkening sky, making her body shift against his chest. "Better take that up with Mother Nature. From the look of the sky, it's going to rain for a while."

"It'll just sprinkle a drop or two. It never rains during the festival. It never—"

It rained, and not just a drop or two. More like a gazillion drops pattered across the faded red bricks. Within seconds, Barrie's shirt was plastered to his chest.

"You don't say," he said. "Glad to hear it. I'd hate to get caught in a downpour."

"How can you be so calm? Because your life's not ruined, that's how!"

He made his way to an alcove as the sky rumbled. "All because of this chap you're supposed to marry that you don't even know?" He set her down gently, where she could lean against the ornate wood door that led to apartments upstairs. "Can't you meet him tomorrow?"

She pushed her wet hair away from her face. "It's only today. The moon is full tonight, it's the first night of the festival, and that's when I'm supposed to meet him." She leaned against the door and squeezed her eyes shut.

"Would this have anything to do with vampires? Or werewolves?"

Her eyes snapped open. Somehow, he looked even bigger when he was wet. "Of course not! It's our... omantic family tradition. Oh, you wouldn't understand! You made it perfectly clear how you feel about that kind of thing.'' She rubbed her nose and shook her head.

"You're not going to cry, are you?''

"No, I'm not going to cry. I know it sounds silly to the…normal, modern world, but it's just that every woman in my family has met her true love in the square on the first sunset of the festival, and I'm the only one who hasn't, and everyone's waiting for me to come home with good news, and I won't have any because… All right, I'm going to cry,'' she choked out. "I can't help it. It's a family trait. We cry easily, okay? Don't you dare call me daft!''

He let out what sounded like a groan and settled his hands on her shoulders. He tilted his head, and his voice lowered to a tone that reminded her of a sweet, rich wine. "I won't call you daft. Just don't cry. It's not so bad. Look, I'm sorry about knocking you into that puddle. I take full responsibility for this mess.''

She wanted to move out from beneath those large hands, but found she couldn't when she looked up at him. Compassion warmed his eyes, and that made her want to cry all the more.

He patted the damp jeans that were molded to his thighs. "I don't have any tissues, not that they'd be much good now, I suppose.'' He ran his thumbs beneath her eyes. "Don't cry.''

How could the man be so gentle? He looked so…strong. She could only nod, and then shake her head as she remembered his request. He had a serious mouth, not lush like Italian men had, but interesting just the same. Were his lips soft? Beads of water slid over those high cheekbones, down to his firm jawline. She felt her gaze go liquid as his eyes swept over her face and settled on her mouth. A dizzy feeling tickled her tummy.

If she hadn't been so dazzled, she might have registered the sound of footsteps and the click of a door opening. But she *was* dazzled. One second she was wondering how his mouth would feel, and the next, she had firsthand knowledge.

The door shoved her forward, sending her right into him. Before she put her weight on her foot, he grabbed her, chest to chest and—just for a moment before he regained his balance—mouth to mouth.

"Sorry!" the two young men said as they darted off into the rain. Her attention reluctantly returned to the matter at hand, which was her body plastered right up against Barrie's. Worse, her body *enjoying* being plastered against all that hardness.

"You all right?" he asked, though he still hadn't made a move to put her down. Yeah, she definitely liked the way he asked if she was all right. It almost made it worthwhile not being all right.

"Mmm?" She blinked. What was going on here? "Yes! I'm all right, just fine and dandy. Maybe you should set me down now."

"Oh. Right." He helped her lean against a wall and slid his arms from around her. "Maybe one of those chaps was the one you're supposed to marry."

"No, they're Gianni's boys. Too young." For a few moments she'd forgotten all about the tradition and her failure to uphold it—again. Now reality washed down over her just like the rain had. "What am I going to do? I can't let my family down." Before she could think better of it, she grabbed two fistfuls of his wet shirt. "I'm talking about a proud and cherished family tradition! They exchange newsletters every season between the family here and the family in Italy. You know what Mama's going to say about me? 'Well, once again Marisa didn't come through. We're probably going to give up on her because, you know, how many times can we dress her up and send her out there?' My brother's taking bets on me! They're going to talk about me for generations, the only woman in the family who couldn't find her true love. I'll be the spinster of the clan. I won't get the job, either, because Pop will think, 'Gee, she can't get a husband, how can she handle a challenging position like sales manager?' and I'll end up being his secretary for the rest of my life. A spinster secretary! Don't you understand?''

He paused long enough to make her realize how desperate she sounded. His perfectly rational reply didn't help. ''Shall I get you a gun and be done with it then?''

She narrowed her eyes. ''That's a fine idea. Only I'll be aiming it at you!''

''Me?'' He had the nerve to look innocent.

''This is all your fault! I would have met him by now if it wasn't for you.''

''I told you I'd take the blame. But there's nothing I can do, short of going round asking every male of proper age and Italian heritage if he was at the square just before sunset.'' He raised his hand. ''Oh, no, get that gleam out of your eyes. I'm not doing it. I've got photographs to make and an article to write. I'm here on business, not pleasure.''

''So am I!'' She crossed her arms beneath her breasts, accidentally pushing them up and catching his eye. She couldn't help but enjoy her power to do that.

''And what's this business about a job? I thought this silly tradition was about love.''

''It is. The job is a bonus. Forget the job.'' She was

from Cerini stock, and they were romantics, so she had to put love first. "I've got to think. I need food. Do you have anything on you?"

His eyebrow quirked. "You need food to think?"

"I need food for everything. That's how my family works. We grieve with food, work out problems—"

"With food," he supplied.

"Right."

He reached into his bag and produced a package of something that looked blissfully like large, round cookies. "They're oatcakes. I have them shipped over from Scotland."

When she bit into one, it was dense and dry. She chewed…and chewed. He watched her, probably waiting to hear how much she liked them. She didn't. Not that she could comment with her mouth full of dry oats. She steered her thoughts back to the matter at hand, which was not Barrie or his cookies. Her eyes widened. Food never let her down. "Pictures! You've got pictures!"

He lowered his head. "Aye. That's what I do. Make photographs."

"Of people!" She found herself grabbing his shirt again, finding the wrinkled places she'd made the first time. "Like the men who were in this square before you knocked me into the puddle."

"I suppose I can send you copies of the photographs. After flying to Barcelona next week, I'll be home putting together the articles. I'll send your copies straight away."

Her soaring hope plummeted. "I can't wait that long. By then my family will know I failed—again. And some of these men will return to Italy or other places when the festival ends. I need the pictures now." She realized she was standing way too close to him, but as she started to back away, she lost her balance and leaned against him instead. "Excuse me."

He chuckled as he set her against the wall. "Can't keep your hands off me, eh?"

She fisted those hands at her side, feeling her face betray her by going hot. "I'd like to get my hands around... Forget that, I don't want my hands around anything of yours. You are so not my type. W-what are you doing?"

He continued unbuttoning his shirt and stripped it off. "I'm ringing out the water." And he proceeded to do just that. "Don't worry, you're not my type, either."

She crossed her arms under her chest again, chastising herself for feeling stung by his retort. "I want a man who doesn't loom over me like the display of chocolate-chip cookies at the grocer. I want a lean, dark-haired Italian...without any freckles," she found herself adding when she saw the sprinkling of freckles over his bare and very broad chest. *Mama mia,* he had the most perfect body, nicely muscled. Lean, wiry, that was what she liked, she reminded herself. Lean, compact, Italian.

He leaned close and said, "I want a tall, thin, *quiet* blonde without any aspirations of marriage or all that other—"

"Don't say it!" She stared at him, lips tightened, chin out.

He leaned close enough to kiss her and said, "F-luff." She'd never heard the word pronounced with three syllables before.

"*Argh!* Well, fine, then!"

"Fine, then."

But he didn't move back. She wished she could read something, anything, in those stormy blue eyes of his. His gaze shifted to her mouth, making her moisten her lips. Making her heart start thudding heavily inside her. *Fluff. The man thinks romance is fluff. Oh, jeez, why do I want to change his mind?* The falling rain created a curtain around the alcove. The rushing sound shut out everything but the muted music of the quartet. If one of them didn't say something, she was going to lose the fight not to lean forward. Finally, she whispered, "Why are you standing there like that?"

"I have the oddest urge to kiss you, and I'm trying to talk myself out of it."

Her heart jumped at his admission. Though there was a slight glimmer in his eyes, he was serious. "Let me help. I'm not your type."

"Very true."

"You're not my type."

"True again."

"And...I wouldn't kiss you back."

"You sure about that?" he asked, making her wonder if he read the doubt in her eyes.

"Very. Well, mostly." She swallowed hard, but her mouth was feeling that soft, warm way it did just before she was going to get kissed. Her stomach was quivering, her blood was racing, and her hands were trembling. This was not good. This was the way she was supposed to feel about Mr. Right. That's what she needed to be putting her energy toward, finding him, not kissing Mr. Wrong. And Mr. Wrong was supposed to be putting his energy into helping her find Mr. Right, not making her want to kiss *him*.

"You're saying that if I kissed you right now, you wouldn't respond at all," he said.

"Does that bother your male pride? Well, too bad. I'm here for one purpose only, and that's to find my true love."

He inched closer. "So if I put my lips on yours, you'd just stand there?"

"Right," she said, telling herself not to moisten her lips and doing it anyway.

"I don't believe you."

"Well, believe it, buddy. I'm no more interested in kissing you than—"

He kissed her, a nice, warm kiss that shot the blood to her temples. Someone must have injected her with a bottle of wine, because she felt giddy and flushed all at once. His mouth moved back and forth over hers in long, slow strokes. She wasn't responding, was she? Her mouth wasn't parted beneath his, and her eyes weren't closed. It had just gotten dark all of a sudden. He captured her lower lip between his, and she was sure, absolutely sure, she didn't sigh. Must have been him. Her mouth wasn't moving back and forth in sync with his, right? That was the earth shifting.

The earth was shifting? She opened her eyes to find Barrie watching her. How had her arms gotten around his neck like that? "Did we just have an earthquake?"

His grin was way too relaxed for someone who'd just experienced an earthquake. "In a way."

She pushed back and wondered when the air had gotten so thin. "See, no response. No pounding heartbeat," she said over the pounding of her heart. "No shortness of breath," she breathed. "And the only reason I was moving was because we were experiencing tremors." Boy, was she feeling confuzzled.

"Ah, I see." He looked too smug; she hadn't convinced him. "Come on, admit it. That kiss knocked your socks off."

"Did not."

"Then I didn't do my job. Maybe I'd better expand—"

"No!" She put out her hand. "Just accept that every woman doesn't fall victim to your charms...such as they are." She cleared her throat. "Back to the matter at hand, which was...oh, yeah, saving my dignity."

"You're insulting my charms?"

She almost laughed at the hurt look on his face. Then she snapped her fingers as the solution clicked into place. "I've got it!"

He moved a fraction closer. "Not yet, but if you'll quit moving around, you will."

She pushed him away. "Not *that.*"

He ran his hand through his damp hair, giving his head a shake. "What then?"

He'd almost kissed her again. Well, she wouldn't have responded that time either. "What?"

"You said you had it."

"Oh. Oh! You know what I'm thinking?"

"If I did, I'd be afraid."

"What?"

"If I understood you so well that I knew what you were thinking, I'd be afraid."

She narrowed her eyes. "Be afraid. Be very afraid. You're going to be my Mr. Right."

That made him back up, eyes wide. "Didn't we just agree that we weren't each other's types?"

"Yeah, right before you kissed me."

"I was only trying to make a point."

She cleared her throat. "But I'm not talking for real, so you can get that Godzilla's-going-to-eat-me look out of your eyes. You're going to pretend, just until we find the real Mr. Right.''

''Wait a minute. *I'm* going to pretend...until *we* find him?''

''I can't believe I didn't think of this before.'' She started to take a step forward, then with a wince remembered her ankle and leaned back against the wall. She rather liked the way his arms had automatically gone out to steady her. ''It'll only be for a couple of days at the most. All you have to do is go along with me. After all, we did meet in the square by the fountain before sunset.'' She looked him up and down, way up, way across those broad shoulders. ''Maybe they won't notice you're Scottish.''

That snort again. ''That's unlikely.''

''You could dye your hair dark.''

A louder snort. ''Very unlikely. There's no way I'm going to play your Mr.—''

''I'll start crying again.''

''You play dirty, you know that?''

''You owe me. You did say you were responsible.''

''Aye, you would throw that back in my face.'' His expression turned grim.

''All I'm asking is that you help me for a few days, to preserve my dignity and my family's tradition.''

''What about *my* dignity?''

She waved that away. ''You won't need it for a few days. It'll be easy. We look over those photos and see who was in the square before you fell on me. Meanwhile, all you have to do is pretend you're madly in love with me, and I'll pretend I'm madly in love with you.''

''How does one look if one is madly in love?''

''You don't know?''

"I'm glad to say, no, I don't."

"If you were in love with me, you wouldn't be able to take your eyes off me. You'd want to touch me in sweet, romantic ways, and you'd compliment me a lot."

"You didn't say anything about Oscar-worthy acting!"

She gave him a smug little smile. "Was that acting a few minutes ago when you were kissing me?"

He cleared his throat and looked out through the curtain of rain. "I was trying to prove a point, that's all."

"And that point was?"

"That I...that you... Uh, it's not important now."

"You can't even remember!"

"And you've lost your head if you think I'm playing along with you."

She lost her head looking at the contours of his back as he shrugged into his wrinkled shirt. She cleared her throat the same way he had.

He leaned back against the brick column, kicking at the bottom of it. "You're too caught up in what your family thinks. We're in the new millennium, for Pete's sake. Tell them the tradition expired in 1999. Tell them you're your own woman and you can't follow their dreams for your life, that you can't be stuck in one place your whole life trying to make them happy, that you've got to explore the world—" He blinked, then added, "find your own mate."

She took hold of his shirt again. "You don't understand. My family lives for tradition. They fight for tradition. Ten years ago my parents and grandparents went back to Italy for a funeral. As sad as my great-uncle's death was, the death of the old ways, traditions and family recipes was even harder. If you'd seen the sadness on their faces, you'd understand. I'm not going to be the one who destroys that. I've already pushed the boundaries far enough. I *need* to carry on the tradition."

"Where does the job you mentioned come into all this?"

"I want to be the sales manager for our family's company, but the position has only been held by the men in the family."

"Isn't that considered sexual discrimination?"

"Yeah, like I'm going to sue my father? The way he is, well, it's just the way he is. He told me if I finally fulfilled the tradition, I could have the job."

"And he thought you couldn't, because you've tried so many times."

"Never mind that."

He got a triumphant grin. "So you're doing this for the job? Ah, that makes more sense."

"I am not only doing this for the job." She fisted her hand at her chest. "Love and tradition mean everything to me. Romance is my family's middle name. Forget the job! Can't you believe I want to fulfil the romantic destiny of my family?"

"No. I think you're trying to fit into their ideals."

Was it that obvious? "I'm a hopeless romantic." She moved closer, rising up on her one good tiptoe, trying to keep her balance without touching him. "And I need your help. I can beg, I can cry or I can throw a tantrum. No, that would be ugly. Much better would be you offering to help me in whatever way you can, because you're such a gentleman." He wasn't buying that, not judging by the skeptical look in his eyes. "And because this whole mess is your fault. If it weren't for you, I would be sitting at that café right

now laughing happily with the man of my dreams.''
He really wasn't buying *that*.

She pulled him down to her level, nose-to-nose with
her. "Then do it because I'm desperate, because I need
you—your help. Because you are the only man..." She
realized just how close they were and swallowed hard.
Push the words out. Don't let the sentence die there!
"...who can help me," she finished with less bravado.
They remained like that for a few moments until she
said, "Well?"

"You smell awfully good, you know that?"

The rest of her argument went right out of her mind.
Barrie drew his finger up her throat and pushed her
chin up to close her mouth.

"Are you...trying to distract me?" she asked.

"Would it work?"

"No. I still need you. To help me." She blinked to
regain her senses. "What do I need to do—"

"All right."

She almost missed it, because he ran the words together just like he did when he asked, *Youallright?*
"What?"

"I said 'all right.' I'll help you, though I'm sure I'll
live to regret it."

She wanted to kiss him in thanks, but that probably
wasn't a good idea. Definitely not a good idea. "Thank
you," she said, instead of kissing him or anything else
that smacked of insanity.

"You're welcome."

"And you won't live to regret it. I mean, you won't
regret it." She took the opportunity to back away.
"You'll help me find Mr. Right, my family won't be
disappointed in me and you can go on doing whatever

it is that you do with your life.'' She smiled. ''It'll be easy.''

MARISA WASN'T SMILING as they drove to her family's home, having nothing better to do than watch the rain dribble down the window and obscure the jam-packed coffee houses, health-food eatery and numerous Italian restaurants. One couple walked hand in hand in the rain, looking so romantic, she wanted to puke. She scarcely had mind enough to think about the dull pain in her ankle. All she could think about was the scene awaiting them. And about deceiving her family.

Technically she'd kept tradition. But when they saw him...oh boy. She glanced at Barrie, who caught her gaze. She looked away, trying not to think about that kiss. Okay, the upcoming scene wasn't all she could think about. The kiss took a close second. Even Barrie looked grim, though she wasn't sure if it was about the impending dinner or their kiss.

''Maybe this isn't such a good idea,'' she said.

''I'm sure it isn't.''

''I hate lying to my family. I don't think I ever have, except the one time I told Mama I wasn't kissing Franco in the car.''

''Franco?''

''I was fifteen.'' She waved away his questioning look. ''This is a big lie.''

''Quite big.''

''Humongous!''

''That, too,'' he said.

''You don't have to keep agreeing with me.''

''Then tell them the truth. Stand up for yourself. Tell them how silly it is.''

''Maybe I should—the truth part, anyway. No, I

can't. And it's not silly, it's just...part of my heritage. If you'd been born in my family, you'd understand." She rubbed her forehead. "I just can't bear to be the Bad News column of the fall newsletter again."

"I say tell them the truth. I'll back you up."

She caught herself almost snorting, the way he did. "While you're backing out the door! No, I've got to make them think I believe you're Mr. Right."

He sat there contemplating her for a moment. "You have trouble making decisions, don't you?"

"No. Well, sometimes. Not a lot. Okay, a lot. Yes, I have a bit of trouble making decisions."

The edge of his mouth lifted in the tiniest of grins. "You sure about that?"

"Positive. But not all the time."

He laughed. Laughed! Then shook his head as he looked out the car window. "I have a feeling this is one decision I'm going to regret." He looked over at her. "So how many people are going to be at your parents' house?"

"Not many." Well, relatively speaking, anyway. Her aunts and cousins, uncles and family from Italy wouldn't be there. Only the immediate family. "There's Nonna, my grandmother. She's the family treasure. My favorite thing in the whole world is watching her cook. She also talks to her dead husband, but we all kind of ignore that. Then there's my Uncle Louie, my great-uncle actually. He's a little hard of hearing and refuses to get a hearing aid. Mama cries a lot, especially now that she's going through menopause. Pop calls it 'mental-pause' because it makes him mental. Pop...well, he's Pop. Then there's my sister, Gina, the perfect daughter, and she'll be the first to tell you. And her husband, Tino. My brother, Carlo, won't be there, because he's still working the booth at the festival. Oh, and you're not supposed to know about the *amore* tradition. The men don't usually know—''

'''Til they've been snagged but good.''

She narrowed her eyes. ''They don't consider themselves *snagged*. As far as the man's concerned, he's hit full in the heart by love, I invite him home for dinner with my family, he loves them, they love him and then it's happily ever after. Don't say it!'' She rubbed her nose, waiting for him to make that snorting noise. For once, he didn't. But she could tell he wanted to. ''That's how it happened with Gina. Tino's a great guy, and he owns his own bakery. How more perfect could he be? Now she's pregnant with my parents' first grandchild.'' Marisa's voice grew lighter. ''It took her a year to conceive, and she was worried about letting my family down. But now she's about ready to pop, and she's even going to be a full-time mom for a few years. My family's so proud of her.''

''Well, I'm not very proud of myself aiding and abetting a lost soul whose only aim in life is to please her family,'' Barrie said. ''Family's supposed to guide, not dominate. Someday you're going to look back on your life and wonder who was really living it. Will you be happy then?'' He guided the Buick through the quaint neighborhood of European-style homes, following her directions. Flowers blooming everywhere looked cheery despite the dreary day. They pulled into a circular driveway in front of a sprawling house with orange tiles on the roof and flower boxes under every window.

Her gaze took in the home where she'd grown up, where Nonna and Uncle Louie and Gina and Tino all lived. Marisa lived ten minutes away in a small apartment, and she knew she was expected to move back into the family home with her husband. Whenever she even hinted that maybe they'd find their own place...oh, brother.

"What exactly is wrong with pleasing your family, anyway? They are the people who put their hearts and souls into raising you."

"Does that mean we owe them our lives? That we have to sacrifice our dreams for theirs?"

This had nothing to do with her family. Her voice went soft. "You said something about living in a whiskey distillery."

"Not *in* the distillery." He looked past her to the blue door with the flowers painted around it, his eyes growing hard in memory. "I grew up in a remote village in the Highlands. The local distillery is everyone's life and livelihood. Family tradition is being manipulated by guilt—and tears—to live the way they think you should. It's never knowing freedom or real happiness or finding out what you want to do with your life." He blinked, snapping out of his spell. "I spent my first twenty years in one place. Now I've got to spend at least that long never staying in one place."

"The right woman wouldn't tie you down. Maybe she'd even travel with you."

That snort again. "Just what I need, a woman tagging along, expecting attention. Some of the places I go aren't fit for a woman. Some aren't even fit for a man. Voodoo rituals in Haiti, sacrificial ceremonies in a live volcano." At her questioning look, he added, "Not human sacrifices. But I do cover the edgier topics. In fact, my features are called, 'On the Edge.'"

"Well, if I were married to you, which of course I never would be, I'd let you go on the edgier trips by yourself, but I'd come with you sometimes and make business contacts. So you see, you wouldn't have to give me attention all the time. But I'd want some attention later." She thought of those sexy teddies in her hope chest—"Given-up-hope chest," Gina called it—and the one she'd worn today for good luck.

Barrie moistened his lips. "Well, I suppose that could be arranged, if we were married, which we wouldn't be, because I don't intend to ever get married. I plan to be one of those seasoned old men who've lived their lives without lies or promises."

"And when you look back on your life, will you be happy with it?"

"Deliriously," he said, pushing open his door. "All I need is my freedom and my photography. I've got no one to answer to at home, no one I have to call once I land somewhere and report in."

"On the other hand, isn't it kind of sad that no one cares?"

He stopped and looked at her. "Of course not." He walked around to her side of the car.

"I can hobble in."

He scooped her up anyway. "Might as well carry you. Since I'm madly in love with you and all."

3

THIS WAS BECOMING way too comfortable, carrying Marisa in his arms, even with the dismayed expression on her face.

Chomp, chomp, chomp. Barrie tried to bring to mind the piranha. Uh-oh, not good, not good at all. It was starting to look like a…*goldfish?* Instead of chomping, it was nibbling. He willed the vicious fish back into his thoughts.

"I know how you feel about traditions," she said, "but please remember that traditions are important to my family. And to me. When you walk through that door, you've got to put yourself into a different mindset. I've been doing it for years, ever since I discovered everyone else wasn't so old-fashioned."

Marisa pushed the door open. He stepped inside the cavernous house filled with tile floors, dark wood furniture, and the aromas of chocolate and garlic. Rich was how he'd describe it, not so much in value but in colors, textures and scents. The left side of the house flowed from a dining room to the kitchen to a family room in the back, all open to one another. The three women and one man in the kitchen and the two men in the living room to the right all came to a halt in their conversations, and twelve startled eyes were fixed on him.

He felt like he'd just stepped onto a stage without a

clue as to what his lines were. From the stereo, an opera singer was letting a high note rip, punctuating the moment. The family's gazes widened. Everyone's eyes shifted to him, then back to her, and their mouths fell open. For the longest moment in his life, nobody said a word. Well, except the opera singer, who continued to wail. Barrie had an almost irresistible urge to take their picture. He restrained it, even though he had a feeling this shot would qualify as having soul.

He whispered in her ear, "I remember a moment like this when I was at a Kombai sago-grub festival in Irian Jaya, Indonesia. When we arrived, five tribesmen burst out of the bush, armed with barbed arrows. This isn't much different. Except your family isn't armed. Or naked."

Marisa glanced at him as her family slowly walked toward the foyer like zombies in *Dawn of the Dead.* "A food festival?"

"Not that kind of grub. Well, sort of. Grub as in larvae."

"Ew, gross!" She now had the attention of her entire family, all gathered for the performance. *"Ciao,"* Marisa said, though he detected a quiver in her voice. "Everyone, I'd like you to meet Barrie MacKenzie." She introduced each member of her family in turn.

And still they all stared wordlessly. Uncle Louie, the oldest man in the group, stepped closer and studied Barrie. His scraggly gray eyebrows bobbed up and down, and then he shuffled back to the pack. He leaned down to Nonna, with the towering hair, and whispered in a loud voice, "He doesn't look Italian to me!"

She patted his arm. "You always were sharp as caterpillar teeth, Uncle Louie." He bared his teeth and growled at her.

Marisa's father, wearing a bright purple shirt, said, "What happened? Did he drag you through the mud? Is he a pig farmer?"

Nonna said, "He's too big, Marisa! Didn't I tell you not to get a big one?"

Her mother, a plumper, older version of Marisa, started fanning herself. "*Madonna mia,* it's hot in here. Is it hot in here, or am I going to faint?"

"Just don't cry, Mama," a very pregnant Gina pleaded, which promptly made Mama start crying.

Uncle Louie tried his whispering tactic again. "He's like an octopus. Got his testicles all over her already!"

"*Tentacles,* Uncle Louie!" Tino, a man about Barrie's age, corrected, wiggling his fingers to demonstrate. He gave Barrie a sheepish smile. "He sometimes gets his words mixed up."

"On purpose!" Nonna said. Louie narrowed his eyes at her and growled again.

Tino leaned forward to shake Barrie's hand, then saw Barrie's hands were otherwise occupied. He wore an apron over his blue jeans and just seemed to realize he was carrying a tray in one oven-mitt-covered hand. He extended the tray of small, round balls. "Deep-fried olive? My own creation. They're covered in a delicate coating of seasoned flour." When Barrie declined, Tino added, "And don't think just because I like to bake that it makes me less of a man. There's not a feminine bone in my body, ain't that right, Gina?"

"That's right, teddy bear."

Not that Barrie would dare argue, but Tino looked a bit like a male version of Shirley Temple with his round face and curly hair.

"She's going to marry a pig farmer," her father said in a stunned voice. "And he's not even Italian!" He ran trembling fingers over his sparse, slicked-back hair making the gray tufts at the sides stick out horizontally.

"I already said that," Uncle Louie muttered. "And don't forget the testicles all over her, and it's not even eight o'clock."

"*Tentacles,* Louie!" Nonna said.

Mama's eyes widened in horror. "He's a pig farmer?" She crossed herself again. "My mama would turn over in her grave!"

"I'm not *in* the grave yet!" Nonna objected, nudging Marisa's mother. She looked upward. "Salvatore, what are we going to do?"

"At least I didn't let you down, huh, Mama?" Gina said with a dramatic sigh.

Barrie looked at Marisa, whose agony over her deception was painted on her face.

"This isn't going very well, is it?" she said as the noise escalated, the pitch rose higher, and the words multiplied in an Italian frenzy.

"About as well as any mutiny, I suppose."

"Mama." Marisa tried to get her mother's attention. "Mama!"

It was only when Gina said on a gasp, "Uh-oh, I think the baby's coming!" that everyone went quiet and blissful silence fell.

For a moment.

And then all hell broke loose.

"Gina! The baby!"

Her husband dropped the tray of olives on the side table and ran out through the French doors. Nonna tromped into the kitchen in—*combat boots?*—and grabbed the phone. Tino slammed into the foyer with a suitcase and slipped on an escaped olive, twisting his ankle. Marisa's father helped him limp out the door.

Everyone was moving, grabbing up things and muttering. In the fastest mobilization of a family he'd ever seen, everyone was out the door.

Marisa let out a sound of exasperation. "They forgot me! Can you please take me to the hospital?"

His eyebrows furrowed. "But *they're* going to be there." His ears were still ringing with the echoes of their voices.

"Please?"

He'd never been a pushover. So why was he turning around and walking back out to his Buick with this soft, damp woman who smelled like roses and mud in his arms?

"HE'S NOT a pig farmer, and no, he's not Italian. You've probably figured out he's Scottish by his delicious—er, his accent." They all crowded into one corner of the waiting room listening to Marisa. "But he's the right one. I'm sure of it."

She had explained the ankle, the cast from hell and the mud-stained dress, everything but the missed appointment with destiny. Uncle Louie strained to read her lips, his eyes narrowing in concentration beneath his bushy gray brows. Barrie, damp and bedraggled, sat off to the side, content obviously to let her do the talking. Poor thing. She'd never forget the shell-shocked look on his face back at the house. But she couldn't let him off the hook. She was on dangerous ground as it was. Lying to her family was only one notch below not following family tradition on the Terrible-Things-To-Do list.

Nonna took her hand and whispered, "Marisa, so big, so big. Will he fit?"

"Fit where, exactly?"

"Through your doorway, of course."

Marisa took a breath of relief. She couldn't handle the thought of talking sex with her *nonna*. "He'll probably have to duck."

Nonna gave her hand a squeeze. "Salvatore had to duck, too." She steadied her tower of hair with her hands and looked up. "Didn't you, sweetheart? But still I walked funny for hours."

Marisa's mouth dropped open, but her mother leaned forward and distracted her. "Marisa, are you sure this was the man at the fountain at sunset? Maybe you missed the right man."

Boy, did she miss the right man.

Nonna put in, "Maybe Barrie was standing in front of him, and you couldn't see him. He's so big, you know."

"Yes, I know how big he is!" Those words drifted in the momentary silence of the room. Barrie had a curious glimmer in his eyes. Could she just die right there? She tried to shrink into the plastic chair. "I mean, I know he's a big man. Yes, Mama, I'm sure."

Mama shook her head. "You've never been sure of anything in your life. Why this? Have I failed as a mother? I've done something terrible and I'm being punished for it!" She started crying again.

Her pop sat so close to her mama, they were almost one. "What're you trying to do, break your mother's heart?"

Barrie watched their cuddling with a look of puzzlement. Louie's loud voice reverberated through the room. "Where's your skirt, then?"

"It's not a skirt," Barrie said without a trace of defensiveness.

"Eh?"

"It's a kilt," Barrie answered again patiently.

"Your skirt was killed, then?"

Marisa had a sudden image of Barrie wearing the kind of garb Mel Gibson wore in *Braveheart*. Not an unpleasant image at all, if she'd been into that sort of thing, but she wasn't.

"They're all at the cleaners," she answered, taking the seat between Louie and Barrie.

"I only wear a kilt when I go home for Robbie Burns Night."

"Who's that?" Marisa asked. Louie was leaning forward, straining to hear.

"A famous poet in Scotland. A bit of a rogue, he was. Had fourteen children, five with different women."

Uncle Louie's mouth dropped open. "You say you have forty children with different women? Why, his tentacles must have been all over the place!"

"Testicles!" Marisa corrected, then with horror realized what she'd yelled out. "Tentacles! I meant tentacles!" She now had the attention of *everyone* in the waiting room. "Oh, my gawd, can I just die right now?" To Louie, she said, "Not Barrie's...tentacles, Uncle Louie. A poet's. Forget the tentacles, okay? Uncle Louie, Barrie's a photographer," she said, trying to change the subject. Desperately.

When Gina and Tino walked—well, Tino limped—into the waiting room, everybody surrounded them. "It's a false alarm," Tino announced when he could get a word in edgewise. "She's not ready to come out yet."

"*He's* just teasing us," Gina said, rubbing her belly.

"And don't think I'm less of a man just because I

want a girl," Tino said, squaring his shoulders. She wondered if he knew he was still wearing his apron.

Mama clasped her hands at her stomach and smiled the smile of a proud mother. It melted away when she glanced at Marisa and Barrie. "I guess we'll go home and have our—" she affected her best noble-but-hurt-and-add-the-sniffle expression "—celebration dinner."

THE RAIN LEFT the evening a dull silver. Marisa watched Barrie take in the town as they drove down Rome Street, the main drag.

"Do only Italians live here?" he asked when he saw the fourth pasta restaurant.

"Mostly. Some came from Italy, some from New York's Little Italy. I guess Chinatown's crowding them out. The founders wanted it to be like the towns in Italy, close-knit, a safe place to raise children. I couldn't imagine living anywhere else." And, by the look on his face, he couldn't imagine living here.

She shifted in her seat. For an old car, the Buick was in great condition. It smelled of ancient vinyl and the pine air freshener hanging from the mirror. It looked good on Barrie, big and sturdy. Her family would love for her to have a car like this, sturdy and old-fashioned, instead of her little convertible Rabbit, which they considered too yuppie. Whenever her Mama got into the car with her, Marisa had to quickly change the radio station from the hip-hop station.

She glanced up as they pulled into their driveway. "Oh, I almost forgot to tell you the cardinal rule. We always kiss Nonna first when we come into the house. It's out of respect, since she's the oldest person in our family. One kiss per cheek."

His eyebrows furrowed. "Look, it's bad enough pretending to be part of your silly tradition, but I'm not going round kissing your relatives.''

''It's just a kiss on the cheek.''

He shifted her, avoiding her gaze. ''I'm not…comfortable with that sort of thing.''

''You didn't have much trouble with the kissing thing earlier.''

He gave her a wry look. ''Are you kidding? I had a mountain of trouble with the kissing thing.''

You and me both. ''If she offers you her cheek, she expects a kiss. Of course, you'll have to lean down a ways. Please, just give her a little kiss. It'll hurt her feelings if you don't.''

''Do I have to kiss anyone else?''

Me! she had the insane urge to yell. The word nearly slipped out of her mouth. ''Probably not Mama. She's not too sure about you.''

He lifted an eyebrow. ''I'm not too sure about any of you.'' His eyes added, *Especially you.*

''You don't have to be sure of us, you just have to…play along. In fact, I don't want you to be too likable, because they might miss you when you leave and the real Mr. Right comes on the scene.''

''Should I sit there with a snarl on my face through dinner then?''

''Do what you did at the hospital, sit off to the side looking confuzzled. That was perfect.''

''What the devil is confuzzled?''

''Confused with a twist.''

He gave her that trademark snort of his. ''That shouldn't be a problem. I have a feeling I'll become very familiar with that state of mind in the next few days.''

''My family's not that bad.''

"It's just that I don't do crowds of people well, especially loud, huggy crowds. Our family meals were quiet affairs, where the only conversation was, 'Pass the tatties' or some such."

"That's what you like?"

"It's what I'm comfortable with. Now I'm used to eating alone."

"Sounds boring." She crossed her arms. "I'll bet your family didn't kiss much, either."

That snort again. "I never saw my parents kiss each other, much less anyone else."

Marisa felt a smile creep up her face. "Well, *you* don't seem to have much trouble with kissing."

The corner of his mouth quirked. "Not with the real kind. None of that cheek-kissing thing."

"That kiss earlier. It was…a nice kiss."

He leaned against the seat and faced her. "There's a difference between a nice kiss and a good kiss. And I only kissed you to prove a point."

"Which you didn't."

"Which I did." He looked way too smug. "Bet if I gave you a good kiss, you wouldn't deny feeling something."

She caught herself swallowing hard. "I'll take your word for that."

"A kiss should be like lovemaking, using all your senses, totally committed to the moment."

"It's not all about kissing, you know," she said, annoyed at the crackle in her voice. "What about holding hands, romantic strolls in the park—"

He got out of the car and walked around to her side. "Not my style, that silly—"

"Don't say it!"

He paused. Smiled. "Fluff."

"Argh!"

Well, what was she feeling so riled about? So what if he wasn't romantic? He wasn't her Mr. Right anyway. And who was she to judge, a woman who wasn't sure if she was romantic enough herself? He hoisted her into his arms and walked to the entry.

Carlo opened the door. "Marisa!" he said in his loud, booming voice.

"Carlo, don't yell!"

His fiery eyes took in Barrie, and his chest puffed out in twenty-two-year-old bravado. "I'm Marisa's brother, Carlo Cerini," he stated. "And I need a word with my sister."

She felt like that sack of potatoes again as Carlo took her from Barrie and marched to his room. "Carlo, put me down! Are you crazy?"

He dropped her on the bed. "Am *I* crazy? First I hear, while working the cookie booth, that my sister is being hauled away by some tall, red-haired—"

"It's auburn, really."

He waved his arms. "Fine, some *auburn*-haired man, and then when I come home, I hear you think he's Mr. Right, and I bet you a hundred bucks you're wrong." He crossed his arms over his chest, mirroring her posture. "He's not Italian."

"Well, duh. Like I didn't notice."

"You're gonna go out there and tell him you were mistaken. I don't care what kind of sparkle he puts in your eyes, you can't marry him."

"He doesn't put any sparkle— There's a sparkle in my eyes?"

Carlo gave her an exasperated look. "Forget the sparkle! Forget that man."

"What, did you lose money on me?" She pointed

to that blasted chart with her name on it. "And how dare you put me up there like some racehorse!"

"It's nothing personal. I gotta meet the public's demand. This has nothing to do with the bets. You know how important tradition is to our family."

"I know that. That's why I've been writing down Nonna's recipes, preserving them." Not that she could actually make them.

"That's not going to mean a lot when you break their hearts." Boy, he was beginning to sound like Pop.

"I hate to break it to you, but he's the right one. So take me back out there this instant before I tell your girlfriend you sleep with a stuffed turtle!"

His eyes widened. "It's not a turtle. How many times do I have to tell you, it's a pillow. A green, furry pillow."

Marisa wrinkled her nose. "With a turtle face."

Muttering, he scooped her up and reluctantly took her back to the living room.

WELL, THAT WAS interesting, Barrie thought as he watched the young man cart Marisa off. In the dining room to his left, a long table was crowded with plates and bowls of food. The air smelled better than any Italian restaurant he'd ever been in.

The opening between the dining room and kitchen was a wide arch decorated with majolica tiles. The kitchen beyond was as large as the dining room, the walls covered with pots and pans, counters cluttered with cooking utensils. On the kitchen windowsill sat a row of potted plants interspersed with old, colored bottles. The women worked together with fluid choreography, filling bowls and plates that Gina took to the table balanced on her belly. The three men sat at the table talking in Italian and gesturing with their hands. They kept looking over at him, not with hostility, but definitely with curiosity as though they still couldn't believe he was there.

Barrie could relate. He glanced at his Buick in the driveway, at the cheerily lit street leading out of the neighborhood, then at the Buick again. For a moment he let himself fancy escaping. Marisa didn't know where he was staying. He couldn't imagine her hobbling around the festival trying to find him. Actually, he could. But he'd promised to help her, and it *was* sort of his fault, so he let out a long breath. He pushed the front door and it closed with an ominous thud.

"Here!"

Marisa was promptly deposited into his arms just as he turned around again. Carlo stalked to the dining room and jumped into the discussion with the other men, gesturing toward the doorway.

"Well," Barrie said, "I think your plan about them not liking me is going forward."

"It's not that they don't like you." She took in her family. "I know this seems crazy to you. Sometimes I feel like I'm part of two worlds: the outside world and my family. But they're not going to change and I'm not going to change them. That's just the way they are."

"You don't have to change them. Would it really be so bad to tell them that you want something different for your life?"

"Yes," she said in all seriousness.

"Would it kill them if you did fall in love with a non-Italian? Not me," he added at her surprised look.

"Out of the question. Besides, I *want* to keep the tradition and marry an Italian. I *want* to be part of the romance of it all. And in my family, that tradition isn't a burden, it's something we're proud of.''

"And I suppose you wanting a career doesn't fit in with the family tradition.''

"Exactly. I know it's normal for the rest of the world, a woman wanting a career as well as a family. I see that, and yet I also see how important giving your all to your family is, because I got all of my mother's love. It's family values.''

Barrie could see in her expression the pain she felt, trying to fit into her two worlds. "But you asked for that job anyway,'' he said, surprised at hearing the pride in his voice.

Marisa had a sparkle in her eyes as she nodded. "I had to, though I couldn't let on how much I want it. But you see now, after asking for the job, how important it is that I get the marriage part right? And, well, that was part of the deal anyway.''

"Deal?''

"Getting the job if I met Mr. Right this time.''

"How many times have you, er, failed?''

"Well, counting this time…six. But I'm going to get it right. And I've got all these great ideas for the company, but I have a feeling Pop's going to keep me restrained if—when I do get the position.''

"And you'll let him because you're a good Italian girl?''

"Oh, put me down! You don't understand at all.''

He set her on her one foot, but she kept her hand around his arm.

"I understand too well,'' he said. "As they say, been there, done that. But I cut loose, because there was no compromise.''

"You took the easy way out. I'm going to prove

myself once I get the job.'' She had a determined look in her eyes, but then it changed to conspiratorial. "Can you keep a secret? I've been taking courses at the community college north of here.''

"You do realize that most parents are thrilled when their offspring go to college?''

"Yeah, I know. They mean the best—they really do. I just completed my two-year business degree and I'm ready to prove myself.''

"What exactly does your family's company do?''

She made a face, as though reluctant to tell him. "Oh, I suppose you'll find out soon enough.'' Her hand tightened on his arm as she balanced herself. Without thinking about it, he put his hands on her shoulders to steady her. Even muddy, she was pretty. What he wanted was to taste her mouth again and get a reaction this time. Get her to admit a reaction, anyway. He was determined to accomplish that. For his ego, of course. She turned and caught him looking at her with what was probably a devilish gleam in his eyes.

She'd been about to say something, but the words obviously escaped her. "Uh…''

"Do you always have this little problem with talking?''

Her teeth clicked when she snapped her mouth shut. "No, only when—yes, yes, I do. All the time.''

He clucked his tongue. "Ah, that indecisiveness again. So, tell me about this company.''

She turned to him, finger pointing. "No snorting.''

"Me, snort?''

"Yeah, you snort. Anyway, my family owns the Amore Cookie Company.''

He caught himself before doing just what she'd warned him about. "Go on.''

"My great-great-grandmother discovered that her husband—whom she'd met at the festival—"

"And no doubt an Italian," he put in.

"Definitely an Italian." Her gaze held his for a moment. She had wonderfully expressive eyes, though he wasn't sure what they expressed right then. She blinked, then turned away, and he found that his stomach had that strange feeling swirling inside again. Could be the flu coming on.

"See that glass bowl over there," she said after a moment, pointing to the mahogany table in the living room that was covered with framed family photographs. He maneuvered her over to it, and she pulled a cellophane package from the red bowl. "These are our cookies. Great-Great-Nonna and her love discovered their mutual passion for cookies, and they started baking these together."

"Not that he was any less of a man because of it."

"Huh?"

He laughed. "That's what your brother-in-law keeps saying."

"Oh." She grinned, too. "I guess he was teased a lot when he took up baking. He tried making manly dishes—"

"Like meatballs?"

She was trying not to laugh, the same way she had when she'd looked at David's willie. He liked that girlish twinkle and the way she covered her mouth. "Right," she said, gaining control over that grin. "Anyway, over in Italy, they only sold the cookies to restaurants and bakeries. When my pop married Mama, and they moved here, they opened a factory. Our cookies are now in most of the gourmet shops on the West Coast."

And she was damned proud, too. He turned the package over in his hand. Two round cookies nestled side-by-side. "And you call them Amore cookies because they come two in each package?"

"That and the poem." She pointed again. "No snorting!"

"You keep saying that, and your family *will* think I'm a pig farmer. Tell me about the poem."

"In each package of cookies there's a poem. It doesn't rhyme or anything. We call them verbal kisses." She opened the package and handed him a cookie. "Try one."

All this talk about kissing had him looking at that lush mouth with the intriguing mole. And she always knew when he did, because she moistened her lips. She never looked insulted; in fact, she looked as though his interest in her mouth surprised her in a rather nice way. Better not think about kissing her anymore. He wasn't a man of impulse, but for some strange reason, this lass had his body leaping in response. He took a bite of the almond-flavored cookie with the drop of chocolate on top. "Not bad."

"Not bad? That's all you can say?"

"I wouldn't die from eating it," he said with a sincere smile. "Where I'm from, that's the way we express things. We use litotes—understatement."

She eyed him, then must have decided to believe him. She held up a strip of pink paper that was in the bottom of the package, and he read the words written in script. "A kiss under the full moon seals the heart in love." He couldn't hold back the snort of laughter this time.

"I suppose you think it's—"

"Don't say it!" He pushed his chin out the same way she did.

She narrowed her eyes at him "—fluff."

"Aye." He popped the rest in his mouth. "But the cookie's not bad."

IN BARRIE'S TRAVELS through Italy, he'd found the natives to be nothing but friendly, warm people, if a bit loud and demonstrative. Marisa's family was no exception, despite the fact that they viewed him as an interloper who threatened to marry their daughter. The men in the family slipped surreptitious looks his way. The women hovered over his plate, more concerned that he enjoyed his meal than eating their own. They must have thought he was storing up for the winter, because every time he turned around, either Nonna or Ninalee, Marisa's mother, was piling on something else.

First *crostini con funghi,* then bread soup with potatoes, three different kinds of bread, a different wine with each course, pasta with arugula and tomato, roast chicken stuffed with olives, stuffed peppers... He was stuffed! And he hated peppers, but he cut his into tiny pieces and tried to blend it in with the rice and salami stuffing.

"*Mange!* Eat!" Ninalee slid another stuffed pepper onto his plate.

"Better eat," Marisa whispered. "It's an insult to an Italian cook if you don't eat all your food." She had cleaned up and now wore a flowered dress borrowed from Gina's pre-pregnancy wardrobe. The top fit tightly across her chest, and one lock of her damp hair lay in the curve of her cleavage.

"Kisses on the cheek, finishing my plate... I need a

rule book in this place," he muttered, but went to work on his food. Eating a home-cooked meal wasn't much of a sacrifice, he supposed. At least he hadn't had to kiss anyone yet.

The conversation at the table rarely stopped, nor did it follow any logical pattern. It seemed everyone threw in their thoughts whether they were relevant to the current topic or not.

"A woman in my Lamaze class wants to cook her placenta in a stew," Gina said, giving Tino a pinch on the cheek. "For good luck, she says."

"Ew, gross!" Marisa said, wrinkling her nose.

"I could come up with a recipe for her," Tino said.

"Ew, gross!"

"We'd already sold a thousand cookies at the booth when I left today," Carlo said.

Marisa told Barrie, "The company closes for the festival, but everyone takes turns at the booth."

"I made chocolate-covered pickles for dessert," Tino said, leaning over to give his wife a sloppy-sounding kiss. "Gina likes them."

"Ew, gross!" Marisa said.

Mama narrowed her eyes at Marisa. "Did you put eye makeup on?"

Nonna leaned over to Marisa, which was easy since she always leaned a little to the right, and said, "What if he rolls over in bed and crushes you? He's awfully big."

"You just called him a pig?" Uncle Louie asked.

"He's big!" Marisa slapped her hand over her mouth and met Barrie's amused gaze. "Oh, never mind!"

He felt almost bad as Tino watched the bowl of

chocolate-covered pickles sit untouched by everyone except Gina.

Gina said, "I'm the perfect wife, huh, teddy bear? I always eat your creations."

One thing he noticed was how much the two married couples touched each other. Between kisses, glancing touches and outright squeezes, he wondered how they had time to eat. Nonna even touched Louie, but it was more of a get-out-of-my-way nudge. Louie growled back at her.

Once the crumbly coffee cake was brought out for dessert, Ninalee pulled a notebook from a mahogany buffet table behind them. Marisa glanced at him, then quickly looked away. Uh-oh. He had a bad feeling about this.

He got an even worse feeling when she poked him in the side and whispered, "No snorting!" He flinched from her jab and grabbed her finger. Her eyes widened in mischief. "You're ticklish?"

"Not a bit."

He liked the shape of her mouth, just the right size, as it quirked in a grin. "A big guy like you, ticklish?"

He held tight to her finger when she tried to wrench it free. Soft hands, nice rounded nails—no painted talons. He rubbed her palm with his thumb. "Don't even think it."

She'd started to sneak attack with her other hand, but stopped and looked down at their linked hands. She tilted her head, a look of wonder on her features. "What are you doing?"

The sight of their joined hands startled him, too. What *was* he doing? *Chomp, chomp, chomp.* Was being around all these kooky romantics stewing his brain? He let go of her hand and looked up.

Everyone at the table was watching them.

Each of the Cerinis wore different expressions. Pop Cerini's slicked-back hair had started to stick out again, and he did not look pleased as he reached for his wife's hand. Ninalee fanned herself. Carlo, with his refined features, put on a good scowl. Gina's head was tilted as she fiddled with her hair. Nonna was actually smiling, and Louie leaned over his plate so he could get a better look.

Marisa looked up, too, and made a sort of giggle/ hiccup noise. Her flushed face matched the plum-and-red tablecloth as she slid her hand free of his. "Love, laughter and kisses, the riches of life."

For a moment, everyone was silent. Then they came to life at once, all wired together, nodding and saying, "Good one!" Ninalee wrote it down.

Nonna said, "Love and chocolate are good for the soul."

Louie said, "Love and prunes, good for the body."

They all started to nod, then abruptly stopped.

"Er…yeah, good one, Uncle Louie," Marisa said, and they continued throwing out romantic sayings.

"Marisa," Barrie said, rather enjoying the way her name rolled off his tongue.

"Love is the cake, kisses are the frosting." She turned to him. "Yes?"

"What, exactly, is it that you're all doing?"

The rest of the Cerinis kept calling out mushy phrases. Marisa said, "They're the verbal kisses that go in our cookies." He caught himself looking at her mouth again, and she ran her tongue self-consciously over her lips. "It's a family tradition. Whenever we get together for dinner, we brainstorm."

He sat back for a few minutes, listening to the words

flying back and forth over the table. These people believed all this fluff. For a man who had no use for romance, he might as well have been dropped into a Hallmark store. "Remind me to throttle Porter."

"Kisses are to life what wine is to dinner. Who?"

"The guy who was supposed to cover this festival. The one who didn't because he fell in love."

Ninalee paused in writing down the phrases and looked over at him. "Do you have anything to contribute, Barrie?"

Carlo said, "Bet you ten bucks he can't come up with one."

"No!" Marisa answered for him, then smiled sheepishly when everyone looked at her. "Now, don't embarrass him. He's only romantic in private."

"What do you do?" Lamberto, Marisa's father, asked Barrie. "Besides pig farming?"

Barrie smiled.

"He works for a magazine, traveling all over and taking pictures," Marisa said, making him wonder if he imagined the pride in her voice. After all, even his own parents deprecated his success. "He's seen naked tribespeople who eat bugs and tried to kill him. Isn't that cool?"

"Charming," Ninalee said with a pinched smile.

"And where do you live?" Carlo asked.

"New York."

"So you travel a lot, then?" Gina put in, still twirling a lock of her hair.

"Aye, quite a bit."

He felt as though the whole family was closing in on him, drilling him with questions about his career, apartment, aspirations. So it came as no surprise when Carlo crossed his arms over his undershirt-clad chest and asked, "What are your intentions regarding my sister?"

He saw her tense, but before she could answer, he said, "Why, I intend to marry her."

4

"WATCH THAT HAND!"

"Oops, sorry."

Being in the small darkroom with Barrie was probably not one of Marisa's best ideas. Even over the vinegary aromas of the fix, his aftershave tickled her senses. In the warm orange light, she could see just enough of him to intrigue her. And sometimes when he passed where she sat on a stool, he accidentally brushed her behind. Or, at least, she thought it was accidental. Some part of her actually hoped it wasn't— but that was a crazy part, so she ignored it.

Barrie had made arrangements to use a darkroom just north of Cortina the next morning. When he'd called to let Marisa know, she had, of course, offered to go and direct him to the place. Out of courtesy, naturally.

And when he'd shown up looking very artistic, with his hair pulled back and a blue shirt that made his eyes look positively dazzling, that crazy part of her didn't feel the least bit courteous. She ignored that too, and the way his white jeans molded to his thighs as he'd walked toward the front porch of her apartment. And just to be safe, she ignored the thrum of electricity that vibrated all the way through her and warmed parts that had no business being warmed by Barrie.

She'd watched in fascination as he'd made contact

sheets from the strips of negatives. Then she'd used a loupe—and felt very professional doing so—to help him choose which photographs captured images of her potential Mr. Right.

"I thought you'd be taking color pictures," she said when she saw the sheet.

"I usually do, but I suggested that since this festival goes back generations, it might be nice to do the piece in black and white with sepia tones to give it an old look."

She watched him go through the process of developing several pictures, the picture magically coming to life in the developer, then into the wash, then to the fix. When several pictures were swimming around in a tub of circulating water he called the wash, he turned on the light and started taking them out.

He squeegeed one print against a slanted piece of glass, then hung it on a line with a clothespin. "So after I left, your parents didn't tie you up in the attic until you came to your senses?" he said, hanging up another photograph.

He had great hands, strong yet graceful. Slowly she realized he'd said something and rewound his words through her mind. "They hung me by my toes and pummeled me with cannoli. I kept wanting to spill everything, but I just couldn't. They'll thank me later for deceiving them now."

"Maybe they'll put their appreciation in that newsletter."

"Hmph." She wrinkled her nose at him. "And you were too much last night."

He lifted an eyebrow. "Really?"

"I mean, you were incredible."

"Why, thank you." He looked way too pleased with himself.

She rolled her eyes. "I didn't mean that kind of incredible. Why'd you go and tell my family all that stuff about it's not every day that you meet the woman of your dreams, and about me being incredible and... beautiful? After the marrying part, which was bad enough."

"I borrowed it from Porter. Isn't that the point of this tradition of yours? What was it you said? The chap is hit full in the heart by love, blah, blah, blah, and they live happily ever after?"

"Yes, but you're not that...chap! Even if you were, you'd never say something so romantic."

"If I were your chap, maybe I'd be moved to say how beautiful you are, but no, not all that other..."

"Don't say it!"

He took hold of her chin and leaned close enough to kiss her. "Fluff."

"You think I'm beautiful?" she asked when his previous words sunk in.

His gaze took in her face, and he stepped back. "If I were attracted to fiery Italian lasses, aye." He pulled another photograph out of the wash.

She checked to see if her mouth was open. It wasn't, but then again, had that really counted as a compliment?

"Hey, that's me." She inched closer. "But how could it be...."

He kept his gaze averted. "It's not you."

She tried to grab for the picture, but he hung it out of her reach. "Yes, it is. Me pre-mud and pre-you."

"Just looks like you." He took the last of the batch of prints out of the wash.

Warmth tickled her belly. He'd taken her picture.

"What do you think of them?" he asked as she surveyed the photographs hanging on a line like laundry.

"Very nice."

"Nice, eh?"

Oh, that wasn't what he was looking for. "They're wonderful, really. Great...composition. Texture. Lighting."

He was looking at them too, and he didn't seem pleased. "Technically, they're not bad. But..." He glanced at her. "Are they missing anything?"

She studied them again, not sure what answer he was looking for. "Maybe..."

"What?" He leaned forward, his hands braced on the counter.

She blinked at the eagerness of that one word. "They might be lacking in, I'm no professional, mind you, but..."

"Go on."

"I don't see any feeling here. Does that make sense?"

He leaned next to her and studied the photograph she was looking at: Saralina throwing the flowered necklaces from the balcony like she did every year. He was so close, his shoulder brushed against hers, and when he turned to her, their faces were only inches apart.

"What do you mean by *feeling*?" he asked.

"Well..." He was way too close for her to think about this, but when she willed her body to shift away, it didn't listen. "There's no passion in them, no connection to the subject."

"Is that the same as soul?"

"Could be. Why?"

"No reason. Just wanted a layman's opinion is all."

"Oh," she said, seeing too well. "You want to talk about it?"

"Nothing to talk about. Light's going out."

He walked around her to the switch. His hip slid against her behind, very slowly.

"Hey!" she said, because she should object, not because she really did.

"Sorry about that. This place is the size of a shipping box." And there wasn't a speck of regret about it in his voice, either. He went through the process again in the glow of the orange light, exposing the negative, bringing the picture to life in one bath, then the wash, and then the fix. After thirty seconds in the fix, he said, "Coming back through," and turned the light on again.

She braced herself against the counter and leaned back the tiniest bit when he passed by again. Then managed to give him another indignant look when his thighs brushed against her. This time he only shrugged, then looked at the photograph in the fix.

"Light's going off again." He threw them back into the orange glow, brushing by her once more on the way back to the enlarger.

"It must be exciting to be a photographer. I mean, not only the taking of the pictures but watching them come to life. It's like magic."

When she turned, he was looking at her. "Magic is a good word for it."

Her throat felt kind of tight when she looked into his eyes in the shadowy room. "I liked that picture you took of me. And believe me, I don't like many pictures of myself."

He looked as if he was ready to deny it was her again, but gave her a roguish smile instead. "I spotted a bonnie lass thinking naughty thoughts and couldn't resist. Little did I know that mere minutes later she'd be lying on top of me.''

She wanted him to repeat the bonnie-lass part. No one had ever called her that and, probably, no one ever would again. ''I wasn't thinking naughty thoughts.''

''You were. You get this sparkle in your eyes when you're thinking something you shouldn't.'' He ran his finger from her forehead down her nose and over her mouth to her chin. ''Like now.''

She blinked, even though she was sure she wasn't thinking anything she shouldn't be, certainly not that she wanted to kiss him again. Nothing like that. ''I never think naughty thoughts. I'm a good, old-fashioned girl.''

''That so?'' She nodded, and he asked, ''So what have you been doing all these years while waiting for your Mr. Right to appear on the scene?''

''I've gone out a few times.''

''So what would happen if you fell for one of those fellows?''

She laughed. ''You've never seen me on a date. I...I can't believe I'm telling you this. I haven't told anyone this. I'm kind of awkward on dates, in those situations. Too many things crowd into my head, and then I go blank and don't know what to say.''

''You, awkward? That's hard to believe. You've not been awkward around me.''

''That's because you're not the right guy.''

He shifted closer. ''I may not be the right guy, but when I kissed you yesterday...''

She slid off the stool. ''And I didn't respond.''

''And you did respond.''

''Didn't.''

He put his hands on her shoulders and gave her a stern look. "I'll not have you bruising my male ego anymore."

"I haven't touched your male ego since—" She caught herself with her mouth open and shut it. "What are you going to do about it?"

She tried her best to put on her don't-kiss-me-again-because-I-still-won't-respond face. Which obviously didn't work because he slid his hands across her shoulders and into her hair, tilted her head and kissed her. Her heart was already slamming into her ribs at the touch of his hands on her neck, and it was pounding away by the time his mouth touched hers. And when he deepened the kiss, and her mouth readily opened to his, and his tongue slipped inside, she was sure her knees were going to give way. He still held her face, and she could feel the heat from his hands.

He moved closer still until she could feel all of him pressed against her. He couldn't hide *his* response, she thought, and then reminded herself that he was still trying to make a point, which was...heck, if she could remember, but it would come to her as soon as her head stopped spinning. Most importantly, she wasn't supposed to be responding to him. That meant she wasn't supposed to be clinging to his shoulders or tilting her head to the left so she could feel every bit of his tongue as it slid against hers. Or pulling the band out of his hair and running her fingers through it.

Mama mia, he could kiss.

Suddenly it was way too hot in that tiny space, and there was no air because she couldn't breathe. She dared to open her eyes. His were closed, and she thought watching him kiss her was possibly the most romantic thing in the world.

He finished the kiss and opened his eyes. She felt damp where his hands had been, then realized she was tipping over because he wasn't holding her up anymore. She steadied herself with the edge of the counter and swallowed, trying to regain her senses.

"I've been kissed like that before," she said, looking everywhere but at him. "No big deal. A nice kiss, sure, but see, no reaction. I am totally cool, calm and collected."

And then she fainted.

Luckily he caught her, and a few seconds later she came to in his arms. "You all right?" he asked, and she couldn't help but smile lazily at the way he said that.

Her thoughts slowly came back to her, and she realized what she'd done: she'd fainted after he'd kissed her. "Must be all the chemicals in here," she said, fanning her heated face.

"Must be," he said, not calling her on it. "Let's get you out of here."

AN HOUR LATER they were headed south again with the photographs and a bag of sandwiches and sodas between them. Barrie glanced over at her. She'd been awfully quiet since her fainting spell.

"You sure you're all right?" he asked, trying to get her to look at him. She hadn't done that since he'd deposited her on the couch in the waiting area and finished developing the rest of the photographs by himself. It hadn't been nearly as fun without her, but it had been more productive. Except when his thoughts strayed back to the way her mouth moved against his.

She only nodded, keeping her gaze on the road ahead.

"It was the chemicals, I'm sure. You're not used to them, and being in a closed room without much air circulation, it's to be expected."

Of course, he'd rather think it was the kiss, but he wasn't going to press. After all, maybe it *had* been the chemicals. He'd just have to try again in a place with good ventilation.

She gave him a quick, grateful smile. "How many times have *you* fainted?"

"Once. I did," he added at her skeptical look. "The first time I was in a darkroom. Fainted straight away. Quite embarrassing, really, in front of my instructor and colleagues. Heard about it for months."

"Really?"

"Really."

The lie was worth the bright look on her face. "Well, all right then."

The road followed the coast. In some places, the ocean was far below them. On the land side, they were passing through a small beach town with head shops, sunglass boutiques and other tourist traps.

"This place is a throwback to the hippie days. Check out the guy on the orange bicycle." He pointed to a man with a long beard and hair, wearing floppy cotton pants in tie-dye design. "Looks like it hasn't changed since the sixties."

"It's kind of nice to know it probably won't change for another forty years," she said. "Any business that wants to build within five miles of the coast has to file environmental-impact reports. To protect the view, they're prohibited from putting any high buildings along here." She laughed at a lime-green VW van with peace signs painted on it. "This is where people get the idea that Californians are hippies. Hey, look! There's a table over there.''

Barrie pulled into the sandy lot and parked next to two surfers in wet suits getting ready to ride the waves. She and Barrie both reached for the bag of sandwiches at the same time, and their fingers intertwined.

''Oops,'' he said.

''Sorry,'' she said.

But neither pulled their hand back. Finally she said, ''I'll get the sandwiches because you've got to come and get me...''

He couldn't help but raise an eyebrow at that statement, intriguing as it was.

''Out of the car,'' she finished in a whisper.

''Right.'' He got out of the Buick.

It was a sunny, hot day with a breeze coming off the ocean. The surfers were climbing down the path to the rocky beach below, surfboards at their sides. He'd have to take some photographs of the beach before they left.

Marisa had already opened her door and was maneuvering her monstrosity of a cast out of the car. Her little red skirt flapped in the breeze and gave him a glimpse of thigh above the cast.

''The problem is,'' he said after clearing his throat, ''we're touching each other entirely too much.''

''Problem? Oh, yes, that is a problem.''

When he slid his arm beneath her, he felt skin. ''But I don't know what we can do about it.''

''It's an impossible situation.''

He hoisted her up, and her skirt slid halfway up her thighs. ''And what were you thinking, wearing something skimpy when I've got to carry you around?''

She gave him a funny look at the irritability in his

voice. "If I wear pants, I've got to cut one of the legs. Skirts are the perfect choice."

He closed the door with his backside. "Did you have to wear one so short? This doesn't look like something an old-fashioned girl would wear."

She'd slid her arms around his neck, which left her face much too close to his. "I've never heard a guy complain about a woman's skirt being too short."

"Well, I've..." What was he complaining about, anyway? It wasn't as if he couldn't control himself. Heck, after a few days, he'd never see her or her nice legs again. "Maybe I'm just an old-fashioned kind of guy."

"Mmm, is that so?" She tugged her skirt down a few inches. "And this is my non-family wardrobe."

"Don't tell me you have two different wardrobes, one for your family and one for yourself."

He set her down on the bench and tried not to notice how his arm had slid across her skin.

"All right, I won't tell you, but yes, I do. I wear this when I go out dancing at the clubs. Not in Cortina, of course. Word would get back to my folks, especially since we only have one nightclub. Believe it or not, I have non-Italian friends from college who know nothing about the *amore* tradition. They think I'm a regular, modern girl." She laid the sodas and sandwiches on the picnic table. "I can't imagine what they'd think of the family version of me."

Barrie caught himself sitting down beside her and headed to the seat across from her. "You know there's a name for that?"

"Do I want to hear this?"

"Multiple-personality syndrome."

"No, I don't want to hear this."

"What's the real Marisa like? *Are* you a hopeless romantic?"

"I am." She reached inside her purse and produced a romance novel. "Never leave home without one. And back at my place I have every romantic movie ever made."

He grabbed the book before she could slip it back into her purse.

"Give that back!"

He held it up until she gave up trying to reach for it. Then he opened it to the middle and started reading. "'He pushed her against the wall, murmuring her name over and over again. She was caught up in the moment, too. Her head tilted back as he kissed the curve of her collarbone. Then he took out the knife and sliced across her throat.'" Barrie turned to the cover depicting a beautiful woman with a flowing mane of hair and a dashing pirate. Then he opened the book to the page with the title...the real title: *Bloodthirst.*

Marisa's face went plum. "Oops. They must have put the wrong cover on it."

Closer inspection revealed the romance cover had been taped on. "Don't women usually hide their romance novels?"

"Why would they? I'm proud to read romance."

"But this isn't romance!"

She grabbed the book and stuffed it in her purse. "All right, I like thrillers. Blood and murder isn't very romantic, so I...disguise them."

"For your family."

She was about to deny it, but gave up with a sigh. "There's nothing wrong with giving them what they want: an old-fashioned romantic daughter. And I am romantic. I love sappy movies and lace and romantic traditions and I want a big, old-fashioned wedding—''

"Who are you trying to convince? Me or yourself?"

That stopped her. "Me. I mean, you. I *know* I'm romantic. I live for it, I dream about it, and I'm ready to find the man I was destined to meet...."

They both looked at each other and said simultaneously, "We forgot the photographs!"

Barrie couldn't get up fast enough to retrieve them. That was the purpose of this stop, not to enjoy the view of the sun sparkling off the waves and each other's company. Certainly not to enjoy watching all the expressions of her face and the way her mole moved every time she smiled. Or the way the breeze was lifting the edge of that blasted tiny skirt as he returned with the box of photographs.

He dropped it on the table. "Let's eat and find your Mr. Right."

"I'M NOT WEARING underwear, by the way," Marisa said once they'd pulled the box between them on the table after lunch.

Barrie choked on the soda he was drinking.

"What I meant was," she hastily added as she realized what she'd said, "is that I'm wearing a bathing suit bottom under my skirt. You seemed disturbed that I'd wear a short skirt when you had to carry me around, and I'm just assuring you that I'm not showing my undies. See?" She lifted her skirt to show him the pink suit.

This time *his* mouth was hanging open. "Would you put your skirt down before..." he cleared his throat and looked away, "people think you're showing me your skivvies."

She smoothed her skirt down and shrugged. "It's California. Nobody cares." For once it was nice to see *him* discomfited. She was enjoying it so much she hadn't even noticed that he'd pulled out the stack of pictures and set them on the table.

"Here you are," he said. "Find your Mr. Right so you can show *him* your skivvies."

"A little testy, aren't you?" She scooted forward and started sorting through the pictures. "I'd think you'd be happy to find him so you could get rid of me."

"I am. Of course I am. I've got a job to do, you know. And if I'm going to cover this 'most romantic' festival right, I've got to get back in time for the kissing contest."

"Shall we enter?" she teased, sure they'd win the hottest kiss prize. At least if they took her temperature afterward.

"And have you faint dead away again? I don't think so."

She narrowed her eyes. "You were making up that story about your fainting, weren't you?"

"I got a knot on my head when I hit the counter on the way down. Now go on and look."

She was sure her faint was because of the chemicals and the hot, small space, and not the hot, grand kiss. But it was nice of him not to insist he'd kissed her into a faint.

"Ooh, he's cute," she said, focusing on the pictures and not the kiss.

Barrie hardly looked at the shot. "He's got a big nose."

"In case you hadn't noticed, so do I."

"No, you don't," he said without even looking.

Then she saw that he was looking at the picture of her just after she'd caught the flowers.

She felt warm all over again that he'd taken her picture before he'd even met her. "Why did you take a picture of me, anyway?"

He tilted it back and forth. "When I saw you there, I just knew I had to get the shot." He pulled out another picture, the one of her at the fountain. "This one's going on the cover."

"It is not! Don't you dare put that on the cover, me staring at...David's feet."

"You were staring at his willie and you know it."

"I was not!" But her face was giving her away; she could feel the blush. "Okay, so I was. Someone tied ribbons to it. How could I miss it?"

Instead of teasing her further, he was looking at both pictures of her. "Pretty bad, huh?" she asked. "I take the worst pictures." When he still didn't answer or look up, she said, "Ew, they must be worse than I thought."

"These are different than the rest," he said at last. "I'm trying to figure out why."

"Maybe because you know the subject."

"That must be it." He set them purposefully aside. "All right, we should be looking for your man."

"No PEEKING, NOW," Marisa said, sliding her skirt down over the cast and tossing it in the backseat. She pulled out the longer skirt and wrangled into it.

"I've already seen your skivvies anyway," he said, but dutifully looked out the side window.

"They're not skivvies, and it doesn't matter. Seems more intimate to watch someone changing."

He chuckled. "You can say that when you flashed me earlier?"

"I didn't flash you. I was trying to make a point."

"What? That you have great legs?"

She nearly snorted. "Yeah, right. Okay, you can look now."

"Back into the family personality again, eh?"

She fastened two more buttons on her shirt. "Mama would have a hot flash if she saw me in that skirt. And there's nothing wrong with having a family personality. There isn't."

He was tsking. "I've a mind to tell them about the other side of their daughter."

"You'd better not. Your place is to go along with everything until we find Mr. Right."

"You really think one of those chaps is him?" He gestured to the four photographs sitting on the seat.

"Yes, I do. And when I meet him, I'll just know it. He won't knock me down, for instance. Or insult my family's traditions."

"You have a lot of room to talk. You're a big phony, pretending to be what they want and being your own woman on the sly. Reading grisly novels and pretending they're romances. Pretending to go along with this *amore* tradition just so you can get a job."

"Take it back!" she said, but he'd already gotten out of the car and closed the door. When he came around to her side, she repeated it. "Take the phony part back. I'm not a phony. I'm just...tailoring myself in certain areas. And I'm going along with the *amore* tradition because I want to, because I'm a hopeless romantic."

He stood with his arms crossed in front of him. He looked rather like a Roman god gilded by the sunshine.

His wide, high cheekbones and long chin added to the effect, along with the way the breeze toyed with his shoulder-length locks.

"You were saying?" he prompted, making her realize her mouth was still open but no words were coming out.

"Let's just get going, shall we? I have the real Mr. Right to find."

He stiffened slightly before dipping down to scoop her out. The crowd was back to its usual number, and the sound of laughter and music drifted over the air. She reached into her purse and pulled out the bottle of rose perfume.

"Oh, great, now I'm going to go round smelling like a woman," he said as the spray got him on the side of his face.

"Oops, sorry." She wiped her hand down his cheek.

"Aye, I'll bet you are."

Her giggle didn't help to convince him. He carried her through the corridors between the buildings and into the square. A couple of ladies she knew did double takes when they saw Barrie carrying her, and Marisa shrugged. They kept watching, and she swore she saw a touch of envy on their faces. Well, why not? How many women had a great-looking hunk to carry them around?

Her thoughts screeched to a halt. *She* didn't have a great-looking hunk either. He was only on loan. She looked at him as he maneuvered through the crowd toward one of the café tables. Everything about him said *strong* and *able*. She had to admit she was lucky that, if anyone had to bump into her, it was him. How many men would—or even could—do what he was doing?

"There's the line for the kissing contest," Marisa said. "Oh, boy, there's Carlo."

He was in line with his latest girlfriend, Rosa Carlotti, a lush, long-haired girl from the neighborhood. Carlo didn't have to live up to any tradition, and he could have had the sales manager position if he wanted it. Not that it bothered her. Tradition was tradition, and she was glad to be part of it.

Okay, it did bother her. But only a little.

Carlo was surveying the other contestants and apparently thought he had them beat, judging from the lift of his chin. Marisa looked away when he started to glance in their direction. She didn't want to hear any more of his lectures.

She should have realized she didn't have a chance. People started pointing at them and someone even took their picture.

"How romantic!"

"Why don't you ever carry me around like that, Aldo?"

She glanced at Barrie, who was either being stoic or ignoring it. When she turned back to Carlo, she met his annoyed gaze. Barrie settled her in a chair near the kissing-contest stage, then perched her foot on another chair. A black, wrought-iron fence ran along the outside of the patio.

"Thank you," she said.

He made a sound like, "Mmph," and sat down across the tiny table from her. A waiter materialized, and they ordered two bottles of sparkling water.

"You're not going to enter the kissing contest?" Carlo asked, sidling up next to her with a smug look.

"No," she answered before Barrie could.

"After all that talk last night you don't want to share

your love with the world? I'll bet you two can't beat us."

"Sorry, old chap, we pass," Barrie said.

"You win every year anyway," she said. "Besides, it's silly putting your kiss on display."

"Seriously, I'll bet you fifty bucks you can't get a higher score than me and Rosa." When Carlo glanced her way, she blew him a kiss and wiggled her hips. Marisa wouldn't even attempt on her non-family days the black knit pants Rosa wore.

"Don't bet anything with him," Marisa said. "He's an addict. Even when he was a kid, he'd sit at the window and bet his friends a nickel on the color of the next car to drive by. And he's just mad because he lost a bet on me recently."

"That bet isn't completed yet. I'm waiting to see what happens."

She narrowed her eyes at him, warning him not to say anything else.

"Come on, sis. You finally have a guy to enter the contest with. Let's see what you both got. It's the most romantic gesture in the world, a man and woman showing how much they're attracted to each other."

"All right," she heard herself say. Before she realized the consequences of those two words, she saw the horror on Barrie's face. "We're romantic, aren't we? We can do this."

"Marisa," Barrie said on a low growl.

Carlo jumped to his feet. "Fifty bucks, right? I'll sign you up and tell the coordinator that you can't stand in line because of your leg. You can go right after us." He dodged through the crowd, and then saw him pointing them out to the emcee.

"I am not participating in this contest," Barrie said.

"It's bad enough that I put myself on display by carrying you about, and all because of some silly tradition. I object on principle. I refuse to put myself on further display by kissing you in front of all these people."

"AND NEXT UP," the emcee said in the loudspeaker, "we have Marisa Cerini and Barrie MacKenzie. Because of Miss Cerini's cast, she's going to sit on the stage, so everyone move in close."

Barrie set her on the edge of the stage. His throat was dry and tight, and he wasn't sure if it was because he was about to kiss her again, or because she'd somehow talked him into participating in this spectacle. Still, kissing her in the privacy of a darkroom was a lot different than kissing her in front of a hundred people, and worse, being graded on it.

"Whenever you're ready," the emcee said.

Barrie moistened his lips, and she did the same. "I bet they'd add at least a point or two if you faint again," he whispered as he moved up between her legs and against the stage.

She nudged him in the side, making him twitch. "Funny. Now stop talking and kiss me and get this over with."

"Now that's romantic," he muttered.

"And make it good."

"Thanks for the support. And by the way, you owe me big for this."

She slid her arms around his waist, and he slid his fingers up into her hair and tilted her just so. She wanted it good; she'd get it good.

He stroked his thumb across her cheeks as he moved in. He started out gently, moving his mouth across hers in slow, sensual motions. When she sighed, he had to hold himself back from deepening the kiss right away. If these people wanted romantic, that was what they'd get. He'd been watching twenty couples kissing. He didn't want to admit that just witnessing the act of kissing could get him hot and bothered, but it had. By the time he'd carried Marisa to the stage to the sound of applause, he'd been more than ready to accommodate her. Not that he was going to let her know that.

She elevated the kiss first, opening her mouth and nibbling his upper lip. Now it was his turn to let out a sound he'd never heard himself issue before. She was giving it a good show, too. Her brown eyes looked dreamy as she looked into his. He parted her mouth and ran his tongue along the edge of her teeth. She ran her tongue over his lips, and their tongues touched at the tips.

Forget this romantic stuff, he thought, tightening his hold on her and sliding his tongue inside. He closed his eyes and concentrated on the kiss and the feel of her mouth. She tasted like the lemon she'd squeezed into her water. He'd never been so aware of a woman's mouth before, of all the different textures and tastes and the way it made him feel deep in the pit of his stomach. She moved with him, tongues exploring, then meeting in the middle. He wasn't sure he'd ever gotten this…excited over a kiss, either. Yet, the rhythm of his breathing was increasing, and the interest in other parts of his body was becoming evident, too.

It was just a kiss, he told himself again over the roar of his racing blood. He wasn't quite ready to let go yet. It was intoxicating, she was intoxicating, the way he sometimes felt when he was experiencing an event he knew he'd never experience again, like a total eclipse.

She went slack beneath him and slumped onto the stage before he could rouse his senses to catch her. The crowd threw their hands into the air and roared with applause.

Where had all these people come from?

Marisa blinked as she came awake. "Oh my gosh, I did it again, didn't I?"

"I think you're forgetting to breathe," he whispered.

They turned to the panel of four judges who held up scorecards: 10, 9 1/2, 9, and 10. While the crowd broke into applause again, Carlo stalked over and shoved a fifty-dollar bill into Marisa's hand. "You cheated with the fainting stuff. I'll bet the house you'll realize he's not the right one by the end of the festival Tuesday morning."

Then he grabbed Rosa's arm and disappeared through the crowd.

"That's one bet he'd win," Barrie said as he moved Marisa to the far end of the stage so the last couple could try their hand—er, mouths—at winning.

The glow on her face had disappeared both after Carlo's outburst and then his own words. He felt compelled to add, "After all, I'll be on my way to Barcelona Tuesday. And you'll have found your Mr. Right."

"Yeah," she said wanly, then repeated it more firmly. "Yeah, we both know you're certainly not him."

"Your family would disown you if you announced you were marrying me."

She laughed. "They think I'm going to come to my senses."

"You will. And so will I."

"It was a nice kiss—for a phony kiss, anyway. We didn't mean it, did we?"

"Certainly—not, I mean."

"I guess we'd better find my prospects."

Barrie had been watching the last couple. "Yes, but I suggest you hide our trophy, because we've just won the contest."

5

"CARLO SHOULD BE happier when I tell him you might use his and Rosa's picture in your article," Marisa said.

"Let's just not be anywhere near him tomorrow during the group wedding," Barrie said, finishing off his water.

"Right, like you'd marry me."

They both looked at each other and then away. Marisa focused on the pictures in front of her. The men were looking less interesting, but she was sure they were her best bets.

Barrie scanned the crowd around them. "How about that guy over there?" He pointed at a guy talking to juggling clowns. "He looks familiar."

She consulted her photos. "Yeah, I think it's this one. Good spotting." Hmph. That meant he had to be pretty anxious to dump her on her Mr. Right. Well, she was anxious to meet him too, darn it. "Go over and ask him to join me, will you?" When he gave her a recalcitrant look, she added, "You're not going to carry me over there, are you?"

"I'll get him."

She watched him weave through the crowd toward Prospect Number One. Could he be going *any* slower? *Sheesh*, the guy was going to get away. She just hoped her prospects hadn't seen her kissing Barrie. They'd think she and Barrie were an item, which they weren't, couldn't be. It was all show, and anyone could forget to breathe when they were being kissed. No big deal.

With his height, his auburn hair and light skin, Barrie stuck out in the crowd. Not in a bad way, she decided. Even if she'd never met him, she would have noticed him...and dismissed him, of course, but she would have noticed. He wore a crisp, white cotton shirt and blue jeans that fit him snugly enough to show off his great behind and loosely enough to look comfortable. Just the thought that she'd kissed that man started butterflies flapping in her tummy. For a man who wasn't romantic, he was sure as heck passionate.

Ah, he'd finally walked up to the guy. Even *he* checked Barrie out, probably thinking how out of place he looked, too. They were a contrast in male types. Prospect One was much shorter, with a thin build and black, long hair. His eyes followed Barrie's hand gesture to her, and Marisa was glad to see no disappointment on the guy's face. Even better, he and Barrie headed over. She only hoped this guy didn't think she was so desperate she had to ask men over to meet them. Okay, she was desperate, but only because of the tradition.

"Hi," Prospect One said as he approached the table. His jeans were so snug, she could see almost *everything*. "Your friend said you wanted to see me."

Barrie shrugged. Well, they hadn't come up with a cover story. She smiled. "I thought you were someone I knew. Sorry to drag you over here for nothing."

"That's okay." He started to turn away.

"I'm Marisa." She held out her hand.

"I'm Maurizio." His hands were as soft as butter.

"Nice name." She cringed at her lameness. "Would you like to sit down anyway?"

He glanced at Barrie, then shrugged. "Sure, thanks."

Barrie stepped back and took a chair at an empty table to her right. Maurizio watched him, then sat down to Marisa's left.

"Isn't your friend going to join us?"

"I guess not." Well, he couldn't really sit with them, could he? No, of course he couldn't. She was supposed to get to know Maurizio. "So," she said, turning to him, and failing to think of a thing to say.

"So," he repeated.

She glanced over at Barrie, who was within earshot. He was trying not to laugh at her pathetic attempts at conversation by running his hand over his mouth. He lifted his eyebrows, urging her to go on.

"Nice festival, huh?" Now she remembered why she hated meeting men: small talk. She just wasn't good at this kind of thing. At least her mouth wasn't hanging open.

"Sure. Fun." He winked, sort of.

"Where are you from?"

"New York."

"Oh, so is Barrie. Do you know him?"

He glanced at Barrie and laughed. "It's a big city. I haven't seen him at any of my haunts." He looked over at Barrie again. "He your boyfriend?"

"Him? Oh, no. If you only knew how silly that idea is." *Don't think about that kiss! And don't look at Barrie. Look at Maurizio!* "He's not my type at all. And I'm not his."

This seemed to perk Maurizio's interest. He sat up straighter in his chair. "Really?"

Ah, he must have thought she was with Barrie. Now that he knew she was available, maybe he'd contribute more to the conversation. She glanced over at Barrie, who was leaning way back in his wrought-iron chair. "He wants to grow old without having women around."

"Really?" Maurizio put his finger to his mouth. He had beautifully manicured hands. "So where do you fit into his life, then?"

"Oh, don't worry, we're not seeing each other. We're just friends, strictly friends, if you know what I mean. He's helping me out with a creative project."

He winked again, though not at her. Probably had something in his eye. "Mmm, I like creative types."

She wanted to steer him away from that project. "Oh, I'm not really that creative—"

"What about him? I'm looking for someone creative for my own…project."

Barrie's face had gone white.

"He's very creative. He's a photographer, does edgy stuff like naked people."

Hey, she was doing pretty good. This making-conversation thing was easy.

He winked again. "I'd love to see his work sometime."

Marisa thought of the pictures in her purse, but decided those weren't the right examples. She glanced over at Barrie, who was fidgeting with the silverware. When he glanced her way, he gave her a wide-eyed look. What was his hurry?

She turned back to Maurizio, who had been looking away, too. "Maybe we can get together later, and you can see his stuff."

Maurizio leaned on the table and propped his head up with his hand. "You mean all three of us?"

"No, just two people having a nice dinner, looking at Barrie's stuff, that kind of thing."

He winked yet again, glanced at Barrie, then back at her. "Sounds great. Where do I meet him?"

"I was thinking—what'd you say?"

"Look, obviously your friend is shy about meeting new people, and he has you warm them up for him. No prob. Tell him I'm interested and I'll meet him here tonight at eight." He slowly pulled himself from the table, paused in front of Barrie, then sauntered off.

"Oh...my...gosh," she uttered as it sank in. She hadn't gotten a date for herself; she'd gotten one for Barrie! She turned to him. His mouth was hanging open and his face was flushed so pink she couldn't see his freckles. Their mortified gazes met, held...and they both burst out laughing. He managed to stagger to her table and drop down in the chair next to hers.

"You all right, then?" he asked between gales of laughter.

"Me? I should be asking you!"

They tried to get hold of themselves, but another glance at each other sent them back into laughter. She clutched her stomach and doubled over.

"I told him you were the creative type and that you wanted to grow old without women."

"No wonder he kept winking at me!"

"That's why you looked like you'd seen a ghost. We'll call him Winkie! He asked if you were my boyfriend, and I told him we weren't each other's types. That you were edgy and took pictures of naked people."

He grabbed hold of her chin. "You set me up!"

"I didn't know!"

"Next time leave me out of the conversation, will you?"

Her laughter faded as she realized how close he was to her. "It was easier talking to him when I was talking about you." She looked into his blue eyes. "What do we do now?"

"We—" he blinked, then let his fingers drop from her chin "—we find Prospect Two, I suppose. What else can we do?"

She pasted on a smile. "Not a thing."

BY THE END of the day, Marisa's ankle was throbbing with a dull ache. She was tired of sitting by herself at the table while Barrie roamed the festival in search of Prospect Two. Every time she spotted him across the square, her heart did a little pop in her chest. She propped her chin on her hand and watched him snap pictures as he wandered through the crowd. When the Love Tango line swirled anywhere near him, he scooted far out of the way. She vaguely remembered the dancers whirling around her when he'd bumped into her.

She watched one hapless woman get sucked into the line of people. She obviously didn't know the dance steps, but the others were glad to show her how to do it. So glad, in fact, that they wouldn't let her escape. Finally she darted for the nearest opening, nearly tripping on the uneven bricks.

Marisa lifted her head as it dawned on her. That's how Barrie had come to knock her down. She'd called him an oaf, but he hadn't done one clumsy thing since. He'd tried to tell her about the dance, but she'd cut him off. So he didn't really owe her help after all. In fact, if she was a decent, fair person, she'd cut him loose once he returned.

Fortunately, she wasn't that decent. Truth was, she needed him. He was the only person who could help her. She couldn't turn to her non-Italian friends; they wouldn't understand the tradition any more than Barrie did. And her Italian friends? If word got back to her family…no way. And unfortunately, she liked him. Wasn't that evident by the grin on her face as she watched him glance at the photographs he held and compare them to the men passing by?

And the way she laughed with him. Had she ever laughed with a man like that before? As dire as her situation was—and as embarrassing as the encounter with Maurizio had been—they had still laughed together like fools. Some romantic she was, falling for the wrong Mr. Right.

Not falling, she quickly reminded herself. Maybe just…tripping a little. Her nose itched, and she rubbed it with the back of her hand.

When Barrie glanced her way, she waved him over. He had a nice stride, graceful and confident. The early-evening sun made his hair look redder, and she liked the way it flowed with his movements.

"Did you find one?" he asked.

"One what? Oh, a prospect! Of course, I knew that's what you meant. You know what I'm thinking?"

"I can't even begin to imagine," he said, looking serious.

She waved him off. "It's a rhetorical question!"

"I'm thinking about going home for the night. My ankle's a bit achy and it's wearing me down."

"You sure? One of your fellas might come round tonight."

"Maybe I should stay a little longer. But even if I do find him, I'm too tired to try to make witty conversation."

"Is that what you called your conversation with Winkie?"

She wrinkled her nose at him, then rubbed it. "This is why I never minded the tradition. I'm not that good in dating situations. Ah, that's how I should have known Winkie wasn't the right one. I had to work too hard to get him to talk. I always figured when I met the right guy, we'd hit it off immediately. You know, have instant rapport." She really wanted to go to her parents' house having met the real Mr. Right, though. "Maybe I'll stay a few minutes longer. No more than an hour. Or maybe forty-five minutes." She looked up and caught him tsking. "What?"

"You just can't make up your mind. What happens if you like all three of these guys?" He tapped the pictures in his hand.

"I won't. One will be far and away the only choice."

"All right, are we leaving now?"

"In fifteen minutes. Ten—"

He came around the fence. "Your chariot is ready." And when his arms went around her, she felt the big, ugly cast and the ache in her ankle weren't quite so bad after all.

"I'VE GOT TO COME BACK and take some pictures of the gondola singing contest," Barrie said when they headed out of the parking lot. "Sure you want to miss that?"

That was one of the sillier contests, wherein contestants pretended to paddle a cardboard gondola of their making and sing to a cardboard couple. Every year the gondolas got more outrageous.

"Actually it'd be neat to see what they're doing this year. Maybe…"

"Forget I mentioned it."

She crossed her arms over her chest and decided to ignore him for the rest of the drive. That lasted about two minutes.

"What's the game plan for tomorrow?"

"I suppose we'll be looking for your Mr. Right again." He shot her a sideways look. "Next time I'll not be picking him up for you."

"Well, you've got a date at eight if you want."

His face went red again. "I happen to be keen on women, thank you ever so much."

She rather liked the way his gaze slid down over her and definitely the way his eyes crinkled a little…until she reminded herself that she wasn't supposed to like him at all. "I'm supposed to take the morning shift at the cookie booth. We got a lousy location this year, thanks to Giorgio not being on the ball. He's the one whose job I want."

"I've a feeling if it were up to you, you would have gotten your booth smack in the middle of the square."

She smiled at his compliment and ignored the warm, silly feeling inside. "Yes, I would have, thank you."

"You said you had plans for the company."

"Yeah," she said, touched that he'd asked. "Global domination. Just kidding. I want to get us on airplanes and I want to expand to the East Coast. Convincing Pop will be another story."

"If you came out of the closet, as it were, and really sold him, I bet you could do it. Look what you got me to do."

She smiled, then rolled her lips inward when she realized how much she was smiling. "So, anyway, we're on the east corner of the hotel. Why don't you meet me there at eleven? You won't welsh on me, will you?"

"I live up to my responsibilities."

Of course—she was only a responsibility. He couldn't really *want* to carry her around all day. So why was she disappointed? She redirected her thoughts to something safer.

"Have you been here before?"

He was a relaxed driver, sitting back in his seat with his hand draped over the top of the steering wheel. "Haven't, no."

"Do you like it?"

"It's not bad."

"That means good, right?"

He looked over and smiled. "Right. I could do without all the little wedding chapels and the shop that does custom poetry and the flower vendors on every corner."

"That's part of the allure."

He snorted. "But I like the town itself. The touches of Renaissance architecture, brick sidewalks, very nice. It's my first time in Southern California, actually. I've seen those tall palms in movies about Hollywood," he said, pointing to the spindly trunks that were topped with palm fronds. "Lots of trees everywhere." Eucalyptus trees flanked the highway and divided the road as well. He nodded toward the hills to the east. "These hills remind me of the ones back in Scotland. I don't know what's all over them, but it looks like heather when it's not in bloom."

Brown and dark green brush covered the hills.

"That's sage. When it gets dry, it goes up in flames really easily."

"I know that feeling," he said under his breath.

"What do you mean?"

"Now, you can't say you had no reaction to the kiss that won the contest. The one that made you faint."

She pulled their trophy out of her purse. The big gold mouth shone in the sunlight. "It was only because I forgot to breathe. I wanted to put on a good show." She glanced at him. "Didn't you?"

"Sure. It was a good show, wasn't it?"

She ran her hand over the trophy and wished she'd admitted she'd stopped breathing because she was enjoying the kiss so much. Maybe he would have admitted enjoying it, too. But her insecurity had reared its ugly head.

She looked at the hills and tried to picture Scotland. "Do you miss your home and family?"

He looked as though he were going to say no, but said, "Sometimes."

"You need to make peace with them. I bet if I talked to them, I'd... Well, if I ever went to Scotland with you—which I wouldn't because that would mean we were dating, which we'd never do—and..." She lost track of her point.

"You'd what?"

"Get them to understand, to appreciate you for who you are."

He snorted. "You can't even get your *own* family to accept you for who you are."

"But the difference is, I *want* to be like them."

"You sure about that?"

"Yes. Definitely. Well, some—"

"Eh!"

She blinked at the sharp sound.

"Never met a woman who changed her mind as much as you."

"Hmph." Darn, she hated it when her mama was right. Her indecisiveness did drive men crazy. And as much as she'd like to say she drove men crazy, that wasn't quite the way she wanted to do it.

"When I'm with them, I want to be like them. When I'm not, I want to be myself."

He rolled his eyes. "What's wrong with being the same person all the time?"

"Stop confuzzling me. You're making me sound like I need psychiatric help. And I don't!" she added at his raised eyebrow.

"So you say. You know why you can't make up your mind? Because you're afraid of offending someone by making a solid decision."

"That's preposterous. There, I made a solid decision."

He didn't look convinced. "Am I taking you to your parents' house?"

"It's Saturday night, isn't it? We always go to evening mass. You'd better take me there. I'm in serious need of confession."

"I HOPE YOU SAID all your Hail Marys twice," Mama said, setting out packages of Amore cookies on the booth's table Sunday morning. "Ten, nine and a half, nine and ten—you set a new record!"

Marisa caught herself grinning and tried to look duly embarrassed. "Told you he's the one."

Mama patted her chest and tried, unsuccessfully, to hide the tears in her eyes. "How could it have gone so wrong? Can I help it if I want my daughter to marry a good Italian man from a good Italian family?'' Even caught up in her melodrama, she still had the presence of mind to slap Marisa's hand away from the package of cookies she was subtly trying to open. "I'm going to get some more hearts from the car. No eating the goods!''

The Amore Cookie Company's brochure was a red heart with a poem and the romantic history of the company. Their booth was U-shaped with a large folding screen behind them proclaiming their company's name. On one corner was a large silver tray with crumbled cookie samples. When Marisa tried to grab a crumble, Nonna smacked her hand.

"I'm hungry. Can't you cut a cripple some slack?''

"Some cripple. I heard about the kissing contest, too.'' Nonna snagged one of the crumbs and said, "Did he slip you the tongue?''

Marisa would have complained about Nonna helping herself to the cookies, but her mouth was hanging open. "Pardon?''

Nonna was shaking her head, her sweet, nostalgic expression on her face. "Your *nonno*, Salvatore, he was so romantic, so romantic.''

Marisa released a breath. She must have misunderstood. "You have the most romantic stories about him.'' She smiled at a man who took a sample and mentally compared him to the remaining three photographs. No match.

"Ah,'' Nonna said on a sigh. "He would take my hand in his and kiss each fingertip. He would always ask permission before kissing me on the lips. Such a gentleman.'' She looked up, winked, then used her hand to rebalance her head. *"Si, mi amore.* And then he would put the tiniest kiss right there.'' She touched the tips of her lips. "He would whisper sweet nothings in Italian, beautiful words of love. Then he would hold my face so tenderly and kiss me."

Marisa smiled, then realized she was picturing the way Barrie did the same thing. "A kiss is the most romantic thing in the world."

Nonna was shaking her head and remembering her sweet moment. "He could do such amazing things with that tongue."

Marisa choked, and when she caught sight of the expression on the man who'd sampled the cookie, and was now moving away from the booth, she really started coughing. Why wasn't anyone in the family around when Nonna said things like this?

Nonna was oblivious to Marisa's reaction. "He had the longest tongue, and when he poked it into my—"

"Nonna!"

"—ear, I would shiver all over."

What had happened to all the sweet, benign stories she used to tell? "What about the time you and Nonno danced in the rain?"

Nonna's smile widened. "Oh yes, we twirled and twirled, the rain soaking us, laughing and kissing. I don't know why the police officer threatened to arrest us. We were in our own backyard after all, and how could the neighbors see us through all that rain?"

Marisa choked on the piece of cookie she'd managed to pilfer. "Arrest you?"

"A couple can't even dance naked in their own backyard! What's happened to the state of romance?"

Mama walked up with a box of heart brochures and dropped them on the table. "Sneaking cookies again, weren't you?"

Marisa nodded to Nonna, who was innocently smiling at a couple walking by.

"Lovely day, isn't it?" Nonna said, giving absolutely no indication that she'd just been reminiscing
about her husband's tongue.

Marisa tried to put that and the image of her grandparents dancing naked out of her mind as she arranged
the fresh supply of brochures. She caught a whiff of
sautéing onions and sausage from the booth across the
way. She glanced at her watch: almost eleven. Her
heart lifted, surely because then she'd be free to search
for Mr. Right. Which reminded her to take a sweeping
glance around for him—the shorter, Italian man, not
the tall, broad-shouldered Scot.

"Is *he* meeting you here?" Mama asked.

"Yeah." She cleared her throat, hoping that wasn't
dreaminess she heard in her voice. "We're going to
have lunch and watch the group wedding."

Every year couples lined up and took their vows in
unison in the town square.

"You're not going to kill your mama and get married along with fifty other people, are you? I'd have a
heart attack right here—after I fainted."

"Of course not. We'll have a traditional wedding
like Gina did, with lots of relatives and a fancy wedding dress and you bawling your eyes out in the front
pew." She remembered standing behind Gina at the
altar looking out over a sea of people. She knew she
should want that kind of wedding, and that to make
her family happy, she would have it. Barrie wasn't going to like it much, though. If he'd gotten that glazed
look during dinner, wait until he was surrounded by a
couple hundred of her relatives—

She wasn't going to marry Barrie! She had clearly

taken this charade too far. Her heart started to pound when she spotted him taking a picture of a bride getting ready. His hair was tied back, and the sun lit it a golden red. Even from a distance, she could see the definition of his cheekbones and the strong lines of his face.

"I fainted when Salvatore kissed me the first time," Nonna said. "Had to learn to breathe."

Marisa pulled her gaze from Barrie. "It's good to know I'm not the only one." Except that Salvatore was Mr. Right; Barrie wasn't.

It shamed her to realize that he was probably keeping more of a lookout for Mr. Right than she was. Then it irritated her. Of course he wanted to find the guy! Then he'd be able to get rid of her.

Nonna and Mama watched him approach. Her chest hitched as she took in the blue, faded shirt and white pants, sexy in a comfortable sort of way.

"He's a biggie," Nonna said. "Keep the wind from you, though."

"She'll come to her senses," Mama said to no one in particular.

Yes, she would. This was the worst thing she'd done, even worse than sneaking off to college twice a week. She didn't even want to think about what would happen if she didn't meet the right Mr. Right. Barrie would leave smoke in his trail, and Marisa would look like an idiot twice over.

And she'd never see him again.

"Cheers," a familiar voice said, calling her from her dark thoughts. Barrie nodded to all three women.

Nonna tilted her cheek at him. Uh-oh. The kiss test. Barrie didn't get it until Marisa nodded her head toward Nonna three times. His cheeks flushed, but he leaned over and gently gave her a kiss.

Marisa gave him an "okay" nod and rubbed her nose, which got her a curious look from Nonna.

He looked relieved to have made it through. "Having a bad day? You looked rather sullen."

"She's been looking for you all day," Nonna said.

"No, I have—well, okay, I have." Even Marisa was getting confused about her two roles. To her family, she was supposed to be in love with Barrie, even though they wished she wasn't. And inside, she wasn't supposed to be in love with him. And, of course, she wasn't.

Nonna lifted the tray of broken cookies. "Sample?"

He took one, and when Marisa tried to snag a piece, Nonna pulled the tray away.

"I just wanted a bite!"

"Here." He handed her three dollars for two packages, then handed them to Marisa. "Ready?"

"Yes, I'm starving." She gave her family narrowed eyes and pulled her leg off the stool.

A group of people came up to the booth and started asking Nonna and Mama questions about the cookies.

"So the chap across the way isn't Mr. Right, either?" Barrie whispered.

"What chap?"

"Don't tell me you haven't seen him? He's been right in front of you all morning."

She directed her gaze to the Italian sausage vendor across the way, and her mouth dropped open. Prospect Two was serving a sloppy, overflowing bun to Uncle Louie, who had arrived to take his shift at the cookie booth.

"Something to drink?" Prospect Two asked Louie.

"What do I think? It's messy, that's what I think."

He took a bite of the long roll with tomato sauce dripping down the side. "Good, but messy."

Louie shuffled across the way toward the booth, making people circumvent the sloppy sandwich he held out like an offering.

"Hi, Uncle Louie," Marisa said, leaning over and kissing him on the cheek. He reeked of onions and peppers.

"Eh? Oh, hi. Bite?" He held the roll at her, misjudging and nearly getting her nose.

"No, thanks. We're heading out."

Louie shifted his gaze to Barrie. "Scottish fellow's still around, eh?"

She was determined not to let the conversation lead to either how big he was or his tentacles. "Bye, Uncle Louie." She pulled out her crutches. "I can move around a little with these things, but not long distances." She hobbled over and gave her mama and *nonna* kisses goodbye.

Barrie hovered nearby as she maneuvered around the booth. Prospect Two was watching her. She smiled, and he smiled back. Then she checked to see if Barrie was looking. He wasn't, which meant Number Two was smiling at her and not him.

One obstacle down.

"Why don't you hobble over and give him a package of those romantic little cookies?" Barrie suggested. He couldn't even say the words without sounding facetious.

"Good idea."

He hovered nearby as she made her way to the food trailer, but backed off once she reached the little counter.

"Hey, doll. I been watching you over there all morning, and you didn't once look over here.'' He put his hands over his heart. "I'm hurt.''

Once again witty conversation eluded her. "I'm here now, aren't I? I...brought you a package of cookies.''

"I was wondering what you were peddling over there.'' He looked expectant. Then she realized she was still holding the package. She set it on the counter.

"Aw, that's sweet.'' He popped one of the cookies in his mouth, then discovered the pink slip of paper. Oh, shoot. She hadn't thought about the verbal kiss inside. Which one would it be? Well, she'd soon find out, because he read it. "'For every full moon, someone finds their true love.'''

She could have sworn she heard a snort from somewhere behind her, and she tried really hard not to look. "I'm Marisa.''

"I'm Tony, Tony from Brooklyn.'' He shook her hand, and she could feel the grease on his fingers. "I'm in the pre-loved car business, but I help my uncle out sometimes.'' His gesture included the trailer. "Say, I get off in about an hour. What're you doing then?''

She forced a smile. "Meeting you for lunch.''

"Perfect.'' Okay, he was definitely interested. For one thing, he still hadn't let go of her hand. "Do you want to meet me here?''

It was too far to hobble anywhere on crutches, and she couldn't have Barrie carry her over. *Pardon my big hunk here.* Well, not *her* hunk. But she certainly didn't want to ask Tony to carry her. "Let's meet at the Roma Café by the hotel. I'll get a table,'' she said, giving him a coquettish smile, or what she hoped was. "See you in an hour.''

"That him?'' Barrie asked when she hobbled over to him.

"Don't know. I suppose it could be." She'd forgotten to notice if she'd felt anything when they shook hands—besides the grease. "Maybe I need to, you know, talk to him more. Gina and Mama said that when they met their husbands, it was...*kapow!* They were swept off their feet. It didn't feel like that with Tony."

Barrie took her crutches and swept her off her feet—literally. "Where to, m'lady?"

There was something about the way he effortlessly scooped her up that made her heart go pitter-patter. The *m'lady* thing was a nice touch, too. Then she realized he'd asked her something and she hadn't answered. "To the Roma Café again. I'm meeting Tony there in an hour."

"We'll take the long way around so we don't walk in front of him. Don't want to give him the wrong idea about us."

"Us?"

"Aye. You and me. Me carrying you around in my arms like some romantic sod." His gaze dropped down to her mouth for a second, and his voice grew softer. "We wouldn't want to give him the impression that there's anything going on between us."

"Yes. I mean, no. Of course. Nothing's going on between us." All she could think about was him putting his mouth on hers, and that this time she would breathe. "If there *was* something going on between us, I'd think it was terribly romantic, you carrying me around like this."

"And if there was something going on between us, I'd probably have to admit I enjoyed carrying you around. If I were romantic, of course."

She met his gaze. "We'd better go and get married. I mean, *watch* people get married."

"And very possibly meet your Mr. Right."

"Mr. Right," she repeated, then realized she was looking at Barrie and saying those words in a soft, dreamy voice. "Maybe, just maybe, I've already met him." She brushed back a lock of his hair the breeze had blown forward.

"You think?"

She blinked, realizing what she was doing. He had the look of a rabbit eyeing the stew pot. "Not you!" She laughed. "You didn't think..."

"That you were talking about me. Course not. That'd be silly."

"Real silly."

"Preposterous."

"Outrageous."

"Shall we stop staring into each other's eyes, then?" he asked.

"Probably be a good idea, since we're totally wrong for each other."

"And we are...totally unsuited."

"Exactly."

He leaned forward and kissed her, a quick, solid kiss. Then without looking at her, he headed around the corner, tossing over his shoulder, "Just so we have that straight."

6

BARRIE AND MARISA snacked on stuffed mushrooms and did not talk about the kiss. It was a perfect day, sunny and bright, with lots of opportunities for great photographs. The best opportunity sat across from him at the table, wearing a deep red long dress covered in cream flowers. The bodice wasn't low-cut, but it was wide enough to show an interesting expanse of skin and the slightest hint of cleavage. She was using her hands to express herself as she told him about the time Gina had convinced her to take part in the gondola singing contest.

"That's when I found out I couldn't sing," she finished. "Mama has a voice that can shatter glass when she sings opera. Mine, I'm afraid, only makes people want to chew glass. The thing is, I thought I could sing all those years. My family smiled whenever I sang a song to them, pretending to be my biggest fans."

"At least your family encourages you to sing."

She paused for a moment before answering. "They're supportive about some things, but they like everything done in the traditional ways. Even though you didn't follow your parents' plans for your future, aren't they proud of what you do?"

He snorted, and realized he did it more often than he ever thought. "A couple of years after I'd moved to New York, I went back home to cover Burns Night. Robbie Burns.''

"The rogue poet," Marisa said with a smile. "The one with all the tentacles."

They both laughed, and he realized something else: he'd never laughed with someone as much as he did with her. "That's the one. Every year Scottish men— only men—get together to celebrate him. They wear kilts and someone reads a bit of his poetry—not the mushy kind—and then they toast him with whiskey. I'd been sending clippings of my articles to my folks all along just to show them I wasn't bumming about. After the celebration in Edinburgh, I drove up to my family's village. I didn't expect a hero's welcome, knowing they considered me to have deserted them. But I thought I'd get some kind of welcome. All they could talk about was my sister's boyfriend and how he wouldn't let them down by leaving the village. My father had to dig my articles out of a box in a kitchen cabinet.''

He wasn't sure why he was sharing all this with her, but the sincere look of compassion on her face made it worthwhile.

"That is so wrong," she said.

"That's the way it is. You can't please your family unless you follow their plans for you. See, you met me, but I'm not right for your tradition, so you haven't made them happy. Even if your father does give you that sales-manager position, he'll not be pleased about doing so. No matter how hard you work and how many improvements he lets you make, you won't be doing what he wants you to do."

"You make it sound so hopeless."

"I didn't mean to bring you down. All I'm saying

is to stand your ground now, be your own person, and find your own way in life.''

She was already shaking her head. "I'm too afraid to take the chance of alienating my family."

He couldn't blame her, not really. If she wanted to live by her family's rules, then so be it. It wasn't as if he was in love with her and wanted to marry her. She would never have to choose between keeping her family's tradition and keeping him. The mushrooms were giving him heartburn. That had to be the cause of the burning ache in his chest every time he thought about never seeing this saucy Italian lass again. Why, she'd been nothing but a pain in his behind from the beginning, ordering him about, making him act like some sappy romantic. Making him want to kiss her again.

Marisa popped a mushroom into her mouth and met his gaze. "It must be lonely to travel all the time."

"Not at all." The words rushed out, as though he couldn't get them out fast enough. "Why do you say that?"

"I know it's exciting, all the places that you see, but to go somewhere and not have anyone waiting to greet you when you get home."

"You mean all those people crowding around the gate, nearly running me over to hug their loved ones? Just what I need after a long flight, someone climbing all over me." It usually sounded convincing.

"To hang around strangers most of the time, never really connecting with anyone. Unless...you meet people—women—on trips, for, you know, romantic relationships."

"I never get involved on a business trip. I did a couple of times in the beginning, before I knew better.

But then I realized I wasn't focusing on my job, so I made it a rule: Never get involved.''

"Until me," she said with a smile, but that smile faded. "You are...involved with me, right? I mean, not on a romantic level, but on some level."

He found her awkwardness cute and somehow endearing until he realized he had to answer her question. "I...well, I'd say we were involved on some level. I mean, we did kiss. There must be something there since we won first place." Now she was making *him* awkward! "Let's just leave it that we're involved on some level."

That made her smile, and he hoped it was the words and not his delivery of them.

"But the point is," he continued, because he had to, "to find your Mr. Right, not for us to get any more...involved. Your chap is going to be here in fifteen minutes. I'll just sit off to the side and make sure he doesn't get fresh."

Her smile had faded again, though he couldn't imagine why.

"Maybe this Tony guy will be the one," she said. "Then you can get me out of your hair."

He grabbed his glass of sparkling water and stood. "And me out of yours as well."

They stared at each other for a moment. He had the oddest urge to admit he didn't mind her in his hair. That her laugh put a little zing in his chest. That he liked watching her express herself with her hands and the way that mole moved whenever she talked. But the guy she was supposed to meet was due soon, and there was no point in telling her that, anyway. In a few days he'd be gone, and she'd be dating some Italian who'd make her family happy.

The café was getting busy, but he managed to find a seat at a nearby table. If this guy winked at him, Barrie was going to throttle him. No, Tony was a ladies' man. Barrie could tell by the way he'd rubbed her hand and looked into her eyes. And the way he'd called her "doll," something he no doubt called every woman he came into contact with.

He hoped Tony wasn't the guy. Even if he was Italian, he wasn't Marisa's type. When he glanced over at her, she was mock-frowning at him. He'd probably been sitting there with a grumpy look. He forced a smile, and she settled in her chair and waited.

Tony was a few minutes late, enough reason to discount the guy right there. Sausage and onion aromas followed him as he walked by Barrie. Worse yet, he was wearing a white belt and white shoes with red pants. Marisa merely smiled and waved for him to take the seat Barrie had recently vacated. If she was amused or horrified, she hid it well.

"Hey, doll, good to see you again." Tony took her hand and kissed the back of it.

Barrie caught himself grimacing.

Tony sat down next to her. "What happened to your leg?"

She glanced over at him, and the glint of amusement in her eyes produced that zing again. "You know how they do the Love Tango, where people are sort of dragged into it whether they want to be or not? Well, this poor guy was dragged in, and when he had the chance to escape, he kind of lost his balance and bumped into me."

Barrie blinked. She knew what had happened. But she hadn't been looking in his direction when the dragging/dancing part had occurred.

"Bummer," he said, whipping open a menu. When the waiter appeared to take their order, Tony ordered first, then flipped his menu onto the table, oblivious to the waiter's outstretched hand.

Marisa and Barrie looked at each other, and she had to hide her own giggle behind her menu before regaining control and ordering. This was not the kind of guy who was going to carry his woman around all day.

And Barrie had to admit he didn't want Tony carrying her around. There was something not right about it.

"Say, we ought to go bowling sometime," Tony said, leaning forward to catch a glimpse of her cleavage as she leaned over for another mushroom.

Barrie had already started coming out of his chair, but stopped himself at the image of himself tugging Tony up by the collar and admonishing him for trying to get a quick peek. Hadn't he been guilty of doing nearly the same earlier? Yeah, but he wasn't…didn't… He settled back into the chair. All right, he was just as curious about her lush figure, and he had no right to be. His only excuse was that feeling her thighs beneath his arms, and her body pressed up against his, was destroying his resolve to keep a distance.

"We could do that," she said, actually looking interested in going bowling. "Once my ankle heals."

"Oh, that's right. *Sheesh*, what was I thinking? All right, you could watch me bowl. I've got the highest league average in Brooklyn."

"Wow, really."

He gave her a dazzling smile that was as cheesy as the rest of him. "You ain't seen nothing 'til you seen Tony bowl. I gotta curve that'll knock your panties off."

She gracefully ignored that comment.

Barrie watched them chat and eat, trying to hold back the grimaces and frowns. Anybody but this guy. She could do a lot better. Still, she seemed to be enjoying herself, and she was actually more at ease than she'd been with Maurizio. Great. She was getting over her awkwardness around men.

Every time she looked over at Barrie, he had to check that his expression was neutral. What he really wanted to do was yank the guy out of his seat and tell him to roll his bowling ball in someone else's lane. But he was just the guy carrying her around trying to help her find her Mr. Right. She glanced over at him again and winked. This time he had to hold back his laughter.

Damn, she could make him laugh.

She made him a lot of things he wasn't altogether comfortable with. And she was still looking at him while Tony prattled on about the pre-loved car business. Barrie felt that odd tickle in his stomach as their smiles faded, and then she blinked and focused on Tony again.

What was she doing wasting her time with this guy? She should be with a guy like...him? No, not like him. He didn't want to settle down, abhorred commitment, and envisioned love as piranhas with blood lust.... Damn, the goldfish had permanently replaced the piranhas.

Forget the fish, then. Love was bulls. Barrie stretched out his legs and sank into the mental image of the running of the bulls in Pamplona. He could recall the fear and exhilaration of the men being chased by the rampaging animals. Now, just replace those bulls with the concept of love. Yes, that worked fine. The terror and adrenaline were the same. Get away fast or be trampled. Men diving into the crowds to save their lives.

Filing the image away for future reference, he focused back on Marisa. "So you think you'd like living in a place like this?" she was asking Tony.

He glanced around at the square and then back at her. "You living here makes it pretty tempting."

She smiled demurely, but it wasn't the real smile she'd been giving Barrie. Or was he imagining that?

"Picture me, living in the most romantic town in the country," Tony said, taking her hand and kissing it again. "And dating the prettiest gal in town. Maybe I'll hang around for a few weeks, see if I like it. How many pre-loved car lots you got?"

"A couple, maybe."

He ran his hand through his messy dark hair. "It would be tough, though, moving away from my family. Mama would take it hardest."

That earned a real smile from Marisa. Of course, any man who loved his mother would score with her. Which left Barrie out, since he hadn't spoken with his family in two years.

"Bring her with you," she said. "I bet she'd love the mild winters."

Tony lifted his shoulders. "Maybe it's time for me to move out on my own, you know? Be my own man. I've been living with her my whole life."

Her smile dimmed several watts. "You live with your mother?"

He laughed. "No, not that kind of living. I've got the whole upper floor, my own kitchen and everything. Like an apartment."

"Oh, I see. Well, maybe it *is* time to move out on your own, then."

Why was she encouraging him like that? Didn't she see what a daft wally the guy was?

Tony grasped her hand again, a light in his eyes. "I like you, Marisa. I've only known you, what, an hour, and we click. You've got me thinking about my whole life here."

She had a habit of doing that to a man. Yes, she did have a way about her. Barrie should be looking forward to getting out of Cortina in a few days. Instead, every time he thought of getting on the plane, he felt that ache in his chest. And she had him thinking about family. And loneliness. He'd never minded being lonely or being around strangers, at least not until Marisa had asked him about it. Now he saw her as part of that crowd at the airport.

"Every year," she was saying, "a few people come to the festival and decide to move here. We've got everything here—mountains, beach, great weather, a wonderful town…"

"And a beautiful woman," Tony put in, leaning forward, still holding her hand.

To Barrie's horror, he heard himself snort. Loud enough to make Marisa jump. Barrie felt his face flush as both started turning in his direction. He focused instead on the square where the mass wedding was being set up.

"Well, thank you," she said with a laugh in her voice. "That's very sweet of you."

"I'm a sweet guy, what can I say?"

"You do…seem sweet."

Ah, some of that awkwardness was returning. Barrie should have felt guilty for relishing it, but he didn't.

"Sometimes, though, I'm a bad boy," Tony said.

Marisa's eyebrows raised. "Bad as in...a cuss word slips out? Or you forget to pay your electric bill?"

"Yeah, nothing really bad." He glanced down at their linked hands, then back up in a coy way. "I need a woman who can keep me in line."

Her mouth was hanging open. She clamped it shut. "In line...how?"

He shrugged. "Make me stand in a corner. A little spank here and there. Wash out my mouth with soap."

Her jaw had dropped again. Barrie wasn't sure if he should intervene, but she gathered herself together and asked, "You're kidding, right?"

"I know it sounds odd at first, but most women get into it after a while. After all, you're the ones who do most of the punishing in the family, right? The yelling, the spanking, the discipline."

"You're kidding, right?"

"I like to get this straight up front. You know, get you used to the idea. We can start out with some recreational yelling. Take it at your own pace." She was subtly trying to pull her hand free from his. He kept grasping at her fingers as he spoke. "But I'd really like it if I could call you 'Mommy.'"

"You're not kidding." Marisa had an admirable handle on her mouth now, and Barrie sat back to watch how she was going to handle him. She tucked her hands in her lap and gave him a sweet smile. "That sounds like fun."

Barrie's mouth dropped open this time. He was about to get up and shake some sense into her when her eyes widened as though she'd just remembered something.

"Oh, shoot, you know what? I can't get involved with you. I keep forgetting."

"Forgetting what?"

"I'm pregnant."

He glanced down at her stomach. "Pregnant? You don't look pregnant."

"I'm just a couple weeks along. That's why I keep forgetting."

Barrie almost laughed aloud at the concern that came over Tony's face. "What about the father? Because if he's ditched you, I could, you know, step in."

"That's very kind of you, really. But my family is very old-fashioned and as you can imagine, they're furious. They're sending me off to a nunnery until I have the baby. Perhaps we could write. I could—" for the first time she glanced at Barrie, but quickly looked back at Tony, her mouth quivering with a contained smile "—berate you in my letters."

Tony's shoulders were slumped and his hands were jammed between his knees. "I suppose. I'm still gonna think about moving here, though. Maybe we could, you know, get together when you come out."

"Oh, sure," she said brightly. "You'll love living here. You can write and tell me how you like the earthquakes."

"You get earthquakes here?"

She glanced at Barrie, remembering their kiss. "Oh, yeah. But no more than once a week. It's fun to hear a newcomer's reaction the first time a wall cracks in his apartment or a window shatters from the vibrations. I thought you knew about the earthquakes in California."

"I've heard of them, yeah. But once a week?"

"We don't like to mention them too much around here. Scares away the tourists."

"Yeah, well," he said, pushing himself to his feet, "I better get going."

The waiter arrived with their lunch orders, but Tony didn't sit down.

"Here's some money for mine. I just remembered something I had to do. But I'll be in touch before the end of the festival. You're not leaving for the nunnery before then, are you?"

Her expression had brightened the moment Tony had stood up. "I'll be right across the way."

As soon as Tony walked away from the table, she put her hand over her mouth and dared a look at Barrie. He had already started heading in her direction. Her face was flushed that plum color, and he wasn't sure if it was from embarrassment or holding back her laughter.

"Spanky leaving already?" he said, taking a seat.

He had his answer when laughter sputtered out between her fingers. She put her forehead to the table and pounded her fist.

"Well, at least you're not crushed." He took a bite of Spanky's hamburger.

"You heard everything, didn't you?" she asked in a muffled voice.

"As well as you heard my snort."

She lifted her head. "You were no help at all."

He bobbed his eyebrows. "Maybe you'd better spank me."

She dropped her head and went into another spasm of laughter, and Barrie couldn't help but join her. He hadn't laughed so hard in years.

When they'd finally gotten hold of themselves, he said, "You were amazing."

"I was?"

"Aye." She *was* amazing. The warm tilt of her eyes as she looked at him in surprise. The curve of her mouth. "The way you handled that sod," he said quickly before some other accolade spilled out. "The way you kept your head and played along, and the nunnery thing...excellent." He could have gone on, but decided not to. He didn't want to risk sounding like a sod himself. "At least you're not too disappointed that Number Two didn't pan out."

She rolled her eyes. "To be honest with you, I almost snorted just before you did."

Barrie took her hand in his. "I like you, Marisa. I've only known you an hour, and we click. You've got me thinking about my whole life." When he kissed her hand, he had the uncomfortable feeling he wasn't joking anymore. He looked up, met her gaze, and felt that tickle deep in his stomach. This wasn't good. He'd never felt a tickle before when he'd looked at a woman. Even a woman who *was* his type. She was wearing that old-fashioned rose perfume, and a few strands of her hair had escaped her upswept do and were trailing down her neck. He cleared his throat. "Poor misguided fool," he said, shaking his head.

But as the words came out he realized he wasn't sure if he was referring to Spanky...or himself.

The mass wedding was beautiful, or as beautiful as it could be with fifty couples all taking their vows together. Marisa wanted to cry, because romantic people always cried at weddings. But she was too distracted by the feel of Barrie's hands on her thighs as he held her steady.

He really didn't have to set her on his shoulders so she could watch the ceremony, but he'd insisted. He'd shown her how to use his camera, and she took shots from her elevated position.

The priest gave the couples a final blessing: "May your love shine brighter than the sun, be as constant as the moon, and as enduring as the Earth. Gentlemen, you may kiss your brides."

"No snorting!" Marisa said, nudging him with her good foot.

He twitched. "I held myself back."

She took a few pictures of the couples in their embraces and cheered with the rest of the crowd. As part of the ceremony, all the men swept their brides up into their arms and carried them out of the square.

She realized how darned romantic that was. And how romantic Barrie was for toting her all over the place in the same way. If she'd been a true romantic, she would have swooned. All she felt was a slight light-headedness and a swirling feeling in her chest.

She really needed to find her Mr. Right and let Barrie get on with his business. She was thinking about him far too much.

She felt a tug on the back of her dress, which was bunched up around Barrie's neck. She twisted around to find Carlo standing there.

"It's Gina. She's going into labor."

FIFTEEN MINUTES LATER, the Cerinis were all assembled in the waiting area again. This time Barrie wasn't sitting off to the side; he was sitting next to Marisa.

"You didn't have to come this time," she whispered.

"Aye, but a proper mate would accompany his girl, for moral support."

She gave him a little nudge. "That was very proper of you, then."

"And I suppose a proper mate would take your hand in his." He took her hand as he said, "For moral support as well."

She had no reply to that, because that simple act swept away her words.

Carlo was watching her from across the way with a surly expression. Nothing new there, she supposed. Pop wore a pained expression that said she wasn't going to get that job because she'd met the wrong Mr. Right. She'd never seen his tufts in such disarray. So far he'd dodged every question about whether she'd get the job. Of course, if she could tell him how very much she wanted it... Louie was staring at them, and Nonna, well, she was actually smiling.

"What are you grinning like a fool for?" Louie asked Nonna. "He's not even Italian."

"Like I could forget with you telling me every five minutes. Stop staring at them already."

As though she'd addressed the whole family, everyone averted their gazes.

Louie tilted his head. "Eh?"

"You heard me." Under her breath, she muttered, "Nothing but a big phony, you can hear everything."

Louie's mouth twitched just the tiniest bit. *Was* he faking it?

Tino was getting treated in the emergency room. He'd been experimenting with battered, deep-fried bananas when he'd heard about Gina's labor pains. He dropped a banana into hot grease and splashed himself. By the time this was over, he would have gone through as much pain as Gina. Mama was in the back with Gina this time.

"Don't forget the dinner party tonight," Nonna said. "Barrie, you are invited too, of course."

Marisa caught the brief flash of panic on his face before he gave her a gracious smile. "Thank you."

The dinner party. She'd forgotten all about it in the confusion of trying to complete her derailed date with destiny. The cousins, uncles and aunts from all over, including Italy, would be there. Their backyard would be turned into a mini-festival, with lots of noise and hugging. Barrie was going to hate it. But not bringing him would raise eyebrows for sure. When Gina and Mama entered the waiting area, everyone jumped to their feet. Barrie helped Marisa with her crutches.

"Another false alarm?" Marisa asked.

"Yep." Gina patted her belly. "He's still not ready to come out. I'm sorry to put you all through this. You know how I hate to cause my family stress. Good thing I hardly ever do, huh?"

Oh, brother. Marisa was surprised to find that Barrie had remained close by. He hadn't seemed to notice his participation, and she wasn't about to point it out. His hand was resting on her shoulder, and she wondered if he knew how romantic that gesture was. Probably not.

"Marisa? Hello, Marisa," Mama was saying, waving her hand in front of her face. "Snap out of that daydream and listen. What time are you coming over to help?"

"Whenever you need me." In the race for being the perfect daughter, she had miles to catch up.

"I'M BEGINNING TO GET that panicky feeling right here," Marisa said as they drove to her parents' house. She pointed to the valley between her breasts. In her life of worrying, she'd never felt such an ache before.

"I've got two days to find two men. Tuesday morning you fly out of my life forever...." She cleared the frog from her throat. "And I'll have to confess everything to my family." Barrie's face actually didn't have relief on it. In fact, he looked rather sullen, or maybe she was just imagining it. "I'll bet you'll be glad to get away from me," she said, forcing a laugh.

He didn't look at her when he said, "Ah, you're beginning to grow on me a bit. I'm..." He glanced at her. "We'll find your chap and you'll forget all about me."

"And you'll be in Barcelona and then onto the next assignment and the next, and you'll gladly forget about me. Won't you?" Now she was being pitiful, looking for some scrap of assurance that she meant something to him, even though she wasn't supposed to want to mean anything to him. Darn it, she was confuzzled.

"How can I forget about you?" He patted the camera on the seat between them. "I've got photographs."

"I won't forget about you, either," she said, not looking his way. The ache was growing larger. This was silly. He wasn't Mr. Right, plain and simple. She'd be a disgrace to her family. She'd be in the Bad News section of the newsletter—forever!

Unfortunately, none of those prospects felt as horrible as never seeing Barrie again.

When he carried her over the threshold, the house was in the usual bustle of activity. She'd expected to see him cringe at all the cars parked along the front of the property, but he'd hidden it well. Since being with him, she was more aware of how arriving at her parents' house was like entering another world—of old-fashioned family traditions where women devoted themselves to family first, and it wasn't strange to meet your soul mate at a festival.

"Better take me to the kitchen," she said.

The last of the afternoon sun poured through the large kitchen window, lighting up the leaves of the plants and the colored bottles. On top of the cabinets and in every nook and cranny were Nonna's canned vegetables in their mason jars. Mushrooms, eggplant and a variety of fruits floated in liquid and promised goodies from their garden all year round. Heat emanated from every cooktop and both ovens, but she didn't mind when it was infused with garlic and roasted vegetables. No microwave, no frozen prepared anything—she hid her TV dinners when anyone from her family visited—everything made just like in the old days. She sighed with pleasure. Being old-fashioned wasn't so bad.

Tino, with his bandaged hand, was mixing something in a bowl while the other women moved in the perfect coordination that always awed her. Pavarotti filled the air with the beauty of his voice. Luckily Mama was too busy to give her that look of disappointment—yet.

Nonna lifted her cheek, and Barrie dipped Marisa down so she could kiss her. And then, to her surprise, he leaned farther down and kissed Nonna, too. Without prompting! And even more surprising, Nonna beamed at the gesture.

Mama gave Marisa a hug, and she could tell by the stiffness that Mama was still not pleased. "And no sneaking in any of that low-fat stuff. Do you want to fill mushrooms or ravioli? Never mind, I'll choose. You take too long to decide."

"Mushrooms," Marisa said, just to make a point.

"Can I help with something?" Barrie asked after lifting her onto the stool.

Everyone in the kitchen stopped and stared at him. He looked around, searching for the source of their surprise.

Tino set down a tray of purple pasta using his good hand and said, "They're not used to a man offering to help in the kitchen. Not that there's anything unmasculine about it."

"Of course not," Barrie agreed, sharing a secret smile with Marisa.

"I mean," Tino continued, "I do it for a living. But hey, if you want to help, we could sure use you. Gina's not feeling too well. Are you, honey?" He sent her three air kisses.

She was sprawled in a brown easy chair in the family room, looking pale and tired. Beyond her, through the windows, about forty people enjoyed the late-summer weather and free-flowing wine. Someone laughed, a baby cried, and one of the older men playing bocce cheered.

"Put me to work, then," Barrie said, heading to the sink to wash his hands.

Nonna took him by the arm, then paused when her hand wouldn't even go around the girth of it. "So big, so big," she said, then pulled him over to the counter where she was working. "Tino, bring over your eggplant macaroni. Barrie can stuff the raviolis." She tied an apron decorated with hand-painted tomatoes on Barrie. He started to object, but held back his words.

With all of the activity going on, not one recipe book sat open. In fact, there wasn't one in the entire house. Nonna prided herself on knowing all the old-country recipes by heart. That was Marisa's project, to capture them on paper for future generations. Her ulterior motive, however, was to have them on hand because she needed a little guidance where cooking was concerned. Naturally, Gina knew most by heart and announced it regularly.

While Marisa spooned crabmeat filling into each mushroom cap, she watched Nonna and Barrie working together at the far counter. At first his movements were awkward as he tried to measure out the right amounts. There weren't any measuring devices in the kitchen either. He watched Tino do a few and mirrored his movements. Maybe he was only helping because he would have felt awkward doing nothing—or worse, because if he'd been outside with the rest of her family, he would have been the only non-Italian in the bunch. If she didn't know better, though, she'd guess he was enjoying himself.

"Back in Scotland, our big celebrations call for haggis," Barrie said, now getting the hang of the ravioli.

"Sounds interesting," Nonna said. "What is it?"

"Sheep heart, lungs and liver stuffed into the skin of its stomach and boiled. It's served with tatties and neeps. Potatoes and turnips."

"Ew, gross!" Marisa said, wrinkling her nose.

Barrie looked dismayed by her reaction. "How can you tell if you've never had it?"

"Call it a…gut instinct."

"Aye, very funny," he muttered, but still managed to send her a smile that tickled her deep down inside.

Barrie didn't belong in the kitchen picture. He towered over everyone else, for one thing. And his movements didn't flow synchronously like everyone else's. But somehow, he did fit. When he finished with the eggplant raviolis, Tino put him to work stuffing cannolis, and when he went to sit with Gina for a while, Mama was forced to ask Barrie to help her take out the large pan of stuffed shells. She even smiled at him.

Marisa wondered if he knew how adorable he looked in that apron, even from the back where the ties swung against his behind as he moved.

When one of her cousins came in for some more wine, she stopped short at the sight of him. Well, Marisa could understand that. In Italian, she asked who he was, and Mama pointed at Marisa and explained that he belonged to her. Marisa couldn't help the warm feeling at those words, even though it was followed by the thought that she was misguided and would soon come to her senses. However, the chances of that happening didn't look very good so far, because she'd been sitting there for an hour and only ten mushrooms had gotten stuffed because she'd been watching Barrie the whole time.

Nonna corralled Barrie again and had him cutting tomatoes. "No, too thin," she said, indicating the desired thickness with her fingers. Barrie took the criticism well and earned Nonna's approving nod. "So, is it true what they say about big men?" she asked when he'd finished, taking hold of his hand.

Oh, no, what was she going to ask him? Marisa held her breath as Barrie said, "Depends on what they say."

"That they have big..." Nonna knocked one of the little tomatoes on the floor and stomped on it with her boot to keep it from rolling away. It splattered on the yellow tile. She looked back up at Barrie, who had a tense, expectant look on his face. "Hearts."

Marisa couldn't hold back the sigh of relief, nor the grin when her gaze met Barrie's.

"To be honest with you," he answered, "I don't know. Never been in love before."

Nonna gave his hand an affectionate squeeze before she let it go. "I'd say you do, the way you've been carrying Marisa around. 'Swonderful, being in love for the first time, isn't it?"

He looked over at her and winked. "It's not bad."

Marisa nearly fell off her stool. She grabbed at the counter and forced her attention to the unstuffed mushrooms. "Not bad" meant good, and that meant he was saying he was in love with her, which he wasn't, of course. But just hearing those words, along with his wink, melted her.

Nonna walked over and pinched her cheek. "Never seen her this happy before, either." She surveyed Barrie, then Marisa. "Maybe he's not Italian, and maybe he's big, but I'd say love hit its target anyway. Destiny, it does not always follow tradition."

Several thoughts bombarded her brain. Nonna approved of Barrie, that was the first. And what was that about her never seeing Marisa so happy before? She must really be putting her acting skills to the test then, because she couldn't really *be* that happy, not when she'd met the wrong man.

Unfortunately, Mama hadn't heard a word of the exchange because she was fighting off tears as she continued to tell her cousin about Marisa's failure. For the first time, her look of disappointment didn't hurt as much as before.

A little while later, as Marisa hobbled to the backyard, she came face-to-face with Prospect Number Three. He was walking in while she was trying to go out. He gave her a devastating smile and stepped aside with a smooth, "*Scusi*. I don't believe we've met. My name is Vincenzo. And you are?"

"Marisa Cerini."

"Ah, Carlo's sister. He has told me much about you. I am very much pleased to meet you."

Uh-oh. Maybe she'd finally met Mr. Right.

7

SOMETHING FELT DIFFERENT and Barrie couldn't figure out why. It wasn't a bad difference, but it gave him a funny feeling in the pit of his stomach. As though he'd stepped outside himself and become another person, a person who was part of the scene instead of on the outer fringes.

At one point, he made shots of everyone in the kitchen. Marisa had been stuffing her mushrooms, though she wasn't focused on the task. Probably worried about meeting—or not meeting—her remaining prospects. Still, she looked beautiful, her shiny, dark hair swept up, several strands gracing the back of her neck. Her eyes had a dreamy quality as she stared at the herbs on the windowsill, and before he realized it, he'd taken half a dozen photographs of her.

That something different penetrated his focus, too. Instead of waiting for the right pose, he waited for the right expression. Nonna, for instance, smiled as she placed each black-and-white cookie just so on a platter and sometimes murmured something to Salvatore. Tino squeezed Gina close, and Barrie could feel love emanating from them. Mama took the kitchen business seriously, moving efficiently, yet taking time to assess each dish. Every scene pulled him in, stealing away his objectivity. Had he lost his skills completely? First no soul, and now no polish?

The panicky feeling that assailed him each time he thought of the conversation with his boss didn't come this time. Still, he wasn't focused enough. He'd let Marisa and her family distract him, and it was going to be his downfall. Just like it had been for Porter.

Well, not like Porter. Porter was in love. Barrie was just…unfocused. And wishing his hands and not her mother's were on Marisa's shoulders as she leaned down and said something to her. Wishing it was his hands on Marisa's waist as Tino helped her get a handle on her crutches. She headed toward the backyard, and Barrie fought his impulse to rush to her side to sweep her into his arms and carry her outside.

Because, after all, he wasn't a romantic kind of guy.

A few minutes later, Nonna waved him over and put him to work mixing some concoction—it looked like zucchini to him—and rice together in a big, flowered bowl. He thought about the daft urge to rush forward and help Marisa when she clearly didn't need it. Could it be that he just wanted to feel her curves beneath her clothing?

"You're supposed to use your hands," Nonna said.

He blinked. "Pardon?"

She took away the spoon he'd been using. "Always use your hands. That's the best way to feel the textures."

"Like this?" He sank his hands into the rice mixture.

"Perfetto!"

He was tempted to ask her more about Marisa looking happier than she ever had, but he held his tongue. She was putting on a show for them while looking for the guy who would really put the glow in her eyes. *That* thought gave him a panicky feeling. Not his career

being on the line or losing his touch. No, that she
would meet the right guy who would put the glow in
her face and his hands on her shoulders or her waist
or the other places Barrie had been fantasizing about.

Had she been saving herself for her Mr. Right? Probably. She wasn't polished enough around men to have
sacrificed her virtue. While he had always liked a
woman who knew her way around a man, the thought
of being the first to make her cry out in pleasure... He
shook his head. Maybe it was just lust—had to be
lust—but he ached to be the one whose name she called
out just before plunging over the edge the first time.

"You're pulverizing the rotenza!" Nonna said, in-
specting the mush he'd created.

In a jerk reaction, he pulled his hands out of the
mixture. This wasn't good. What really wasn't good
was that his body had responded to his thoughts. In a
room full of Marisa's relatives, he felt really sinful. He
didn't dare glance down to see how visible those day-
dreams had been beneath the silly apron.

"Er, sorry about that. Guess I got carried away."

Nonna clucked her tongue. "Sometimes I get carried
away too, daydreaming. When you haven't had any for
a long time, it can consume your thoughts. Eh, Salvatore?" she said, glancing upward. Her hair was piled
so high, she had to use her hand to right herself.

Barrie felt his face flush when she looked at him.
"Salvatore was your husband, then?"

"*Si*, a good man. He died while we were making
love." She shook her head. "He didn't even get to
enjoy it."

Barrie glanced around to see if anyone else was listening. Everyone was caught up in their own conver-

sations or tasks. "Heck of a way to go," was all he could come up with and stay respectable.

"He always was a little too fast for me." She tried to fix the mess he'd made, then pushed the bowl of rotenza back at him. "Take it out back. Everything is almost ready."

He covered the choking sound in his throat and carried the bowl outside.

People were scattered around the large backyard enjoying the warm breeze and music. Hanging lanterns added atmosphere as they swayed from the branches of trees and posts. A long table was covered with bowls and platters of food and bottles of wine.

"Got your balls now!" Louie called out, and Barrie was relieved to see he was playing bocce.

Just about everyone looked his way, making him realize how much he stood out. Clearly everyone knew about Marisa's mistake in thinking he was her Mr. Right. He nearly missed the edge of the table with the bowl as his gaze sought and found her. She was sitting at a table near a eucalyptus tree with her brother, Carlo, and another man. Her gaze met his, and she held up three fingers.

Then he recognized the man: Number Three.

Marisa surprised him by waving him over. Three wasn't paying any attention to Barrie at all, focusing on Marisa. He had dark, wavy hair and a cupid's-bow mouth. He wore a white cotton shirt that was buttoned only halfway, showing off a mat of dark hair. Thinking of his own mostly bare chest, Barrie couldn't help but wonder if she preferred the dark, hairy type, then decided she probably did, and it didn't matter anyway.

"Barrie," she said as he drew near. She captured his hand in hers. "You've met Carlo," she said, dismissing her brother with a wave. "This is Vincenzo. Carlo met him at the cookie booth yesterday and...invited him over. Vincenzo, this is my friend, Barrie."

Friend. Somehow that sounded inappropriate. They weren't friends, really. Then again, he had so few, he wasn't sure what qualified as a friend. Perhaps wanting to tuck a strand of her hair behind her ear was friendly, but wanting to sink his tongue into her mouth probably stretched the definition a little.

Carlo looked pretty pleased with himself. Barrie would bet even odds that Carlo figured this guy to be the proper mate for his sister.

"Sit down," she said, patting the chair next to her.

He didn't belong at that table. "Why don't I get you something to eat?"

"I'm not hungry."

Great, the guy had stolen her appetite. "How about some wine then?"

"Sure. Red, please."

He nodded at the two men, who declined his unspoken offer. How long could he drag out the task? He meandered through the crowd, then stepped back and took some pictures. Again, he felt the loss of distance and objectivity as he was drawn into snatches of conversation. Nonna was seated at the head of a long table. She waved at him, and Marisa's parents glanced over at Marisa and then guiltily back at him. Before he knew what had happened to him, he'd been seated between Lamberto and Ninalee in front of a plate of food that must have included a sampling of everything on the table.

He knew a diversionary tactic when he saw one. Whenever frustration levels soared—which was whenever he saw Marisa talking to Vincenzo—he reminded himself that this was his role. He was the wrong Mr. Right and her family wasn't supposed to like him much anyway. And, more importantly, he wanted her to meet Mr. Right so he could get back to his lonely life.

Lovely life. That's what he'd meant.

So he settled into his role and tried not to look at her too much. When their gazes met, hers was filled with questions. Maybe she was wondering where her wine was. Then Vincenzo had touched her shoulder, and she turned back to him. Carlo had left them alone.

For the first time that he could remember, Barrie lost his appetite.

"SO I ASKED your brother who was the beautiful woman working at the booth this morning, and he told me all about you," Vincenzo said.

Marisa smiled, but couldn't think of anything to say. Not that she felt awkward. For some reason, her mouth hadn't dropped open all night. She just wasn't in a talkative mood.

"Your friend must have forgotten about your wine. Wait, and I will get you a glass."

He wove through the tables to the wine. He was beautiful, no doubt about it. Not terribly tall or big…just what she liked in a man, she reminded herself. No way could Vincenzo carry her anywhere. He had refined features and an Italian accent. He'd lived in Rome for the past ten years, but was looking for a change of scenery.

So far there'd been no sign that he'd been more interested in Carlo than her, or that he had any inclination to be punished. She tried to muster up some excitement about him being a very viable candidate for Mr. Right.

Her gaze strayed to Barrie. That he would rather sit

with them and let her get to know Vincenzo bothered her. No doubt he was tired of the charade she'd foisted on him.

Her father walked over. Uh-oh. He never left the table in mid-meal unless he had indigestion or something important to say. He was smiling, and she wondered if he'd tell her that Barrie wasn't such a bad guy after all, even if he was Scottish. But that would be a bad thing, because he was leaving in a couple of days.

"*Cara,* you are doing all right?" he asked, planting a kiss on her forehead.

"Yes, Pop. Are you being nice to Barrie?"

He waved away her concern. "Your *nonna* seems to like him." This was said in the way you'd comment on someone's strange taste in foods. "But this guy Vincenzo—Carlo tells me he is very nice."

She watched Carlo take money from cousin Emilio. "He's taking bets, isn't he?"

Pop tilted his head back and forth. "He bets on everything. Are you sure this man wasn't in the square during sunset and you just didn't see him?"

"It's possible," she found herself saying. "But there's no…feeling."

Her pop gave her shoulders a squeeze. "Sometimes feeling comes later. If this is your true *amore,* the salesmanager position is yours."

After another kiss, he departed.

"It's nice to see such affection in a family," Vincenzo said, as he returned with two glasses of wine. "My family is very close, too."

"You don't live with your mother, do you?"

"No, why?"

She waved it away. "No reason."

"Are your parents from Italy?"

"Yes, from a small town called Cortina."

"Really? My father comes from there, too." He clinked his glass against hers. "A coincidence or fate?"

Her gaze slid to Barrie, who was engaged in conversation with Nonna. She really did like him. Then she realized Vincenzo was still talking and tuned in. "Hmm?"

"I said, I'm usually awkward around women."

"No way."

He gave her a shy smile. "You think because I wear designer clothes, have money and a Ferrari at home and travel a lot that I'm smooth with the ladies, don't you?" He leaned closer. "But that's all a front. I was born into a rich family and people expect me to act a certain way. Whenever I'm around a beautiful woman I'm attracted to, I get nervous." He gave her the most genuine smile she'd ever seen. Well, other than Barrie's. "But with you, I'm very comfortable. Why do you suppose that is?"

She wanted to say, *Because you're full of it?* Instead, she said, "I don't know."

"Would you like to visit me? I could show you all of Italy—Venice, Florence and Naples. No strings attached, nothing expected in return."

"Don't they have a lot of sewage in Venice?" she heard herself asking, then cringed.

"I won't be noticing the water if I'm with you," he said.

"That's nice," she said, trying really hard to sound flattered.

Something was wrong with her. She was sitting across from a rich, handsome, Italian man who would make her family proud and she couldn't muster up one iota of excitement.

She shifted her gaze to Barrie. It was all his fault. He'd warped her thinking somehow. As he started to look her way, she looked at Vincenzo. She should be thinking about kissing those lush lips, not Barrie's un-lush mouth. But it didn't matter if he didn't have a lush mouth, he had a lush kiss that consumed her and made her forget everything—like breathing.

"Maybe," Vincenzo was saying, "we could get to know each other better alone. I'm staying at the Piazza Hotel. We could have a drink in the bar and see where it leads."

"Sure," she heard herself saying and realized she was watching Barrie again. He was making Nonna laugh. And she was squeezing his arm. What were they talking about? The way she dropped verbal bombshells, Lord only knew.

"Why don't we meet downstairs in the bar at ten?" Vincenzo said, rising to his feet. "I'd better get going. I promised to call home." He took her hand and snapped her attention back to him. "I'll see you at ten."

"Downstairs at ten." She tried to get hold of the conversation. "I look forward to seeing you," she said, then realized she was looking at Barrie again.

"I'll lay two-to-one odds that's the guy you were supposed to meet in the square," Carlo said, sliding into the chair Vincenzo had just vacated.

"Maybe."

"Look how happy the family is now that you've finally met the right guy."

Pop pumped Vincenzo's hand in farewell once he'd failed to get him to stay. Louie was smiling, but Louie was always smiling. Nonna was too busy talking with Barrie to even notice, and Mama...well, she looked bothered. She glanced guiltily over at Barrie, then back at Marisa.

"Pop's the only one who looks happy. And you."

Carlo looked smug. "I saw you today. Tell me this: If you're so in love with the Scottish guy, why are you talking to other men?"

"Good question," she answered glumly.

"So HE'S THE PERFECT MATCH, then?" Barrie asked as he carried her to the Buick.

"Seems like it. And as an added incentive, I get the job if he's the one."

"Sounds like bloody blackmail to me," he muttered, kicking open the door and setting her on the car seat with a little more force than necessary.

"Pop thinks he's doing the right thing."

"They always do." He scooted her back on the seat and made her forget for a moment that she was defending her father and think instead of how neat it would be to make love in a car. An old car, with a big, bench seat.

He untangled his arms from around her, leaving his face only an inch from hers. "Do you think he's doing the right thing? Is that what you want, some slick Armani guy with a line?"

"I think he was being sincere. It's nice when a guy admits his true feelings."

She could still smell the scent of roasted vegetables on his clothing and the heat coming off his body.

"It was a load of pish. A man doesn't go around spouting his feelings to impress a woman."

"What do you do to impress a woman?"

He paused for a moment, caught off guard. "I'm honest with her. You can tell when a woman's interested, and— Wait a minute. We're not talking about me, we're talking about this Armani guy. All I'm saying is, don't be taken in by his smooth talk. He's going to ply you with drinks and get you to his room."

"What are you so grumpy about? Isn't that what you want? Then you'll be rid of me."

"I don't want to be rid of you— I mean, I don't want you to be taken in by the wrong guy. You're so caught up in this silly tradition, you can't see what you're doing."

"Huh?"

His hand had gotten tangled in the skirt of her dress, and he struggled to free it. "I mean, you've been saving yourself for the right guy, and I don't want you dazzled by the wrong guy. If you want to go along with this tradition, well then, I want it to be right for you. There's still one more guy to find, so don't blow everything on this one. You've waited this long...." He shook his hand. "This is not coming out right."

His hand was getting further tangled, and he was pulling her skirt tight around her. She reached out and disengaged his hand with hers.

"How did you know I was saving myself?"

"I...well, I assumed, since you were an old-fashioned girl and all. At least half of you anyway. Have you?"

"Well, I suppose I have. It wasn't that hard. I haven't met anyone I wanted to...well, you know." *Until now.* She met his gaze. "And why do you think this guy is going to get me into bed now?"

Their noses brushed. "Because he's the perfect guy. Your perfect guy, and your family's."

She could feel a tightness spreading from her chest up to her throat. Her arms were still up around his neck, and his thigh was pressed against hers. She could hear the music and conversation drifting from the back of the house, but the front yard was quiet.

"Thank you for caring." Her words came out a whisper against his cheek.

"That's what friends are for. I just don't want you to sell your soul for some tradition. I've been there, and it's not worth it."

"Would you kiss me again?"

Clearly that wasn't what he'd expected, because he started to respond and stopped himself. "Pardon?"

"Kiss me again." This time it wasn't a question.

His gaze dropped down to her mouth. "Why?"

Now her heartbeat was hammering in her throat, and her fingers involuntarily tightened against his warm neck. "Because I like the way it makes me feel."

He didn't need any more prompting. His mouth pressed against hers and deepened the kiss. Her fingers slid up into his hair, pulling at the silky strands as his tongue ran along the edge of her teeth and tickled the roof of her mouth.

This was the feeling she was after, the helium-inside-her-chest, close-your-eyes-and-savor-every-sensation feeling she'd been missing with Vincenzo and never realized it. She knew this kiss, or feeling, wasn't going to lead anywhere. She might marry Vincenzo or maybe Prospect Four and have three children, and she would read Barrie's articles and daydream about these moments.

But this was what she'd been thinking about—needing—when she'd smiled at Vincenzo and kept looking over at Barrie.

Her breath caught when his hand traced the neckline of her dress. Very lightly his palm skimmed her breasts, and she arched to his touch. She felt sinful and wanton and she'd worry about penance later. But the feeling wasn't just lust or the culmination of waiting for years to experience a man's touch. The feeling was waiting for the right man's touch and the way her whole body screamed *Yes, this is the one!* and didn't listen at all to what her mind was saying.

She hadn't thought big and hunky was her type, but the feeling grew as she ran her hands over his shoulders and down his biceps. He tilted her head back and kissed her throat, and she unbuttoned his shirt and slid her hands inside.

He was hot and smooth. When her pinky fingers grazed his nipples, they were already hard. She loved the way his muscles were defined and the way they moved beneath his skin as he shifted her to the side. He unzipped the back of her dress and slid his hands all the way down her back. She wasn't sure how he'd unsnapped her bra, but his hands slid around her sides and then over her bare breasts. Desire shimmered through her, curling around her nipples and between her thighs. She had dreamed of kisses and romantic strolls, but never this heated passion between a man and a woman.

He tilted her back, kissing down her throat to her collarbone and then to the valley between her breasts. Her dress was loose enough for him to nuzzle beneath it. He took his time, kissing the curve of her breast, inching toward the peak that was burning in anticipation. She involuntarily put her hands on the back of his head, urging him to hurry and put his mouth there. He still took his agonizing time, though his tongue flicked the outer edge. She couldn't believe how much she wanted to just shift herself beneath his mouth, she who should be relishing every touch. He twisted, and she thought, *finally!*

When the horn blared, she jumped and pulled her dress together. Barrie had jumped, too, but was now looking chagrined.

"Hit the horn with my elbow."

She glanced at the front door. "We'd better go. We'd…" He was sliding out of the car, and his shirt gaped open as he did so. She wanted to see more of that beautiful body.

Barrie circled the car and slid in on the driver's side. He pulled out of the driveway and headed into town.

"I guess it's a good thing you hit the horn." She twisted around to zip herself up. "Who knows what would have happened if you hadn't?" Like any one of her relatives coming out and finding them groping each other in the driveway.

He looked flushed, but still hadn't buttoned his shirt. "Nothing would have happened." She liked the way he sounded breathless and really liked that she had made him that way.

She had the nearly irresistible urge to slip her hand inside his shirt again, but then his words sank in. "Why?"

"Because you're saving yourself for your Mr. Right, and I am not him. I like kissing you too, but we can't let that happen again."

"You like kissing me?" There she was, getting caught up in one part of the conversation and not paying attention to the important part. "Why not?"

"Have you gone daft? I'm not the right guy for you."

"And I'm not the right girl for you."

"This has nothing to do with me. This has to do with your tradition and making your family proud and all that pish."

After zipping up her dress, she crossed her arms over her chest and tried to quell the aftershocks of his touch on her breasts. "It doesn't matter, because soon you'll be on your way to Barcelona and then another place and then another."

"Right," he said with a little too much force. "And you'll be doing what we almost did with the man you're supposed to be with."

But what if... She wanted to speak the words that hung between them. What if she didn't want the right Mr. Right, and what if she had enough guts to buck her family's love tradition? What then?

Barrie would still hightail it out of there and never look back. He was just using her tradition as an excuse not to make any kind of commitment. And he'd made it perfectly clear how he felt about commitment.

"We've got fifteen minutes before Smoothie arrives," he said, finally buttoning his shirt. "And you don't want me carrying you in if he's there waiting for you."

She was about to ask why not, then realized he was right. *Focus, Marisa.* Darn, how was she supposed to focus when he was slipping his arms beneath her and then lifting her into his embrace? How was she supposed to focus when all she wanted to do was get back in the car and feel his hands on her skin?

Unfortunately, Vincenzo was already there. He was at the far end of the bar talking with someone, but she couldn't see who it was.

"Let's go in the side entrance," Barrie said. "I'll

carry you to the bar, and you can use the crutches to go the rest of the way.''

She would have wondered if he had forgotten the whole episode in the car, except she could feel he hadn't, right against her hip. Before she could think better of it, she shifted against him.

''Don't be a bad girl,'' he said in a strained voice.

She tilted her head. ''You think I'm a bad girl?''

''You have your moments.''

''I like that. 'Bad girl, bad girl...''' She sang a few bars from the Donna Summer song.

''Shh,'' he whispered in her ear, then let his mouth stay there for a moment as though he were fighting the urge to run his tongue around the edge of her ear. She shivered at the thought of it.

As it turned out, Vincenzo was talking to an attractive blonde. Periodically he glanced at the clock and then the front entrance. After another check, he leaned closer and they could just hear him say, ''I'm so glad you agreed to meet me for a drink but I've got to call home tonight. I'd like to see you again though. It's funny, but usually when I'm around a beautiful woman, I get nervous. But with you, I'm very comfortable. Why do you think that is?''

Barrie's body tensed. ''That slimy—''

She urged him to duck back out the side door before he said any more.

''Con artist,'' he continued, then looked at her. ''You all right?''

For a moment she was distracted by the way he ran those words together with his accent. Then she realized she wasn't all right. She should feel disappointed, not relieved. She should feel dashed that she hadn't dazzled Vincenzo enough to cancel his first date. Mostly she should feel devastated that she had failed once again. But all she could think about was being alone with Barrie.

"Just take me home, please," she said.

The short drive to her apartment was made in silence. The night had gotten breezier, and palm trees and shrubs danced as they pulled into the parking lot. Her apartment building held only eight units, and luckily hers was on the ground floor. When he scooped her into his arms, the world felt right again, even though it was more wrong than ever.

"Want to come in for coffee?" she asked once he'd unlocked the door with the key she handed him.

"You sure about that?"

Usually he set her down on the door stoop, and she watched him walk down the sidewalk to his car.

"The thing in the car was a fluke, right?" She managed to get inside on her crutches and turned on the light. "It's not like we can't keep our hands off each other."

He shrugged. "Of course we can't. Can, I mean." He looked around the apartment, and she followed his gaze and wondered what he thought. It was a small place and looked even smaller with all her stuff. Her family had donated the brocade couch and the dining set. The wood floors were covered with braided rugs in colors of wine, mushroom and peach.

She'd been collecting pictures for years. It didn't matter where they came from—magazines, old photographs, her own sketches, they were taped to the walls and even the blinds. Many were of Italy, and some were flowers or men and women on the verge of a kiss. He was looking at one of those.

"That's my favorite moment, when two people who

want to kiss are just about to,'' she said, hobbling up to him.

When he looked at her, his gaze involuntarily dropped to her mouth, then went back to the pictures. ''I wish you hadn't heard that jerk.''

''It's all right.''

''No, it's not. You're upset, and you've every reason to be.'' At her grimace, he added, ''You're not going to cry, are you?''

She looked away as she set her crutches next to the couch she was leaning against. ''I'm not going to... Okay, I'm going to cry.'' She wiped her eyes as tears sprang to them. ''It's—''

''I know, a family trait.'' He wasn't grimacing, at least.

Still, she said, ''Look, it's probably best if you leave. I'm not going to be much company, and I know you don't like crying women.''

''All right then.'' He walked to the door, then stopped. ''Will it make you feel better if I go pound the chap?''

She laughed through her tears. ''It wasn't him.''

He walked back to her. ''It wasn't...something I did, was it?''

His genuine concern made her laugh again. ''It's not you. It's me. I'm a failure. I can't even fall for the right guy. Okay, maybe that is your fault, a little. You didn't make me fall in love with you, after all. But you knocked me into a fountain, ruined my dress, kept me from my date with destiny, and you're all wrong for me and I'm wrong for you, and still...''

His face kept changing as she spoke, as each word connected with the next and he realized what she was saying. At least he didn't look horrified. In fact, his blue eyes had softened as she'd let her sentence trail off.

"And I know," she continued, "that I'm not your type, that you look at commitment and love as something akin to…"

"Pirhanas," he offered when she couldn't come up with a word.

"Thanks. Yeah, pirhanas. I'm probably a little too heavy for you—"

"You're not too heavy."

"And I do want romance and commitment and babies and you're going to be an old salt or some seasoning and never settle down."

He moved closer, and with every word she spoke, her voice became more passionate.

"I know we're totally wrong for each other, but I still can't help wanting you to kiss me again because I've never felt the way I do when you kiss me. And I know in another day you're going to walk out that door and I'll never see you again, but it doesn't matter how many times I tell myself that, the thought of it—" her voice went thick with emotion "—tears me up inside."

He cradled her face in his big hands. "If I kiss you now, will you stop crying?"

She took a deep breath. "If you kiss me now, will you never stop?"

8

MARISA FELT as though she'd had twelve cups of espresso injected into her veins. She felt dizzy and high and anxious all at once. Barrie carried her—or maybe she was floating, she wasn't sure—to one of the closed doors and opened it.

"Bathroom," she whispered.

He nodded, then tried the door next to it. Her bedroom, where no man had ever been. Light from the living room spilled in and framed her bed in its glow. He set her on the multicolored coverlet, his gaze never leaving hers.

"Are you sure?" he asked as he climbed onto the bed with her.

"As sure as an incurably indecisive person can be."

His laugh was low and sultry.

He ran his hand up the side of her neck and into her hair. She was mesmerized by the intensity of his eyes and the knowledge that each touch would take her closer to something that would change her life...and shatter her heart.

His thumb grazed her mouth, sliding across the lip gloss she'd put there. She placed her hand against his chest. His heart was beating fast. When his hand pushed up her skirt to expose her good leg, it was shaking.

"Why are you shaking?" she whispered. "You can't be nervous."

He looked at his hand, then squeezed her thigh. "I am, a little."

"But this can't be the first time..."

He tilted her head back. "It's the first time it's...mattered. I've been making photographs without being involved, and those photographs have come out without soul. Now I've seen the difference—capturing you and your family, knowing them, it's different. Now I understand why. My soul is involved. And making love is the same. With you, my soul is involved."

And then he kissed her, immediately deepening the kiss and exploring her mouth. She didn't know the difference between making love while being involved and not, but she did know kissing. His kiss was different than any other man's kiss, and not necessarily because he was a better kisser. There was something else there, something undefinable.

Her heart and soul were involved.

She unbuttoned his shirt and pushed it back over his shoulders. She loved the feel of his skin, smooth and soft over delectable muscles. While he continued to kiss her, he unzipped her dress and pushed it down over her shoulders. She was wearing a bra and panties from her given-up-hope chest, and she only hoped the frilly lace would compensate for the extra flesh on her stomach and thighs.

He broke the kiss to maneuver the dress over her cast, which reminded her that she *had* a cast on, and that nearly naked she was not going to look very pretty.

Except that he wasn't looking at her with repugnance. In fact, his hands glided over her skin as his eyes took her in with something akin to awe.

His voice was thick when he said, "Don't change a thing about yourself." His gaze met hers, and she saw that he wasn't being solicitous or even casual. "You're beautiful, Marisa, just the way you are."

She felt tears spring to her eyes again, but she smiled to assure him they weren't tears of anything but pure joy. "Thank you."

He stood and unzipped his pants, then pushed them to the floor. She wanted to tell him how beautiful he was, too, but the words caught in her throat. His white briefs did little to conceal him, and in fact, the tip of him strained right out of the top. She couldn't breathe when he pushed them down, too.

First she was overwhelmed by his perfection. He was more beautiful than Michelangelo's *David* or any piece of art she'd ever seen. And then thoughts of Nonna talking about doorways and walking stiffly for days afterward flitted through her mind before she sent them on their way.

He crawled onto the bed again before she'd had enough visual satisfaction, but then she could probably look at him for hours and feel that way. She saw him push something to the head of the bed, but then he was kissing her again and she didn't think about anything but the way his tongue lathed her own and the way his hands touched her body. He unsnapped her bra and then used his tongue in wonderful, amazing ways that made her release sounds from her throat she'd never heard before.

Since all she could reach was his head, she ran her hands through his hair and relished the feel of it sliding through her fingers. His tongue made a warm, wet trail across her stomach and teased at the edge of her panties.

She'd thought she'd be nervous the first time a man

touched her down there, but she was wrong. When his fingers dipped into her hair, she caught her breath, and when they slid lower yet, she let out a strangled groan. He stripped away her panties with one hand while the other continued to tease her. She moved with him, body tensed and arched, eyes squeezed shut. Her breathing came in little puffs. The man knew what he was doing, even if it was all new to her. He gently pressed his palm on her pubic area and sent a warm feeling through her, and when he touched her again, it felt twice as wonderful.

The sensations coursing through her were building in intensity, rising in a crescendo, and when his mouth came down on her breast, she went over the edge in a spasm that engulfed her whole body.

"More?" he whispered against her skin, sliding his finger through her wetness.

She shook her head, crazy with the intense sensations, and when he touched her again, she went over...again.

"How...how..." She didn't care how it could happen twice. She just wanted to relish the sensations rocketing through her again.

He chuckled softly, and the sound reverberated through her. She opened her eyes and saw him watching her with satisfied amusement.

"I want to touch you," she said, rolling to her side.

He lay on his back and let her touch him, obviously comfortable with himself. She loved every inch of him, from his small, taut nipples to the faint freckles scattered across his chest. She traced lazy eights over his stomach, building up her courage to go farther south.

She inched closer, grazing the moist tip of him and eliciting a nice, soft groan. She moved her fingers back and forth against the velvety tip of him, and before she knew it, she'd slid her hand down the length of him. Which elicited another long groan from him.

"But you're so big," Marisa said in an imitation of Nonna, and they laughed. She kept stroking him and then he wasn't laughing anymore.

"Maybe...you...should know it's been...awhile since..." With another groan, he grabbed hold of her hand. "No more."

He reached up for his wallet, which was sitting on the pillow, and pulled out a little package. After he'd opened it, she watched him roll it down over himself. He kissed her again while positioning himself over her. She wanted to wrap her legs around his hips, but the cast made that a difficult proposition. Instead, she wrapped her arms around his neck and watched the expression on his face as he very gently found her.

"Remember to breathe," he said, making her realize she was indeed holding her breath.

A fine line between pleasure and pain—now she knew the meaning of that phrase. But when he filled her, she forgot all about the pain part and lost herself in the feeling of totally, completely belonging to a man.

To Barrie.

"You all right?" he asked.

"I love...the way you say that."

"I love the way your face looks right now."

He started the rhythm, and she caught on, moving in sync with him. He watched her, and when he was sure she wasn't in pain, he closed his eyes. She kept watching him, the expressions on his face, and the way his hair swung with his movements.

Then she closed her eyes and lost herself to the sensual feelings pulsing through her body and the way she felt deeper inside. That was scarier than everything else, because she didn't want to let go of him.

Then she couldn't breathe again, and her insides felt as though they were imploding, and then they did. His body jerked too, and he squeezed her tight against him.

Several long, sweet minutes later, he pulled back and looked at her. "You all right?"

"I am so all right, I can't even tell you."

He rolled her around so that she lay on top of him. "Me, too."

She loved the feel of her body pressed against his from her breasts all the way down to her toes. "So, what do we do now?"

"Eventually we'll have to pull apart, and then—"

"No, silly, I mean...now. Did we have soul?"

He reached up and twirled a strand of her hair around his finger. "So much, I can't even tell you."

She grinned. "You know, if we were meant to be together, we could just stay here for days and let the world march on by."

"If we were meant to be together, that's exactly what we'd—"

A sound intruded. Knocking.

"Marisa, are you in there?"

"Mama!"

She struggled up with his help and pulled on her dress. He pulled on his briefs and jeans.

"You stay in here!" She smoothed down her hair. "You're not here, all right?"

He helped her to her crutches and then went back into her room. By the time she'd hobbled to the door, her parents had already used their key. They were looking around the room.

"Is Barrie here?" Pop asked.

"No, why?" Oh, jeez, she sounded guilty.

"His car's outside."

"He said he wanted to get some pictures of the area, so he probably just left his car there."

That they trusted her without question dug right into her heart.

"We need to speak with you," Pop said, making himself comfortable on the couch. "It's about Barrie."

BARRIE QUIETLY cleaned up, straightened the bed, arranged her dainty underthings, then decided to tuck them beneath her pillow. He'd already assessed the window situation. He wasn't sure he could get out the double-hung window, so he sat on the bed and listened to the conversation in the living room.

"He has no intention of marrying you, Marisa," her mother said.

Her father said, "We bought one of the magazines he works for, and that's all he does, travels from one place to another. He's not the one, *cara*."

Mama said, "He's only here to cover the festival, which is over in two days. Then he leaves, and what happens to you?"

He could picture them leaning over her, pounding in their points. And they had points. He couldn't stay here, in one place, drowning in a family that kept their nose in their daughter's business. And there were the piranhas...no, they were still goldfish.

All right, bring on the Pamplona bulls then. Except they'd become a pack of puppies chasing him down the winding streets, ears flopping.

"Vincenzo isn't the one, either," Marisa said. "He was hitting on some woman."

Her father said, "Good, because we've found the one."

"Fabiano Ferruccio," her mother said. "He looks just like *the* Fabian! He's a third cousin twice removed, from the town just north of Cortina, Italy. His family moved here last year—you know the Ferruccios. He's come over to see about moving here."

"He's industrious," her father said. "He's been working as an accountant at his father's factory in Italy. I may have a position for him."

"But I like Barrie," Marisa said. "I...really like him."

"Has he made any promises to you? He says he intends to marry you, but has he made plans?"

"No."

"You're infatuated with him because he's different," her father said.

"Do you really think he's going to settle down here and take you with him when he travels?" Mama asked.

Barrie leaned against the door and waited for her answer.

"No," Marisa said at last.

He had the urge to burst through the door and tell them he did plan to marry her and make her part of his life. But he wasn't supposed to be there.

"Fabiano is the one, Marisa," Mama said. "He was supposed to be in the town square at sunset, but he didn't see you because Barrie had already knocked you down. He's from a good family, he's decent and caring—"

"And Italian," her father said.

Barrie waited to hear Marisa's protest, but after a few moments she said, "Is he straight? Normal? Not a **womanizer?**"

"We know his family. He's a good man. The right man. And you're going to meet him tomorrow."

"Well..."

"Make your family proud," he said. "We want the best for you. And think how happy you'll be in your new position with a man who makes everyone so happy for you, and doesn't break your mama's heart."

Barrie hated the way her "All right, I'll meet him," made him feel.

He wasn't her Mr. Right, and he was leaving in a day, and he couldn't settle down. So why did he sag against the door?

He pushed away and walked around her room, not wanting to hear any more. He was glad he hadn't seen the photographs on her dresser earlier. He saw different versions of Marisa, changing from a child, laughing in the sunshine, to a young woman probably on the verge of looking for her Mr. Right the first time. The photographs weren't professional, but they had the elusive soul he'd been searching for. It was obvious that whoever had taken them loved her. As there had been at her family's home, there were an array of family photographs, some sepia-colored. Many were of couples clearly in love.

She had a big, feminine bed with white posts at each corner. At the foot of the bed was an old, ornate wood chest. He knelt down and examined it.

"It's my given-up-hope chest," she said from behind him.

He spun around, surprised to find her leaning on her crutches in the doorway.

He stood. "Sounds like your family hasn't given up hope yet."

"You heard?"

"Nothing else to do. Look, I'd better get going, in case any more of your relatives pop by." Before he said something he'd regret, and she'd regret as well. She had her destiny to fulfil, and he wasn't part of it.

He couldn't pass her without leaning close and kissing her again. He knew what she meant about wanting another kiss because he'd never felt the way he did when he kissed her.

As he started to open the door, she said, "Will I see you tomorrow? Will you take me to the café?"

"If you want."

"Yeah, I do."

They settled on a time, and he walked into the warm night air and thought how free he should feel.

That relief was beginning to feel a little like heartbreak.

FABIANO WAS definitely Mr. Right. He was poised, gorgeous, classy, and Marisa had made it through a whole lunch with him without being grossed out or floored by some sexual deviance. He was polite, didn't kiss her hand, or show any overt interest in any other man or woman. As for herself, she didn't act awkward, nor did her mouth hang open once.

Better yet, Fabiano was interested in her and loved her family. Heck, he was part of her family in a twice-removed way. She had found the perfect man.

And she was miserable.

She *should* be miserable, because she'd given her body to the wrong Mr. Right instead of waiting. But unfortunately, that wasn't why.

Barrie was in the square taking pictures of the winners receiving their trophies for the best spaghetti sauce. He occasionally glanced her way, usually catching her watching him. This time when she looked up, he was taking her picture.

"So when cousin Rosa came home," Fabiano was saying, "there was sauce all over every wall and counter!"

Marisa laughed, picturing her cousin's face at seeing such a mess. Fabiano was funny, too, and her laughter was genuine. But it lacked...something, compared to the laughter she shared with Barrie.

"It's been really nice meeting you," Marisa said, glancing at her watch. "But I need to get to the cookie booth and help out for a couple of hours."

"A rich life is filled with good food and love." At her surprised expression, he said, "That was the saying in the cookies I bought yesterday. What fun you must have coming up with the sayings. I even thought of a few myself, though I'm sure they're not as good as yours. Hey, why don't I help out at the booth for a while?"

Now Marisa's mouth *was* hanging open. Could this guy get any more perfect? "Sure, that'd be...fine."

He took her crutches and helped her to stand. "Here, you can lean on my shoulder."

She was glad he didn't offer to carry her. He probably *would* grunt with the exertion, because he wasn't nearly as big as Barrie. She gave Barrie a look that tried to get across the fact that she was heading to the booth. He saw Fabiano helping her and nodded, and before she knew it, he'd disappeared from sight.

Something felt empty inside. She had to see him again before he left. She wanted to beg him to stay with her and love her, but there wasn't a chance of that. Still, she was sure she'd die if he left without kissing her one last time.

BARRIE STOPPED by the booth after he'd watched Fabiano help her hobble along the brick street. Not only was Fabiano still at the booth, he was actually working behind it. Mama Cerini and Nonna were laughing with him, though Marisa was sitting in the corner fiddling with a package of cookies.

Her face lit up when she saw him. Before she could say anything, Nonna lifted her cheek to him. The simple gesture warmed him, and he remember how uncomfortable he thought he'd be with it. He pecked her on both cheeks.

Mama Cerini actually looked a little guilty and even offered him a smile.

"You will come to the last family dinner tonight?" Nonna asked.

"Uh…" He glanced at Fabiano. "No, I can't. I've got a few more events to cover and then I'm off to Barcelona early in the morning."

"Please come," Marisa said, reaching out to touch his arm, then apparently thinking better of it. Even the briefest brush of her fingers sent warmth up his arm.

"Well…" Her indecisiveness was rubbing off on him. "I'd better not." For her and for him. There was so much he wanted to say, but he had to hold the words in for both their sakes.

"What about the breakfast tomorrow?" she asked, and he wondered if he really detected the trace of desperation in her voice.

The festival ended with a community breakfast in the square. "I'll be gone by then." The urge to take her hand in his felt strange, foreign, and yet overwhelming. So he did, just for a moment. She squeezed his hand back and didn't let go. He pulled away, because in her world of hope chests and family traditions, she shouldn't be holding hands with a Scotsman when her true love was standing right there.

"Be happy," he said quietly. "Have lots of kids, make your family proud, and show them what you can do at the company."

She gave him a tremulous smile. "Be happy. Take lots of beautiful pictures with soul, see the world, and think of me once in a while."

For a moment he couldn't swallow. "Goodbye," he said to her, and then nodded to the rest of the group.

As he wove through the crowd, he told himself he shouldn't look back. If she wasn't looking, he'd feel crushed. If she was, he'd want to go back and sweep her off her feet, family tradition be damned.

He looked anyway. She was watching, finger in her mouth. The look on her face really made him want to go back, but he forced himself onward. Fabiano was a great guy, the perfect guy, and she'd fall for his charms and live up to her family's expectations. She'd get her job. She'd be happy.

And he'd be happy, he quickly added. He'd be doing what he wanted, going where he wanted, unencumbered by commitment and responsibility. And love. No one to call when he arrived. No one to greet him when he returned home.

When he felt a tug on his shirt, he quelled the hope that it was her. Nonna stood there, looking dismayed.

"You going to give up, just like that?"

"You of all people should understand why."

"Perhaps. But I know true love when I see it. And you can't help it if you're not Italian."

"Her being happy with me isn't the same as true love."

"But the itchy nose is—part of the tradition, though

Marisa doesn't know about it. When we meet the man of our hearts, our noses itch.''

He looked at Marisa, who was watching the scene and...rubbing her nose. She'd been doing it a lot, now that he thought about it. "Her nose probably itches with the other guy, too."

Nonna shook her head. "Only one true love."

"I appreciate what you're trying to do. But your family—'' He took in her fierce expression. "The rest of your family isn't going to accept me, and Marisa's not going to risk losing their acceptance. I...have to go now." He leaned down and kissed her goodbye. And tried, as he made his way through the crowd, to forget about the whole itchy nose business.

He made a few photographs of the meatball-eating contest, then checked the schedule for the evening's event: an outrageous proposal competition at eight. He glanced at his watch. He had enough time to develop some of his photographs before then.

As he drove up the coast, he remembered all the things Marisa had told him about the area. He thought of her every time he saw a place she'd pointed out. He saw the golden hills in the distance and remembered her saying that California was named the Golden State for them, and not for the gold rush as some people thought.

Mostly, he remembered the kiss in the darkroom. He'd worked alone for years, going through the routine, and he'd never felt this...emptiness before. And something else. What had she called it? Confuzzled.

Later, he laid out the photographs and found what he'd been missing all this time: soul. It was there in the shots of Marisa, of her family, at the party the night before, and in the longing expression on her face this morning as she sat with Fabiano and looked at him.

Was it really longing?

Maybe he was reading his own feelings into it. He'd been wrong about keeping a distance from his subjects. Not that he'd get as close as he had to Marisa. He wasn't sure he could get that close to any woman again.

She made him feel things he'd never felt before. A longing, yes, a longing for things he'd never wanted before: love, family, and a sense of belonging. She'd even made him crazy enough to want to go home and make peace with his family.

What would she think of Scotland? He wanted to see her experience his world, a world of hairy cattle and rugged, remote mountains and seaside villages where people spent their whole lives in one tiny area.

After he'd gathered up his photos and slid into the Buick, he had a terrifying realization: Marisa was his Miss Right. She made him laugh and made him want to see her when he stepped off the plane.

When he returned to his room, he immediately rang up Porter and was surprised to find him home. "Back already?"

"Yeah, I'm back."

"And your lady is with you?"

"No, she finally admitted she couldn't marry a guy who was shorter than she was. You're right, Barrie. Love stinks. I made a big mistake mixing business and pleasure, and believe me, I've learned my lesson. Never again."

"Good, I'm glad to hear that. Now, can you do me a favor and cover Barcelona?"

"What? You said you wanted to cover it. In fact, you were dying to cover it. What's up?"

"I have some, er, business to attend to here."

"Business. Wait a minute. Female business?"

Barrie rolled his eyes. He might as well be honest. "I've met a woman here and I can't come back until I convince her I'm her Mr. Right."

"Shall I bring a gun and be done with it?" Porter asked, reminding Barrie of his own brusque words just days before.

"Aye, but only if she takes up with the right Mr. Right."

"Huh?"

"Never mind, just get ready for Spain." He gave him the travel information and hung up. That was the easy part. Convincing Marisa's family was going to be the real challenge.

TONIGHT'S FAMILY gathering was really only a way to get rid of all the leftover food from the previous night. When Marisa had suggested once that they simply make less food, she'd created an uproar about changing how things were done and how they'd always been done.

She sat with her family at the long table and kept quiet. It wasn't much of an effort, really. She didn't have the initiative to do otherwise. She caught parts of conversations that indicated her relatives thought Fabiano a much better choice than her "date" of last night, but gaining their approval brought no satisfaction.

"He's a nice young man," Pop said, nodding to where Fabiano was playing bocce with some of the other men.

She shrugged. "Perfect."

"Are you feeling ill?" Mama said, placing her hand on her forehead. "Not warm."

"She's lovesick," Nonna said, "for the Scotsman."

Mama rolled her eyes. "But how can that be? He's not the right one."

"Look how she mopes tonight. She didn't mope around him yesterday, did she?" Nonna said.

"I saw the way you were looking at him," Carlo accused his sister with narrowed eyes. "All gaga."

"Not gaga over that one." Nonna pointed at Fabiano. "*Si*, he may be perfect in many ways." She squeezed Marisa's chin. "But no passion here. And no passion in him, either."

Mama whispered, "Don't talk about passion at your age!"

Nonna looked up. "Salvatore, do you hear this? A woman my age isn't allowed to have passion. Let me tell you something, daughter. I have much passion. And I know passion when I see it. With Barrie, Marisa had passion. With Fabiano, no passion. And she rubbed her nose with Barrie. Proof enough." She crossed her arms over her chest.

"Huh?" Marisa was lost on that part, but smiled for the first time in hours. Since Barrie had walked away from the cookie booth.

"Barrie was a nice man," Mama acceded.

"And so big, so big," Nonna said, this time obviously not bothered by the idea, judging by the admiring grin on her face.

"He seemed all right," Carlo said. "But he isn't Italian."

"And he did carry you all over the place," Pop said. "Never seemed to bother him."

"And he helped out in the kitchen," Mama said. "Even seemed to enjoy it."

"Not that there's anything wrong with that," Marisa said in Tino's absence. He was overseeing the bakery for the morning breakfast.

"But he can't be the one," Pop said. "This guy, it has to be him."

Marisa followed her pop's nod to Fabiano. "I don't know. Maybe he is." She remembered Barrie attributing her indecision to the fear of disappointing others. Three days ago, Fabiano would have been the one. She would have embraced him as such and never known what she'd known with Barrie. Barrie encouraged her to be herself, to fight for what she wanted. And she wanted him.

"Fabiano isn't the one," Marisa said. "In the beginning, Barrie was the wrong guy. He accidentally knocked me into that puddle and didn't blame the dancers who'd pushed him. He carried me everywhere even though he had a job to do. He put up with my worrying and even pretended to be my Mr. Right. Yes, he pretended because I asked him to. I didn't want to let you down by not meeting my *amore* again, so he stood in and helped me try to find the real one. And in the process..."

She met her family's gazes. "He became my *amore*. So no, he doesn't plan to marry me and take me with him on his travels, and he probably doesn't even plan to see me again. But it's time you knew the truth: I'm in love with him. And I don't care if he's Scottish. In fact, it's one of the things I love about him. And the way he kisses..." She put her hand to her chest. "Carlo, you have to admit we beat you in the contest fair and square."

He ducked his head. "Yeah, you two burned up the stage."

"I'm not going to keep the tradition. I'm sorry, I really am. But I can't make myself fall in love with that man over there, and I'm already in love with the wrong man anyway, even if I don't end up with him." She had to focus on something else before she started bawling. "And Pop, I really want that sales job. I'm qualified, I've got a business degree, and I want to take the company to new heights. I want you to hear me. Don't dismiss me because I'm your daughter. I'm not just your daughter. I'm a woman with her own ideas and dreams, and I'm sorry if I let you all down, but this is who I am."

They all sat in stunned silence, and she felt a great weight lift off her shoulders. If only Barrie had been there, everything would have been perfect.

Just as everyone was about to open their mouths and throw their four cents' worth in, Tino ran up to the table. "Where's Gina?"

"She and Louie took the last shift at the booth." Pop looked at his watch. "They were supposed to be here by now."

Tino's round face went white. "Louie's in the house. And Gina's not with him."

9

THE SQUARE was busier than ever when Barrie returned. A crowd had formed around the fountain where the proposal competition was underway. Colored lights added to the atmosphere as each couple took to the stage and crooned romantic words. He wondered what would have happened if Carlo had bullied them into entering that contest. Would he have proposed to Marisa?

"You are the moon to my sun, the clouds to my sky, and relish to my hot dog. Please be my wife."

Barrie snorted at that, but took a photograph anyway. If he proposed to Marisa, he'd say something simple, like, "Marry me." *If* he were proposing, of course. At the moment her family was probably celebrating their daughter's accomplishment, and she was probably getting to know her real Mr. Right and thinking about her new promotion.

He had the sudden image of himself barging into the party and carrying her off into the sunset. Now that was romantic.

He wasn't sure what he was going to do. These things didn't come naturally to him. All he knew was he couldn't leave without trying to convince Marisa that he was, indeed, the right Mr. Right. He'd make everything else work. Cortina wasn't such a bad place to live, and Marisa's family, well, he could get to like them if they could accept him.

"Barrie!"

His heart tripped as he searched for the source of the voice that sounded a lot like Marisa's. He had a moment of disappointment that it was Gina until he realized she was huddled on a bench in extreme pain. Her long hair hung in damp tendrils.

"Oh, am I glad to see someone I know," she said with a sharp gasp, grabbing his arm. "Louie and I were closing up the booth, and then he disappeared, and the pains started really bad."

"Let's get you to the hospital."

He scooped her up and headed to the car.

"Just like that?" she said between breaths. "No panic or rushing around? No hurting yourself?"

"I just get things done."

It wasn't the same as carrying Marisa, but he had the motions pretty well down. He slid her onto the front seat and got around to his side.

"Thank you so much," she said. Her hands were clutching her enormous belly. "I didn't know what to do. There were so many people, I couldn't see anyone I knew, couldn't get to the phone, nothing."

"You're fine now. Just hold on."

She wasn't fine. She threw her head back and screamed in pain. All he could do was pat her shoulder. She let out several puffs of breath.

"I didn't even want to have a baby yet," she said, twisting to get comfortable. "I wanted...to be an actress."

"Why didn't you pursue that, then?"

"Do you know what my father would have said if I'd told him that? This is what he wanted, and I never wanted to let him down. I love Tino and the baby, don't get me wrong. But...I'm not ready for this yet. Marisa's the smart one. She wants a career, went to college.''

"You know about her going to college?"

"Yeah, but she doesn't know I know. She pretends to try to find her *amore* and continues going for what she wants.'' She looked over at him. "She wants you.''

Those three words sent a gush of warmth through him. "Me? You're sure about that?''

"I've never seen her look at a guy the way she looks at you. I'm going to tell her...'' She grimaced in pain. "If I live through this, I'm going to tell her not to sacrifice what she wants to make the family happy.''

"But she's met the guy, the real Mr. Right, a removed cousin or somesuch.''

Gina shifted again. "The next time you see her, which will be at the hospital I'd guess, you look at her and see if she's still crazy about you.''

He pulled into the hospital emergency entrance and carried her in. She gave him her parents' number just before they wheeled her to the maternity ward. When Ninalee answered the phone, and he told her Gina was in labor, he could hear screaming and chaos in the background. No one even bothered to hang up the phone.

"YOU'RE SURE it was Barrie who called?'' Marisa asked as everyone helped her into the maternity ward waiting area.

"For the hundredth time, yes,'' Mama said. "How many men with Scottish accents do we know?''

Marisa couldn't stop smiling. She was happy that Gina was in labor, for real this time. But she couldn't deny that a good part of that happiness came from the expectation of seeing Barrie once more. And this time she wouldn't be that fifty-percent traditional girl and fifty-percent modern girl. Not that that would change his plans.

They came to a stop in the doorway of Gina's birthing room. Barrie was standing next to her bed, holding her hand and talking softly.

"You're doing a bang-up job. Keep breathing like that. I think that's how it's done. Nice and calm."

Now she was sure she loved him. Her body filled with it, lifting her up.

Gina was breathing in puffs and gripping Barrie's hand in a death clutch. She glanced beyond Barrie and saw her family. Her agonized groan activated them into their usual chaos. Tino ran ahead, dumping out the contents of her suitcase. Mama rushed forward to hug her and Nonna started picking up the scattered clothing.

Barrie met her gaze over her scrambling family members, and they shared their secret smile. Could she love him any more than right at that moment?

Then he took hold of Mama's shaking shoulders and said, "Everyone needs to be calm for Gina. She's been doing well and focusing on her breathing, but now you've got her stirred up again."

Mama wiped her tears and took a deep breath. Tino stopped jabbering on the other side of the bed, and everyone else stopped rushing around. Gina calmed down, too, and even managed a smile. She looked at Marisa, then at Barrie. "See?"

His shoulders lifted, making him look even larger than life. His auburn hair was mussed, and Marisa wanted to run her fingers through it and push it back from his face.

The only sounds in the room were the beep of the monitors and Gina's even breathing. Marisa hobbled through her family to Barrie. "Thanks for doing this. For taking care of Gina."

"Anything for your family." He reached out and grasped her chin.

His touch filled her with a warmth she'd never felt before. She swallowed. "If you were to ever think of relocating to another town, which I know you wouldn't, but if you were, would you consider moving here?"

His thumb slid back and forth over her lower lip. "If you were ever to break your family's tradition, which I know you wouldn't, would you consider marrying the wrong Mr. Right?"

She nodded, trying hard to keep a serious face when her heart was soaring. She pulled her family closer until they formed a half circle around them. Then she said, "Fabiano is the wrong Mr. Right, and I certainly don't want to marry him. Right, Pop? Mama?" They shook their heads, then nodded. "You see, I'm not breaking tradition. I'm just changing it a little. The Italian part goes."

"Italian?" Uncle Louie said. "He doesn't look Italian to me."

"He's not Italian," she said loudly. "That's only one of the things I love about him." She kept her gaze on Barrie. "I told them everything, the charade, how it wasn't your fault you fell on me, my horror novels with romance covers, and how unromantic I am."

Barrie snorted. "You're the most romantic person I know. In fact, you've rubbed off on me. Let me see if I can get this right." He looked up, as if trying to remember, then took her in his arms. "You are the moon to my sun, the clouds to my sky, and the relish to my hot dog."

Her family digested the words, then quickly nodded, "Good one, good one."

They shared a laugh, and he pulled her closer. "How about, 'Marry me,' and I'll work on the sappy stuff later? But wait," he said just as she was about to say yes a thousand times. "This should be traditional." He set her away, made sure she was balanced, and walked up to her father. "May I marry your daughter?"

The whole family nodded in unison, even Gina.

Marisa pulled him back over. "I don't need their approval. I'm my own woman." She leaned back toward her family and whispered, "But thanks anyway." She turned back to Barrie. "And I say yes to your proposal."

"Are you sure? I don't want you changing your mind and breaking my heart."

"I have never been so sure of anything in my life." And she proved it by pulling him down and kissing him with all the passion of a woman who knows just what she wants.

No one even noticed when Gina's water broke.

Never Say Never!

BARBARA DALY

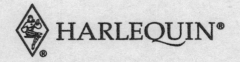

HARLEQUIN®

TORONTO • NEW YORK • LONDON
AMSTERDAM • PARIS • SYDNEY • HAMBURG
STOCKHOLM • ATHENS • TOKYO • MILAN • MADRID
PRAGUE • WARSAW • BUDAPEST • AUCKLAND

Dear Reader,

I can't stay away from Vermont for long. There's something about those gently rolling mountains—whether they're summer-green, brilliant with fall color, or white with the first snow of winter—that gets into a writer's bloodstream and compels her to set a love story there. When the ground thaws in those same gently rolling mountains and the dreaded mud season sets in, this is a different story.

Sheriff Zeke Thorne, who's dedicated to bachelorhood and non-violent village law enforcement, is hunkered down beside the muddy road trying to catch a chicken thief in the act, while runaway heiress Tish Seldon is futilely attempting to chug up that same muddy road in the truck she's stolen from the family gardener....

You can guess what happens next. She gets stuck in the mud. How long can it be before she's stuck on the sheriff? Who says mud season in Vermont isn't romantic?

Happy reading!

Barbara Daly

To Sheridan, my bright and beautiful daughter,
who succeeds even though it always rains
on her birthday. Thank you for being my friend.

1

Early afternoon, Newport, Rhode Island

NOW THAT SHE'D burned her bridges behind her, Tish Seldon was having second thoughts. Was her bridegroom really trying to kill her, or had eighteen years of living with paranoids finally caught up with her?

Music shimmered out from the house, a romantic dance melody that thrummed against her eardrums like a death knell. All because of that look on Marc's face as he reached toward her, calculating and determined, so different from the tender expression he usually wore. And before that, his sister's anxious question, not meant for Tish's ears— "She'll be here in a minute. Are you ready?"

Worrying, Tish chewed on her lower lip. Lorraine could have meant anything by "Are you ready?" Like *Are you dressed?* But she could see with her own two eyes whether Marc was dressed or not. Or, *Do you have your billfold?* Just an overprotective sister making sure her brother had himself all pulled together. And Marc had often forgotten his credit cards, or found himself short of cash.

She might even have meant, *Do you have your pocket comb and handkerchief?*

Well, Marc had his handkerchief for sure. And

there'd been an urgency in Lorraine's voice that most people didn't waste on pocket-comb-and-handkerchief issues.

Tish wavered among the crabapple trees. A thin shaft of sunlight dissected the stormy gray of the Atlantic as it pounded against the bulkheads of Seldon Point. The lawns that sloped down to dune grass and sand were shyly green, and the sweet scent of blossoming trees competed with the last bluster of winter. Almost spring but not quite. What an appropriate date they'd chosen—April, the cruelest month, because Marc just couldn't wait for a traditional June wedding.

As far as she was concerned, they didn't have to wait for the wedding! "He's showing his respect for you," her brother Jeff said when she went to him for counseling. Big deal. Respect was nice, but a really hot-and-heavy kiss leading to goodness knows what would have been a lot more fun, would have reassured her that marriage was going to be all that she'd hoped. And she'd given Marc every opportunity to overwhelm her with that hot-and-heavy kiss.

Behind her, the large white clapboard houses of the family compound stood straight and tall like sentinels, forming a protective semicircle against anyone who was out to harm a Seldon. So why had no one in her ever vigilant family suspected that Marc Radcliffe had exactly that in mind, to do harm to a Seldon?

To her, Tyler Staley Seldon. Tish.

Unless that wasn't what he had in mind.

Was it or wasn't it? Any second Marc would find her skulking in the orchard and she'd have to explain that she'd run away because she thought he was trying to kill her. Great start to a honeymoon. And she'd been so looking forward to it.

She'd thought he was, too, the way he'd insisted they sneak away from the reception and catch an earlier plane. But would a bridegroom so eager he wouldn't even give her time to change clothes be all that bothered by a smudge on his bride's professionally made-up face? Bothered enough to wipe it off with that huge white hanky....

Darn it, he *was* trying to kill her, knock her out, anyway, so he could kill her later. If that wasn't chloroform she'd smelled on his hanky she'd eat her veil.

Tish wrapped her arms around herself, nervously stroking the smooth white silk of her sleeves as she sorted out her options. There was no point in attempting a daring dash back into the house to consult her father, her brother Jeff or the Seldon family lawyer. She'd taken her early concerns to them, and they'd told her she was having prenuptial jitters. They'd say the same thing now, except they'd say post. Postnuptial jitters. And her mother? Forget it. Her mother practically wept with pride, joy and pure motherly satisfaction every time Marc's name came up in conversation. Marc had all of them, the entire extended Seldon family, thoroughly snookered.

She frowned. There was always the slight possibility that they were right about him. Again she wavered. *Loves me, loves my money. Loves me, loves my money.*

If Grandmother were still alive, she'd know what to do.

Of course, if Grandmother were still alive, she wouldn't have bequeathed her fortune to Tish and none of this would be happening.

The truth was, if Grandmother were still alive, she'd be over a hundred and probably none too reliable in a crisis.

Tish had no one but herself to look to for help. She would have to use her own judgment about Marc and accept the consequences.

The very idea took her breath away. Make a decision for herself? That would be a first. Her fingertips tingled, her heart pounded, half with panic, half with excitement. It was the Seldons themselves, not merely their houses, who had formed a circle around her, made her decisions, programmed her life. Now it was up to her.

It was a heady thought. She waited a moment for the dizziness to pass. Okay. What she was going to do was...

She heard furtive footsteps and hushed voices. A man's deep tone. A woman's softer whisper. Marc and Lorraine, tracking her down, coming closer and closer.

Her feet were screaming for help in her four-inch stilettos. Thank God her parents had conceded that even rich girls should learn to drive. She would need a relatively inconspicuous vehicle, unguarded and unoccupied, with the keys in it, and she knew where to find one.

So what she would do was...what she was going to do was...

...run now, explain later!

Pulling the lace and satin panels of her wedding dress tightly around herself, she skimmed through the cloud of lush pink blossoms toward the gardener's cottage.

Nightfall in Wild River, Vermont

NOPE, nothing more fun than a good stakeout. An occasional thrill like this was the reason you got into law enforcement.

Deputy Sheriff Zeke Thorne squatted down and shuffled his feet in their heavy shoes, trying to get himself centered on the green plastic garbage bag he'd laid down in the clearing. It sank under his weight, curled up around him. That bag was the only dry spot in what would otherwise make a good cranberry bog.

Rain was collecting in his ears. He wrenched his sou'wester farther down on his head and hunched under his absolutely-guaranteed-waterproof slicker. Surveillance work was especially nifty in mud season, when the thawing earth sucked at the tires of your car, buried your boots, pulled your spirit right out of your body. The rain, well, that was just frosting on an already soggy cake.

But this assignment was worth the sacrifice, by golly. Jasper Wedgelow alleged that Crockett Highcrest was stealing his chickens, or rather his wife Hortense's chickens, and selling the eggs for cold, hard cash, cash that rightfully belonged to Jasper, or rather to Hortense. An injustice of this magnitude could not be allowed to continue. Jasper had insisted that Sheriff Thorne stake out the Wedgelow property, wait for Crockett to make an appearance at the Wedgelow henhouse and catch the thieving bastard in the act.

"Hard as it's raining, he's sure not going to show up tonight," Zeke had reasoned with the irate Jasper.

"That's where you're wrong," Jasper said, shaking his fist in Zeke's face. "Tonight's exactly when he will show up, because he knows you're saying to yourself, 'He won't show up tonight, not as hard as it's raining.' That's how the man's mind works," Jasper concluded. "Low and mean. Take my word for it."

The bottom line was that Jasper Wedgelow was a Town Selectman with the say-so on who was going to be Wild River's Deputy Sheriff. And when it wasn't mud season, when it wasn't raining chipmunks and woodchucks, Zeke was crazy about his job.

Except for the uniform. *Stone,* they called it. Stone, for God's sake, like pants from a yuppie catalog. And a car to match. But the uniform aside, Wild River, where a crime worse than chicken-thieving was a rare occurrence, was a sheriff's dream.

This sheriff's dream, anyway.

Wild River folks still talked about that murder in 1961, but what they said about it was that old man Abernathy deserved to die and his long-suffering wife Abigail deserved the honor of killing him. She'd accomplished it neatly, too, without even messing up the house, by scaring him to death in a grizzly bear costume she'd rented in Burlington. A jury of twelve local citizens had declared temporary insanity and had put her in the care of her daughter in Calais, who had four of the cutest kids you ever saw, the story went. Abigail had ended her days a happy and cherished grandmother.

The Murder, though, had been reason enough to send the Wild River community leaders running to the sheriff of Whitewater County to demand their own live-in deputy sheriff to bring down the sudden rise in the crime rate. All that happened before Zeke was born, but once they got themselves qualified for a deputy sheriff they stayed qualified, and now he was out here in the mud on a stakeout because the alternative was worse. If he were a Boston lawman like his brother Cole, he might have to do things he didn't care to, like point guns at people.

Which reminded him of the one good thing about mud season in Vermont. For a whole month every spring, sometimes even six weeks, Zeke could be sure Cole wouldn't show up in Wild River to yell at him about his lack of ambition. Cole didn't seem to mind pointing guns at people, but he sure hated for the underside of his car to get muddy.

Patiently Zeke waited. The rain pattered on his slicker, turned his garbage bag into a pond. A different kind of sound put him on the alert, although a second later he realized it wasn't anything like a chicken-stealing sound. It was the sound of a truck laboring up the road, squishing, sliding, grinding, squealing through the mud. Must be a flatlander to be out on a Vermont country road in anything but a high-riding tank like the Pathfinder Zeke drove during mud season instead of his official sheriff's car. Dread filled his heart even before he heard the ominous whirring of tires that had finally met mud deeper than they were.

The whirring went on for quite a while, long enough to warn Zeke that the driver was a stubborn SOB, then all was silent. Zeke stayed silent, too. After all, he had a larger mission than pushing some guy out of the mud when he should have known better than to be in the mud. But when the silence broke, what broke it was the sound of sobbing.

Now sobbing was something else again. Forced to reexamine the crucial nature of this stakeout, Zeke was pretty sure sobbing ranked way above Hortense Wedgelow's egg money. When he heard the car door slam, he unfolded himself to a standing position and took a couple of tentative steps off the garbage bag.

He was looking at a red truck that was about half the size of his. In the glow of its headlights he saw a slip of a woman dressed in white. Not a good color choice for mud season, was Zeke's opinion. Still sobbing, she took a step into the muck of the road, sank in, sobbed harder, then stubbornly took another step.

"Hold on, lady," he said, emerging from the forest.

Her scream was a good fifteen times bigger than she was. She seemed to leap straight upward as she flung herself back into the little truck. Even before she started the engine Zeke knew what was going to happen. The wheels started whirring again, faster and faster, with an eggbeater effect that slung mud in every direction, including Zeke's.

He was fishing a clod out of his eye when the whirring stopped, the sobbing recommenced and he could tell she was back in the road. "Don't be scared, ma'am," he tried again. Half-blind, he edged along on the freeze-dried grass parallel to her futile steps, figuring the fewer of them stuck in the mud, the better. She was trying to run, and it sounded like, *thwuck, thwuck,* said slow and steady.

"Don't come another step closer to me," she said in a low, dangerous voice that carried across to him as well as if she'd spoken into a megaphone. "I'm armed." She wasn't sobbing any more. Now she was mad.

"Well, good," Zeke said. "You did right to have a little protection out here in the dead of night on a lonely country road." By now he was closer to jogging than edging. She'd gotten some kind of magical hold on the mud, and the *thwuck, thwuck* had speeded up. "But if you don't mind my asking, why the hell are you out here in the dead of night on a lonely country road?"

"That is absolutely none of your business." *Thwuck, thwuck, thwuck.*

"Fine. Want me to go home and leave you out here all by yourself?"

Silence. Even the thwucks got quieter.

"Look," Zeke said, taking a chance on stepping out on the road, hoping she wouldn't shoot him before he could offer to help. "I'm the law around here. If you'll just hold on a minute, I'll try to get your truck moving again."

She halted, her arm raised and her hand gripping a pair of pruning shears big enough to clip a limb off a maple tree—or off him. "A likely story," she said. In the beam from the headlights he could see her pointy little chin trembling. "You'll say you're the law, gain my trust, and the next thing I know..."

He moved even closer and opened his absolutely-guaranteed-waterproof slicker. This netted him another piercing scream, as he should have known it would. Out of the corner of his eye he saw lights go on in the Wedgelow house. "I was trying to show you my badge," he protested. "Hey, you didn't think I was trying to show you—"

Just as he was wishing he hadn't gotten that far into a sentence he had no intention of finishing, a ruckus broke out in the vicinity of the Wedgelow chicken coop. First there were shouts, then the *pop-pop-pop* of a BB gun going off, then screams and shrieks, chickens squawking, dogs barking, even the cows got into the act and started mooing. With one last cry that was halfway between a sob and a scream, the woman flung herself into his arms.

"What was that?" she babbled. "I can't handle one more thing all by myself. I can't I can't I can't!" She started sobbing again, holding on to him as though he were her very last hope.

For a minute he stood stock-still, trying to adjust to the fact that he was holding the softest, silkiest little woman ever to cross the Wild River town line in his arms, in a torrential downpour, in eighteen inches of mud, in the middle of the road. Her hair was light-colored, and even dripping wet it smelled like honey and almonds. Her bones were so small and fine it was like holding a kitten, light as a feather but zinging with pent-up energy. He couldn't see her face, but she just had to be pretty. Her soaked dress slipped and slid under his hands it was so satiny, but not as satiny as the underside of the arm she had slung around his neck.

The only downside was the pruning shears. If he wasn't mistaken, when she flung her arms around him she'd stabbed straight through the sleeve of his absolutely-guaranteed-waterproof slicker, pretty much canceling out the warranty. If it hadn't been for the rain pouring through the hole and drenching him straight to the skin, this might have been about the most perfect moment in his life.

Also the most stressful. He was entertaining thoughts and fighting urges unbecoming to a sheriff in the process of saving a damsel in distress. "My guess is," he said in a strangled voice, "that Jasper Wedgelow just caught Crockett Highcrest in his chicken coop."

It silenced her, but since she wasn't privy to the facts of the situation, he supposed that was understandable. Sensing that she was beginning to regret throwing herself at him, he eased her away with considerable regret of his own, put his hands at her waist and lifted her straight up in the air. It was clear that she was thinking of screaming again, so he hurried her over to the side of the road and set her down on the grass before she could get her lungs primed.

She stood there trembling, staring at him. A lightning flash lit up the sky long enough for Zeke to come to a couple of firm conclusions.

One, she wasn't just pretty, she was a knockout, with a slim face and skin that looked just as smooth as it had felt, with big eyes that were some pale color, not brown.

Two, the job of being Deputy Sheriff of Wild River had just gotten a little more complicated. The muddy white dress she wore was definitely, inarguably, a wedding dress.

The flash subsided and Zeke got practical. He announced that the weather wasn't right for pushing trucks out of the mud. They would go to his dry, warm office in his dependable Pathfinder and address her various problems in an atmosphere conducive to logical thinking and sensible decisions.

He didn't say it like that, of course, he said it a whole lot plainer.

"The truck can wait. Get in the car," he said, pointing at the Pathfinder. "I'm taking you in."

For some reason, she didn't argue.

2

ON THE WAY to the sheriff's office, Tish sank into deep and weighty thought. Relying on your own judgment worked better when you had some—judgment, that is. She'd made the first big decision of her life and had fallen flat on her face in the muddy consequences. She wished she'd fallen flat onto her powder-blue crocodile going-away handbag while she was at it, but as she'd been running away rather than "going away" in the traditional bridal fashion, she hadn't been thinking accessories.

In that bag—which matched the crocodile slingbacks that matched the Chanel suit—there was a twenty-dollar bill, she thought, a couple of major credit cards, she knew, and her cell phone, she was positive. If she'd had the phone she could have called for help. She wouldn't be right back where she'd always been—at someone else's mercy.

On the other hand, AAA would never have found her here. She wasn't sure the FBI could find her here. Nobody could find her here, because even she didn't know where she was.

It was a town of sorts. And she took great comfort in the sign attached to the picket fence that surrounded the white house the sheriff was ushering her into. Deputy Sheriff, Wild River, Whitewater County, it said.

His home and the sheriff's headquarters were apparently one and the same, and he was apparently for real.

Real, and really good-looking in the light, even wet and mud-spattered. His dark hair curled over the collar of his uniform shirt, sending little rivulets of water down his back. There was a lot of that dark hair. It brushed across his forehead above eyes that were dark, too, and thick-lashed. His eyebrows were expressive, his features strong, and Lord, was he ever tall! And broad in the shoulders. And long in the legs! Under the uniform, which was an unusual, pale stone color instead of your ordinary khaki, muscles rippled all the way up and down his body.

But it was absolutely not true that her first good look at him was making her weak in the knees. She was merely noting his physical characteristics in case she ever needed to identify him in a lineup.

For the moment, which would probably last about two decades, she was through with good-looking men. With men, good-looking or not. Make that through with *love*. Someday she might need a man to lift or open something, but that was as far as she was willing to go when it came to involving men in her life. She wouldn't even ask a man to lift or open until she'd exhausted her own lifting and opening resources— that's how little she trusted them after the way Marc had scared her.

Of course, this man could probably lift or open anything that had ever needed lifting or opening, which was another good thing to remember about him. "I'm hysterical," she said, and realized too late she'd said it aloud.

"That's a positive sign," the sheriff said. "Knowing you're hysterical. It means you're sane."

"Of course I'm sane," Tish snapped. "I'm just upset."

"Anybody would be in your situation."

Tish narrowed her eyes. He had a nice voice, deep and soothing. But that's how men lulled you into thinking you could trust them, with their nice, deep, soothing voices. "What do you mean by that?" she asked him suspiciously. "What do you know about my situation?"

He seemed puzzled by her question. "You're away from home, you're wet and you're stuck in the mud. Enough to make anybody hysterical."

"Oh, that," Tish said, waving a dismissive hand. When she saw his gaze slide down the length of her ruined wedding gown, she wished she'd just gone ahead and agreed with him.

They stood dripping on a thick pad of newspapers in an entryway that looked as though it had been designed for people to drip in. Beyond the newspapers was a brick floor. On the wide, board walls of the long, narrow room were hundreds of antique-looking brass hooks, with something or other hanging from every one of them—coats, hats and fishing gear, baskets, buckets, brooms and snow shovels. A pegboard held a neatly organized smorgasbord of tools.

Where things weren't hanging, other things stood—skis, sleds, snowshoes, boots. On a shelf was a stack of gloves—gardening gloves, leather winter gloves, an enormous pair of gloves he probably used for strangling wild mountain cats or engaging in some such Vermont recreational activity. While she scanned this dizzying array of equipment, a deep shudder rose through her body.

"You need to warm up," he said in the slow but still bossy voice he'd used out on the road. "Take a shower. I'll loan you some dry clothes. You'll catch cold before you get a better offer."

She eyed him while he hung his slicker on the one vacant hook she hadn't noticed, thinking hot shower versus the possibility that this mountain man might crash through the shower door and jump her bones. But he didn't look like your standard, run-of-the-mill mountain man, not with those erect shoulders and proud, graceful carriage. If she was going to lose her virginity in the shower, it might as well be his shower. Another shiver attacked her, but this one, surprisingly, was hot, more a quiver than a shiver. She squelched it at once. "Thank you," she said. "I accept."

"I'll call Lester Martin about towing your truck."

"Thank you for that, too."

"Then we'll do a little talking about your..." He paused and a take-charge expression skated across his face. That look redefined him, totally eliminated the image of slow-moving, slow-talking, slow-thinking mountain man. "...your situation."

Tish eyed him thoughtfully. Here was a man who would assume control over her "situation" as soon as he knew what it was. She was determined not to let that happen. The heady feeling of having escaped her family's control was still with her—temporary setbacks notwithstanding—and she intended to blunder through the Marc situation on her own.

So she wouldn't tell him the truth. She eyed him again. On the other hand, here was a man who wouldn't be easy to deceive. So, Tish decided as she dripped away in the direction he pointed her, while she showered she'd invent a "situation" that would keep the sheriff entertained until she figured out a way to deal with her real problem.

THE SMELL of coffee brewing drew Tish back down the hallway from a plain, white, surprisingly clean bathroom. She passed a bedroom on her left and another on her right, each with that same whitewashed-wall, blue-and-white decor. Everything was very plain, but the absence of frills gave the old, low-ceilinged house a fresh, light look.

The aroma had a cheering effect on her. So did the fact that she no longer had to fear romantic attack, not in the clothes he'd loaned her. The red-and-gray-plaid wool shirt came almost to her knees. She didn't even need the coordinating gray sweatpants, but she'd put them on anyway, rolled up the legs into big sausages around her calves and pulled the cord up as tight as she could around her waist. In this ensemble and a huge pair of his gray wool socks she billowed silently toward the smell of his coffee and the sound of his voice.

"Tomorrow? Tonight sure would be preferable, Lester.

"Tomorrow. I know, Letha always thinks you're going out to see another woman, sexy devil that you are." He sighed.

"Yeah, bring it here. I'm not sure where she'll be. I'm about to call Bess Blakeley and see if she can—"

Tish crept up to the doorway just in time to see him frown. "She did? She is? Well, bless her heart. That's a hell of a note. I'll check in on her tomorrow. Is

Doobie Winslow still taking in guests? Oh, yeah, she's in Florida. Hmmm.''

Her gaze wandered around his office. It was different from the rest of the house, with dark wood-paneled walls, lots of bookshelves and a pair of brown leather armchairs. A little round table sat between them. On it was a glass dish filled with candy.

He looked up from a battered wooden desk and caught sight of her. "Got to go, Lester. See you." His frown deepened as he hung up the phone. "Sit down. We've got a problem."

Tish sank into an armchair. The leather was cracked with age, but it was comfortable and felt very cozy. She tucked her feet up under her. "I'm aware that I have a problem," she said. "What's yours?"

"You. I mean—I mean Lester can't tow your truck until tomorrow," said the sheriff, sounding frustrated about it.

"I heard," she said. "Letha has a jealous streak."

It pleased her to see him flustered. A chink or two in his armor might give her an opening to slip through. She'd had the shower, but he'd worked some kind of miracle on himself, and as she'd read in a book once, he cleaned up real good. He looked even more appealing in snug jeans and a black turtleneck than he did in his uniform, and the dark shadow of beard merely increased the display of pure maleness that made little tickles run out to her toes and fingertips every time she allowed herself to look him over.

When she looked at Marc, she'd had a relieved, "I'm finally getting married!" sort of feeling, but she couldn't remember any tickles.

She wriggled against the chair and decided she'd

better not look the sheriff over any more. What was she doing, having tickly feelings about a strange man? There wasn't a man on earth appealing enough to make her feel like relying on him at the moment.

"It looks like you'll have to spend the night in Wild River," he blurted out. His voice was thickening up. Maybe he was the one who'd caught cold.

"And I can't spend it with Doobie Winslow or Bess Blakeley. What happened to Ms. Blakeley?" She had to admit it; she was curious, even a bit worried.

"She—" He halted. "How did you know anything was wrong with Bess?"

"I was eavesdropping," said Tish. "I couldn't help myself. You learn such interesting things that way."

"Oh. Well, Bess slipped on a piece of waxed paper and sprained her ankle."

"What a shame!" Tish sympathized. She paused, studying an old photograph that hung behind his desk. Anything to keep from looking into those dark eyes. "But why did she have waxed paper on the floor?"

"It blew off a cookie sheet. Bess bakes cookies for the—" He halted again, which drew her gaze toward him for a split second. "We don't have time for thumbnail sketches of the townsfolk," he said, tightening up a mouth that was even fuller and more enticing than she had first noticed. "We were talking about what to do with you. Closest motel's thirty miles away. Doobie Winslow's in Florida for the mud season. Left her house closed down and locked up like Alcatraz. It's too late to call the preacher's wife. You'll have to stay here."

That got her complete attention. "Absolutely not!" she said instantly. The idea simply melted her from the waist down. "Honestly," she scolded him, putting her feet flat on the floor and willing them to hold up her knees. "I thought you'd be different, being a sheriff, but here you are, just as I predicted, gaining my trust and then taking advantage of me!" Yelling at him helped, but she still didn't think she could stand up.

He seemed to prefer sitting down while he yelled at her, too. It was the one thing they had in common. "If you don't trust me," he said through clenched teeth that showed up very white against his tanned face, "I'll sleep in the car and you can lock me out of the house. Perfect end to a perfect day."

She couldn't lock him out of his own house after he'd rescued her, and if he wouldn't admit that there was someplace else she could stay, she certainly couldn't find one on her own. In a desperate effort not to think about spending the night with six-feet-plus-several-inches of high-octane testosterone, she remembered a loose end they hadn't wrapped up. "What was Crockett Highcrest doing in Jasper Wedgelow's chicken coop?" she asked timidly.

"He... No," the sheriff said suddenly. "I'm not going to let you get me off the track. The subject is you. Who you are. What you're doing here. Why you're doing it in a wedding dress. Okay, I'll start. Name's Zeke Thorne, Deputy Sheriff of Wild River. What's yours?"

Jolted by his staccato tone, she looked him full in the eyes. Her lips parted. Her face felt hot and her chin quivered. "I don't know," she said in a small voice. "I can't remember."

"You can't remember." He gazed at her with those wide, dark eyes. His eyelashes floated down, then up again. A hushed, expectant stillness filled the room. "You're telling me you have amnesia?"

"Is that what you call it?" Tish said piteously.

"Amnesia?" He leapt up so suddenly from the old wooden desk chair in which he'd been swiveling that it kept right on spinning. "You spent enough time in the shower to use up five dollars worth of propane, and you couldn't come up with a better story than *amnesia?*"

That stung. In fact, she'd been struck by the pure genius of the idea. The sheriff would get to work figuring out *who* she was, and she could get to work finding out *what* Marc was.

"The woman who remembered a name like Jasper Wedgelow can't remember her own name?" he ranted on, his eyes wide and wild with outrage and disbelief. "Come on, give me a break!"

"I've read," she offered hastily, "that the amnesiac has random memory, that he or she might remember the dog's name, but not..."

"You made up the amnesia story to keep from telling me who you are and what you're doing here." He fixed her with a condemnatory stare. "I knew you were up to no good. Nobody up to any good would have been out on that road at that hour in that rain."

"Sure she would," Tish protested. She mentally ran through her favorite television series for examples. "A doctor would, or an emergency repairman, or a minister with a crisis in his flock."

"Are you a doctor?"

She gazed thoughtfully into the distance. "I really, really doubt it."

"I really, really doubt that you're an electrician, either, or, God forbid, a minister!"

"Or a sheriff," she added pointedly. "You were there."

"Of course *I* was there! *I* had a job to do! But *I* sure as heck wasn't wearing a wedding dress! So why were you..?"

"I wasn't in my right mind?" Tish ventured. "I was fleeing from the new unknown?"

"'The new unknown.' Oh my stars and **gar**ters," he groaned.

"It's okay to use real swear words," Tish said politely. "I don't mind as long as you're not swearing at me." She remembered her claim not to be able to remember anything at all. "At least," she added, "I don't think I do."

He answered her with a glare, then sank back into his chair and ran a hand over the stubble on his chin. "Okay," he said, "we'll play it your way. First thing in the morning I'll check out the registration on your truck. Then we'll know who you are."

Unaccustomed as she was to being on the lam, it hadn't occurred to her that license plates were like fingerprints to today's modern, electronically linked lawman. When he found out that the truck was registered to the Seldon gardener, the cow patty would hit the windmill. She wrinkled her forehead, realizing her story still needed work. "Actually," she said slowly, "I seem to recall that the truck is not mine."

"A breakthrough! Praise the Lord!"

She ignored his sarcasm. "It's coming back to me now." She placed her hand delicately over her forehead. "Just a fleeting memory—I was running and running, and my feet were killing me in those high heels, and there on the street I saw this truck...."

"What street?" he barked. "Where?"

Tish was starting to worry that his head was as full of brains as his body was full of muscles. "I don't remember that part of it," she said. "My first awareness of location was when I passed a sign that said Welcome To Vermont, and I remember thinking, 'Oh, my goodness, whatever am I doing in Vermont?'"

That much was true. The only thing on her mind had been to get as far away from Newport as she could before she ran out of gas. Filling a gas tank was not something she'd ever had to think about. Next time she'd remember it took money.

He was staring at her. "Go on about the truck."

She went on. "So I saw this little red truck that didn't look too intimidating. The owner had left the keys in it—and those big..." She made an overblown scissoring motion in the air to indicate the pruning shears.

"How do you know he was a he?"

The man was a serious sheriff. Fortunately, she'd read enough mystery novels, seen enough reruns of *Murder, She Wrote,* to keep up with him. "I don't, of course," she said in that patient tone the guilty party always used when being cross-examined. "But the seat was pushed way back, and the scissor things were so heavy I could hardly lift them—I just figured he was a he."

"So you stole the truck and started driving."

"Uh-huh." She nodded.

"You had no idea where you were going."

"Uh-uh." She assumed an expression she hoped was woebegone.

He answered with a deep, frustrated sigh. "Want some coffee?" He seemed to be giving up, which was encouraging.

"I'd love some," she admitted.

"It's fully leaded. Sure it won't keep you awake?" His gaze was wide and innocent. The question was a trap.

"How would I know?"

He flung his hands in the air in the classic gesture of defeat. "We're wasting time. Lester will bring the truck around in the morning and I'll go on from there."

"No," Tish said firmly, "I'll go on from there. My amnesia's not your responsibility. When Lester brings the truck, I'm hitting the road."

"Not in a stolen vehicle you're not," he said, then smiled.

Tish's mouth opened in a wide O. It was clear she wasn't cut out to be a fugitive. The amnesia story that had seemed foolproof in the shower was going to require constant vigilance on her part to avoid the sheriff's sly traps. The truck story had gotten her more deeply into trouble than she'd been before. On her first day of making her own decisions, she'd dug a great big hole and promptly fallen in.

She couldn't help wondering what would have happened if she'd told him the truth.

He wouldn't have believed her, that's what would have happened. If her own family, her own legal counsel had dismissed her suspicions, why should a total stranger listen to them? He would have called Marc and asked him to take her off his hands. She couldn't take that chance.

"Which cell is mine?" she asked glumly.

He handed her a cup of coffee and laughed. That really made her mad. The fact that it was a warm, rich, enveloping sort of laugh made her even madder.

"It humiliates me to ask," she added, snapping the words at him, "but do you have a ditch I could dig in return for something to eat?"

His smile was a little kinder this time, a little less smug. "I'll get out the stuff. You can make yourself a sandwich."

"Thanks ever so much," she said as the cold fingers of panic clamped around her heart. How hard was it, she wondered, to make a sandwich?

3

"BREAD. Ham, cheese, mustard. Lettuce. Tomato's from the grocery store and not very ripe. I wouldn't eat it, but if you're really keen on tomato..." The blank look he was getting from the misplaced bride made him wonder if she might actually have a couple of short circuits.

"Grab a knife." He gestured toward the knife block. "To slice the tomato," he explained when her look turned quizzical. "And the ham and the cheese."

The ham was your usual half ham, and the cheese, a big wedge of sharp cheddar from Floyd's General Store. He always had ham or turkey and cheese, lettuce and tomato in the refrigerator. His father had always kept these things on hand. Good, solid, plain food a hungry kid could fix for himself. Until Dad married Adele, anyway. Adele thought quiche made good snack food.

Tish riffled through the knives and chose one. Clutching the tomato in her left hand, she approached it with the knife, which she gripped in her right.

"Hold on," Zeke said. "Put it on a cutting board. And get a better knife." He put a small square of hard maple in front of her while she went through the knives again. Just watching her *hold* the knife had made him nervous, but dammit, he wasn't going to start waiting on her. Putting her up for the night was his good deed for the day. Even top-ranking scouts only had to do one.

His eyes widened. "Not like that," he yelled as she brought a cleaver down with a whack on the cutting board. She missed the tomato. It flew at him. "I've got it," he called out with a confidence he didn't feel. A split second and a loud *splat!* later, he doubled over, his arms clenched to his crotch. "Nice curve," he muttered hoarsely.

"Omigosh, I'm so sorry," she cried. "Here, let me help...."

Anybody else would have grabbed the paper towels. She'd grabbed the first thing she saw, he guessed, and it was a pot holder, the kind you slid your hand into, and she was sliding her hand into it.

"Don't help!" he gargled. "I'm fine. Just..."

He wasn't sure just what. All he knew was that he wasn't letting her clean him off with a mitt that had her little hand inside it. He turned his back, crab-walked to the kitchen table and grabbed a clump of paper napkins. The udder on the Holstein cow napkin holder, the one young Josh Rountree made for him after he got the Rountree cat down out of the tree, fell off again.

"I feel terrible about this," she said mournfully, hovering, first to his left, then to his right. "I guess I'm not very good at slicing tomatoes."

"In the first place, you don't slice a tomato with a cleaver." His voice still felt a little strangled, but he was getting himself under control. A tomato wasn't going to affect his virility in the long run. It was just that it was still pretty green and it had hit the bull's-eye, so to speak, at short range. "You put it down on the board, then you start a cut with the tip of a serrated knife..." He paused, then turned to gaze at her, his hands full of tomato-splotched napkins. "You've never sliced a tomato?" he said.

She was still hovering, and so close behind him that he found himself staring down into eyes so blue they didn't look real. Her pink, surprisingly voluptuous mouth tilted up to him. He ran his tongue over his lower lip. It felt dry.

"I don't know whether I have or not," she said. "In fact, I can't remember how to make a sandwich."

She turned a look of pure satisfaction on him, the little liar.

"Otherwise," she continued, gathering steam, "a sandwich, I mean, anybody can make a sandwich. Can't they?" An odd flash of uncertainty crossed her face.

"I thought so," Zeke said, "until a minute ago." He eyed her for another moment, suspicion growing inside him. She did *not* have amnesia and he was *not* about to let her use it as an excuse for turning him into her house slave, not even for one night. "Okay, we'll have a retraining session."

"Are you sure you're up to it?" she asked him.

She was so innocent, she didn't even blush. "I'm fine," Zeke said, forcing himself to straighten up, then packing the napkins firmly into the trash can beneath the sink. "We're going to make a sandwich or die trying."

"That's the spirit," she agreed. "I want to be sure the mustard ends up on the inside," she added. "I guess it would taste the same, but it would be a lot less messy if it were on the inside. Are you sure that tomato didn't—"

"Forget the tomato!" Zeke barked. "We'll concentrate on getting the mustard on the inside. Now. Here's how you slice ham...."

"STOP FUSSING. It's only a surface wound." With the hand that wasn't bandaged, Tish took a healthy bite of the excellent sandwich Zeke had made for her.

"It's a gash that goes almost to the bone." He was on the floor, halfway under the kitchen table, mopping up blood with the rest of the paper napkins, and the words were muffled. "You should have a couple of stitches."

Tish was admiring his rear end while he worked, and at the same time, wondering why she wasn't too heartbroken to admire another man's taut buttocks. "Oh, no, thank you," she said absentmindedly, "but I appreciate your—" Her eyes drifted across his backside again. "—concern."

He reached up from the floor and placed a bit of white-painted wood on the table. Tish examined it curiously. It looked sort of like a tiny clown glove, splintery at the wrist, with fat white fingers.

"Of course I'm concerned." His head shot upward. "I'm a sheriff, you're a car thief."

"Truck thief," Tish corrected him. She left off trying to figure out what the clown glove belonged to and reached for her mug of coffee. *Maybe I never loved Marc. Maybe I just wanted love.*

"I should probably get you to sign a waiver," he muttered, and followed up with a deep, depressed sigh.

She was sorry she'd depressed him. He'd rescued

her from a cold, wet night on a godforsaken road, and she'd rewarded him by bombing him with a tomato. He made a great sandwich and he had a great... "Don't worry," she said to distract herself. "I promise I'll..."

She saw his keen gaze light on her just in time to keep her from saying she'd never sue him for not insisting on those stitches. A waiver was something she knew about, from her books, from listening to her father talk about his law practice. "...sign any waiver you're passing around," she concluded. "Whatever the cause." A little time to think and she could have come up with something more creative. But apparently she'd done enough.

"It's your bedtime," he said, still sounding gloomy. "I'm exhausted."

BY THE TIME he'd shown her to the spare bedroom and fished out the new toothbrush he kept on hand in case he ever got lucky enough to need it, Zeke was as sure as he needed to be that this woman was going to ruin his life.

He changed his jeans for sweatpants, went back to his office and did a few therapeutic spins in his chair. Now that the soreness was going away, he was sorry not to be looking at his houseguest anymore. All that long blond hair had dried into a curly cloud that reminded him of cotton candy. Her eyes were as blue as the Bachelor Buttons Adele planted in his garden every summer just to irritate him, and without any of that dark stuff women used on their eyes, her lashes were long and pale and floated up and down like feathers. The only thing competing with her eyes was her wide, full, pink mouth. Looking at it made him remember how long it had been since he kissed a mouth like hers.

All in all, she was as cute as a june bug—and not all that great a liar.

Purposefully Zeke got up. Aware that thinking about his houseguest was having an unsettling effect on him, he decided he'd look around for some clues to her identity. If he were a policeman in Boston like Cole instead of a sheriff in Wild River, he would have thought to write down the license plate number of the truck while he was out there looking at it. But no, all that was on his mind was that Lester wouldn't need a license plate number, because there was only one small red truck stuck on Winsom Hill Road.

What else might give him a clue? She didn't know how to make a sandwich. What with the liberation movement, that didn't tell him much. In the world outside Whitewater County, women didn't join the 4H Club at birth, didn't learn to cook and can and quilt.

When she'd cut her finger there'd been plenty of blood to do a test, but asking her to bleed into a clean measuring cup hadn't seemed right at the time.

The wedding dress. What had she done with it?

He checked the bathroom. She was about the messiest guest he'd ever had, but the dress wasn't on the floor with the towels. It wasn't in the silly white wastebasket Adele had insisted on buying for him, either. It wasn't...

Quickly Zeke averted his eyes. It wasn't stuffed over the towel rod. What was hanging on the towel rod was the smallest pair of panties he'd ever laid eyes on. And next to them was a bra that wasn't quite as little as he might have expected it to be, but not big, either. Nothing more than bits of white lace, both of them. They'd dry fast.

He left the bathroom in a hurry and continued his search in the kitchen, where he found the dress wadded up in the trash can under the sink.

He pulled it out. It looked like a few thousand dollars worth of silk cleaning rags. He checked the label: Priscilla of Boston. He'd call Cole in the morning and ask him if that meant anything, like did it mean she came from Boston? He held the dress for a minute or so, remembering the way it had felt under his hands when she was inside it, then smoothed it out and folded it carefully.

Exhibit A, Your Honor.

No doubt about it, this woman was bound to mess up his life. He could feel it coming. Let a woman walk in and take over and before you knew it, you were living differently and eating differently and finding slipcovers on your favorite leather chairs.

Neither he nor Cole had gotten married, knowing full well that marriage was a garden path toward sit-down dinners with tablecloths and napkins that had to be ironed. But that was just the beginning. Marriage turned a strong man into putty. It had turned his father into a besotted, foolishly grinning wimp who was all of a sudden telling him and Cole to get their feet off the coffee table. It had not been pretty.

He would not let the same thing happen to him. And Cole, who'd been younger and had to hang around longer and snack on a lot more quiche and fruit cups, apparently felt the same way.

Zeke put Cole, who was doing fine now, to the back of his mind and returned to contemplation of his houseguest, who wasn't. Some guy too dumb to know what he was in for had lost himself a mighty good-looking wife. Was it his fault? Or had she taken a notion at the last minute to run from the idea of being a wife and mother? How'd the guy feel right now? Sad? Mad? Embarrassed?

Frustrated enough to knock out a wall of the honeymoon suite with his fists, that's how Zeke would feel.

No, *he* wouldn't. Relieved, that's how *he'd* feel. But that guy, the one the amnesiac had run away from, probably liked quiche and slipcovers. Zeke shook his head to clear it. He was tired, getting spacey.

He was hiding the spare keys to the Pathfinder in various unlikely spots in his office, in case his houseguest took a notion to run again, when the phone rang. He grabbed it on the first ring, hoping she was asleep and not lying awake plotting her next attack on him. "Jasper?" he said. "Jasper!" He'd almost forgotten about the drama of Jasper and Crockett and the egg money Hortense was saving to go to the quilting convention in Charleston.

"Hey, sorry I had to walk off the job, but— Oh. You already heard about her." He frowned. "Well, how'd it all turn out?" He listened to Jasper's high, excited voice for a while. "No!" he said when Jasper finally got to the punch line. "She wasn't! You didn't! Where'd you shoot her? Aw, no, not in the— How's she going to quilt? Can't quilt standing up. Jasper, honest to…"

Out of his other ear he heard the *plop, plop* of small bare feet on the broad planks of his hallway. Before he could prepare himself for seeing her again, his mystery woman burst into his office wearing his plaid shirt over the T-shirt he'd given her to sleep in. For such a short person, her legs were long and beautiful, the skin as smooth and rich-looking as a freezer of Bess Blakeley's homemade vanilla ice cream.

"Is that Jasper Wedgelow?" she said breathlessly. "What *happened?*"

"Go back to bed," he yelled. It was all he could do. He didn't dare stand up like a gentleman when she came flying into the room, because no gentleman would react the way he had to the mere sight of her. The mere sight of his cantilevered sweatpants would confirm her fear that she wasn't safe spending the night in his house.

"You heard me, Jasper," he said sternly when she'd scurried away. "Go to bed and think things over. Tomorrow morning you'd better go up to the hospital and give Hortense an apology to remember. Crockett too, for mean-mouthing him. Flowers would be good. Not for Crockett, for Hortense. Okay, Jasper. Okay. G'night."

The Wedgelow Fiasco having more or less settled itself, he put a stack of muddy stone-colored uniforms into the washer to soak and got to work on The Case of the Extra Bride. He logged on, accessed his data base and consulted it. He phoned the county sheriff's office and the state police. Then, figuring that in this day and age the press might know something the police didn't, he watched the news. There wasn't a word about a runaway bride in a stolen truck.

He knew the police made all sorts of scared-out-of-their-minds supplicants wait twenty-four hours before they'd post a missing-persons report, but this had to be a special situation. There was only one place she was supposed to be, with her bridegroom, and the bride-groom must have realized by now that she wasn't.

He sat there, wide-awake, for a long time, puzzling over the omission. How could anybody lose this particular woman and not notice she was gone?

IN THE HIGH brass bed in Zeke's guest room, Tish floated on a cloud of old, soft white linens with crocheted edges and listened to the rain pattering on the roof. Alone for the first time in several hours, with no hope of attacking her problems until morning, she felt the day crashing in on her.

As wedding days went, hers had been a bummer.

Five hundred people came to see legendary local heiress Tyler Staley Seldon marry Marc Radcliffe in a formal ceremony to be followed by a lavish reception at home; 540 people sent gifts—china and silver, toasters and blenders. Unimaginable amounts of money had been spent on flowers, a catered dinner, musicians and the wedding dress every girl dreams of wearing when she faces the minister with the love of her life by her side.

And then...

Tish buried her face in a pillow that smelled of lavender. "And then" was the bummer. It seemed that Marc wasn't the love of her life.

What if she was wrong? What if she'd caught her parents' paranoia about fortune hunters and read something into Marc's behavior that wasn't there? What if she'd humiliated her family for nothing?

But that sickeningly sweet smell that filled the car—she couldn't have imagined that smell.

Tish shuddered. She wouldn't think any more about Marc tonight. Instead, she would think about...

Sheriff Zeke Thorne. The way his biceps bulged beneath the sleeve of his black turtleneck as he held the telephone to his ear. The muscled tightness of his rear end as he bent to hide a set of keys in the back of the bottom drawer of his desk while she spied on him from the hallway. The size of his hand as it made a dive to the bottom of the candy dish with another set of keys.

The man had a presence, no doubt about it, a blatantly male presence. When she was with him she was aware of his heat, his strength, the sexuality he exuded. Too bad she couldn't just put herself in those big, strong hands, the ones that had bandaged her finger so gently, so carefully.

Tish sent a rueful smile into the pillow. He trusted her about as much as she trusted him. They were starting off even; it was the first time in her life she'd started off even with a man. It would make a change. She might learn something from the experience.

4

"YOU MEAN Hortense was stealing her own chickens?"

"And giving them to her daughter Cordelia." Zeke
broke eggs into a pan. The pan sizzled. A light rain
beat against the kitchen windows and tapped on the tin
roof.

Cozy sounds. "But why, for heaven's sake?"

"Cordelia's saving her egg money to leave her
worthless, no-good husband—that's Hortense talking,
not me—and go to New York to be an actress."

"That's inspiring," Tish said, wondering how many
eggs they were talking about here. "But...why didn't
Hortense just give Cordelia the money?"

Zeke broke two more eggs into the pan. "Jasper
wouldn't let her," he said. "He's as dead set against
Cordelia going to New York as her worthless, no-good
husband is."

"You men," Tish said feelingly. "Hortense just
wants her daughter to follow her dream."

"Hortense," Zeke said, "has a secret hankering—"
He halted. "Why do you want to know all this stuff?"

"Because it's so interesting," Tish breathed.
"Please go on. You can't leave me hanging here on
Hortense's hankering."

Zeke expertly flipped one pair of eggs, then the second pair, forked bacon onto paper towels and toast into a basket. "Breakfast," he said. "How's your finger feeling?"

"Fine." She wished he'd go on talking. Even though his voice was gruff she was sure he cared about the people in his town, got inside their lives. How else would he know what Hortense hankered for?

She felt a stab of envy. She'd never been allowed to get inside the life of anyone outside her family, and their lives were too predictable to be interesting. Her mother secretly hankered for a face-lift and wouldn't get one because it would be admitting she had the Staley family jowls. The excitement topped out right about there.

In his shirt and sweatpants, Tish sat at Zeke's small, round kitchen table, resting her arms on its scrubbed-looking top. She had devised a plan for the morning and the timing was crucial. One little detail was putting everything else on hold. She didn't have a dime. She did, however, have a diamond, several of them, the big solitaire in her engagement ring and the row of smaller ones in her wedding ring. She'd read about people pawning their valuables and getting money for them.

The rings were in the pocket of the sweatpants even now. But she couldn't buy gas for the truck until she pawned the rings, and she couldn't pawn the rings until she found a pawnshop, and the gas gauge was already on empty when she got stuck in the mud.

She would have to pursue a life of crime, of theft and lying, for a few more hours, long enough to get to a big town, pawn the diamonds, hole up in a motel and begin her investigation of Marc Radcliffe. Later she would go back over her tracks and make amends to everyone she'd wronged. Especially to Zeke Thorne, whom she'd barely begun to wrong.

"You have a way with eggs," she complimented him, her guilt increasing as she contemplated what she was about to do to him. "How do you cook them? You break them into the pan, I know, then put the pan on the stove...."

"Other way around," Zeke said. "Heat the pan first. And if you have any interest in getting the eggs out of the pan, put in some butter first."

"How interesting," Tish marveled.

The gas fumes must be getting to him, Zeke decided. Cooking eggs for the spare bride who sat at his kitchen table was making him lightheaded.

When she got so caught up in Hortense's situation, she didn't seem as much like a woman who was out to make trouble. She seemed like a curious waif who'd never sat at a kitchen table waiting for the toaster to ping. It touched a chord in him he'd just as soon not have touched. Sometimes it only took a touch to break a string.

Yep, gas fumes. Had to be.

He cast a more critical eye over the spare bride in question. She looked soft, sweet, warm with leftover drowsiness. That could only mean one thing. She was moving in for the kill. He narrowed his eyes and studied her through the slits. "You prefer your eggs over medium?"

Tish heard the peculiar undertone in his offhand remark and saw the squinty look he was giving her. It could only mean one thing. He was moving in for the kill. "Is this breakfast or an interrogation?"

"Both."

"Just can't resist it, can you?" Tish sighed. "Get a girl softened up with perfect eggs and crisp bacon and she's sure to lose her iron control and rat on the gang."

"You don't have amnesia," he snapped at her, slamming his knife down on the table, "and I want you to admit it."

"Why?" Tish put her cup down with a similar bang.

"To clear the decks. To wipe the slate clean. To..."

"What a brilliant conversationalist you are!"

"I do fine when I'm having the conversation with an intelligent person!"

They glared at each other, picked up strips of bacon and made simultaneous loud crunching sounds.

They finished the bacon at the same time, but Tish still heard crunching sounds. Lester Martin had arrived with her truck.

"Excellent breakfast," she said briskly, scooting her chair back. "And now, if you'll excuse me—"

"Hold it!"

Tish held it, her knees bent and her rear end hanging above the chair seat. "I was going out to thank Mr. Martin."

"Lester's going to want a little more than thanks. Twenty-five dollars, to be exact."

She stood all the way up, biting her lip. "I don't seem to have any money."

"Figures. So I'll pay Lester. You just sit tight."

"If you insist," said Tish, and sat. She picked up a triangle of toast and took a dainty bite from one corner.

Casting a frown over his shoulder at her, he stalked out the front door. She dropped the toast and leapt up to follow his progress through the kitchen window. Lester had pulled his mud-caked tow truck up in front of the house, right outside the picket fence, with her mud-caked little truck hiked up behind it. Some kind of thingy held it there so it didn't block the driveway. That was a stroke of luck. She whirled from the window and went directly to the sheriff's office, fished the keys up from the bottom of the candy dish and slid cautiously out the mudroom door.

So far, so good. Zeke and Lester appeared to be negotiating. She tippy-toed up the drive, feeling the moisture from the thawing earth soaking through Zeke's wool socks while the rain soaked her hair. She made it to the garage, which must have been a barn once, and tugged open one of the big doors. It squeaked so loudly that she thought it must have given her away, but a moment later she was sitting in the Pathfinder, unchallenged and ready to roll.

Talk about a seat pushed way back. Tish adjusted it, then fiddled with the rearview mirror. In it she saw the rear end of the red truck, still hiked up. She said a brief prayer, then jammed the key in the ignition, started the car, jerked it into reverse and flew backward down the driveway.

"Okay, Lester, let her go," Zeke called out. Lester released the cable from the winch and the red truck rolled back across Zeke's driveway. Too stunned to do more than watch with his jaw hanging open, he saw the rear end of his Pathfinder crash into the truck, heard the hideous thud and the screech of ripping metal.

Wild River had just had its first car wreck since 1989. The woman he'd cooked breakfast for leapt from the Pathfinder, screaming something so incoherent that the only word Zeke could identify was *truck*. At least he hoped that's what she was screaming, considering that the neighbors had begun to take an interest in the event and were wandering one by one out onto their porches. When she finished screaming, she whirled and took off at a run.

"Guess I'll just tow 'em on to the garage, Sheriff," he heard Lester say before his feet finally began to move.

She was mad and she was fast. It took him two blocks to catch up with her. He grabbed her in the middle of Royal Rountree's vacant lot and spun her around to face him, his hands gripping her shoulders. Expecting rage, he saw she'd gone back to sobbing.

That did him in. He knew something worse than a cut finger had happened to this pretty little woman yesterday and in time he'd wring it out of her. So instead of yelling, he panted, "You are one stubborn woman, Madame X," and wrapped his arms around her. The sensation of holding her the night before came back in a painful, aching rush. She was so slight she felt boneless. He was afraid of crushing her, and he didn't want his height to scare her, so he slid his arms down almost to her waist and lifted her gently against himself, up and up until her teary face was level with his.

Bad idea.

Even the slight pressure of her weight against his swiftly swelling groin was enough to awaken the cave man that slept just beneath his civilized exterior. The next thing he knew, he'd brushed his mouth against hers, and then it wasn't just a brush anymore but a hungry search for the sweetness, the depth he knew was there. And it was. She offered it to him and took what he had to give, as hungry as he'd ever thought about being.

Her sobs faded into a soft moan, and something about that moan brought him back to real life, the life of a sheriff in Wild River, Vermont. If he were her lawyer, he'd sue himself.

It should have taken him no more than a second to put her down, but he wanted so badly not to put her down that it took more like five. "I'm sorry," he said. "I overstepped my bounds. I lost my head. I got carried away. I—"

She tilted her head up to look him straight in the eyes. "You got a glimpse of the new unknown." But her voice shook, just like his.

"Something like that," he muttered. "Okay, lady, it's time to stop playing games. I want the truth."

She put her hand to her forehead, which scared him, although he didn't let on. Then she said, "The wreck...I think I'm starting to remember...yes, I'm definitely beginning to remember...."

She just wouldn't give up on it. He ought to turn her over his knee and spank her. The thought made him tingle all over, as though his hand already rested against that small, shapely bottom, caressing it, though, not...

At the moment he wasn't even sure he wanted the truth. He just wanted her.

THE SHERIFF was certainly acting peculiar. He banged a plate on the counter. He slammed a pot on the stove. He sloshed stuff into the pot and whipped it violently.

She was so edgy, every move of his body jarred her. His kiss had rocked her from scalp to toenails. It wasn't the wreck that had made her decide to tell him the truth, it was the impact of all that maleness. Marc's kisses had never made her feel the way Zeke's kiss had.

Realization struck her hard. The sensations Zeke's kiss had awakened in her, that aching, longing need she had felt all through her body—that was the way a woman should feel about the man who would share her bed for the rest of her life. Until Zeke kissed her, she'd been too inexperienced to know that Marc wouldn't— couldn't—give her that feeling.

"Why did you kiss me?" she blurted out.

He gave her a look that made her wish she hadn't asked. "I don't know." He sounded frustrated. "Men do weird things when they've just watched a loved one die."

"Who died?"

"You totaled my car. Same thing."

"I didn't total your car," Tish protested. "I just banged it up a little."

"If you want another take on it, I'll show you Lester's estimate." His voice level went up. "I have insurance. With a *thousand dollar* deductible."

The thousand-dollar part seemed important to him. "I'll pay the thousand dollars." She paused. "When I can put my hands on some money."

"While we wait for that wonderful day, I want to know who I'm loaning money to." He shoved a plate of cookies at her. The spin he put on the plate made her jump.

"We just had breakfast," she protested.

"Have one to satisfy your curiosity," he snapped. "They're Bess Blakeley's."

"Oh." She got a grip on a huge, thin, crisp cookie that smelled like peanut butter.

"Start at the beginning," he commanded. Turning his back on her, he returned to stirring wildly. A delicious hot-chocolate smell filled the kitchen.

The beginning. Tish absentmindedly took a bite of the cookie. *Um. Yummy.* She chewed for a moment, thinking. "I was a breech baby," she said at last.

"Not that far back," he barked at her.

She'd intended to make a point, that she'd simply meant trouble for everyone from birth—from before her birth! Of course, after her mother recovered from the C-section, Tish had apparently given her family ten fairly trouble-free years. Maybe she should start at the point when those ended.

"Well, first my grandmother died and left me all her money. Then I met Lorraine, and she introduced me to her brother Marc, and we got married, then he scared me, so I ran away. And here I am."

"You had a big day yesterday." The facts of the situation, stated so bluntly, had left him looking stunned.

"You know perfectly well all that didn't happen yesterday," Tish said. "I was trying to be brief."

"So brief you still haven't told me your name."

"And I'm not going to."

"Why not?" he asked, his wooden spoon poised above the saucepan. "Are you a celebrity? A big-time crook?"

"No. My family has made quite a lot of money over the last few generations, but they're not well-known, and I've only been a crook since yesterday. I haven't really built up a reputation." She hesitated. "What I'm afraid of is that you'll call my father, or worse, call Marc, and the next time we meet I'll be dead or locked up in an attic somewhere and Marc will have ten million dollars, which I guess is a lot if you don't really have the three hundred million you said you had."

He stared at her until his eyes crossed. "I'm missing something here." He poured hot chocolate into a cup and set it down in front of her as though he dared her not to drink it. He redirected his stare toward the pot, poured a cup for himself and eased himself into the chair opposite her. It creaked under his weight. Their knees touched. He shoved the chair back, causing it audible distress.

"You're missing a lot," she said, still feeling the brief contact of his leg against hers. "I've barely begun."

He gave her a lawman sort of smile that wasn't even close to being as warm as his touch. "Don't. Begin. This time I'm going to do the job right. I'll question you."

"Like I'm a criminal?" The notion caught her interest.

"Worse than that. One car theft made you a first offender. Your recent attempted theft made you a repeater."

That sounded bad. "I do intend to make amends," she assured him.

He clenched his teeth. "And I admire you for it. But I have to figure out what to do with you between now and then. So go back to the part about Grandmother's money."

Her shoulders slumped. "You, too," she said, shaking her head. "I thought you'd be different, but no. All you're interested in is Grandmother's money, just like everybody else."

He turned so red she began to worry about him, afraid he might implode. "I am interested in the way the money relates to your story." He dropped each word like a rock into the quiet of the kitchen. "Although…"

He was actually getting madder. Tish's nervousness increased. She'd read a lot of books about communication skills and knew they weren't fighting fair, the way the books said to. She was holding back, he was resorting to rage. They'd never Get to Yes this way.

"…I am relieved to hear that you'll be able to repay me for having your car towed…."

This was better. They were just talking money. "Twenty-five dollars," Tish readily admitted. "Of course, as soon as—"

"*Seventy*-five," he shouted. "Two more towing charges this morning! Remember?" With visible effort he did what appeared to be a calm-down routine—silence, deep breath, resume relaxed position in chair. Then he pulled a notepad toward him and scribbled on it. "Seventy-five dollars for towing. Plus the repairs to your car and the deductible on mine." He looked up. "That's how much of Grandmother's money I want. Do I make myself clear?"

"Perfectly," Tish said.

"But I do want to know what happened after you inherited it. Is that equally clear?"

"Yes. It is now."

"Well?"

"Well," Tish said, deciding she'd better hurry along, "there were all these cousins and aunts and uncles who stood to inherit from Grandmother, too, but she left everything to me. I don't know why. I was just ten. I felt bad about it and tried to divide it with everybody, but they all said, 'No, no, dear, we must honor Mother Seldon's—'' She clapped her hand over her mouth.

"Seldon! Your name is Seldon. Now we're making progress." He reached for the notepad and wrote down Seldon.

She glared at his smug expression. "Surely you've realized I don't have the skills to be a criminal."

"I'm softening my stand on the subject," Zeke admitted. "But we haven't gotten to the punch line yet."

"All *right*. Let's see, they said we had to honor Grandmother's wishes," she muttered. "But they hated me for it, I know they did." It upset her just to think about it. "I mean, everybody in the family has plenty of money, but Grandmother's net worth was really, really..." She hesitated. She didn't want him to think she was boasting.

"I get the picture," Zeke said. "Then what happened? You got paranoid about fortune hunters?"

"I didn't," Tish said morosely. "My family did."

"I may hate myself for this later, but could you clarify that?"

"They built a wall around me," Tish said. "A bodyguard chauffeured me back and forth to girls' schools, and on the few occasions I managed to dredge up a boyfriend, they found some reason to be suspicious of him."

Humiliating memories suddenly rushed through her. "Can you imagine," she burst out, "how a naval academy cadet must feel when he shows up in sparkling white for his first date with a girl whose father demands a financial statement before he'll let them leave the property?''

''Funny,'' Zeke said.

''It is not!''

''I meant he'd feel funny,'' Zeke explained. ''Did that really happen?''

''About fifteen times. Not all naval cadets, of course. There was considerable variety. I have eclectic tastes.''

''None of them had more money than you?''

''One appeared to. My father hired a private eye who learned that his father was overleveraged in real estate, and that ended that.'' She sighed. ''It wasn't the only time Father knew best, either.'' She didn't want the sheriff to know how many times—or that a couple of them had broken her heart. She thought Marc had broken her heart, too—until Zeke kissed her. The memory of the kiss buzzed through her again.

''So the years rolled by.''

He was getting impatient. She hurried on. ''I met Lorraine Radcliffe at a *tea,* for heaven's sake. On my first date with Marc, she chaperoned. Proper, proper, proper,'' Tish said glumly. ''Mother was thrilled.''

''What about Father and his financial statement phobia?''

Tish gazed at him in sudden admiration. ''That was wonderful alliteration,'' she complimented him, ''father, financial, pho—''

''Go...on!''

''Oh. Yes. Marc actually volunteered his financial statement. Every penny checked out. He didn't have as many pennies as I did, but enough that he surely couldn't have needed my little ten million dollars.''

She couldn't begin to interpret the sheriff's expression. "We signed a prenuptial agreement," she explained. "In the event of divorce or death, each of us bequeathed the other one a token ten million dollars. That would have been just a drop in the bucket for a man with three hundred million."

"Drop in the bucket," Zeke muttered. He glanced at his scratch pad.

"I guess he could have faked the statement. But how he could get a fake statement past my father and all the lawyers, I can't imagine."

"So now the days are rolling by," Zeke prompted her.

"...and I got worried about a few things," she confessed. "Like Marc wasn't interested in buying a house."

"Men don't feel the same way about houses women do," Zeke interrupted. His voice was low and he sounded almost absentminded.

"Just what the family lawyer said," Tish admitted. "You've got a house," she reminded him. "You must care about—"

"We're not talking about me," he growled.

"We were for a minute there."

"We aren't anymore." He sounded definite about it.

"Anyway, what Marc wanted was to lease a condo in Boston, so I did."

"You paid for it?"

"Well, yes. It didn't matter who paid. Who paid wasn't the point. The point was—"

"What else bothered you?"

"Well, he and Lorraine don't seem to have any family or friends. He *said* they were all on the West Coast.

He *said* the wedding was for my family, that his family wanted to give us a big party after the honeymoon.''

"Sounds reasonable," Zeke said.

She folded her arms across her chest. "Amazing," she remarked. "That's just what Father said." She was getting pretty tired of his lack of sympathy to her cause. She had done right to hold back, trust no one but herself. Men were for opening, lifting and kissing, but you couldn't rely on them to act in your best interests.

"Anything else?"

"No," she lied.

The expression that moved across his face was avuncular. It was kind. No, it was condescending. Tish felt an unfamiliar fury rise up inside her even before he spoke.

"Are you sure," he said in a mild tone, "that you didn't decide all of a sudden that you didn't want to live the life of a married woman?"

She leapt up from the table. "I was dying to live the life of a married woman," she yelled. "It was Marc who insisted on waiting!"

Heat rose to her face. She'd been determined not to share that with the sheriff. It was too humiliating.

"Don't you think he was just showing his respect for you?" Zeke asked in that same maddening, mild tone, delivering the last and final blow.

"That's what my brother said!" Now she was shrieking. "Do you men ever have an independent thought? Or do you have a mass-produced tape playing inside you?" She paced around him, watching his head swivel as his gaze followed her. "Well. Listen to this."

She suddenly wanted to tell him what happened yesterday so he could see for himself just how much Marc "respected" her! "Marc wanted us to sneak away from the reception early, take an earlier plane to the Cayman Islands. And I thought, 'Oh, boy, he's finally acting like an impatient bridegroom.'"

What a romantic fool she'd been!

"When I slipped away to my room to change, Marc and Lorraine were both there, and they said I didn't have time to change. They hurried me down to the garage and stuffed me into Lorraine's car, not a limo, Lorraine's car. I was sitting in the back seat feeling sort of breathless because everything was happening so fast, and Marc said, 'Oh, look at you, you've got a smudge on your face,' and he whipped out this big white hanky and came at me with it..."

The words got harder. She began to doubt herself again, to see how melodramatic the story must sound to a third party. To Zeke, who listened so alertly. The tension in his big, virile body electrified the very air of the room.

She went on desperately. "...and a horrible smell filled the car, and I just...just..."

"...ran."

His voice was so quiet it quieted her. Her hands dropped to her sides. She slumped back into her chair, put her elbows on the table and buried her face in her hands. "Yes," she whispered. "I know I should have stayed to see if it really was chloroform I was smelling, but if I'd stayed and it *was* chloroform..."

"Have you ever smelled chloroform?"

"No. But mystery writers say it has a sickly sweet odor, and this was a sickly sweet odor."

Her despair deepened. The story did sound silly today, with cookies and cocoa, but yesterday, in the quiet garage with Marc and Lorraine, with hundreds of people just a few feet away having such a good time they'd forgotten she was the cause of it all, she had been certain Marc was going to clap that handkerchief over her nose and then—and then what?

"Besides," she said, fighting back tears, "do you think a man who's anxious to be away on his honeymoon would be worrying about a smudge on his bride's face?"

"I don't know."

"Would you?" She peeked at him through her fingers.

"No."

5

WOULD HE BE worrying about a dirty spot on this woman's face? Hell, no! He would have been waiting in her room stark naked with only one thing on his mind! How clean her face was would have been way, way down on the list.

Zeke's heart was doing scary pre-heart-attack things. He'd known she was going to be trouble the minute he laid eyes on her.

In the first place, it upset him entirely too much that she'd gone through the wedding ceremony. She was a married woman. He'd lost his head and kissed a married woman, and worse than that, she'd enjoyed it.

She'd as much as said that she and this Marc person had never made love. She had to be lying. No red-blooded man could have waited until after the wedding for this luscious—and apparently willing—sliver of femininity.

The luscious sliver was waiting now, looking puzzled by his blunt, ''No,'' and undoubtedly hoping he'd tell her she'd done right to run. Here Zeke saw a slippery slope. What probably had happened was that she was all keyed up after the wedding, and she'd had a lifetime of her parents' warnings against men who were after her money, and she'd overreacted.

Marc *was* eager to be off on their honeymoon.

Zeke paused in his reasoning process to grit his teeth over *that* prospect. The poor guy had bought a new aftershave for the honeymoon—too bad his bride didn't like the way it smelled—and he was holding a handkerchief...

...because he was the kind of guy who'd have a clean white hanky on his person, just in case, while Zeke was the kind of guy who kept a roll of paper towels in whatever vehicle he happened to be driving, just in case. His just-in-case situations probably tended to be greasier, bloodier and muddier than Marc's. The things Zeke got into could ruin a white hanky forever.

It was unlikely that a guy with a white hanky intended to kill his lady for her money. Zeke was starting to hate the guy with the white hanky, whether he had doused it with chloroform or some fancy-schmancy aftershave. The fact that he hadn't admitted he'd lost his woman was a plenty good enough reason to hate him.

"Why didn't you tell your parents, your brother, somebody, before you took off? You told me they were overprotective. Wouldn't they have run him off right away without waiting for him to explain?"

She dipped her head, stared at her cookie. "I didn't think I could get back into the house without Marc catching up with me. But even if I had, I was afraid they were too happy and excited to listen." She glanced up. "If you think I was relieved to be getting married at last, you can't imagine how relieved they were to get me married to a man they'd decided was perfect."

He couldn't imagine any of the things she was talking about. "Okay, enough questions for now," he said. "Time to make some decisions." My, but he did sound calm and professional, just the way law enforcement training taught you to sound. He took a sip of no-longer-hot chocolate. He didn't know why he'd wanted to give her cocoa and cookies instead of more coffee. Something about her lost-little-girl look, he guessed. "There may be a simple explanation for what happened, and what we're going to do, we're going to call Marc and ask him what it is."

"I knew that's what you'd do," she cried. "I knew you'd want to call Marc!"

"Why are you so dead set against just asking the man what he was up to?" Zeke argued.

"Because he *will* have a simple explanation. He'll be lying, but you'll believe him because you men stick together like Super Glue and fingers. You'll tell him where to find me, and he'll come and get me and then he'll finish doing whatever he planned to do with the chloroform."

"Really."

"Really." She glared at him, daring him to make the call.

Which, of course, he intended to do. Eventually. For the moment, he was going to pretend to buy her story and see what she did next. "Okay, I believe you," he said. "If you don't want to call Marc, what do you want to do?"

Just look at the way she got down to business now that she thought she was getting her own way. "I'd like to call my mother first. She and Dad must be worried sick."

"Okay," Zeke said. At least it wasn't as harebrained as her previous ideas. In fact, a call to her mother might be very informative. He wondered what she'd do when her mother told her Marc was wringing his hands. Pining away. Wondering if it was something he'd said. Willing and eager to explain. Would she be ready to run right back to him? He hesitated, then asked, "Do you mind if I listen in?"

"I guess not," she said.

"I'll add the long-distance charges to your bill." He reached for his notepad.

She eyed him for a moment, probably trying to retrieve information about long-distance charges from her overprivileged brain. If she didn't realize that ten million dollars was a lot of money, she couldn't possibly know about ten-cent versus seven-cent long-distance plans.

He handed her the kitchen phone, then brought a portable in from his office. "The sheriff's office has one line," he told her. "If you hear a beep, it's call waiting. It could be an emergency, so put your mother on hold."

Her eyes narrowed. "I'll be happy to do that, but I'm not paying for the time you're on the phone."

Wow, she learned fast! "I'll time my part of the call."

"Fair enough," she said briskly. Still eyeing him, she punched buttons rapidly, and when he thought the moment was right, Zeke put the portable to his ear.

"Hel-lo-oh." The voice that answered was not the voice of a woman worried sick.

"Mother? Hi, it's me."

"Tish, honey!"

Tish! Zeke thought triumphantly. Her name was Tish Seldon! He reached for his notebook.

Tish sent a murderous glance toward the receiver. "Mother, I'm really sorry I—"

"You stinker!" said Tish's mother, laughing. "You sneaked away from us yesterday. How did you manage it?"

"Well, I felt that I had to—"

Zeke heard the uncertainty and fear that crept into her voice. He couldn't figure out where this conversation was going, and apparently, neither could Tish.

Tish. It was a good name for her.

"I know, honey. Marc told us when he called last night. He said it was his idea and he apologized for whisking you away from the party. But he sounded so happy we just couldn't be mad at him."

Across the kitchen, Zeke stared at Tish. Her eyes were wide. They darkened as she stared back. He watched her run her tongue over her lips before she finally said, "Marc called you?" She reached for a paper napkin, fiddled with it and reached for another.

"While you were changing, he told us. He wanted us to know you'd gotten to the Caymans and were fine. What a lovely man he is. So thoughtful."

"Yes, isn't he?" Tish said in a shaky voice. "Did, ah, Jeff talk to him?" The paper napkins were starting to stack up in front of her.

Zeke made another note on his pad. "Who's Jeff?"

"Oh, no, honey. Jeff's gone off to climb Mount Kilimanjaro, remember? He took Stephanie with him. No, that can't be right. Ellie's the mountaineer. Well, anyway, he took one of his girlfriends. I can't keep them straight."

Lucky Jeff, Zeke thought. Must be a brother, or a

cousin. Whoever he was, he had a kind of freedom Tish had apparently never known.

"Natasha is the mountaineer," Tish said dully. "Stephanie's the social worker, Ellie's the stockbroker, Kaye rides horses, Jennifer…acts. But he might have taken any of them because I've read that Kilimanjaro is just a long steep walk." Her voice trailed off in a little sigh. "Well, goodbye. I'll call again soon."

"Marc said he was going to keep you too distracted to call." Mrs. Seldon giggled. "This is your honeymoon, sweetheart! Don't worry about us. My goodness. This is the first time I haven't been worried about you in as long as I can remember. Just have the time of your life. Love you."

Tish hung up. In the shocked silence of the kitchen her gaze met Zeke's and held it for a long, long moment.

That was one mystery solved. There was no missing-persons report on runaway bride Tish Seldon because nobody had reported her missing.

ZEKE CHEWED on his lower lip for a moment. "Okay," he said finally, "I'm willing to admit you have a problem."

"So am I," Tish assured him, letting her heartfelt concern spill out.

The look he gave her was odd, to say the least. "I mean," she explained, twisting her fingers together, but only for something to do, "that I've gone over and over the thing with the handkerchief and the chloroform in my mind, because I was afraid I was accusing Marc unjustly, but when Mother said he'd called to say everything was terrific…"

"Yes. You—"

"...which implied we were having a heck of a honeymoon, when we certainly aren't, and to tell you the truth, I don't think we would have had in the best and least threatening of circumstances..."

"I said you—"

"...well, you just have to wonder, don't you? What Marc is up to? Maybe he's just embarrassed. Wouldn't you be embarrassed if you'd misplaced your bride somewhere between 'I do' and 'Let's do it?'" She paused, feeling tension in the air although she herself was quite calm. "Was there something you wanted to say?"

"Yes! I mean, yes," Zeke said. "What I wanted to say, what I already *said,* is that you have a problem."

"Well, I know *that,*" she said. What was making him look so annoyed? She'd agreed with him, hadn't she?

"What I'm saying is that I think this Marc person's behavior is pretty strange, and whatever I may think of your behavior..."

She watched, fascinated, as he took a deep breath, which expanded his already expanded chest, then let it out slowly, which only made his tempting mouth more tempting. She could reach up right now and catch those lips just as they were blowing out breath sweet with chocolate and peanut butter, sort of a Ben & Jerry's Peanut-Butter-Cup-Ice-Cream kiss. But she had a feeling this wasn't quite the moment for spontaneity.

"...I still have to admit you have a problem. Imminent death, probably not. But something's wrong."

"So we've reached consensus."

"Yes." The way he ground out the word made her

want to loosen him up a little, let him know she appreciated what he'd done for her and that she'd pay attention to any advice he might want to give her. Humility, that was the key.

"What do you think I should do?" she said. Humbly. It pleased her to see him regain a little strength.

"First thing I think you should do is sit tight, so I can keep an eye on you." His tone was one of deep regret.

"Stay here in Wild River? But how will I ever find out what Marc..."

"That's my point," said Zeke. "I don't want you trying to find out. You're a loose cannon. Anything could happen. You could end up damaging Marc, going to jail. *My* plan—" his jaw muscles had stopped working as though he were grinding his teeth and had stiffened into a hard line "—is to keep you off the streets while *I* find out what Marc is up to."

There. He'd said it. He'd make her decisions for her. She didn't need to bother her pretty little head at all.

She wanted to stamp her foot and scream. She'd never learn to take care of herself if people kept doing it for her. But she was flat out of cars to run away in.

"We'll stick to the amnesia story with the townsfolk," Zeke was saying. "No names. No details. I'd trust them with my life—" He paused. "—but not with yours."

Be humble. Be grateful. Mutiny later. "That's awfully kind of you," she said.

"It's my job. Sort of." He frowned.

"Well, while you do that," she said decisively, "I'm going to get an annulment. Then I'll be a free woman." She smiled up at him.

ZEKE FACED an ethical quandary of enormous propor-
tions. He looked at her, then looked even harder inside
himself. He thought about the sense of lightness, even
joy, he had had while she sat at his kitchen table, her
blue eyes taking in his every motion as he performed
a task that was a complete mystery to her—frying eggs.

His inward smile faded as hot, aching tension drove
its way through his body. He thought about the way
she felt in his arms, small, satiny, innocently seductive,
about the way her mouth had felt under his, so giving,
her generosity as large as she was small. He thought
about how much he'd like to taste her sweetness again.
And more than her mouth would be sweet. That little
hollow in her throat, the spot where her breasts began
to swell...

He realized he was looking her over for more sweet
spots. If she were a free woman...

If she were a free woman, she'd be dangerous, a
serious threat to life as he knew it.

"Ah," he said, snapping his gaze back up to the
relative safety of her eyes. "An annulment. That's a
major step. Yes," he continued, "a step that will affect
your whole life. Shouldn't you wait until you've
calmed down before you make a decision that big?"

"I am perfectly calm," Tish assured him. "I'm disturbed by that phone call, certainly. Who wouldn't be?
But I'm quite rational, and I know now I should never
have married Marc."

She had a tic in her left eye, he noticed, and it fluttered at him a few times. Her fingers were in knots he
wasn't sure she'd be able to untie, and while she talked
to her mother she'd folded half the package of paper
napkins he'd used to refill the cow holder into fancy

little shapes. He didn't know how he'd ever get them back between the cow cutouts. But they were cheap, and he had another package.

Yeah, she was *real* calm. What she was was vulnerable. It would be so easy to take advantage of her. And he wasn't going to do that.

"How do you know you'll feel that way in a couple of weeks?" he argued. "You're still afraid of the man. What if I find out you have no reason to be afraid of him?"

"I will be very relieved," she said, "and I will apologize to him profusely for being too inexperienced to realize I didn't love him."

Now she sounded assured, a lot calmer, not so vulnerable. Zeke cleared his throat, then took the plunge. "All right, then." He swallowed hard, giving his conscience one last chance to talk him out of it, but not getting any nudges from it. "I'll take you to see a lawyer."

6

THE SKIES DARKENED and the rain started up again as Zeke hurried Tish the few blocks up Main Street to the old Sykes house. Clarence Wedgelow had practiced law there for thirty-five years, but to Wild River it was still "the old Sykes house" and would probably stay that way until Clarence passed on, when it would suddenly be "the old Wedgelow office."

Clarence was Jasper Wedgelow's first cousin. He would have been a farmer like Jasper if he hadn't had asthma that was particularly aggravated by corn tassels, hay, chicken feathers and cow dander. "Surely do appreciate this rain," he said as he ushered Zeke and Tish into his office. "Settles down the pollen."

"Yes," said Zeke, "It does do that."

"You have allergies?" Tish said with ominous interest.

Zeke saw Clarence's pale-blue, watery eyes light up and knew he couldn't afford the man's hourly rate if they were going to get into the topic of his allergies. "Yes, he does," he said curtly, "and someday he'll tell you all about them. But not now."

"So what can I do for you?" Clarence said, gazing warmly at Tish, cutting a less warm glance at Zeke, then fixing permanently on Tish. "You the amnesiac?"

"Yes and no," said Zeke. He reached into his shirt

pocket, pulled out a folded check and handed it over. "This'll be your retainer, Clarence."

"Now, Sheriff," Clarence said, "you know you don't have to pay me a dime. Up front," he added after a brief, uncomfortable pause.

"But this retainer guarantees me that anything the lady tells you will be kept confidential," Zeke said. "Am I right?"

"Well, sure," Clarence said, "but I'd keep her confidence with or without a retainer." He seemed hurt that Zeke might be suggesting otherwise.

"But this retainer means," Zeke repeated, rising and stepping to the door, "that Mabel won't repeat anything she overhears, either." He flung open the door.

Since it had been nothing more than a good guess on his part, he was gratified to see Mabel Withington, Clarence's first cousin on his mother's side and his secretary from the day he hung out his shingle, standing on the threshold.

"Coffee?" Mabel said brightly.

"No, thanks," Zeke said.

She scurried away. Zeke closed the door and returned to his seat. When Clarence had finished harrumphing, Zeke said, "She doesn't have amnesia."

"I want an annulment," Tish chipped in. "As fast as possible."

"Her life may be in danger," Zeke added. "She's hiding from the man she married."

"Oh, my," said Clarence. He stared at them for a moment, apparently trying to get the news straight in his head. Then, to Zeke's relief, he cut to the chase. "Why don't you get a divorce?"

"Why should I get a divorce from a man I've never really been married to?" Tish argued.

"Because it's easier to get a divorce. Annulment's a shaky thing." Clarence wobbled his hand in the air to illustrate shakiness. "Nobody does it much any more except for religious reasons. You wanting to marry somebody else right off?" He gazed hopefully at Zeke.

"No!" Zeke said when he thought Tish had waited a second too long to answer.

"Well, then, I vote for divorce."

"You don't get a vote," Tish said crossly. "I want an annulment. I want the marriage never to have happened."

"Well, well, well," Clarence said, making a church steeple of his fingers. "We'll see what we can do for you. When you get married in the state of Vermont—"

"Rhode Island," Tish corrected him.

"When you get married in the state of Rhode Island," Clarence sailed smoothly on, "you have to have sufficient grounds for annulment." He paused to give Tish a sharp glance. "Are you of age?"

"Way over," she muttered.

"Were you forced into the marriage?"

"Sort of," she temporized.

"Was the groom diseased or insane?"

"There was something sick about him," Tish said.

"Were you mentally ill at the time of the marriage?"

"If I'd been in my right mind I wouldn't have married a man who wanted to kill me."

"You *allege* he wanted to kill you," Zeke murmured. The glance she shot him would have withered a weaker man.

"Did you get married under the influence of alcohol or drugs?"

Tish narrowed her eyes. "I took an aspirin that morning. And the wedding party had a champagne toast before we—"

"Is the groom already married?" Clarence asked.

"Not that I know of," Tish snapped. "But—"

"Was the marriage ever consummated?" Clarence said abruptly, like he really hated to ask but it seemed he was going to have to.

"No!" she said triumphantly.

"Ah. Now we have grounds," Clarence said.

Zeke wished that somebody besides him could see the flaw in her reasoning, but apparently she didn't, and Clarence couldn't without having more data to go on. "She ran away before the honeymoon," he said.

"Hmmm," Clarence said, frowning.

"Of course I did," Tish declared. "He was trying to—"

"You *allege* he was trying to…" Zeke ventured.

"Will you please shut up?" Tish snapped.

"Look, Tish, give Clarence some time to figure out your options, find out if you have to establish residency in Vermont—"

"I'll handle this," Clarence spoke up. "Miss Tish, give me some time to figure out your options, see if you have to establish residency in Vermont…"

Zeke blinked at him, but Clarence had some original material to add.

"…what the waiting period is, whether the young man has to sign—"

"Waiting period!" Tish exclaimed. "Marc has to sign? You mean I can't—"

"I'll find out," Clarence soothed.

Tish moaned. She'd thought getting an annulment would be easy. "What am I going to do while you're finding out?"

"Catch up on your reading?" Clarence suggested. "Wild River's got a fine little library."

This suggestion made her feel even more despondent. "I *am* caught up on my reading."

"What about doing some volunteer work?"

Tish thought glumly of her many experiences as a proper young socialite doing volunteer service in the community. Somehow it never resulted in meeting actual people from the community, just other proper young socialites. Like Lorraine. "Would you like me to organize a charity ball?" she asked without much interest.

Clarence chuckled. "Not likely. But we do have somebody who needs help."

"Clarence..." Zeke murmured.

Tish gave him a sharp glance. Her lawyer had finally said something interesting, and Zeke seemed to be sending him a warning not to say anymore. "An actual person who needs help?" she said.

"Clarence," Zeke said again. "I don't think—"

"Who?" Tish interrupted.

"Bess Blakeley," Clarence said.

"What a wonderful—" Tish managed to say before Zeke leapt up and started yelling.

"For God's sake, Clarence, she's already sprained an ankle!"

Tish gazed at him in silence. So did Clarence. "Well, I know that, Zeke," Clarence said at last. "And every woman in town stands willing and ready to do something for her, but they've got their lives and their husbands and their kids to keep up with, too. That's why I was suggesting Tish here might help her out."

"I would be thrilled to—" Tish continued before Zeke got control of the conversation again.

"Help her into her grave is what she might do," Zeke snapped. "Ruin her reputation, end her career!"

"How's she going to do that?" Clarence asked.

"Clarence," Zeke said firmly, standing up and motioning to Tish to do the same, "you've been very helpful. Tish and I will discuss this further in private." He backed up two steps and opened the door. "Understand that, Mabel?" he warned. "Don't go calling Bess."

"Why, I wouldn't dream of it, Sheriff," Mabel replied, swishing past him with a file in her hands. "How could you suggest such a thing?"

Zeke stuck his head back through the doorway. "Either of you know anybody Tish could stay with for a few days?"

"Not offhand," Clarence said.

"Me, either," Mabel added.

He didn't like the way they smiled at him.

"I THINK it sounds like a great idea," Tish said. She was wearing yet another pair of his thick wool socks, and they made a slapping sound as she trotted along beside him. "Where are we going?"

"To the bank," Zeke growled, heading them up the steps of a small brick building next to the old Sykes house. "Hey, Violet," he said as he went up to the single teller's window, pulling his savings passbook out of his jacket pocket.

"Why are you so negative about it?"

"You can't cook! Yeah, Violet, I need to transfer..." With a few strokes of the pen he transferred a considerable sum of money from savings to checking.

While he did this Tish gazed at him purposefully, biding her time. As soon as he'd put one fingertip to her elbow and whirled her around and out the door of the bank she piped up.

"I can be her legs."

The rain had gotten serious again. Zeke gave up and opened his oversize umbrella. "What do you mean, her legs?" he said. Rain, mud, runaway heiresses and lawyers with less judgment than queen ants. What was he doing here in Wild River, anyway, trying to drive himself crazy?

"That's what my grandmother called it," Tish explained, ducking her head under the umbrella, which brought all that curly, blond, cotton-candy hair to a position just under his armpit. "She said I could be her legs." Her tone indicated that she'd made herself crystal clear, which from his perspective, she hadn't.

He glanced down to see water droplets clinging to her curls, making little rainbows around her face. "Let's get back to the house," he said. "Then we can talk about your legs." From a spot way up under the umbrella, too far up, he hoped, for her to see him, he flushed hot and red. "I mean, your grandmother," he said, wishing he could sink straight through the mud to China.

SHE COULDN'T TELL what was going through Zeke's mind now as he sat in his swivel chair trying not to swivel. She'd describe his expression as "bemused."

"Almost every day in the summertime I'd go to her

house. It was just two houses down from ours.'' Tish took off the wet wool socks and tucked her feet up into the leather chair, rubbing them to warm them up. ''Her nurse would bring her out to the garden. She'd sit there in her wheelchair and tell me exactly what to do.''

''This would be Grandmother Seldon,'' Zeke said.

''Yes. She died when I was ten. It just broke my heart,'' Tish said, feeling sad all over again. ''I'm so glad she lived long enough for us to get to be friends. She had a gardener, but there were things she'd always preferred to do herself, like deadheading and pruning and picking flowers for the house. Those were the things she taught me to do. Now I realize Bess Blakeley doesn't garden. She makes cookies, and I know I haven't had a whole lot of kitchen experience.''

''One, would be my guess,'' Zeke said. ''Last night.''

He was fascinated by what she was telling him. Was she gaming him, or did she really not realize that this Grandmother Seldon left her fortune to the one family member who really seemed to care about her?

''I can see you've made up your mind,'' she said, sighing in a resigned way. ''So let's just drop the subject. I've already figured out what I can do instead.''

''What?'' Zeke asked as tension began to freeze his spine, one vertebra at a time.

''I'm going to keep house for you,'' she declared. ''I'll learn to clean and wash and iron. And cook. I especially want to learn to cook.''

This idea seemed to infuse her with new energy. She leapt out of the chair and began to flit around his office, straightening a picture here, a book there. ''I love ethnic food, don't you?'' she enthused. ''Especially sushi.

There must be someplace around here to get good fresh fish. Because the one thing I know about sushi is that if you're going to eat fish raw, it has to be really, really—"

Placed against sushi, quiche sounded good. It was at that moment that Zeke threw Bess to the dogs. "Come to think of it," he interrupted the aspiring sushi roller, "Bess might enjoy having somebody around just for the company. I'll give her a call, see what she says."

"You will?" His tormenter whirled away from the picture frame she was dusting with one fingertip and gave him a look of apparent delight. "Well, if you insist, but while you talk to her I'm going to get into a pair of dry socks and get started on the housework."

"You shouldn't be doing housework with that cut on your finger."

"My finger's fine." With a heart-stopping smile, she flew out of the office. Zeke gave himself a ten-count to ask himself if he was doing the right thing. Alarming noises from the kitchen made him stop at seven and dial Bess.

Could he really be acting this selfish?

Yes. "Bess!" he said warmly when she answered. "Hey, I heard about your accident. Gosh, I'm sorry. What can I do for you?"

"How would you like to make and deliver sixteen dozen cookies by five tomorrow afternoon?"

She sounded down in the dumps. Bess lived in a huge old Victorian house which she tried to maintain on the little bit of money her husband left her plus her Social Security, plus taking in roomers, plus the money she earned baking gourmet cookies. They were big sellers at Floyd's General Store and everywhere else within a fifty-mile radius—one great big monster cookie for a dollar, and Bess got to keep fifty cents of it. She netted about a quarter a cookie, Zeke figured.

"I'll get you somebody to deliver," he promised her. "As for making them...well, how do you feel?"

"I feel fine," Bess snapped at him. "I just can't stand up! Think about it, Zeke. I can't reach the kitchen counters, I can't reach the flour canister..."

"Yeah. Well, listen, Bess, why I called..." A million reasons not to go on with the sentence tripped through his head, but doggedly he forged on. Bess's life was already temporarily ruined. He didn't think even Tish could make it any worse. Clarence was right. Every woman in town would like to help Bess, but he—and Bess—had tasted their cookies. Nobody had died from them, but nobody had offered to buy them, either, except at the church jumble sale where they all bought each other's.

"Why I called," he repeated, "is that I've got a woman here—"

Unexpectedly, Bess's voice brightened. "Well, praise the Lord," she said. "At last!"

"That's not what I meant." Every woman in town had tried to marry him off at one time or another. The men just seemed to envy his life-style. "She got stuck in the mud last night, and this and that happened, and well, she's got to stick around for a while, get her truck fixed."

"Oh, the amnesiac!"

Zeke gritted his teeth and did *not* ask how she'd heard. "The very same. She's bored as all get-out and she wondered if she could help you get those cookies made."

"Can she cook?"

"No," Zeke said. "She's...forgotten most of the basics, but she—"

"Tell her about me being her legs."

Zeke had thought he was going to be allowed a private conversation in his own office. The sound of Tish's voice sent him leaping sky-high, inside, anyway. He turned to snarl at her, and saw her wearing his enormous barbecue apron over his plaid shirt and holding a dish towel with a pottery plate clutched inside it. *Protect me, Lord. She's doing my dishes.* But she looked so silly and so cute that he didn't feel like snarling any more. What he felt was helpless.

"She says she can be your legs," he told Bess.

"Oh," Bess said. "Well, I hadn't thought of— You know, Zeke, now that I am thinking about it, maybe she could do just that. Bring her over."

"Now?" said Zeke. He glanced at his watch and couldn't believe it was only one o'clock. He felt as if he'd lived half his life this morning.

"Of course now. I've got cookies to bake." Her mood was swinging way up. That was good, anyway.

"We're on the way," he said. "You two can talk. See if you can work something out."

"Oh, goody," Tish said from the hallway, apparently on her way back to the kitchen to break all his dishes. "A project."

"THE FIRST THING I need to know," Tish said, "is how you make cookies."

Bess looked Tish up and down. Zeke could almost hear her mind ticking off the details of Tish's bizarre appearance—his clothes, his socks, no shoes. "You start by creaming the butter...." Bess began. She wore an uneasy but brave expression that made Zeke feel sorry for her.

"No, what I mean is, you probably put together the raw stuff and then you bake it, right?"

"*After* you shape the *dough* into cookies and put them on a *cookie sheet*," said Bess.

Zeke was happy to see that Bess was going to take Tish's memory loss seriously. She was introducing vocabulary words with a vengeance. He guessed she found amnesia easier to believe than not knowing how to make cookies.

"Like the one the waxed paper blew off," Tish said. "Now, let me think how you're going to do this. Your kitchen table is great for putting things on, but too high for you to work at. Do you have a card table?"

"Well, yes, but..." Curiosity seemed to get the best of her. "Zeke..."

Zeke hurried away to get the card table out of a closet in a room on the second floor. Eventually he located it, dug it out and hurried back. He found the two women in animated conversation.

"That will be perfect for the ingredients, but we need a low table, too," Tish informed him, "so Bess's arms won't get tired while she stirs the dough."

"Girl's got a head on her shoulders," Bess said.

"Yep," Zeke growled. "Just not a whole lot in it." They'd been here five minutes and it was already "Bess" instead of "Mrs. Blakeley." He hurried away again, returning with the coffee table from the parlor. It had been made from a bellows and weighed about three hundred pounds. He'd brought his beeper. He was starting to hope for a major crime to call him back to his real job.

"...light the oven now, so we'll have a nice even heat by the time the first sheets are ready to go in," he heard Bess say.

"I'll light the oven! Then don't anybody turn it off." Bess would soon know why Tish should not be lighting any gas ovens, but she didn't know yet. He was the sheriff. It was his job to protect her. He lit the oven.

"What may I call you?" he heard Bess say. He whirled.

"Oh, call me Tish," Tish said.

"That's what I've been calling her," Zeke interjected in a hurry.

"Tish?" Bess was understandably curious.

"Yes. After a cat I used to have."

"I didn't know you had cats," Tish said.

"Had one when I was a kid," he stated, making faces at her. "Tish was short for...for..."

"Letitia, I bet," Tish supplied, finally getting it, finally realizing she was supposed to be a no-name amnesiac. Her eyes sparkled with mischief. He shot an ice water glance in her direction.

"A delightful name. Suits you," said Bess. She gave Zeke a smug smile. "You can run along now, dear," she told him. "Tish and I have everything under control."

Tish looked smug, too, like a kitten that was being petted. As Zeke returned to his last remaining vehicle, his official stone-colored, uniform-matching sheriff's car that wasn't worth a damn in the mud—four-wheel drive and antilock brakes notwithstanding—he was sorry he'd come up with that particular comparison, a

kitten being petted. Tish reminded him too much of a
kitten, wild, mischievous, but scared, too, of the new
world it had come into. Knowing it was scared was
what made you want to pet it, to snuggle it up against
your chest and feel it start to settle down, start to purr.
That was what he wanted to do to Tish. He wanted to
pull her to his chest and run his hands through that
silky, curly hair, and down her back, feeling all the
little bones beneath her skin. He wanted to feel her
nuzzle his throat and make contented little sounds, kitten sounds, aroused woman sounds....

Zeke slid into the car, and the windows fogged up.

There had to be a town even more peaceable than
Wild River, a town that hadn't had a murder in 1961
or a car wreck in 1989. He'd find it, look it over, see
if they might be wanting their own live-in sheriff.

In a black uniform.

7

"I BAKE every day and deliver on Tuesday, Thursday
and Saturday afternoons," Bess explained to Tish as
she spread out a huge blob of dough on the parchment
paper lining a cookie sheet. "It's a full-time job."

The kitchen was alive with activity and perfumed
with the scent of cookies—cookies baking, cookies
cooling, bowls of creamy dough waiting to be shaped
and put into the oven. Bowls, pans and spatulas, measuring cups filled with plump raisins, chocolate chunks
and chopped nuts covered the surface of every counter
and tabletop.

"There, dear, this pan's ready for the oven. I'm going to take a little break. Would you like a cup of tea?"

"Sounds wonderful," Tish admitted. "I'll make it
as soon as I get that batch in and this batch cooling."
She paused. "How do you make tea? You boil it,
right?" She slid the next pan into the oven, then
mopped perspiration off her forehead before she wres-
tled another enormous, perfect cookie—chocolate, with
chunks of more chocolate and studded with toasted pecans—onto a cooling rack.

What she'd really like to do was stretch out on a
rack herself. Her hair stuck in clumps to her scalp.
She'd long ago traded Zeke's wool shirt—no longer
quite as clean as it had been—for a T-shirt of Bess's

that said Burnham Falls Union High School on the back and Go Lions! on the front above a stamped-on picture of a ferocious mountain cat.

She was hot and sweaty, her back hurt, about twenty-five little burn marks decorated the backs of her hands, and she was having the time of her life.

She turned to Bess and smiled. "All done."

"Light a burner and put some water on to boil. The tea's in the caddy over the sink. It goes in later."

Tish wished Bess didn't use so many foreign words, but otherwise she felt as comfortable with her as she had felt with Grandmother. In a few minutes Bess had steered her toward the teakettle, had taught her to light a burner and had introduced a new meaning for the word *caddy*.

If a few leaves escaped the tea ball Tish had stuffed, Bess didn't seem to mind. "Okay," Tish said briskly when they'd settled down to tea and a warm, melt-in-the-mouth Chocolate Whopper cookie, "we've covered the Wedgelows and the Highcrests. Now tell me about the Rountree family."

It had been a productive afternoon in more ways than one. Family by family she was learning all about the people of Wild River. Bess knew everything about everybody. She even knew what Hortense Wedgelow had always hankered for. Tish had listened and had made herself a promise. She was going to help Hortense get what she hankered for—when the time was right. And Cordelia Wedgelow. And...

"Bess," she said after Bess had covered the real estate holdings of Royal Rountree and the remarkable spelling abilities of young Josh Rountree, "you need a bigger stove."

ZEKE DRAINED the muddy water off his uniforms, added detergent and started running clean, hot water into the washer. Would have been good if the designing women of Wild River had thought about how *stone* would hold up in mud season. He was going through two or three uniforms a day. And next to pointing guns at people, he hated to iron.

Next he logged on to the Justice Data System, typed in "Radcliffe with an *e,* Marc with a *c*" just the way Tish had spelled it out for him and clicked the mouse on Go.

He found a Marc Radcliffe who was in prison for forgery. While Zeke would have liked him to be the man, it wasn't likely he could have courted and married Tish on a weekend good-behavior pass.

When he went on a search for God-fearing, law-abiding Marc Radcliffes, he found six of them in the continental United States plus Alaska and Hawaii. If Tish was right about the man, he'd probably be using a false name, but you had to go with the facts you had on hand. None of the Marc Radcliffes had a Rhode Island address, so he'd start with the one in Boston.

But not yet. The Marc Radcliffe he was looking for probably wouldn't be at home. Before he began ragging total strangers, he'd look for Radcliffe where he was supposed to be, in a honeymoon suite in the Cayman Islands. And he couldn't do that until he'd taught his bicycle safety class at the school.

Twenty minutes later he looked out at the group of kids, some looking earnest, some looking for mischief, who'd gathered in the lunchroom. "We'll learn the rules in here," he told them. "When mud season passes, we'll go out to the parking lot and practice what we've learned. Okay, folks, if you use it right, your bike is—"

A hand shot up. The hand belonged to Josh Rountree whose cat he'd rescued and who'd made him the Holstein napkin holder with the unstable udder. Zeke's big smile slipped a little. "You already have a question, Josh?"

"Yeah. We heard you have an amnesiac at your house."

Zeke felt that old impatience-with-small-town-gossip sour his good mood. "Well, yes, a young woman who—"

"Why'd you tackle her in Dad's vacant lot?"

The room didn't even buzz. The kids had already heard. He felt his face heat up. "We'll talk bikes now and discuss amnesia…some other time. If you ride your bike according to the rules—"

Another hand. Lester's boy. "Sheriff Thorne, Dad said she stole your car and wrecked hers with it."

"She is very upset," Zeke said, frowning repressively. "A person should never drive when he or she is upset. You should never ride your bicycle when you're—"

"Was her wedding dress pretty?" sighed one of the older girls. "Did it have a train? Was she wearing a veil?"

"Your bicycle," Zeke said loudly, "is your best friend, but if you don't follow the rules of bicycle safety…" With an amazingly steady hand, he flipped down the first page of his chart.

"Maybe the children would rather learn about the causes and effects of amnesia today and take up bicycle safety later," the second-grade teacher piped up. "We encourage them to explore their current interests."

Zeke gazed at her vulturous face and wished upon her the worst-behaved class in the history of Wild River.

When he got home a frustrating and misinformative hour later, the phone was ringing. "Don't worry about finding anybody to deliver the cookies," Bess informed him. "Tish and I can handle it on our own. We'll drive the route tomorrow afternoon, right on schedule."

An alarm bell went off in Zeke's befuddled head. "Uh-uh," he said firmly. "Get the lady out in a car and she's bound to—" he caught himself just in time "—get lost," he concluded. *Leave you sitting in your wheelchair in front of the Speedy-Shop in Burnham Falls and run away in your car is what she'll do. If she doesn't wreck it first.*

"Not with me navigating," Bess said decisively. "I'll keep an eye on her so she doesn't forget what she's doing and wander off. Don't you worry. If you want to be helpful, you might come around at one o'clock and help me into the car."

"Now, Bess…"

"You men just hate it when we work things out for ourselves," Bess complained.

What she said had the ring of truth, not that he intended to admit it.

"If you'd loan her a little money, she could buy a few things at Sally's Fads and Fashions in Burnham Falls while we're there," Bess suggested.

Zeke ground his back molars together. "I intend to do that myself," he protested. "First chance I get."

"Don't be silly. You'd have to guess at her size and her color preferences. We've got time. We'll do it."

He had a pretty good idea what Tish would do. Buy out the store, that's what, with his money. In a frustrated gesture, Zeke flung his hands up into the air, forgetting the receiver was in one of them. It boomeranged on the coiled cord and caught him right above the eyebrow. He grabbed at it and put it back to his ear just in time to hear Bess say, "We'll be through here by seven. Come over for supper, why don't you. The church ladies have brought enough food for an entire nursing home."

"Well, thank you, Bess, I'll do that. Um, Bess," he said cautiously, "I was wondering if you wouldn't be safer if Tish stayed over there with you. Not like a guest, just like a friend. There must be things you need help with...."

"Oh, no, Zeke, that's not necessary. She's all settled in with you, and the visiting nurse comes by twice a day to help me dress and whatnot. I'm just fine here alone."

A beaten man, rubbing the spot above his eyebrow, he mumbled something, couldn't remember what, and plopped himself down in front of his computer. Time to download a list of Cayman Islands hotels. His life was going to keep sliding downhill until he got the little lady back where she belonged—into the honeymoon suite with Marc Radcliffe.

It was his only hope of preserving his chosen lifestyle, but every time he thought about Tish and the mysterious Marc in the honeymoon suite, he felt those molars grinding against each other again.

"MEN," Bess said disgustedly as she hung up the phone and wheeled herself back to the bellows table. She began to cream the butter for the peanut butter cookies, slamming the beaters of the handheld mixer against the bowl with a vengeance. "Control freaks, all of them."

"Isn't that the truth?" Tish said, pressing out an oatmeal cookie on a baking sheet. The first day on the job and she'd been promoted to shaping. It was clear she'd been born to bake. "But you talked him into it, right? You and I can handle the deliveries?"

"And do a little shopping," Bess said.

"I'm going to owe him a lot of money before this is over. Before I remember who I am," Tish amended herself.

"I'm sure he can handle it," Bess said comfortably.

"I have the wedding rings. I wonder if I could sell them," Tish said, trying to sound as financially challenged as possible. After all, she was.

"Pawn them," Bess suggested, taking Tish's bait.

"Pawn them. What a clever idea. That way, if I change my mind, I can get them back. Is there a pawnshop in Burnham Falls?" She held her breath.

"Afraid not," Bess said. "Get Zeke to take you to Burlington one day. That's your best bet."

Another plan down the drain. She didn't intend to tell Zeke about the diamonds. Once she had money, she'd run away to investigate Marc on her own.

"So," she said brightly, "all we have left are the peanut butter cookies." A timer pinged. She lifted two pans of oatmeal-raisin cookies out of the oven, dumped them on the granite countertop and scrubbed back a sweaty clump of hair. Afterward it felt more gunky than wet. She examined her hand. Might have been a good idea to wash the cookie dough off first. She shrugged and put two more pans into the oven.

"We'll bake those in the morning while we wrap the Whoppers and the oatmeals. Can you get over here at six?"

"Six?" Tish said weakly, then stiffened her backbone. "Six. Of course."

Bess looked as fresh and perky as she had at the beginning of this cookie marathon. Her pale, unlined skin was flushed with roses from the heat, and her beautiful white hair waved perfectly around her face. Tish was getting the idea that an hour a day with a personal trainer didn't prepare you for hard work the way hard work did.

And romance novels didn't prepare you for the impact of a man like Zeke Thorne. "You've told me about everybody in town except Sheriff Thorne," she said. Turning her back on the sudden twinkle in Bess's light-blue eyes, she began to slide the spatula under an oatmeal cookie. "I'm just curious. He doesn't talk much about himself. What brought him to Wild River?"

"We don't know how we got so lucky," Bess said. "Zeke just moved in and wrapped those big long arms of his around the town, and we knew right away we would never have anything to fear with him on the job."

The image of Zeke's big long arms wrapped around the community served as an uncomfortable reminder of his big long arms wrapped around her. It made Tish feel twitchy and oddly irritable. "You wouldn't have anything to fear anyway, would you?'' she challenged Bess. ''There's no crime in Wild River.''

''That's because Zeke is here,'' Bess said comfortably.

Tish's head swam around for a moment with Bess's circular reasoning. ''But...'' She gave it up, realizing the woman's mind was set. ''Is he your first deputy sheriff?''

''No. The third.''

''Was there any crime while the first two were here?''

''Well, no,'' Bess admitted, ''but Zeke does things they didn't do, like work with the kids, look out for the old folks and the sick ones, patrol the elementary school looking for unsavory characters. He's as fine a young man as I've ever known,'' she declared. ''Except for his one fatal flaw.''

She halted so abruptly that Tish sneaked a look at her. Bess wore a disapproving frown. Whatever Zeke's flaw was, it must be terrible. ''What flaw?'' she whispered, mesmerized.

''We can't get him married,'' Bess said.

Tish collapsed in a relieved heap against the countertop, afraid she might start giggling. ''Oh. That is a problem,'' she said. ''Come to think of it, it's amazing he's been single this long. He's fairly attractive...'' *Fairly* attractive? He was a breathing, walking dream. Tish fanned herself with an empty cookie sheet. ''...and he must be...what? Thirty-three or four?''

''Thirty-three. And believe me, he's not the one being rejected,'' Bess said, looking frustrated. ''When we hired him we hoped we'd get one of the local spinsters married off, but no. The list is as long and hopeless as ever.''

''What's his problem?'' Tish asked, stifling a quick and surprising resentment toward the town matchmakers.

''I'm sure I don't know.'' Bess sniffed. ''Royal Rountree told everybody his oldest girl was as good as engaged if we hired Zeke. A disappointed man, Royal is.''

''Maybe something in his past...'' Tish ventured.

''He did lose his mother when he was just a little boy, but his dad's second wife is a lovely woman. She comes to town now and then, works in Zeke's garden, brings him things for his house. You can tell she's crazy about him and Cole, and I hear she made their dad a happy man again.''

''Cole?'' Tish tipped another cookie onto the rack.

''Zeke's younger brother. Policeman in Boston. Just as good-looking as Zeke and just...as...single.'' She growled the words.

''Two of them—with the same fatal flaw.'' Tish shook her head.

''A terrible waste is what it is.'' Bess fell silent.

The hairs on the back of Tish's neck began to prickle. She turned to see Bess gazing at her. Was her expression thoughtful, reflective—or scheming?

''All we really want,'' Bess said, ''is to see Zeke happy and settled. Settled here in Wild River. Not looking around for a better place.''

''I understand,'' Tish said understandingly.

''I don't suppose you...well, no, you came to us in a wedding dress and wearing the rings, so you must have a husband somewhere. And he'll find you and help you get back your memory and you'll go away with him and…'' Her ramblings came to an abrupt halt. ''Dear, did you set the timer for the two pans of cookies you just put in the oven?''

''No!'' Tish groaned. Not born to bake, born to burn! She flung open the oven door and gripped the rims of the pans, thinking of nothing but the condition of her cookies. Bess had spoken up in time. With two pans of perfect oatmeal raisin cookies plunked down on the countertop, the sensation in her fingertips became her top priority, and she screamed.

''THAT WAS a scrumptious dinner,'' Tish said. ''The cheese-and-pasta thing was real comfort food.'' She leaned back against the car seat and patted her tummy.

Zeke racked his brain for a memory of a cheese-and-pasta thing. ''Macaroni and cheese?'' he asked her.

''That was it. It was a little like *linguine quattro formaggi,* but better. Smooshier.''

''Macaroni uno formaggio,'' Zeke murmured. His gaze drifted away from the road for a second to rest on her hands. Now she had a bandage on her cut finger and a Band-Aid on each fingertip. Good thing he'd arrived just in time to hear that first scream. He didn't like remembering the way his heart rate sped up when he heard it, the way his right foot had tripped over his left one as he raced up Bess's stoop and practically broke down an unlocked door to find out the reason for that scream. Just what any normal, ordinary lawman would do, he reassured himself. Good thing life in Wild River hadn't slowed down his reaction time.

The car wove forward through the muddy, tracked-up street. ''Bess says you were doing great until you burned yourself. Think you'll be able to drive her around tomorrow?''

"Oh, absolutely. I don't know what that was you put on my fingers, but I went straight from agony to...feeling okay.''

He had to admit it. He'd gone straight from feeling okay...to agony. Seeing the pain in her eyes had made him hurt all over. But as he'd rubbed some magic potion of Bess's onto her soft little fingertips, he'd felt a new kind of shock to his system. It had made him put his arm around her, want to comfort her. At that moment he'd have let her mess up his life any way she wanted to. He had to be alert for spells of weakness like that one. They signaled the beginning of the end, for sure.

"Burning myself really made me mad.''

"Mad? Well, sure. Burns hurt.''

"Not because it hurt. Because it was my own fault. Because I can't blame it on lack of experience—I used the pot holders about sixty-eight times. Why not sixty-nine?''

"Yeah. Why not?'' Zeke murmured, wondering where this conversation was going.

"Because for that one moment, I let my attention wander.'' She half turned toward him, her face filled with zeal. "Cooking isn't something you can do while you're filing your fingernails.''

"Guess not.'' She was too crazy to argue with.

"It requires intense concentration. You have to take pleasure in the very act of cooking, not merely a satisfying result. And I think...'' She paused. "I think it must help to care deeply about the person you're cooking for.''

Zeke felt a vague push below the belt, followed by a not-so-vague spiral of heat that rose dizzyingly to his head. He closed his eyes tight and opened them again, but she was still there, and still talking.

"And of course cooking isn't just the *cooking*. It's everything that comes before it, too. The selection of ingredients, the chopping..."

Zeke uttered a quiet "oof" as the car sank into someone else's tire track. Carefully he edged it out and wobbled onward.

"...the mixing, the tasting, the perfect heat—immersing yourself in the experience and living it to the fullest..."

Her voice had taken on an unnervingly breathless quality. Zeke wiped his forehead and peered into the darkness, looking for traps set by the hardening mud.

"...building something beautiful as you cook, building and building—toward that first incredible taste of the thing you've been building toward! Zeke..." She turned fully toward him. Her eyes glittered in the darkness. "I want you to teach me everything you know about reaching that moment, that glorious moment when it all comes to a climax!"

The car slid. He stamped on the brake—and hit the accelerator.

"Zeke! We're skidding! Omigosh, look out for that tree!"

8

ZEKE SURVEYED his most recently totaled car in stony silence. The right front headlight was smashed, the hood rose to a rooflike peak on the right-hand side and the right front fender was crushed against the tire in a way that let you know right off that tire wasn't going to be moving without a little help from Lester.

Tish would probably say it wasn't totaled, that three-quarters of it would drive just fine.

The tree was one of those skinny, fast-growing, short-lived ones. It was looking none too good, either. Even Tish might be willing to admit it was totaled.

There had been that one car wreck in Wild River in 1989, and two in the last twenty-four hours, both involving his cars. That'd sound good when the topic of his performance came up in town council meeting.

Staring at the headlight gave him a minute to address the really important question. Had Tish been talking about cooking? When she said she wanted him to teach her everything—well, it didn't sound like she meant everything about frying the perfect egg. The memory of her words coming at him in the darkness shortened his breath, set his pulse to racing, did a whole lot of other things that made him glad he was wearing his Woolrich zippered coat that went down almost to his knees.

"I don't know how you're going to get the air bags back into those little slots," Tish said, popping out of the passenger side of the car quite unharmed. "Is it something like folding a parachute?"

"You don't fold them," Zeke said. "You buy new ones." Of course he knew she wasn't hurt. That was the first thing he'd checked on. He wasn't completely cold and unfeeling. Lord help him, he'd never felt warmer or more feeling. But he had to douse it right now. That's how she'd ruin his life, by getting him all warm and touchy-feely and then taking over, changing things, complicating his life.

"I'll pay for the new ones," Tish said, looking sincerely concerned. "I feel that this was my fault, that I sort of distracted you and you lost control of the car."

He'd lost control of everything. "I'll add it to your bill," he assured her. "Put this on," he said, keeping his voice gruff, hoping to scare her a little even as he flung his Woolrich zippered coat around her. He hated giving up that coat, and not because there was any chance of him getting cold. "We have to walk the rest of the way home and call Lester."

He stalked away in the direction of his house and Tish scurried along beside him, his coat trailing through the mud. "I've really got to get some shoes, Zeke," she said. "The way things keep happening, I'm going through your wool socks at a pretty rapid rate. I wonder if Cordelia Wedgelow's feet are anywhere close to my size. I was wanting to meet her anyway, talk to her about this acting thing. Bess says Sally's Fads and Fashions doesn't sell shoes. Do they carry shoes or boots at the General Store? If you wouldn't mind loaning me...enough...money to..."

He guessed it was the way he'd stopped walking and started glaring at her that made her trail off like that. He delivered himself of a big, resigned sigh and spun, stalking off in the opposite direction toward the General Store, feeling the breeze as she swirled, sticking with him all the way. "Should've done it first thing this morning," he growled.

"Will the store be open now?"

"I'll open it."

"Floyd!" he shouted a few minutes later, pounding at the wooden frame of the battered screen door. "I know you're in there!"

"How do you know he's in there?" Tish said.

Was there no end to her curiosity? "Because tonight's poker night. The guys play in the back of Floyd's store because their wives won't tolerate poker in their parlors."

The door creaked slowly open and Floyd of Floyd's General Store gazed at Zeke through the screen that still separated them. Floyd was a big man with sandy hair and freckles, but seeing Zeke, he scraped his feet like an overgrown kid. "Aw, Sheriff," Floyd said, "you know we don't have a gambling operation going on in here. We just—"

"What you've got in there are rubber boots," Zeke snapped. "Open up and sell me some."

"Why, sure, Zeke." Now that Floyd wasn't feeling threatened, he couldn't have been nicer. Floyd dearly loved a sale. He unlatched the screen door and bowed them in. "For you, Sheriff, or…"

He'd caught sight of Tish and his eyes were nearly bugging out of his head. "This the amnesiac?" he said.

Zeke had long since given up wondering how news

got around in Wild River. It just did. "The very same. Got anything in small sizes? And I need to use your phone."

He left Floyd practically curtseying while he inquired about Tish's shoe size and style preferences, and dialed Lester.

"Hey, Letha," he said. "Lester there?" His gaze went toward the back room. "Lester's here. I mean, I'm here, too. Well, bye, Letha. I'll just talk to him in person."

Disgustedly Zeke hung up the phone and sought out the poker players, one of whom was Lester, as he should have figured out for himself. He ignored the surprised greetings that came his way from the poker table and pulled Lester over into a corner.

"It's not funny," he told the ungrateful man whose business he'd tripled in twenty-four hours.

"No, sir, Sheriff. Not funny at all."

"Then stop smirking, dammit! Go get my car and take it in. And do a rush job on it, you hear?"

"You could drive the Pathfinder while I'm fixing the Buick."

Lester uttered these words of deliverance in such an offhand way that it took Zeke a minute to realize what he'd said. "I can drive the Pathfinder?" He felt like weeping from joy.

"Didn't get that much damage. Too big. Got her hammered out. Needs a little paint, but that could wait."

"Best news I've had all day," Zeke said. "Okay, Lester, bring me the Pathfinder and tow in the Buick."

"I was thinking I might do it in the morning. I'm winn—"

"Or I could call Letha back and tell her you're not here after all."

He had him nailed. "I'll get right on it," Lester promised, flung on his coat and got right on it.

Zeke went back to the front of the store to watch Tish modeling knee-high rubber boots. While she tried on about a dozen pairs, every member of the poker club came out into the store, clearing his throat, grumbling a little, pretending he was after a beer or a cola or a bag of chips when he was really out there to look Tish over.

Jasper came out first.

"Mr. Wedgelow," Tish exclaimed when it didn't seem like Zeke could get out of making the introduction. "How's Hortense? Is Mr. Highcrest here? Why not? Doesn't he play poker? Oh, my. Now Jasper," she said persuasively, settling right down to first names, "you and Crockett have to make up. Why, you're neighbors! And you started it, Jasper. It's up to you to make things right."

Each of these slices of wisdom was punctuated by mutters from Jasper, so inaudible that Tish might have been talking on the phone. As Zeke glowered at her behind Jasper's back, the Congregational minister two-stepped out.

"Just the advice I've been giving Jasper and Crockett," the minister said gravely. "I feel that higher powers have directed your path toward our community. Tish." He held out his hand for Tish to shake and gazed benevolently at her.

"How the hell do you know her name?" Zeke exploded. "Sorry, Reverend," he mumbled.

"My wife dropped in to check on Mrs. Blakeley

today," the minister said primly. "Tish was there, helping out."

"Irene's your wife?" Tish exclaimed. "What a lovely person. And she makes a wonderful cheese and macaroni."

"Macaroni and cheese," Zeke growled. "Actually, Reverend, I was thinking of calling you and Irene, see if Tish might be able to—"

"They don't have room," Tish whispered to him. "Irene's parents are coming to visit tomorrow."

The elementary school principal sidled up beside the minister and gently nudged him aside. "Well, well, Tish," he said jovially. "Hope you'll be hanging with us for a while. If you have time to volunteer at the school, we can always use another...warm body."

"She's forgotten how to read," Zeke said grimly.

Floyd's dad, who was probably filling in for Crockett Highcrest, crept out on his walker. "Don't suppose you remember how to play chess," he cackled. "Come by the store tomorrow, little lady. I'll jog your memory, nudge those gray cells, tickle your—"

If it had been one of the younger guys, Zeke would've plugged him one, but he couldn't quite bring himself to knock Floyd Senior off his walker. "She's busy tomorrow," he said through his teeth. "I'm busy tomorrow, too. I'm busy now, if you want to know the truth. Can we get on with the shoeing?"

"She's not a horse, Zeke," Floyd said reproachfully. "Well, now, Miss Tish, how're those boots feeling?"

Zeke leaned against the cash register counter, maintaining a threatening sort of silence that guaranteed him no further questions. The poker players retreated to the back of the store. They had looked at him like he was the luckiest so-and-so in town. Maybe one of them would like to teach her about "cooking." He ought to follow them back there and just throw it open to discussion. "Hey, the little lady needs a man to teach her *everything*. Who's game?"

"Sure, I can fit you in some jeans," he was alarmed to hear Floyd saying.

"You're buying clothes tomorrow," he reminded her.

"But I might as well buy jeans tonight," she said with a sweet little smile at Floyd. "I'll look more professional when I'm representing Bess tomorrow."

Professional? Which profession? The reason Zeke had wanted to make the trip to Sally's Fads and Fashions himself was that he'd been planning to bring home a few chin-to-toe dresses in some heavy material like cotton flannel—not jeans. But no, there was Floyd pulling down a teeny-tiny pair of jeans off the shelf and handing them to Tish. Now he was waving her behind the curtain that covered what he called his try-on room and making a point of standing with his back to that curtain, like he wouldn't dream of peeking while she slid into those tight little jeans. Zeke knew he was dying to, though, and kept a keen eye on the man.

"They're perfect," he heard her call out. She trotted out into Floyd's Store with Bess's "Go Lions!" T-shirt knotted up at her little waist, those jeans as snug as a banana peel around her way-too-curvy bottom, and her new rubber boots pulled up to the knees. Her eyes were shining. She was smiling a big, open, happy sort of smile, and all that curly blond hair turned into a halo in the harsh fluorescent light.

For a second he swore his heart wasn't beating.

It started beating again, a little bit too fast, when she began window-shopping in the sock bins and the turtleneck stacks and he began figuring how much money he was already out, even before she decimated Sally's inventory. He was going to be broke if he didn't get her back to the bosom of her family pretty soon. She probably ought to have more than one set of underwear, too.

Sally carried underwear. In her ads in the *Whitewater County Herald,* she called it "lingerie for the trousseau."

Zeke was desperately trying to shimmy away from the thought of Tish in "trousseau" underwear when everything happened at once. Tish finalized her purchases with a black cotton turtleneck sweater and a pair of thick black socks to go under the boots, and Floyd was urging payment of one sort or other. Lester came in and handed him the keys to the Pathfinder.

Tish handed him back his Woolrich coat with mud all over the bottom edge of it, and he hurried her in her new clothes to the car. They headed for home while the poker game, presumably, resumed with everybody having a whole lot more to talk about than they'd had before he opened up the store to a little late business. Specifically, what he and Tish were apt to do *after* they got home.

Speaking only for himself, he was going straight to bed. This had been the longest day of his life.

TISH LOITERED in the mudroom for a moment, examining her all-new persona in the splotchy old mirror that hung there. The evening had ended well, but she was sorry Zeke had wrecked his car and suspected it was something she'd said.

True, she'd gotten wound up in her excitement about learning to cook.

True, she'd realized halfway into the conversation that she was excited about learning all sorts of new things.

She slumped onto a wooden bench and began to pull off her boots. True, she'd started remembering how she felt when Zeke stroked her fingertips with the cool salve, then put his arm around her and cuddled her against him. His hug made her remember his kiss and how different it was from kissing Marc, and on the spot she'd made her next big decision—that Zeke was the very man to teach her about making love.

She might have gotten a little confused at that point, might have sounded as though she were talking about sex instead of cooking.

Because, face it, she had been. And he'd known it! That's how smart he was.

She leapt up, mad at herself all over again. She'd blown her chances with the sheriff, springing it on him the way she had. What she had done was no different from a man saying on his first date with a girl, "Let's go to bed."

All she'd accomplished was to scare him so thoroughly that he'd run into a tree. She should have seduced him the way any decent man would seduce his girl. That's what she'd do now.

Romances formed the bulk of her reading material, so she had a reasonably clear idea of how other women went about it. But where she'd find a red lace teddy she couldn't imagine, or how she could get him to catch her deep in a bubble bath. This situation would call for a lot of improvisation.

It felt good to be working toward a goal. In her sock feet, she tiptoed off in search of her quarry.

She found him in his office, standing over his desk and writing in his notepad. Probably adding on what she owed him for the clothes and the repairs to the sheriff's car and the two new air bags. Perhaps estimating what he'd need to loan her for clothes from Sally's Fads and Fashions.

His eyes had a wild look about them. She decided not to mention that she intended to give Bess a new stove, a big commercial range with two ovens like the one the Seldon cook used in their kitchen at home. No need to worry him about advancing her the money until the stove was delivered.

His head jolted upward as she stepped into the office and curled up in the leather chair, dangling her legs over one arm. "Better add dry cleaning your plaid shirt to that bill," she said to open the conversation.

"What happened to it?"

"Chocolate."

"Oh." He scribbled on the pad.

"Thank you for my new clothes. I'm ever so much more comfortable."

I'm not, Zeke groused to himself. The black turtleneck framed her chin, making her face look like a heart. It clung to her breasts....

He sat down hard in his desk chair. No, he wasn't going to look at her breasts, because in the first place they were way too curvy for somebody that small, and in the second place, he knew how thin that lacy little bra of hers was. If she was even the slightest bit cold, he would see the little points her nipples made when they pushed against the cotton.

He was pretty sure she'd have small, pink nipples.... No, he was *not* going to think about her nipples and that was that. But the turtleneck was an outrage and the jeans were worse. Her hips were the kind that flared out from a small waist. He'd always been a sucker for the kind of shape she had. Her new clothes were driving him crazy, and he'd been forced to pay for them!

The money didn't matter one way or the other. She'd pay him back or she wouldn't—he didn't care. He'd bought clothes for people before, people who came wandering through Wild River not quite knowing what they were looking for and out of money and hope both. But not one of them had ever plopped into a chair right in front of him looking as if they'd like to eat him alive.

He was embarrassed enough to crawl under his desk when he realized he'd groaned. And she didn't even pretend not to notice.

"I bet your muscles are sore from the wreck," she said, all sympathetic-like.

He grabbed at the excuse she'd offered him. "Not too bad. A kink here and there."

She swung her legs off the arm of the chair, did a little snakelike wriggle and slung them right back over the other arm. "Let me give you a massage," she said invitingly. "If I had some baby oil, I could warm it up and rub it into your shoulders and your back and your thighs...."

A hot, hard ache rose up inside him, accompanied by a sense of need so urgent it was scary. "No," he snapped. "I don't need a massage. I don't want a massage. And I don't have any baby oil."

He had a sudden vision of himself bullying his way back into Floyd's store and asking for a bottle of baby oil—and shuddered. "It's time for bed," he said. "Time for me to go to my bed," he added for clarification, "and time for you to go to your bed." He hoped he sounded calm and firm, not desperate, which was how he felt.

She swallowed a little yawn, stretched her arms way up over her head, then damned if she didn't arch her spine back over the other arm of the chair, dangling her arms and her hair almost to the floor. She'd gotten some kind of gunk in her hair, right above her forehead, but instead of looking disgusting, it revealed a dainty little widow's peak he hadn't noticed before. The mounds of her breasts rose alarmingly beneath her turtleneck and if he was looking at them, which he had no intention of doing, every question he might have had about her nipples would have been answered.

"I *am* tired," she said in a sleepy, sultry voice. "I guess I'll take a shower, wash my hair, buff my who-o-ole body with a towel until it simply tingles, then slip into another one of those soft, soft T-shirts of yours and go right off to dreamland."

Just when he thought he couldn't stand it anymore, she added, "Mustn't forget to wash out my panties and bra. It will be so nice to have some new lingerie. Do you suppose Sally carries pretty things? I hope she has a teddy."

Zeke whooshed a sigh of relief. He was back on solid ground at last! "Teddies? You want bears, we've got bears," he said enthusiastically. "Maybe not at Sally's, but there's a teddy bear store in Waitsfield just up the road. You won't have any trouble finding a teddy bear.''

For a moment the gaze she turned on him carried a hint of impatience. Then her face smoothed out into a languid smile and she slowly rose from the chair, swinging her legs at him again, arching out her breasts as she stood. With her hands on her hips, she did a little shoulder roll that pulled her turtleneck tight across her chest.

"Wonderful," she said. "I'm dying for some company in bed. Well, I'm off to the shower. Can you spare another sleeping shirt? Do you have anything in blue?"

"Cole, I need help," Zeke whispered into the receiver. He could hear the shower running in the back of the house. Sweat streamed from his armpits down his sides into his trousers.

"The way you sound," his brother said, "you ought to call 911."

"I am 911." He wiped his forehead on his shirt and blinked his eyes to clear them.

"Oh. Yeah. What's up?"

"I've got a situation here."

"Oh, come on. In Wild River?"

"I'm serious, Cole. It's a situation. I've got a runaway I've got to get back home before it's too late."

"Too late for what?"

"She's after me." Those words were guaranteed to get Cole's attention.

"Hey, careful with that one, Zeke." Cole sounded gratifyingly nervous. "You know the kind of trouble you can get into if a kid accuses you of—"

"She's not a kid."

"Uh-oh."

"She's married."

"Uh-oh." Cole's voice rose a little.

"Says her husband tried to kill her."

"Uh-*oh*."

"Says she wishes she'd never married him. Wants me to teach her about making love. Or eggs over, but I think it's love."

"*Uh-oh.*"

"I could sit here all by myself saying 'uh-oh,'" Zeke snapped, losing patience. "I was hoping you'd say something that would help."

"Sure I can. Find the husband. Send her back. Know where he is? If you don't, I'll pull out all the stops here...."

"I can find him," Zeke lied for the sake of his pride. "Problem is, I don't know if it's the right thing to do. What if he *was* trying to kill her?"

"Of course it's the right thing to do. So he wants to kill her. Arrest him, but send her home! Zeke, friend, brother, fellow stepson, you keep this lady around and before you know it you've got doilies."

Doilies—plus love with a beautiful, warm, willing...

"Doilies," Zeke snarled, remembering that sappy, goofy grin his dad starting wearing after Adele came along and slapped lace doilies down on every chair in the house.

"So what do you want me to do?"

"You just did it," Zeke said. "Thanks."

He hung up on a spate of, "What? Wait a minute. Zeke? Zeke!" coming from the receiver. Cole had said the secret password, *doilies*. It was all he needed to remind him of the way their lives had changed when

Dad married Adele. Now Zeke was his own man again, happy with his choice to remain a bachelor and enjoy a plain, simple, uncomplicated life with time in it for everybody, not just one person.

His control regained, Zeke marched down to his room, stripped and got into bed. Damned if he was going to start wearing pajamas and a robe just because a woman was sleeping next door. Adele had put him and Cole into pajamas and robes and said never to jog down to the bathroom naked again.

Lots of things they couldn't do after Adele moved in, like have Dad's total attention, tackle him in bed to wake him up in the mornings, sneak in to talk things over late at night. Nope, she'd changed everything.

Zeke frowned. Tish had fallen into his life and he couldn't jog down to the bathroom naked now, either. He was afraid to. He was afraid to take a shower—his own house, and he was afraid to get into the shower. It was a crime what that woman had already done to ruin his life.

9

THAT NIGHT Zeke dreamed that his plain white down comforter had climbed up to his throat and tried to smother him. He woke up to find that his comforter had climbed up until it wasn't covering anything but his head and that it was in fact doing a pretty good job of smothering him.

With a growl, he hoisted it like a dumbbell and tossed it down to his feet. Wasn't a dream a psychiatrist could have much fun with. But then he'd never thought of himself as a person with much imagination. Or ambition, Cole said. He wondered what it was he did have, if anything.

He was responsible, punctual...

His eyelids flipped up and his gaze went straight to the clock. Six-ten. He yawned.

Six-ten! Bess had been expecting Tish at six. He leapt out of bed, stuck one foot into the sweatpants that were hanging on the bedpost and hopped his way into the other leg. He had to wake her up, take her to Bess.

When Tish was safely at Bess's house, he'd be a free man, for a few hours anyway. Free to stroll down to the bathroom naked and take a long, hot, invigorating shower. Free to leave the bathroom door open if he wanted to. Free from the fear that she might launch an attack on him—and win.

Free to find Marc Radcliffe, clear the poor guy's name and send Tish running back to him. He hurried across the hall and pounded on her door. "Tish," he yelled. "Time to get up. You're late."

No answer. He pounded a little harder. "Bess is counting on you. Get dressed. I'll start the coffee."

Still no answer. Zeke stood in the hallway chewing his lip. He sure hated to open that door, to see her lying in bed, her hair spread out over the pillow, those pale, pretty lashes lying on her cheeks. Maybe he ought to put on a shirt first.

Why should I put on a shirt? This is my house, I'll dress any way I want to. He opened the door fast, not sneakily. "Tish," he said, using a firm tone and looking anywhere except at the bed, "time to get up."

Then there was nothing left to do but look at the bed. It was empty. He darted back into the hallway. The bathroom door was open and the room was as empty as the guest room. His bare feet splatted on the floorboards as he jogged into the kitchen, the office.

Holding his breath, he went out to the garage, shirtless and barefooted. The Pathfinder was there. But Tish wasn't.

He clumped back into the house, stopping at the kitchen door to clean the mud out from between his toes. She was gone. Gone without a word. Gone without saying please or thank you. Gone without learning how to fry eggs.

So what? Let Marc teach her to fry eggs.

But where the hell was she? Had Marc tracked her

to his house? Kidnapped her? Zeke grabbed for the kitchen phone and dialed Bess.

"Havacookie," Bess answered.

"What?"

"Good morning, Zeke," Bess said warmly. "Tish and I were just sitting here wrapping cookies and talking about a catchier name for my business. How does 'Havacookie' strike you?"

"She's there?" Hearing the weak, relieved sound of his own voice, he revised his list of attributes. *Ir*-responsible, *un*-punctual and *over*-emotional.

"Why, yes," said Bess. "Want to talk to her?"

"No."

"You don't?" Tish's voice crossed the blocks between them.

"No need to," he grated, "now that I know you haven't been kidnapped."

"Of course I haven't been kidnapped. Since I have boots now, I saw no reason for you to wake up early to drive me to Bess's," she said, sounding pleased with her thoughtless behavior. "I walked."

"What did you have for breakfast?"

"A peanut butter cookie."

"You might have left a note," he growled.

"I did."

He examined the kitchen table, the space in front of the coffeepot. "Where?" Probably on his bathroom mirror. In lipstick. Which he'd have to clean off before he could shave.

"On your face. I mean, on the comforter you had over your face."

Zeke breathed out a shuddering "a-h-h" before he

could stop himself. An image of himself, stark naked, spreadeagled, flashed through his head. He opened his mouth, goggled like a fish, felt himself go hot, then cold and sank down into a kitchen chair. It crunched under him, as it always did.

She'd opened his door, she'd walked in and she'd put a note on his face.

No way could she not have seen him. He was too big not to see. His body, that his. His height, his weight...*oh, hell.* One more time, Adele had made her point. Pajamas weren't such a bad idea when you shared a house with unrelated persons of the opposite sex.

Sinking his scratchy face into his shaking hands, he added another attribute to his growing list. He was irresponsible, unpunctual, overemotional—and *dumb.*

There was only one way out. One of the many things Adele had preached to him and Cole was that there were certain things you simply pretended hadn't happened. Getting caught in your natural state had to be one of those things.

He straightened in the chair. The back swayed behind him. *Act casual.* "Sorry," he said, "I didn't see it." He tilted the chair back on two legs. "So I guess you and Bess are..."

The chair splintered beneath him, the legs collapsing, stretchers flying, landing him hard on the kitchen floor. "...making progress with those cookies," he groaned.

"What was that sound?" Tish said, sounding worried.

"What sound?"

He ended the call as fast as he could, before every

curse word he and Cole had learned between them went flying into her little pink shell-like ear. Then he rolled up off the floor and gazed down at the shards of what had once been a good, plain, old-fashioned kitchen chair.

It was an omen. It wasn't just one chair. His whole life was falling apart.

He cooked himself a big breakfast and wondered why the pleasure had gone out of it, why it was so tasteless.

TISH SMILED serenely while Zeke gently lifted Bess into her gray Subaru station wagon, folded the wheelchair and slid it between the front and back seats.

His face was stony. "All set, ladies?" was all he said.

"Wonder what's got Zeke's tail in a twist?" Bess said.

Me, I hope. "He has a lot on his mind," Tish said, backing cautiously into the semiliquid street.

"More than usual, I'm sure," Bess said, "trying to find out who you are."

"Mmm," Tish said. *Some enchanted eve-ning, you may meet a stran-ger, you may hear him yel-ling a-cross a mud-dy road...* She was the one with a lot on her mind—an image of Zeke lying in his bed, manliest of men laid out before her like an unwrapped Christmas present enticing her to drop everything and play games. Plus he didn't need batteries.

The heat bubbling inside her was intense enough to bake a Chocolate Whopper. The word *whopper* made her wriggle against the car seat, and wriggling against the car seat intensified the sensations she couldn't quite shake. Out of the corner of her eye she saw Bess's sharp glance and returned another serene smile.

"At least you're in a good mood," Bess pointed out.

"I enjoy having a job," Tish improvised.

"Work is good. When I lost Mr. Blakeley, I don't know what I would have done if I hadn't had the cookie business on my mind for so many years."

"You didn't start the business until you lost Mr. Blakeley?"

"No." Bess gave her a little sideways woman-to-woman smile. "Calvin always pooh-poohed it. Said I'd never make any money. He was missing the point. I always stop at Floyd's first," she interrupted herself. "No need to haul his cookies all over kingdom come."

Tish pulled up to the general store and tugged a large white box labeled Floyd's out of the back of the wagon. "Won't be a minute," she told Bess, and hurried in.

Floyd stood behind the counter visiting with a young woman, perhaps in her mid-twenties, while he counted out change into her hand. "How's Hortense getting along, Cordelia?" Tish heard him say.

Cordelia Wedgelow, at last! Tish hovered behind the canned vegetables, clutching the big white box and eavesdropping. Cordelia was tall and slim, with long blond hair tied back with a ribbon.

"Oh, Mamma's doing fine," said Cordelia. Her voice was lovely, Tish noted, soft, but every word carried across the store. "Still standing up to quilt, of course, and still mad at Papa, and he's still siding with Seth, and Seth's still mad at me, and the whole thing's my fault."

"Now, Cordelia—" Floyd began.

"Hi," Tish burst out, suddenly covering the distance to the counter. She put down the box and gazed earnestly at Cordelia. "You have a right to realize your hopes and dreams," she said.

Two pairs of glazed blue eyes stared at her. She had clearly violated every rule of Vermont etiquette by saying something so personal. Well, she had sort of jumped the gun, but Bess was waiting, and they had a schedule to meet, and she was so, so interested in the lives of the Wedgelow women.

Cordelia's eyes suddenly came to life. "Oh," she said, "you're the amnesiac."

"Tish," Floyd said with the smugness of the first-to-know.

"Tish. Wow," Cordelia continued, "we all feel so sorry about what happened to you. It must be terrible to have forgotten even the simplest things."

Like my manners. "It is," Tish said fervently. "But I'm learning. Relearning."

"Is there anything I can help you with?" Cordelia asked.

It looked like genuine concern on her face, and Tish's heart went out to her. "Well, yes. Did your high school stage experience teach you anything about hair and makeup?"

Cordelia glowed. Outside the general store, a horn honked.

"Omigosh," Tish said, "that's Bess." She shoved the box into Floyd's hands and spun.

"Don't you want me to pay for these?" Floyd asked.

"Well, of course," Tish said, spinning back toward him.

Time passed as Floyd wrote out a check. Cordelia continued to smile shyly at her. She had a beautiful, radiant smile. She was a lovely woman. She deserved to be on the stage! And by golly, Tish would put her there! "Could we get together late this afternoon?" she whispered to Cordelia.

"After the chickens or after the cows?" Cordelia said.

Tish gazed at her, mystified.

"About four, after I feed the chickens, or about six, after we milk the cows," Cordelia said. Her smile widened.

"After the cows would be better for me," Tish said. "Bess and I have a lot to do this afternoon. Come to her house at six." Neither Zeke nor Cordelia's husband Seth needed to hear what she wanted to discuss with Cordelia.

The horn honked again. Twice. Tish pocketed Floyd's check, gave Cordelia a last conspiratorial glance and ran to the car.

"Sorry," she told Bess, who appeared to be wavering between worry and exasperation. "I got caught up in planning a career on the stage for Cordelia."

"What?" Bess exclaimed as Tish sped off in the wrong direction.

HE COULD ONLY GUESS at the mischief Tish and Bess had made during the day, Zeke thought glumly. Doggedly he turned his attention back to the list of Cayman

Islands resort hotels and dialed the last number. He got the same answer he'd gotten from all the other hotels.

No one had a Mr. and Mrs. Marc Radcliffe registered. No one had a record of a reservation made by a Marc Radcliffe. Zeke was starting to entertain the idea that there was no Marc Radcliffe.

But there was. There were six of them. Now it was time to start ragging total strangers. And it might be a good idea to call in some bigger guns—the Rhode Island State Police, the Newport Police Department and the Newport County Sheriff's Office. And Cole. Tish had leased an apartment in Boston for herself and Marc, so the Boston Police Department had a little interest in the case, too. With all that computer power behind him, he'd make quick work of this business and get back to life as it ought to be lived.

Which included his self-defense class at the Senior Center, where he was due right now.

After that, it wouldn't be long before Tish would be home. At that thought, something exploded inside him, sending insidious flashes of heat to parts of his body he'd been giving stern lectures to all day.

A few minutes later he faced a group of three over-the-hill dynamos, Hattie Highcrest and Anabel Wedgelow, who appeared not to be speaking, and Nell Rountree.

"Anybody tries to take my purse dies," Hattie crackled, raising one quavery white hand and bringing it down through the air with a vicious slash.

"Her son's more likely to take her purse than anybody I can think of in Wild River," Anabel said with a sneer.

"*Her* boy's too busy ripping off his own wife's purse to bother with mine, I hear," Hattie retorted.

"Why, you..." Two pairs of watery eyes flashed and two sets of claws reached out.

"What?" Nell quavered. "Crockett's carrying a purse now? Well, doesn't surprise me in these troubled times."

The claws and the watery gazes turned as one upon Nell.

"Ladies, ladies," Zeke said soothingly. "Our neighbors are not the enemy. But outsiders come through town, and you never know," he pontificated. "You just never know. So this afternoon we're going to practice getting your whistles in your mouths and blowing, even if your attacker is attempting to restrain you. Everybody have her whistle?"

"Everything's different today," Nell rattled on as though he hadn't spoken. "Time was a man could choose to be a bachelor without everybody wondering if he, well, you know what I mean. But now..."

Zeke was startled to find three pairs of watery, accusing eyes looking straight at him. "It's important for your whistle to be on a fairly short chain," he persevered. "That way you can duck your chin, like this...."

"We hear the amnesiac's a nice-looking woman," Hattie said. Her voice was hard. No crackle.

"Tish," said Anabel with the smugness of the first-to-know.

"Don't have to tell me her name," Hattie snapped. "I already knew it. And a kind woman, too," she continued, the hard tone softening unexpectedly. "Why, she's saved Bess's career, helping her out like this."

"Bess has a career?" Nell said. "I thought she made cookies."

For a moment it was two against one again. Zeke was almost relieved. He began thinking of other ways, less dangerous topics, with which he could pit them against each other instead of against him.

"But what you don't know," Anabel said even more smugly, "is that she asked my granddaughter Cordelia to help her fix up a little, make her look nicer. Cordelia's meeting her at Bess's house after milking time. Wonder why she's wanting to look nicer."

Zeke's heart was thudding in his chest, so he thinned out his mouth to compensate for it. What was Tish up to now?

"Duck your head like this and grab for that whistle with your mouth. Okay, Hattie, you pull Anabel's hands behind her back and hold tight, and Anabel, you reach for your—"

"Just because she was wearing a wedding dress doesn't mean she actually got married," Hattie said to Anabel instead of grabbing hold of Anabel's hands.

He'd thought she'd love to pin Anabel's hands behind her back, but no, the Three Witches had unfortunately united again and were stirring the pot.

"Heard we had an amnesiac in town," Nell whispered. "You don't think she's here to steal our purses, do you?"

"Yes!" Zeke said too loudly. They turned toward him, obviously surprised by his unusual vehemence. "I mean," he floundered, "like I said, you never know. Now, back to your whistles…"

He'd forgotten to ask if any of them might have a spare room Tish could stay in.

"CORDELIA, you have such talent."

Tish admired herself in Bess's dressing table mirror. Cordelia had insisted on a soft, natural look, and had pulled Tish's hair up in a casual twist with lots of curls hanging down around her face. She'd produced light-brown pencils and mascaras from a box and applied them to Tish's blond brows and lashes, and had finished her off with pale-pink lip gloss.

"You look absolutely lovely," Bess declared. "Your hair, your makeup, your stylish new outfit… Zeke's going to—" She stopped right in the middle of her sentence. "—going to be glad you and Cordelia are making friends."

Cordelia blushed a little. "It was fun," she said, and began to gather up her tools.

"You must have a cup of tea before you go," Bess said, lifting an eyebrow at Tish. "Tish already put the kettle on. I can do the rest."

Tish responded by lifting her own eyebrows. "Thank you, Bess. Cordelia and I will sit in the parlor and chat."

Bess wheeled away, and Tish wasted no time in getting to the heart of the matter. "I hear you want to leave Seth and go to New York to be an actress," she said.

Cordelia only looked shocked for a second or two. She must be getting used to having her life pried into.

"Yes and no," Cordelia sighed. "I don't really want to leave Seth. I love him to pieces, but—"

"Just as I thought," Tish said, nodding. "All you want is a chance to be on the stage."

Cordelia nodded, looking miserable.

"But Seth can only imagine that acting would take you away from him," Tish persisted.

Another nod.

"And I think your mother has the same problem with your father," Tish said.

"Isn't it funny?" Cordelia said. "What Mamma wanted to do with her life was design clothes, but Papa wouldn't let her, told her she'd never make any money out of it and he needed her to help out on the farm."

A gasp from the hallway outside the parlor informed Tish that Bess hadn't been able to resist listening in. She hid her smile as she said, "Well. I've figured out a way for you and Hortense both to follow your stars."

"How?" Cordelia said, sounding more nervous than excited.

"While Bess and I were in Burnham Falls today," Tish said, "we asked Sally—you know, Fads and Fashions—about opportunities in the area for people like you and Hortense, and guess what we found out."

HE'D MADE A PLAN not to look at Tish at all when she came home from Bess's, just sit her down to a bowl of chili and go back to his office to call the Marc Radcliffes of the world. But he could feel something different about her the minute she breezed in through the door of the office like she owned the place, and the first thing his eyes lit on was her skirt.

"Do you like it?" she said, twirling. "It's not as short as a lot of women wear their skirts, but I figured I ought to dress conservatively in Wild River."

If that skirt was conservative, he'd be dangerous around any woman wearing an unconservative one. It was black, looked like denim, and fit her tightly from her waist down to...he had to admit it cleared the panty line, but not by much. He was grateful for the stockings she wore with it, even if they weren't plain and thick the way stockings ought to be. They had a diamond pattern that kept him looking at them longer than he needed to, following them down into her high-topped boots.

He whipped his gaze up to the top half of her. Thankfully it was covered by a nice white shirt that buttoned up the front and came down to her elbows and slid on past her waist to hang out over the skirt.

Don't look at the skirt.

"See how practical this is?" Tish said happily. He watched in horror as she unbuttoned the shirt he'd been so relieved to see and whipped it off to reveal a little white top that would have crushed her ribs if it had been any tighter. It looked like a man's undershirt, but whiter, and prettier, and face it, no man ever looked that way in his undershirt.

Real men don't swoon.

Zeke flexed his mental muscles and attempted to quash his baser reactions. "You intend to go out in public like that?" he queried, frowning at her.

"Not unless the weather warms up. But the tank top is all I need when I'm...cooking," she explained. "I bought three of them, white, baby-blue and a really tarty red one.'' She smiled at him. ''Sally helped me stretch my clothing dollar to the max. Now I have jeans and a skirt, and the blouse goes with both, and the tank tops and the turtleneck go with both. Wasn't that good wardrobe planning? I'm all set, and I didn't spend a cent.''

He realized he'd forgotten to give her any money. ''How'd you manage that?'' he asked her. *Probably held up the Speedy-Shop.*

''No problem. Sally opened a charge account for me. No payments until May, and surely I'll have my own money by then.''

Uh-huh. Sure.

''I borrowed a jacket this morning,'' she said. ''A blue windbreaker you had hanging in the mudroom.'' Her eyes narrowed and her tone cooled perceptibly. ''It's a small size.''

He returned her glinty stare. The windbreaker belonged to Adele. She kept it here because she liked to drive down from St. Johnsbury in the spring and turn his perfectly fine yard into a garden that had to be weeded and watered. It was her ''mess up Zeke's life'' jacket. She usually dragged his father along so she'd have somebody to boss around and do the messiest parts.

Tish actually sounded jealous of the owner of the windbreaker. Okay, he'd let her wonder who it was. Served her right. ''You're welcome to use it for the short time you're going to be here,'' he said gruffly. ''What happened to your hair?''

''Cordelia fixed it.'' Her sunny mood returned. ''Oh, Zeke, wait'll I tell you what happened. Bess and I talked to the community theater director in Burnham Falls. He teaches an acting class on Thursday nights. He's dying for more students, and of course he puts them right into the theater productions. Isn't that wonderful?''

"Well, it's interesting, but—''

"Here's where Hortense comes in. She's always wanted a career in clothing design. So I talked to Sally, and she was just thrilled at the thought of having original designs to sell. Cordelia and Hortense can drive up to Burnham Falls together on Thursday evenings after the cows and neither of their husbands will get jealous—''

She paused and took a deep breath. Zeke took one, too, just in case he needed air when she got to the end of this. He needed it now, actually. While she talked nonsense, the little curls bounced around her face and her eyelashes fluttered up and down at him. He was getting a fine, warm feeling deep down inside, which made him remember that nothing about his body was a mystery to her any more, while he could only guess at what lay beneath her tank top and tight little skirt.

What would have happened if he'd woke up just as she walked in? He was rock-hard inside his uniform trousers. He sure couldn't make chili until he'd calmed down.

"...and a seven-week acting class term only costs $325!''

Now he was calm. "Cordelia can't afford it,'' he said flatly.

"I know. I told her I'd pay for it.''

"You don't have any money.'' He glowered at her.

"Oh, but I do! If you'll just loan me $325 for the time being, the first class of the term is next Thursday night." She smiled another sunny smile, then shoved his notepad across the desk at him. "Add it to my bill."

When she leaned over to reach across the desk, her breasts peeked at him over the low neck of the tank top, edged by the lace of her original trousseau bra. They looked round and firm, two small handfuls, and the skin looked even softer and smoother than the skin on her bare shoulders. He wished he could remember what had happened before to calm him down.

Money, that was it. But now not even the thought of his impending bankruptcy could calm him down. His fingers jerked at the pen as he added $325 to the lengthening list on the notepad. They shook as he made himself a note to transfer more money from savings to checking.

"Do we have any dinner plans?" she asked him next, apparently unaware of the turbulence building inside him to a national-disaster-level storm. "Bess wanted to give me dinner, but I told her I intended to start cooking for you."

"Don't need to," he croaked. "We're having chili."

"Oh, chili. That sounds wonderful. Show me how to make it." She smiled fetchingly.

"I'll do it. Won't take long. It's a mix." Something was wrong with his voice. Something was wrong with his legs. Something was wrong with his mind. There was nothing wrong, unfortunately, with his sex drive. He hauled himself up, suggesting to his knees that they show a little of the spunk other parts of him did, and rolled up his shirtsleeves.

Tish trotted along behind him as he made for the kitchen. Once there, she opened a bottom cupboard and rattled his pots and pans.

"No, really, I can—"

"I have to learn, Zeke." From her position on the floor, she looked up at him with pleading eyes. Her skirt rode way, way up, and any man crass enough to look could have seen way, way down inside her tank top. "Come on. Just tell me which pan."

He firmed up his jaw. How much trouble could he get into if he showed her how to brown beef, dump in the packet of Texas Pete's Chili Mix and add water. "Get out that big pan in the back," he instructed her, reading the packet like it was the Bible just to keep his eyes off her.

Beef. He took a big package of ground chuck out of the refrigerator and dumped it in the pan as soon as she'd straightened up and put the pan on the burner.

Onions. He leaned down to open the crisper drawer, then thought about the likelihood of Tish's surviving an onion-chopping experience. It wouldn't hurt him to eat chili without onions as long as it only happened once and he wasn't looking at a lifetime of chili without onions. "Turn on the stove—no! I'll turn on the stove."

"Don't be silly," Tish said. "Bess taught me how to light a gas stove."

The smell of gas filled the kitchen. "Turn it off," Zeke gargled. "Bess's burners have automatic pilots.

Here you light them with a match." He handed her the big matchbox. "But you ought to wait a minute for—"

With an explosive whoosh the burner lit. "—for the fumes to die down," he finished.

"I'll remember next time," said Tish, unfazed. The pan began to sizzle at once. "What next?"

He handed her a wooden spoon. "Start moving the meat around the pan."

"Like this?"

"No, like this. Break up the meat." He moved up behind her and stretched his arm out alongside hers. His hand covered hers, added pressure as he took control of the wooden spoon. When she pushed back against him, he felt the tickle of her hair on his chin, felt his body responding to the sensation of cradling her—and wished to high heaven they had a place to eat out in Wild River.

10

THIS WAS WHERE she'd longed to be from the moment he'd hugged her close on the muddy road the night they met. It was what had filled her thoughts from the first touch of his lips. It was all she'd been able to think about since she tiptoed into his room this morning and found him lying there, so strong and powerful, invulnerable even in sleep. She'd looked away at once, but the image was tattooed on her brain.

She leaned into the firmness of his chest, the tautness of his stomach, tilted her head back and closed her eyes. The dark hair on his arms brushed against her skin, awakening every nerve end to feverish awareness. His arousal pressed against her. He wanted her. She wanted him.

She knew it was too soon, too sudden. She was still a married woman—married, but unloved, unsatisfied. Marc could never satisfy her. She knew that for a certainty, just as she knew she'd never loved him.

But now, surrounded by the masculinity of Zeke, she felt the ache of unbearable longing, originating where his promise of pleasure pushed against her and spreading into the depths of her tummy. She felt heavy, as though the bottom might drop out of her, but lightheaded, too, dizzied by desire.

She rejoiced in the knowledge that he wanted more, that he couldn't resist touching her. His free hand went to her shoulder, caressing it with a maddening, circling stroke before it slid down her arm with a featherlight touch to entwine with her fingers. His breath cooled her forehead as his mouth began a slow slide to her temple, her cheekbone and the hollow beneath. Her lips parted, and she whimpered with the pure deliciousness of his touch. His breath quickened.

The hard, urgent beat of his heart told her what he wanted. The delicacy of his touch told her of his uncertainty, how he struggled to stop himself, hold himself back. His mouth almost touched the corner of hers. It was pure animal instinct that made her reach for him, turn to him, seek the heat of his kiss.

"Stir."

The word, spoken so raspingly, was a jarring note.

"I'm stirring." She could barely manage the two words.

"I mean stir the beef."

"I am stirring the beef."

"No, you're not, you're playing in it. Like a kid in a sandpi—"

Their lips connected, hard at first, out of sheer relief from deprivation, then more softly, moving together as he bent from his great height to reach her, to tangle his tongue with hers, to spin her toward him so that all the parts of them that belonged together were together, close and warm, reaching, demanding, tempting, promising. She flung her arms around his shoulders, giving everything she had to give, asking even more.

A distant *splat* awoke her from her dream of know-

ing passion at long last. As they stood so close together, only their soft panting sounds broke the silence
of the kitchen. Drifting through some other world she
wished they could move to and dwell in forever, she
watched a large glob of gray-brown ground beef fall
from the ceiling onto the bridge of Zeke's nose.

He blinked hard, closed his eyes and groped blindly
for the roll of paper towels. The ground beef in the pan
made a new sound, a snap, crackle and pop rather than
a soft sizzle. She stared at the wooden spoon in her
hand, the spoon that had been in her hand when he
swirled her toward him.

Zeke lay down a wad of paper towels, grabbed the
spoon and began to scrape the bottom of the pot. He
flung in the packet of mix, sloshed in some water, and
voilà, ten minutes later, dinner was ready.

Tish was ready for much more than dinner. But the
night wasn't over yet.

ZEKE THOUGHT the evening would never end, but at
last it came to a logical stopping place. He showered
noisily, went to his room and closed the door with a
bang he was sure would make a statement. His bedroom needed a lock, and the county ought to pay for
it. He'd bring it up by e-mail tomorrow with the Whitewater County Sheriff's Office. A self-defense measure.

He could hear the shower running. It made him feel
so insecure that he decided to sleep in a clean pair of
briefs. What had possessed him to curl himself around
her and nibble on her sweet, soft skin? They were
cooking chili, for God's sake. Hardly an aphrodisiac.

But *she* was an aphrodisiac.

The shower stopped running. Now she'd be drying herself, patting her body with one of his towels, her firm little breasts, her curvy bottom. Zeke groaned. He wanted to march into the bathroom and pull her into his arms.

Instead, he was going to go to sleep. Determinedly he turned off his bedside lamp and buried his face in his pillow.

He lay there for almost a minute, then did a full roll, ending up in the same position. He stayed put for another minute, at which time he flung himself onto his back and pulled the pillow over his head.

He felt hot, prickly, restless. He flung back the comforter, then pulled it over himself again in a hurry. He'd wake up off and on all night and check on it, make sure it hid all the important parts of him.

Now didn't that just say it all? A week ago he'd have said his brain was the most important part of him. He growled deep in his throat.

His door softly opened.

He closed his eyes and held his breath. Then he realized he wanted to feign sleep, not death, and let himself breathe, deep and slow. *I am a soundly sleeping man. Don't wake me up.*

"Zeke?"

He took in a big snortling breath and let it out in a gurgling snore. Instead of putting her off, it seemed to encourage her. Next thing he knew, he felt the bed sag as she sat down beside him.

She was staring at him. He could feel it. With a disgusting show of snorts and honks, he turned over on his side, away from her.

"Good, you're awake," she said. "Zeke, I've been thinking about you."

He opened one eye, then the other. "Wha, wha?" he said drowsily.

"About why you're afraid of women."

That was too much. He rolled over. "I am not afraid of women." He was just afraid of her. She was resting on her knees, her entire little body tucked up beside him so she could lean over him and tell him something ridiculous like he was afraid of women. He loved women. In their place.

And their place was not in his bed uninvited with their curly blond hair flying all around their faces, their blue eyes gleaming in the darkness and wearing...

Oh, my God, what is she wearing?

He squinted. It was a one-piece bit of nothing with straps over the shoulders and no longer than a pair of panties. In the ray of light that came in from the hallway, he saw that it was red.

He sat bolt upright, clutching his comforter all the way up to his shoulders. "What are you doing in here? And what is that...garment...you have on?"

"This?" she said, daintily stroking one strap. "It's a teddy."

"A teddy?"

"Like the bear, but different."

"Well, put something on over it," Zeke said crossly.

"I didn't think I should spend your money on unnecessary items like robes," Tish said sweetly. She wriggled her knees a little closer into the curve of his body.

Every inch of him reacted to that wriggle. He

clutched the comforter. "I'm very tired," he said, aware that his remark didn't fit any too well into the conversation. "I want you to take yourself and your teddy back to your own room and let me go back to sleep."

"See, you're afraid of me," she said sadly.

"I am not...."

"Yes, you are. You're afraid some woman is going to chase you and catch you. And I say, what's wrong with that? Why are you so stubborn about getting married?"

He sat up a little straighter. "Who says I'm stubborn about getting married?"

"Everybody," Tish told him. "The whole town talks of nothing else."

"What if I just don't want to get married?"

"We women can't accept that as a reason."

Zeke stared at her, exasperated. "Well, it's not your call. It's mine. And I choose to—"

"But why? The inquiring feminine minds of Wild River want to know."

The bizarre nature of the moment was not lost on Zeke. He, nearly naked, and a beautiful woman, nearly naked, were having a therapy session in his bed in the dark, exploring the reasons he wasn't married to somebody else. But then Tish seemed to specialize in bizarre moments. Fortunately, he was a strong man, a man with willpower. Any other man would have jumped her the minute she appeared in his bed. But not him. Not Sheriff Zeke. He thought over the question and decided to deliver a straight answer.

"I like the bachelor life. I like the freedom to live

the way I want to, with plain, simple furniture and plain, simple food. You get married and the standards change.''

''Really.'' She seemed as interested by his answer as she was by everything else. He was almost able to ignore the enchanting shape of her body in the red teddy, the gleam of her blue eyes, by turning this into a serious conversation. Except for the fact that interest made her wriggle even closer. Her face wasn't a foot from his now, and her knees nudged his hipbones. Any closer and she'd be on top of him.

''Really. At least it did when Dad remarried. Everything got more...more formal. We'd been doing fine without any help. Adele changed everything.''

''I have to tell you, Zeke, I'm relieved,'' Tish said, but she didn't just say it, she sort of breathed it at him, her face so close to his that he could almost taste the mintiness of her mouth. ''I thought you were afraid of sex.''

''Well, I'm not,'' he snapped. ''I'm afraid of doilies.''

She drew back an inch, for which he was grateful. ''That's a peculiar thing to be afraid of,'' she said slowly, but then she brightened. ''As far as I'm concerned, though, I'm glad you're afraid of doilies. I mean, I'm glad you're not married.''

Deep dread and suspicion rose up through the heat inside him. ''Good, we're agreed,'' he said briskly. ''Now if you would please go back to your—''

''Because if you were married, I wouldn't say this...''

''Don't!''

"...but since you're not, I can tell you how insecure I'm feeling right now, because of Marc, you know, and..." She hitched herself closer.

"I'll find you a therapist." Hang the cost!

"...and disappointed, because I, well, to be very frank..."

"Please don't be frank. Just go back to your—"

"...was ripe for the taking, so to speak. In fact, I've had plenty of time to think about this, and I know I just wanted to be married and Marc was the first person my family had ever approved. I should have realized he wasn't interested in me. Oh, Zeke, I want to know what it's like to make love, I want that so much. But I wonder if any man will ever want me, just me."

A thin ray of moonlight slanted through the window and landed on her face just long enough to show Zeke the big, wet tear sliding down it. As he watched, hypnotized by that tear, she sank her head to his chest.

She was like a cat the way she'd sneaked forward, hardly seeming to move, yet coming ever closer and at last landing on his chest, right where she wanted to be. A cat. A kitten. A kitten needing to be petted.

His arms rose of their own accord, slid around her shoulders. His hand trailed through her hair. The silky strokes as it slipped between his fingers were maddening, teasing, made him think crazy thoughts, do crazy things.

Like say to her, "A man would have to be dead not to want you."

"You're not dead."

She was right. He'd never felt more alive.

Her voice was muffled. "You could teach me about

making love, I just know you could, and I want you to. I want to stop feeling disappointed and insecure and fatalistic about my hopes of ever experiencing—this.''

First he realized that her voice wasn't muffled any more, then he felt her soft, sweet breath on his face. Before he could assemble his forces of resistance, her mouth covered his and her slim, loose-jointed little body pressed against as much of him as she could cover.

Dear God, he was lost. Her lips were as rich, lush and sweet as he remembered from their first kiss. Her body sought his and he gave it unthinkingly, fitting her to himself and giving in to the intense ache of longing he'd been fighting, denying. They rocked together, their mouths discovering, their bodies blending. He relished the soft kitten sounds she made, the way her mouth opened so generously to him.

With his fingertips he traced a path across the invisible little thing she called a teddy—down the back and over soft mounds and valleys to her thighs. His heart raced in anticipation of the moment he would let his hand stray up and beneath the silky red fabric. She shivered under his touch. He stroked her harder, raking her skin, felt her wild response in her kiss, in the touch of her hands on his shoulders, his chest.

Only the comforter kept them apart, and he realized he was starting to work it down with his feet, clear it away, leaving nothing between them but the heat of desire that, more and more, was the only thing on earth that mattered. The covers tangled around them, gripping him, strangling him...

Strangling...

Without warning, Zeke had a vision of his all-white down coverlet covered in chintz. The image didn't lessen his desire, but it did wake up his brain. He lifted his hands slowly from the small, curving mounds of her buttocks. As he slipped out from under her he felt her cling to him and experienced a deep regret about the step he was taking. Edging himself to the side of the bed, he rolled out.

He didn't expect her to roll right out with him, but she did, and before he could stop her, she was in his arms again, nuzzling his neck because she wasn't tall enough to reach his mouth and dimming all the resolve that had just been building inside him.

"Of course," she murmured. "Protection. We should use... Do you have..."

He did, but he didn't dare think about it, much less admit it. "We can't do this," he muttered into her hair. His hands slid down her back, feeling the silkiness of the teddy over even silkier skin. "You're still a married woman, your future is still unresolved, I'm responsible for you, I can't..."

"Don't be silly," she said, an edge of aggravation appearing in the purr of her voice. "We can, we will, we almost already did." Her hands slid from his back down his sides, her thumbs brushing his hardened nipples, moving down, down...

With an animal-like groan, he put both hands at her waistline, picked her up and held her at arm's length as easily as if she were a rag doll. "Behave yourself, Tish," he said, giving her a little shake, hating the hoarseness of desire that thickened his voice. "I'm about out of willpower."

"Then why won't you just give in and make love with me?" she reasoned with him, struggling in his grasp in a way that just made everything cloudier in his mind. "We're two consenting adults, after all."

"I'm not consenting to anything!"

She stopped struggling. He let her feet down to the floor, but he didn't let go. She was too...dangerous. "You want to," she said, narrowing her eyes. "I can tell you want to. I can *see* you want to. You're just being..."

"Respectful," Zeke interrupted her. "You don't know what you want. You're a babe in the woods. You're inexperienced. You're—"

She folded her arms across her chest. "I," she said in a cold, clear voice, "have had about all the respect I can handle." And with a determination he wasn't sure he could win against, she reached for him again.

"Zeke, open up!"

The familiar voice, the hard thuds against the front door, were enough to bring Zeke fully back into the real world. He made a leap in one direction for his uniform trousers, in the other direction toward the bed, which he restored to its normal middle-of-the-night state. While he dashed around he was aware of Tish dashing around beside him, babbling unhappily. "What was that? Who's here? What are you doing? Don't go to the door. Zeke! Talk to me!"

"Zeke, wake up! Open the door." *Thump, thump, thump.*

Zeke paused in mid-pillow-fluffing and gave Tish a considered look. She was so beautiful, so warm, her mouth so compelling, her small, perfect body nearly irresistible. "That's my brother Cole, come to rescue me, is my guess," he said. "And in the nick of time, I'd say."

He sighed, then moved by something he didn't understand, he picked her up in his arms, carried her across the hall and deposited her in her bed. "And stay there," he said. Her eyes still gazed at him wildly as he closed her door with a firm click and went forth to save the entire front of his house from Cole's fist.

11

"I HOPE I've interrupted something."

Amazing how calm Cole got as soon as he was in the house. "Only my sleep," Zeke growled. "Nothing important."

"Mmm," said Cole, looking him over from head to toe in a way Zeke found extremely annoying.

So he did the same thing to Cole. Cole was two years younger than Zeke and they could have been twins, except that if Cole had his hair cut any shorter it would stand straight up like a flattop. When they'd finished staring each other down, Zeke stalked toward his office, which felt like the safest place in the house, with Cole right behind him.

"What brings you to our fair city?" he asked when he'd settled down behind his desk to show Cole he was in charge.

"Your phone call," Cole explained. "It bugged me."

"Must've."

"Did."

"Why?"

"There was something in your voice."

"Something in my voice? You drove up from Boston, got your car all muddy because of something in my voice? What if I'm just coming down with a cold?"

"Not a cold you're coming down with."

His eyes widened as Cole rose and came around the desk, brandishing a tissue. "What are you do-ing? Ouch!"

"Getting the lipstick off your ear." Cole displayed the evidence and sent Zeke a meaningful look.

"It's not what you think," Zeke mumbled.

Cole went into therapist mode, a habit of his that really drove Zeke crazy. "Hey, you can live your life any way you want to."

"Gee, thanks," Zeke exploded.

Cole ignored him. "I just want to meet the lady, make sure you're buying good quality doilies, that's all."

"I'm not buying any—"

"Methinks he doth protest too much," Cole said.

This was Cole at his condescending worst. Tish would bring him down a notch. "You can meet her in the morning," Zeke conceded.

"Good enough," said Cole. "Where can I sleep?"

"The back half of my bed," Zeke said. "Good enough for you when you were a kid, good enough for you now."

Someday, Zeke thought as he sat straight up against his pillow, wide-awake and watching Cole sleep like a baby even with a light shining in his eyes, it would be Cole's turn. An enchantress—short or tall, blond or brunette, troubled runaway or Back Bay debutante— would turn that peaceful slumber into the same hot and tortured insomnia Zeke had been enjoying recently. Then Cole would understand.

"YOU FOLDED the paper napkins?" Cole stared at the Holstein holder filled with Tish's origami.

"No," Zeke said unwisely, "she did." He poured buttermilk into a measuring cup.

"Aha!" said Cole. "That's the first step. Want me to glue the udder back on the cow while you cook?"

Zeke handed him a tube of epoxy. "She was nervous," he told Cole. "She needed something to do with her hands, I guess." So did he. Pancakes had been a good idea for breakfast. Gave him something to beat up on.

"Uh-huh," Cole said.

"She was talking to her mother and getting the scare of her life," Zeke snapped.

Cole sighed. "Okay, Zeke, tell me everything you've got on this case."

That only took a minute or two. Zeke didn't know any more about Marc Radcliffe than he had when Tish got stuck on Winsom Hill Road. "I alerted every office in Vermont and Rhode Island and I was going to call you in the morning," he concluded. "I can't get anybody very interested in a twenty-eight-year-old woman who's safe and unharmed and a man who doesn't appear to exist. Of course, they didn't hear the conversation with her mother."

"If that was her mother."

Zeke stared at him.

"What I'm saying," said Cole, "is that—"

"What you're saying is she could be lying about the whole thing," Zeke said flatly.

"You got it," said Cole. "She ran away for whatever reason, you rescued her, she took a good look at you and said, 'Whoo-ee, here's a guy I can move in on.'''

"She didn't say that," Zeke said abruptly. "I mean, not even to herself."

"She folded your paper napkins," Cole said. "Doesn't that tell you anything?"

Zeke's entire body was telling him something. Merely hearing little footsteps coming toward the kitchen made him feel hot and aroused. He stirred away at the pancake batter.

"Hi, Cole," said Tish. She looked at Zeke, then back at Cole. "There is a certain resemblance," she said, giving Cole a sunny smile.

"Hi, Tish," Cole said without returning the smile.

The room fell into silence.

"May I help?" Tish asked Zeke.

"No," Zeke said. He was relieved to see that she was wearing her jeans and white shirt with the blue tank top under it. Nice and modest. Modest—and sexy as all get-out, but at least she was covered.

"I'll set the table."

Out of the corner of his eye, Zeke saw Cole's I-told-you-so expression.

"I can put out the butter and warm the maple syrup," she added, having no idea she was sealing her fate with Cole.

"Warm the maple syrup," he hummed.

"Shut up," Zeke muttered.

"What?" Tish said. "If you'll move your elbow just an inch, Cole, I'll put down the place mats."

"Place mats," Cole murmured.

At that moment Tish set a little arrangement of dried strawflowers in the precise center of the kitchen table.

"Oh, my God," Cole breathed, and got up.

"What brings you to Wild River?" Tish said as she poured syrup into a saucepan and edged around Zeke to put it on the stove. She smiled up at him. His heart did a flip-flop.

"I'm going to work on your case," Cole said suddenly.

"Great!" Tish said. "What are you going to do?"

"I'm going to help Zeke find this—this man you married, figure out what if anything he's up to and get you back safe and sound to your family. Soon."

It was clear that his cold tone startled Tish. Zeke felt bad about it, mad at Cole, mad at himself for ever letting Cole in the house, mad at himself for letting Tish into his life.

"Pancakes?" he said, balancing two giant ones on a spatula.

"Oh, Zeke, you forgot to warm the plates," Tish said.

The look in Cole's eyes let Zeke know that as soon as she was off to Bess's house, he was in for it, big time.

"HE HATED ME at first sight," Tish mourned. "I'm used to men not loving me, but I don't think anyone's ever felt instant hate." She tossed off her borrowed blue windbreaker, then remembered no one was picking up after her any more and quickly hung it up.

"Cole doesn't hate you, dear," Bess comforted her. "He's just very protective of Zeke, and let's face it, those boys have a thing about..." Her eyes widened. "What did you say about being used to men not loving you?"

Tish paused at the closet door, feeling the flush rise to her cheeks. For a moment she floundered, then made a decision. "Oh, Bess," she burst out, "I've been wanting to tell you the truth since the day we met."

THE NEXT FEW DAYS slid into a pattern that was both comforting and frustrating. The days with Bess, who had already moved up from wheelchair to cane, provided Tish her only pleasure.

Everybody in town dropped in to visit with "the amnesiac." Their stories were better than novels. Jasper and Crockett had called a cease-fire and their mothers were speaking again. Seth and Cordelia had made up, and Cordelia hinted that having an actress wife had aroused Seth's—interest. Hortense was too involved in designing a perfect church-wedding-funeral-type dress to waste time being mad at Jasper for shooting her in the rear end.

Tish was keeping a list of things she would do when she had money coming in again. The youngest Highcrest needed braces on her teeth. Josh Rountree's family should go to Washington to watch him win the national spelling bee, which Myrna Rountree was sure he was going to do. Clarence Wedgelow was keen to visit the Mayo Clinic, convinced that his would be the most intriguing asthma they'd ever encountered. Her life was going to be a lot more fun when she could use her inheritance to do things for real people instead of just signing checks over to this charity or that.

Unlike the days, the nights were dreadful. Dinner was ready when she got home in the evenings. They ate in silence, Zeke insisted on doing the dishes himself, and afterward he retreated to his office and closed himself in.

From the low mutters and hissing sounds she heard through the door, she inferred he was ironing uniforms in there. The television set in his spartan living room received three channels with snow flurries and one under blizzard conditions. Still, the sound of human voices was comforting.

She couldn't sneak up on him in the middle of the night, either. She'd stood right there and watched him install a lock on his bedroom door. So she rinsed out her red teddy, hung it on one of the posts of the antique guest bed to dry, then put it away for the right moment. She was certain that one day it would arrive.

"YOU NEED a check for *what?*"

"For Bess's new stove. The store in Burlington can deliver it today. It's just a loan," she reminded him.

"How much?"

Her answer wrung a cry of agony out of him. The tension in the kitchen was thick enough to spread on the blueberry muffins Zeke was baking for breakfast. She was tired of borrowing money from him. She was tired of his locked bedroom and his darned sense of ethics. If she had to watch the Wheel of Fortune spin one more time she'd scream. The situation with Marc had to be brought to a head.

She had an idea for speeding things up. It was the sort of idea one didn't check out with Zeke, because he'd say no. She'd have to spring it on him.

"Mother and Father are expecting Marc and me to come home this Sunday," Tish told him when they'd settled uneasily at the table.

He frowned. "Wonder how Marc will handle that."

"I was wondering the same thing. May I call Mother? Maybe she'll let something slip."

He gestured toward the phone. "Give it a try."

"Hi, Mother," Tish said gaily when the familiar, sleepy voice answered.

Zeke tiptoed out of the room. In a moment she heard the soft click of the portable phone being lifted off the hook.

"Oh, honey, I know you're having a good time, but I miss you. I almost wish you weren't staying another week."

Footsteps, and Zeke stood in the kitchen giving her his *"what?"* look. Tish made a circle of her thumb and index finger and thrust it at him. *Bingo.* "That's why I called," she said. "So do I."

"You don't want to stay longer?" asked Mrs. Seldon.

Tish delivered herself of a stagy sigh. "Not that I'm not having the most wonderful time of my life, but I'm ready to come home and start nesting. You know, finish decorating the apartment and put all our beautiful wedding presents away." She thought she'd better hurry on. Zeke was already starting to look cross.

"So the next time Marc calls," she said swiftly, "would you help me out by trying to explain it to him?" Zeke shook his head violently. "Tell him I want to come home Sunday, the way we planned, not because I'm not happy, just…"

Zeke's glare was burning two holes in her forehead.

"Why, sure, honey," her mother said. "I know just how you feel. I'll talk to him. These little communication problems often happen between newlyweds."

"Thanks, Mother," Tish said.

"Aunt Amelia said she got the sweetest thank-you note from you," Mrs. Seldon said. "I'm glad you're getting a few of them out of the way."

Thank-you notes? Marc was desperate enough to start writing the *thank-you notes?* Bemused, she hung up. Now she had to face the Vermont country music.

"What are you trying to do?" Zeke raged at her. "Get yourself killed?"

"No," she said calmly, "I'm trying to flush him out."

"Great. Good thinking. Then what?"

"Figure out what he wants. I mean," she amended herself, "you can figure out what he wants." Zeke was awfully red. She hoped his family didn't have a history of aneurysms.

His square white teeth bit down viciously on a muffin, and he stalked around the kitchen while he chewed it. "I can't be everywhere at once," he grated. "He may know you're here, might come after you. How do I know what he'll do? Oh, my God," he said suddenly, throwing his hands up in the air, "what have you gotten yourself into?"

Love. That's what she'd gotten herself into. She'd gone way past admiration of a beautiful male body, way past a need to experience sex with an infinitely desirable man. She'd fallen in love with Zeke Thorne, but he wouldn't even take a good look at her until she got the matter of her inconvenient, unfortunate marriage to Marc out of the way.

And that's what she intended to do, whatever the risk. One day passed, then two, and she began to fear that her plan had failed. On Friday morning as she walked toward Bess's house in the light of early dawn, still hot and tremulous from nothing more than glimpses of Zeke, brief conversations and one of his delicious pancake breakfasts, she wondered how she could last another day under this much stress.

"SHERIFF THORNE? This is Marc Radcliffe. Is Tish with you?"

His heart pounding, Zeke stared at the phone. His first thought was to race to Bess's house, make sure Tish was all right. He forced himself to calm down. "Where are you?" he said coldly. "I want to talk to you."

"I'm here in town," Marc said. "I've had the worst two weeks of my life, lying to her parents, following every little lead, praying Tish wasn't hurt or..." He ended with a husky sob. "God help me, have I found her at last?"

Zeke frowned. The man had a pleasant enough voice. He didn't sound like a chloroformer. He sounded like a man who always had a clean white handkerchief in his pocket.

"Come to my office," Zeke said. The moment he'd waited for, written scripts for, practiced for, had arrived. At last he'd know what he was dealing with, a dangerous man—or a neurotic woman. But for some reason, now he was dreading to find out.

Five minutes later, he met the bridegroom. "I can't imagine what you must think of me," Marc said with a sad-sounding laugh.

At the moment, neither could Zeke. The man was well-dressed, brushed and combed, appeared to have good teeth and his ears didn't stick out. His manner was mild and his gaze direct. There were bags under his innocent brown eyes.

"Tell me how Tish is," Marc said next. He leaned forward, looking anxious.

"She's fine. Just...afraid of you."

"Why?" He wrung out the cry in a truly pitiful manner.

"You and I need to talk about what happened," Zeke said, steeling his heart. "Tell me about your wedding."

"It was a beautiful wedding," Marc said ruefully. "Tish was a perfect vision in her—"

"I'm sure she was," Zeke snapped. "But what *happened?*"

Marc jumped and began to speak rapidly. "I couldn't wait for the honeymoon to begin. I found out we could take an earlier plane..."

"I know that part." Zeke was damned sick of hearing about Marc's honeymoon plans.

"Okay. So we sneaked away from the reception and ran down to the garage...."

This was familiar material, too. "Why was Lorraine driving? Why didn't you have a limo waiting?" He was trying, he really was, to see it from Tish's point of view.

Marc looked puzzled. "Somebody might have noticed an extra limo. In that crowd, one BMW more or less wasn't going to attract any attention."

It made sense. Zeke had hoped it wouldn't, but it did. "What about the handkerchief thing?"

"Oh, Lord," Marc groaned. "Well, she got in the car, and she was so beautiful I couldn't keep my eyes off her. Then I saw she'd gotten something on her face..."

"...which you decided to wipe off..."

"Yes. I just wanted to touch her, to tell you the truth, and it was sort of awkward with Lorraine there in the car. Wiping her face would give me an excuse to touch her. I got out my handkerchief, but when I moved close to her, she freaked out and ran!" His voice actually shook with emotion.

"She ran," Zeke growled, "because she smelled chloroform on the handkerchief!" He stood, towering threateningly over Marc. Towering threateningly was the only weapon he had on hand. He should have taken time to find his official sheriff's pistol. Maybe even load it. What had he planned to do when the man turned mean? Hit him between the eyes with a peppermint from the candy dish?

Fortunately, when he towered, Radcliffe looked threatened. "Chloroform? What are you talking about?"

"I'm talking about chloroform on the handkerchief. I'm saying you tried to knock her out! Abduct her! Demand ransom! Or worse!" He leaned over the desk. "Maybe you intended to kill her."

Marc's eyes widened. "Why would I want to kill her? Why would anyone want to kill her? Wouldn't get him anywhere, not with the clause in Grandmother Seldon's will."

Zeke straightened up. "What clause?"

"The will states that if Tish dies under suspicious circumstances, her entire inheritance goes to the Newport Garden Club. She doesn't have anything to be afraid of. If one of the garden club ladies hoed her to death, that would probably cancel out the terms of the—'' Marc halted. ''Tish didn't tell you about the clause?''

Hell, no, Tish didn't tell him about the clause. If she had, he wouldn't have kept her under his roof for nearly two weeks, causing himself all kinds of grief, to be sure nobody tried to kill her. Zeke felt numb, his energy sapped, his rage dissipated by his sickening disappointment.

She'd lied to him. Just like Cole said, she'd run away for some reason of her own and after he rescued her, had played on his sympathy.

''I don't know what Tish smelled,'' Marc was saying, ''but it sure wasn't chloroform.''

Zeke's muscles tightened as Marc reached into his trousers pocket, but all he brought out was a clean, folded white handkerchief, which he handed across the desk to Zeke.

Zeke sniffed. He detected the slightest hint of bleach that hadn't come out in the rinse water, and something else, musky and a little bit sweet. ''Sandalwood?'' he said.

''Vetiver,'' Marc corrected him. ''I don't use cologne,'' he said haltingly, ''but I do keep a sachet in my handkerchief drawer.'' He blushed a little.

Zeke stared at him dumbfounded. He knew two people could tell the same story and come up with two entirely different interpretations, but this time it meant something to him personally.

''Why didn't you tell her parents she was gone?'' Zeke said. ''Why'd you call them, make them think nothing was wrong?'' No way the man could talk his way out of that one.

Marc collapsed into depression. "I didn't want to scare them. Her father—" He pressed a hand to his chest. "And her mother—" With his finger he made a little spinning motion beside his head. "I even flew Lorraine out to the Caymans to mail a few thank-you notes, just to make them think everything was all right."

Zeke whooshed out a big breath of pure frustration and sank back into his chair. He'd longed to nail this man to the wall, and here he sat, listening to the man nail Tish to a wall. What was he supposed to think? What was he supposed to do now? Except forget Tish, forget her sunny smile, her touches like tickly little feathers, her slim, lovely legs slung over that very chair Marc Radcliffe, castoff bridegroom, now occupied.

He had one last ace to play. "You didn't even have a reservation in the Caymans!" he thundered.

Marc gave him a look of wide-eyed innocence. "I used a false name. The wedding announcement was in the newspapers," he explained. "I didn't want Tish harassed by reporters, so I used a different name and wired cash for the deposit."

Of course. Why hadn't *he* thought of that?

Marc leaned back into his chair and sighed despondently. "I should have realized Tish was too immature for marriage," he said. "She probably told you how closely her family guarded her. She never had a chance to grow up."

Zeke just listened. Unfortunately, the man was still making sense.

Marc went on. "I think she realized for the first time that we would actually be man and wife, and as her bridegroom I would have certain...expectations..."

He paused, looking at Zeke as though he wanted to be sure Zeke knew what he was talking about. Zeke did. Wow, did he ever.

"...and the sexual repression that resulted from her parents' overprotectiveness motivated her to flee from the reality of marriage and all it entailed..."

Sexual repression? Tish? *Sexually repressed?* The woman was a ravenous tiger! Were they talking about the same person?

It occurred to him that Marc's language was stilted, as though he were giving a speech. Of course, it was possible he'd just gone over and over it in his head while he searched, frantic, worried, trying to reassure himself.

"...and I understand, I really do. I'm guessing Tish wants to go back home, and I've decided—" he paused to shake his head in a defeated way "—to agree to an annulment." He put a document on the edge of Zeke's desk and gave it a push.

Zeke stared at it. It was an annulment agreement like the one Clarence still hadn't drawn up. Zeke thumbed through the pages. He scanned the Cause section, his eyes lighting on "failure to consummate marriage," and at last found the Financial Agreement section.

Marc wasn't asking Tish for any money. He didn't want anything except to release Tish from her marriage to him.

12

ABSENTMINDEDLY Tish reached for the bowl of raisins and poised it over the Chocolate Whopper dough. "No raisins," Bess screeched, flattening herself over the huge mixing bowl.

Tish stared at the bowl in her hand. "Oh. I thought these were the pecans."

"You're off in another world this morning," Bess said. "We're going to have a whole new product to market if I don't keep a close eye on you."

"The waiting's getting to me," Tish moaned. "Sorry, Bess." She dumped in the pecans and Bess had begun to work them vigorously into the dough when the phone rang.

"Get that, will you, dear? Try out our new name."

Tish picked up. "Cookies Anonymous," she said lifelessly.

"Marc's in town," Zeke said.

Tish gasped and gazed wildly around, expecting Marc to leap out of the nearest closet.

"It's all right," Zeke said. His voice was low and noncommittal. "He's willing to annul the marriage."

"At what price?" Tish snapped.

"He doesn't want anything," Zeke said.

"I don't believe it!"

"I'm looking at the agreement right now."

"Where is he?"

"He's driving around, looking the town over. You can meet him at eleven at Clarence's office for the signing."

"But—but what did he say? About what happened?"

Zeke sighed. "Sounds like the two of you had a little misunderstanding."

"What do you mean—a little misunderstanding? I misunderstood his need to chloroform me? He thought it would help me relax?"

"He has an explanation for everything that happened," Zeke said. He sounded tired.

"And you believed him?"

"Hard not to," Zeke said. "Look, Tish, I don't care what the truth is. All I'm sure of is that Marc is willing to give you an annulment. If you want his side of the story, you can talk to him in Clarence's office."

He believes Marc. He doesn't believe me. He's lost what little faith he had in me. "All right," she said slowly, "I'll be at Clarence's office at eleven. I'll look over the agreement myself, and if it seems all right, I'll sign. Will you be there?"

"If you'd like me to be."

He didn't seem to care one way or the other. He just wanted to close the case and send her home. Tears blinded her. What had Marc said to win him over so easily?

"Don't bother," she said, trying to sound as though she didn't care, either.

She hung up and turned to Bess. "Marc wants an annulment, just like me."

"That's good news. Isn't it?" Bess said.

"I don't know." Tish wrung her hands. "It's too easy. Something's wrong. He told Zeke some story and Zeke believed him. And he's not asking for a financial settlement."

"If anything's wrong with the agreement, Clarence will know," Bess declared, then blushed a little.

Bess and Clarence? Everybody in the world could find love, Tish thought sadly, except her.

The doorbell rang. She peeked out the parlor windows and not seeing a car, decided it was probably one of the townspeople come for a visit. She didn't feel like listening right now, but opened the door anyway—and confronted Marc.

At the sight of him she felt a revulsion so intense she wanted to gag. He was as handsome as ever, as neatly dressed and groomed, but the tender expression was gone.

"What are you doing here?" she said. "We're supposed to meet at Clarence's office."

He pushed his way smoothly through the door. "Your sheriff made the appointment," he said. His smile had a terrifying quality about it. "I have other plans."

He reached out for her. She backed away. "How did you find me?" she said. What did he intend to do, and how could she stop him?

"In Wild River? Or at Bess Blakeley's house?" He gave a humorless laugh. "Wild River was hard. The rest was easy. I would have been here earlier, but I had to get your sheriff taken care of."

"Taken care of?" she gasped.

"He's fine." He gave her that horrible smile again. "I gave him a good story to chew on and showed him an annulment agreement to get him all relaxed. Right about now,'' he said, glancing at his watch, ''he's being picked up for questioning in the matter of your abduction. And if he tries to run, he won't get far. I took care of that, too.''

''But I haven't been abducted,'' Tish said, struggling to follow what he was telling her.

''You're about to be.'' He seized her wrists and locked them behind her. ''I'm taking you hostage until you sign the real annulment agreement and deliver the money.''

''The money?''

He spoke softly from behind her. The words blew across her cheek. ''The hundred million dollars the heiress wants to give the man she left at the altar in return for getting their marriage annulled.''

She tried to jerk her wrists out of his grasp. ''One hundred—''

''Tish?'' It was Bess. Tish wanted to call out to her, tell her to run, but Bess couldn't run. ''There's a blue car pulled way up in the driveway beside mine. Oh,'' she said as she came into the parlor and saw Marc, ''you have company. Hello, young man. May I serve you tea and cookies?''

Marc gave Tish's hands a warning little jerk.

''This is Marc, Bess,'' she said weakly. ''He—he came by to take me to Clarence's office. We're going now, so...''

''Not without your windbreaker you're not,'' Bess said firmly. She held it up. ''You young people. Too impatient to wear a coat in this damp weather. Never worry about getting a chill.'' She held out an arm of the windbreaker for Tish to slide into, and as she did, gave Tish's hand a surreptitious little squeeze.

Tish felt the reluctance with which Marc released first one wrist, then the other. While he was still trying to put on a show of normalcy for Bess, she thrust her hands into the pockets of the jacket. Her fingertips encountered her wedding rings, and then a crisp bill Bess must have put there. In the other pocket was a set of keys. Bess's car keys.

Marc gripped her elbow tightly. "We really must go."

As he started toward the kitchen door with Tish in tow, Bess clomped along after them. The door was open when Bess said suddenly, "Oh, I forgot! I put up a box of cookies for Clarence. Since you're going over there anyway—" She grabbed Marc's arm, pulling him back into the kitchen. "Here, Marc…"

Tish knew she had only a split second to act. As Marc reluctantly accepted the box of cookies, she flew out the kitchen door, slid down the back steps, recovered her balance and scrambled into Bess's car. She heard his inhuman roar as he tumbled down the steps, his face a black mask of rage.

What, she wondered, had Bess put on the steps? A full quart of canola oil would be her guess. And Bess was usually so thrifty!

Once again, Tish ran. But this time she had no doubts.

ZEKE SAT at his desk, his face buried in his hands. Poor little rich girl. Who knew what the real story was? But that clause in her grandmother's will was the clincher. She'd given him a cock-and-bull story about Marc trying to kill her, when that was the last thing a fortune hunter would want to do.

There was one big hole in Radcliffe's story. Tish was *not* sexually repressed. He had a sudden vision of her in the red teddy and broke out in a cold sweat of longing.

Zeke didn't know what to make of it. And he didn't much care. That unnerved him. All he cared about was Tish.

Now that was a really scary thought. He lifted his head from his hands and fished his savings passbook out of the top desk drawer. When he made this next transfer, he'd have about a hundred dollars left to show for years of careful saving. But who cared? Money was the least of his worries.

Marc had forgotten to take his handkerchief with him. Thoughtfully Zeke picked it up, unfolded it. It was very white. Marc had a drawerful of handkerchiefs like this one.

So what? He had three new rolls of paper towels!

Zeke laughed softly at himself. He had to accept that Tish might be changing her mind about Marc right now, realizing she'd been born to learn about love with a white handkerchief kind of man, not a paper towel guy.

Fine linen pocket squares like this one would be monogrammed. He ran his fingertips along the hand-rolled edges of the square, looking for the raised letters. Not finding any, he frowned and rubbed the edges a little slower, a little harder as he stared at the fabric. No monogram.

Well, that was hardly a clue. Maybe the guy's vanity stopped just short of having his clothes monogrammed.

On the other hand, if you didn't always go by the same name, that would be a very good reason not to monogram your clothes.

Again Zeke felt that instinctive, urgent need to see Tish, to know she was all right. It was almost eleven. He'd show up at Clarence's after all. He'd use Tish's wedding dress as his excuse for being there—just came to return it in case she, well, in case. It was a mess, but if you had enough money, you could get anything fixed. He pulled it out of the closet, where he'd stored it in the plastic envelope his white down comforter had come in. Exhibit A, Your Honor.

The phone rang as he left the house, but he ignored it. He was halfway up the driveway when Marc's rental car, badly mud-splattered, slipped and slid down Main Street. He was going way over the speed limit, but Zeke got a good look at the man behind the wheel.

He wore an expression of such rage, such frustration, that Zeke knew he was finally seeing the man Tish had fled from. Zeke's pulse rate sped up. It looked as though she'd fled from Marc again.

Zeke intended to be there when Marc caught up with her. Panic heated his blood, muddled his brain while his body went into fast-forward mode. He wasn't in uniform, he wasn't wearing his badge, and he still hadn't looked around for his pistol. Sir Galahad in a blue blazer, armed with a wedding dress. Feeling like a pitiful excuse for a lawman, he leapt into the Pathfinder and gunned it.

He was going ninety-five on the mountainous road to Burlington and had just gotten his first glimpse of Marc's blue car sailing over the next rise when the Pathfinder began to wobble. Zeke cursed as he gripped the steering wheel and slowed down, willing the car to shape up. The wheel fought against him, the car pulling toward the narrow, muddy shoulder with a determination greater than Zeke's. At last he couldn't fight it any more. He had to stop before he lost control altogether, skidded down the steep slope on his right and crashed into a tree. Again. He stomped on the brake. He jumped out and ran around the car to find his right tires, front and back, flatter than Adele's famous crepes.

But luck was with him. A car pulled up behind him. He'd buy the stranger's spare and be on his way in five minutes if the guy would cooperate. Zeke rushed toward the man who stepped out of the plain brown sedan, a man in a tan uniform, the uniform of the sheriff's department in Whitewater.

"Deputy Sheriff Ezekiel Thorne?" the man droned.

A sheriff! A sheriff who recognized him! That would speed up the transaction. "Yes," he said swiftly, "and I've got an emer—"

"I'm taking you in for questioning in the matter of the abduction of Tyler Staley Seldon of Newport, Rhode Island."

Zeke could only stare. "The what?" he said stupidly. "Of...what did you say her name was?"

"Deputy Sheriff Ned Eskin, Internal Investigations," said the officer, presenting a badge.

"No, no," Said Zeke. "Her name."

"The sheriff's department has received a complaint from Marc W. Radcliffe in regard to your— Oh, my God," he said suddenly, staring at the bag that held Tish's wedding dress. "Have you got her in there? You fiend! You disgusting—"

Zeke stared, too, realizing he was clutching the bag as though it were a security blanket, and then he exploded. "What in the hell are you talking about? Stop babbling and help me get these tires off."

"I don't do tires, you scumbag,' said Eskin. "I do interrogations, and I'm going to see you put away for life!"

Another car screeched to a halt dangerously close to Eskin's. "Zeke, .hn-n-nh, hn-n-nh!" honked a familiar voice through the open window.

"Here's your inhalator," said another familiar voice. "Breathe, Clarence, breathe."

Zeke's jaw dropped as Clarence and Bess emerged from the car, Clarence clutching his inhalator. "What are you two—"

"You've got to find Tish, hn-n-nh, hn-n-nh," Clarence panted. "She's in trouble."

"*She's* in trouble!" Zeke snorted. "Wait until you hear what kind of trouble I'm—"

"Who are these people?" said Eskin. "Folks, I have to ask you to stand back. This man is a dangerous..."

"The Newport County Sheriff called," Clarence managed to get out. "Tried to reach you and couldn't. Marc's not Marc. Lorraine isn't his sister." He ran out of breath and paused to take a deep whiff from the inhalator.

Bess took over. "She's his wife! Marc and Tish were never legally married! But he's filed a complaint with Internal Investigations..."

Clarence, now recovered, interrupted her. "Oh," he said, staring at Eskin. "I guess that's who you are."

"Tish isn't married?" Zeke said.

A jaunty sports car squealed onto the shoulder behind Clarence's car and Cole unfolded himself from the driver's seat, already yelling. ''Get off my brother's back,'' he shouted. ''He didn't abduct anybody. Radcliffe's a con man. That damned financial statement of his belongs to a Marc Radcliffe in Montana, a filthy rich rancher who—''

''Tish isn't married, Cole,'' Zeke said.

A gleaming Lamborghini skidded past them and pulled over in front of Zeke's Pathfinder. A man with curly blond hair leapt out and rushed Zeke with flailing fists. ''Let me at 'im,'' he shouted. ''He abducted my sister!''

''Stand back, young man,'' Bess snapped, hobbling toward him with her cane aloft, ''or I'll crack your skull open! Who are you anyway?''

''This must be Jeff,'' Zeke said, trying hard to come out of the stupor he'd sunk into. ''Tish's brother. What are you doing here? I thought you were up a mountain somewhere?''

''Ha!'' Jeff yelled, making a leap for Zeke's throat. ''He knows everything about us. How long have you been stalking my sister, you—you— Oh, my God,'' he said, staring at the plastic bag that Zeke still hung on to. ''You killed her! You butchered her—in her wedding dress!''

''Let's take him!'' Eskin shouted.

Zeke warded both of them off effortlessly with his free arm, fear for Tish and fury at the circumstances warring within him. ''While we stand here trying to get it all straight in our minds,'' he growled, ''Marc who isn't Marc has probably caught up with Tish, who isn't married to him after all, and God knows what's happening to her. Doesn't anybody else care what's happening to *her?*"

It silenced them. Bess was the first to recover. "Let's go," she said shakily.

"I'll ride with Cole," Zeke muttered. He gestured toward his flat tires, then glared at Jeff. "I suspect your sister and an ice pick."

"I suspect the false Marc Radcliffe and a Swiss Army knife," Bess snapped at him.

"You two come with me," Officer Eskin ordered Clarence and Bess. "I'm holding you hostage until we get this straightened out."

"I'm gonna straighten you out, buster," Cole threatened him.

Engines roared to life. "Wait a minute," Zeke shouted over the noise. "Anybody know where we're going?"

Heads emerged from opened windows. "Tish was going to a pawnshop," Bess cried out.

Jeff's mouth moved. "A pawnshop?" He looked dazed.

"Top Dollar Pawnshop in South Burlington," Zeke yelled. "Follow me!"

"DON'T KID AROUND," Tish snapped. "I'm in a big hurry." She glanced back at the pawnshop door.

"I'm not kidding, lady," the pawnshop owner said. "These aren't diamonds, they're zircons. Nice platinum settings, though. I'll give you a hundred dollars for both rings. Now those earrings you're wearing—"

Tish clasped her hands to her ears. "I won't sell my earrings. They were my grandmother's!"

The pawnshop door opened and Marc walked in. His

brown hair was no longer perfectly smooth, or his clothes perfectly neat. In fact, they were splattered with mud. His tender smile was strained. "She doesn't need to pawn her rings," he said to the pawnbroker. "Poor girl. She's upset right now. I'll take care of her."

"Lovers' quarrel?" said the pawnbroker, nodding.

Marc sighed. "A little more serious than that." His expression grew sad. "Sweetheart, if you'll just come with me, we'll get these papers signed and I'll send you home to your mother. You've broken my heart, but I'll agree to the annulment. Okay, honey?" He linked his arm through hers. "Understand what I'm saying?"

Tish came out of the frozen state she'd gone into at the sight of Marc, at the knowledge that he'd caught her, that her last hope was gone, that she'd made one more very bad decision. Tugging away from him, she folded her arms across her chest. "I'm not going anywhere with you," she said, narrowing her eyes, "and I'm not signing those papers."

Marc rolled his eyes at the pawnbroker. "But you were the one who wanted the annulment," he said patiently, returning his gaze to Tish. "You're not being reasonable, darling. Look, across the street. That little coffee shop. We'll go there and sit down in a nice, cozy—"

"I'm not even going to cross the street with you," Tish said. She had to stall for time. Time for Zeke...

But Zeke wouldn't be coming after her. Zeke was through with her. He believed Marc. He thought everything she'd told him had been a lie. He was probably at home, changing the guest-bed sheets. A cold lump in the pit of her stomach told her she'd never see him again.

She forbade herself to think about Zeke. She needed time to figure out a way to save herself—and keep one hundred million dollars out of Marc's greedy hands. It wasn't just herself she had to consider. She had to think about the next woman he'd victimize if somebody didn't stop him.

"You gave me zircons," she accused him.

"No!" Marc said. "You mean the jeweler lied to me? I'll sue!"

"Oh, get off it, Marc," she said crossly. She would not allow her voice to shake, and her hands wouldn't shake, either, if she kept digging them into her own ribs. "This whole thing was a scam. You get me to think I'm in love with you, we get married, you scare me into asking for an annulment—and demand a lot of money in return for signing the papers. Well, it's not going to work. I'm not buying it." She gave him a reproving look. "And to think you'd involve your own sister. What a cad you are."

The pawnbroker's gaze zoomed from Marc to her. He was too interested to be any help, and Marc was unmoved.

"She has such an imagination," he said fondly, directing his remark to the pawnbroker. "Like a child. She was just too young to get married."

"I'm twenty-eight," Tish snapped.

"Too immature, I meant," Marc said kindly. "We'll talk about it over a hot cup of—"

He broke off as the screeching of brakes pierced the quiet of the pawnshop, the sounds of car doors slamming and at last, the voice Tish had been sure she'd never hear again.

"Hands up!" Zeke said, his voice cutting like a whip. "Nobody move!"

"Oh, my goodness," said Tish, watching the posse pour through the pawnshop door. "It's a party!"

"Tish, you're alive!" breathed Jeff.

"Then who's in the bag?" growled Eskin.

"Do you have a gun?" Cole hissed over Zeke's shoulder.

"Of course not. I thought you did."

"You thought wrong."

"Why the hell don't you?" Zeke said, taking another step into the pawnshop.

"This was private business."

"Was for me, too. Eskin? You have a gun?"

"Internal Investigations don't carry," Eskin simpered.

"Anybody got a gun?" Cole whispered down the line.

"I have," Marc said smoothly, and waved a pistol at the little group huddled in the doorway.

"You planning to shoot all of us?" Zeke asked, taking a step forward.

"Hold it!"

Zeke halted. His heart sank to the toes of his hiking boots as "Marc" slung his arm around Tish's waist, pulled her up close in front of him and put the gun to her head.

"Get the point, Sheriff?" he drawled. "I'm walking out of here with Tish. Try to stop me and I'll shoot her."

"But Marc," Tish said in a strangled voice, "if you

shoot me, I can't ever sign the papers or give you the money, and all these people will just pile on you and carry you off to jail. This is not a well-thought-out plan.''

Zeke's eyes widened. The fact that Marc's plan had flaws was not the point here. When his hands clenched into fists, he realized he was still hanging on to that damned wedding dress. Without taking his eyes off Marc, he unsnapped the plastic bag, letting his fingers slide through the silk for reassurance.

"Tish,'' he said, putting a patronizing twist into his tone, "I think you'd better just go with the man, sign his papers and give him the money. I mean, what's a hundred million to you? Drop in the bucket, right? Make Marc, or whatever his name is, happy and he'll let you go.''

Condemning silence came at him from Tish's direction and from the group at his rear. *Sheriff Cops Out,* they were thinking. "He won't shoot you because of the clause in Grandmother Seldon's will,'' Zeke explained.

"What clause?'' Tish said.

She must know what he was talking about, but he repeated it anyway for the benefit of the rest of them. "The clause that says if any suspicious circumstances surround your death, your money goes to the Newport Garden Club.''

"Grandmother didn't put a clause like that in her will,'' Tish said. "Did you tell Zeke she did?'' she said, trying to look at Marc. "What a dumb story! What's The Garden Club going to do with a billion—''

Marc suddenly tightened his hold on her and dug the

pistol more firmly into her scalp. It was such an effort to hold himself back that Zeke almost failed.

It must have scared Tish, too. "Zeke is right," she squeaked to the group at large. "I'll leave with Marc. He won't hurt me. All he wants is money."

At that moment her gaze locked with Zeke's. He was amazed by her courage and tried to tell her without words. No, he would show her. He would think of something. *Think of something!* As he nervously fingered the silk of the wedding dress, it came to him. The oldest trick in the business, but he could make it work. Had to.

He fell silent, staring at a spot behind Marc and Tish as he began to gather up the dress fabric into his grip. He nodded at the spot, gave it a slight smile.

Marc's gaze shifted uneasily.

Zeke's smile widened. "Tell us, Marc, about your former conquests," he said in an artificially loud voice. "I bet nobody's given you the trouble this one has." When he had a tight hold on the dress, he let the plastic envelope fall. It slithered to the floor with a little swishing sound.

"That's the truth," Marc muttered.

Tish gave Zeke an irate glance. "Give us a brief history of your career," Zeke said coaxingly. "Fill in the gaps, so to speak." He gave the imaginary person behind Mark a subtle thumbs up sign. He could see how badly Marc wanted to turn around. He'd almost edged Tish to a point that he could see where Zeke was staring. Zeke would have to move fast.

"Take him," he shouted suddenly. When Marc yielded to impulse and cast a startled glance behind him, Zeke leapt forward, flung the heavy wedding dress over Marc's head and jerked Tish away from him. The gun flew out of Marc's hand and landed in the pawnbroker's outstretched one.

Marc untangled himself from the dress and sprang at Zeke. Zeke sprang for Marc at the same time. They met in the middle, collided and crashed to the floor.

All that mattered to Zeke was that Tish was all right, and he'd landed on top.

"It's a stage prop. A fake," the pawnbroker said disgustedly as he examined the pistol.

"Just like everything else about him," Tish said as Jeff and Bess both tried to hug her at once.

13

MARC WAS IN CUSTODY. Unnaturally calm and admitting nothing, he obviously intended to put up a fight in court. He'd lose. Zeke would see to that.

Lorraine turned herself in to the Boston police at Logan Airport rather than having to write another thank-you note. She faced a charge of aiding and abetting her husband.

Getting everybody else organized was like herding a bunch of cats. He was getting tired of Jeff's dramatic story about the messenger who ran up Mount Kilimanjaro to bring him the news of Tish's abduction and the helicopter pilot who started him on his long journey home. Cole kept trying to top Jeff with his own story of getting the call from the Newport Sheriff and speeding recklessly to Zeke's defense and Tish's rescue. Personally, Zeke suspected Lamborghini-envy.

Outside the corner coffee shop, where Clarence had treated everyone to lunch while Zeke listened with one ear, he began to deal them into cars and send them on their way.

"I'll take Tish home," Jeff insisted, hugging his little sister for about the fiftieth time.

"I'll give Tish an official escort home," said Zeke.

"You're taking me home?" Tish said in a small voice. She'd barely spoken during lunch except to share her praise and gratitude equally among her rescuers. She'd only gazed at him, doubt on her face, and he didn't know the answer to the question her expression was asking him. He wasn't even sure what the question was.

"It's in my job description," he growled.

Jeff yawned. "That'll work, too," he agreed.

"I have to fill out a report and get you to sign some papers," Deputy Sheriff Eskin said.

"Fax them," Zeke said.

"Well, okay, I guess I could do that," Eskin agreed reluctantly, "if you won't leave the state until you sign."

"I'm leaving for Rhode Island as soon as I put new tires on the car," Zeke growled.

"Then I'll catch you when you get back." Eskin vaporized.

"But I don't want to go home," Tish said. "I—"

"I have…things to discuss with your parents," Zeke said firmly. "Cole, drive us to the car and help me put on the tires?"

"Sure."

"Then go back to Boston."

"Aw, Zeke…if I hung around here for a while, you and I could talk about your future, and Tish, and get some things worked out, you know what I mean?"

He squelched Cole with a single glance.

"Oh, all right," Cole said, looking disappointed. "Back to Boston."

"And thanks," Zeke said gently.

"No problem. I'll buy you a couple of tires over there at the filling station. You get Clarence and Bess on the road."

Zeke found Clarence and Bess engaged in low-voiced conversation as they gazed into each other's eyes. Clarence clutched his inhalator. Bess clutched her cane. "You two all right?" Zeke asked.

"Why, yes, Zeke, we're fine." Clarence sounded dreamy. He must be on antihistamines.

"Deputy Sheriff Eskin's waiting to take you to your car. Ready to get back to Wild River?"

"Oh, yes," Bess breathed. "I'm going to take Clarence home and make him a big pot of boiling water with eucalyptus oil in it."

"Sounds great," Zeke said absentmindedly. "Save some for me."

TISH WATCHED Zeke interrupting Clarence and Bess in the process of falling in love and smiled a small, sad smile. He wanted his money back. Maybe he even wanted a reward. She couldn't blame him, but it hurt to realize that once again, all a man wanted from her was her money.

Hurt? What a small word. This was heartbreak as she'd never known it. But she'd keep a stiff upper lip until he'd taken his money and gone, or die trying.

Things could have been different. She'd run away this morning because he didn't trust her. He thought she'd run away because she didn't trust him, or maybe because she'd used him all she needed to.

She'd blown it with the sheriff and had almost given Marc a chance to make off with a hundred million dollars of Grandmother's money, money that should be used to make people's lives better.

To make good decisions, you needed experience. That was one of the many things she'd learned over the past two weeks. But to get the experience, you had to have some practice in making decisions. It was a puzzling, frustrating matter.

"Tish…"

She retreated from her thoughts at the sound of Cole's voice. He was carrying a tire on each shoulder.

"Hi, Cole. What a day, huh? Bet it's not much more exciting than this in Boston."

"Not much." He fell silent.

"Cole, do you happen to know whose windbreaker this is?"

He peered at it. "Oh. It's Adele's, our stepmother's. She keeps it at Zeke's house. Wears it when she plants his annuals. Why do you ask?"

That was one worry off her mind. "Why do you think?" she said pointedly.

"Oh," Cole said. "Oh, yeah." He retreated into silence again, then said, "Tish, I, um, I owe you an apology. I was wrong about you and Zeke." He sounded flustered. "I'm afraid I encouraged Zeke to, ah, to…"

"Keep me at arm's length?" Tish said softly.

"Yes. But now I wish I hadn't. Now I wish…" He chewed his lip for a minute. "Just go slow with the doilies, okay?" he burst out all of a sudden.

"The *what?*"

He grew even more flustered. "I mean, don't try to rush him into a lot of changes."

"There's only one change I'd like to make in Zeke's life," Tish said.

"Slipcovers?"

The Thorne brothers had the oddest thought processes. "No. His marital state. But I guess it's not going to happen." She sighed, then held out her hand. "Bye, Cole. I'm glad I got to meet you."

"Me, too. Tish...I wouldn't mind, ah, having you as a sister-in-law," Cole blurted out, and ran with the tires toward his car.

Nothing she'd love more than to be Cole's sister-in-law. But it would take a miracle. She could tell from the look in Zeke's eyes. Party's over. Guest of honor goes home. Host restores order to his life. The world keeps on turning.

It was all wrong, but she didn't know how to fix it. Zeke didn't even seem to know he needed repairs.

"I'M STOPPING FOR GAS."

"Thank God."

The drive from Wild River to Newport had been punctuated with witty, brilliant repartee like this most recent exchange. But that was fine with her, Tish thought, because she didn't feel witty, or brilliant, and if she tried to talk, she'd probably cry.

Zeke pulled up to a pump and Tish hotfooted it to the women's rest room. When she returned, she found him waiting at the entrance of the convenience store. "Coffee?" he said.

"Please." She glanced at the wieners turning on spits in an electric rotisserie. Tension had made her ravenous.

"Hot dog?"

"Yes, thank you." She was suddenly fed up with feeling like a beggar. "Bess loaned me some money. I'll pay."

"Forget it." His jaw hardened. "I'll add it to your bill. Send Bess's money back to her."

The fury that stemmed from her frustration leapt hot and high inside her. "I am aware of my indebtedness. I'll take care of it."

Bearing cups of coffee and hot dogs, they marched back to the Pathfinder, Zeke in the lead. Tish gave herself one last chance to look him over, to memorize the crisp curl of his dark hair, the way his shoulders rolled when he walked, his long stride, the flex of his muscles as he moved purposefully toward the only thing that seemed to matter to him—exchanging her for the money she owed him.

When she felt tears welling up in her eyes, she shook them away and concentrated on not getting any mustard on herself, the car or above all, Zeke.

He cut a dashing figure in his street clothes. Even that depressed her. She didn't know where he'd dredged up a double-breasted navy blazer. With his snow-white turtleneck and snug-fitting jeans, it was practically formal wear. It coasted lightly over his broad shoulders and skimmed in a little at the waist, outlining his shape in a way that made her remember the body beneath the clothes, how it had quivered, hardened under her caress, how he'd—

Stop it. It's over. You lost. She sank her teeth into the hot dog as though she were biting a bullet, but the pain persisted, and would, she knew, for the rest of her life.

"TISH! MY BABY!"

The petite blonde who flung her arms around Tish had to be her mother. The tall, handsome, graying man who hovered beside her waiting his turn to hug was probably her father. Jeff stood close behind him, smiling.

It struck Zeke that Jeff was smiling that same smug smile of the first-to-know he'd seen so often on the faces of Wild River folks.

They stood in a large hall that rose several stories high. Forming a tight, protective circle around the principals in the drama of Tish's homecoming was a mob of well-dressed, well-groomed Seldons. They looked as though they belonged to the semicircle of handsome houses he'd just driven past. They would be at home in the carefully designed gardens, the sailboats tied up to the piers. They were born and bred to live behind the high stone wall, the wrought iron gates of the compound.

They made dignified little cries of happiness, relief, comfort. These people cared about Tish. This was where she belonged. He felt good about bringing her back.

The emptiness that stole through him came as a shock. He had business here, and that was all. When he'd finished it, he'd go back where he belonged, to the life he'd chosen. Yes, that was exactly what he planned to do. He swallowed hard and folded his arms across his chest.

He didn't know why that slight movement suddenly focused all the attention on him. He gazed down into a collage of eyes, all of them curious, assessing. It was a lot like looking down at the bicycle safety class.

"And who...are you?" said Mr. Seldon.

"Father, this is Deputy Sheriff Thorne," Tish said in a hurry. "He rescued me, took me in, apprehended Marc—"

The man stalked slowly toward Zeke. His eyes were clear and vivid blue like Tish's, but nowhere near as warm. "Took her in...and kept her there," he said, low and threatening.

"Father," Jeff spoke up, "it was what Tish wanted to—"

"I can speak for myself," Tish said. The hall fell into hushed silence. "He was dying to send me home." She sent an inscrutable glance toward Zeke. "I wouldn't let him. I wanted to flush Marc out from whatever rock he was under, and I couldn't do that unless he thought I was out somewhere on the loose."

"On the loose," Mrs. Seldon gasped. "Tish, that is hardly—"

"And we did it," Tish continued. "Marc will never victimize a vulnerable woman again."

"Vulnerable?" Mr. Seldon's laugh was a short bark. "You're not vulnerable to anything, sweetheart, not with your money and your family behind you all the way."

"Vulnerable to love," Tish said softly, almost to herself. Then her gaze drifted to Zeke, and the expression on her face socked him a punch low in the belly.

Her father gave her a puzzled glance and turned back to Zeke. "Well, thanks, Sheriff, for bringing her home safely. Maybe I can donate a little something to the—"

"No. Thank you," said Zeke.

"I owe Zeke a lot of money," Tish whispered to her father.

"How much?" The blue eyes went cold again.

"I've prepared a bill," Zeke said, and opened his black leather document case.

"What is all this?" Mr. Seldon said, staring down

at the handwritten list. "Towing charges—seventy-five dollars."

A memory flashed through Zeke's mind—Tish, a small, lost kitten on a mountain road, flinging herself into his arms. She'd fit as though she belonged there, and he'd known at once that he wanted to take her home and care for her.

"Insurance deductible. One thousand dollars."

She'd asked him to teach her everything he knew. She'd been willing to entrust him, Zeke Thorne, with that precious task. Zeke closed his eyes, remembering, wanting, wishing.

"Long distance charges, rubber boots, *Viking gas range? Acting lessons?* What the hell is this all about?"

It was all about Tish fitting into the community by doing the one thing she knew how to do well—care about people. Just as that little girl had cared about, and cared for, her grandmother, she had set about to care for the entire town of Wild River.

She hadn't come to town to ruin his life. She'd come to town to fix the lives of everybody who lived in it.

Zeke felt an emotion welling up in him that he didn't know how to handle except by clenching his jaw so hard he felt his molars cracking. Maybe that was all Adele had intended, to fix the lives of a man and his motherless boys, make things neat, pretty, stable, secure. But all he and Cole had been able to see was that their father wasn't their private property any more. As for Dad, Zeke had a new take on that sappy, goofy smile. The man was happy. Happy with quiche. Happy with *doilies,* for God's sake, because...because...

Because he was in love. Zeke's knees tried to buckle under him and he locked them in place. *In love. In love.* The words hummed through his head.

His ears buzzed with dizziness. Distantly he heard Tish reminding the Seldons that they'd taught her to contribute to society, and she'd found a lot of truly worthwhile ways to contribute in Wild River. But she wasn't looking at her father, she was looking at Zeke, and in her face he saw puzzlement, then realization, then understanding.

He wished he knew what she realized and understood, because he was totally in the dark.

In the dark. Tish in the dark, slipping onto the side of his bed, offering herself, asking for the love she'd figured out she couldn't have with Marc...

...but apparently thought she could have with him. Why? What did she see in him that he couldn't? Maybe she saw... Good Lord, maybe she knew he cared about her!

"Well, of course," Seldon was saying gruffly. "Now that I understand, of course, honey, you should ask your accountant to draft a check—no, I'll write the sheriff a check on my account so he can be on his way."

"I don't want your check." Zeke heard a voice come out of nowhere. It was his voice, butting in a step ahead of his brain. "I want your daughter."

The collective gasp started with Tish, then moved like a wave through the Seldon family. Zeke shot a glance toward her, trying to read her face, trying to figure out if he was just about to make a first-class fool out of himself. Hard to tell. Right now she just looked pale and shocked.

He forged on. "Here is my financial statement," he said, pulling a second sheet from his case and handing it to Seldon. "You didn't take a close enough look at Radcliffe's. Take a good look at mine." His financial statement. Had he planned all along to present Tish's father with his financial statement?

Seldon slowly turned the paper around, staring at the numbers. "Is this a decimal point, here in the middle of the—"

"Yes."

"Would this be in millions, or thousands…"

"Dollars."

"You have $42.79 in your checking account?"

"Yes. But it's not a problem," Zeke added. "I have a paycheck coming in at the end of the week."

"Your sheriff's salary," Seldon said, and rolled his eyes at Mrs. Seldon.

"Deputy sheriff's salary," Zeke corrected him.

"Yes, yes. And $103 in your savings account?"

"The numbers were larger before your daughter came along," Zeke said. "Of course, I still have some shares of stock."

"Stock shares." Mr. Seldon consulted the sheet of paper, then looked directly at Zeke, his eyes glittering. "This is some kind of joke, isn't it? Well, Thorne, I'm in no mood for jokes. You can take your financial statement—"

Zeke was beginning to realize that he'd just asked Tish to marry him. He was already halfway wishing he could take it back. Seldon was offering him a way out—on a silver platter.

But he didn't want out! The next thing he admitted to himself was that he loved her, loved her for the real and wonderful person she was, loved her in spite of her money and her family, who would undoubtedly make his life miserable. No way was this controlling father going to tell him to leave!

"Hold on, Father," Jeff said. "Tish may have something to say about—"

"You hold on, too, Jeff," Tish said. Her voice was clear and strong. "Nobody else gets to decide. I do."

HER HEART had pounded a rat-a-tat tempo from the moment he said, "I don't want your check." When he said, "I want your daughter," she thought it would burst from her chest.

They had wanted each other from the beginning, but hadn't known why. Now she, at least, knew. He was the most caring person she'd ever known, and he didn't plan it ahead of time or even realize what he was doing. He just did it. He brought cats down from trees and coddled the women at the Senior Center, he worked with the schoolchildren and kept the peace among their parents.

He was also the most real, down-to-earth person she'd ever known. Love with Zeke would be just that real, just that down-to-earth. A shiver traveled down through the center of her body, a shiver of delicious anticipation—followed by a chill of doubt. At least it would be if...

They had one little matter to clear up before she

made her decision. "I want to talk to Zeke privately," she said, drawing herself up to her full height. "Zeke, will you come with me?"

She closed the library door behind them and turned to confront the man she loved and desired. She loved him even more for his stubborn, defiant expression that said, "Take me as I am or forget it."

"Did you really mean it?" she said quietly. "That you wanted me?"

"I must have, or I wouldn't have said it." He wasn't giving an inch until he found out what she had to say to him.

Her gaze went briefly to the library door. "Because if you intend to support the Yankees instead of the Mets," she said loudly, "our relationship doesn't have—" she flung the door open "—a chance," she said as her mother toppled into the room.

Mrs. Seldon righted herself. "Coffee, either of you?" she said brightly.

"No, thank you," Tish said, and giving her mother a stern glance, she closed the door again, put her ear against it and listened for the sound of departing footsteps. They were a few seconds coming, but at last they did. Satisfied, she turned back to Zeke.

His eyes were wide. "Your family's not much different from the folks in Wild River," he said, sounding surprised.

"Of course not," Tish said. "Why did you think they would be? Zeke," she continued without waiting for his answer, "there's one thing I have to know before I can give you an answer."

His mouth tightened. "How I feel about your money."

She tried to interrupt, but he couldn't be stopped.

"Well, here's how I feel about it. I'd like you to put the whole sockful into a trust fund and share the interest with your family. You can put your share into another trust fund for…well, for…"

"Our children?" she whispered.

"If we…that is…"

"Sounds like a great idea to me," she said, letting him off the hook. She moved a step closer, so filled with longing she could barely keep her hands off him.

"We'll live on my salary," he persisted, backing up a step. "And I insist on a prenuptial agreement. You'll have an equal right to everything I earn, but you can't touch my forty-nine shares of Microsoft stock."

"Everyone needs some money of his own," she agreed. She hesitated a moment, then said, "I could buy the groceries for a while, until you get back on your feet financially."

He appeared to be thinking it over. "Okay," he said grudgingly, "but just the groceries. Is that all you need to know?" He folded his arms across his chest.

"No."

He shifted his weight a little, looking uneasy. "What else?"

"This is really important to me."

"Okay. I understand."

"I need to know…oh, Zeke, this is very difficult to say."

"Say it."

The firm line of his mouth made her want to run her

fingertip over it, see if she could make it twitch. "I want to be sure you really do want to make love with me," she said all in a rush.

He took a step forward.

She took a step back. "I have to know that sex will be an important part of our relationship..."

"Our marriage," Zeke growled. He took another step forward, a bigger step.

Another step backward and she'd be crushed against the door. "...because I must tell you very frankly that..."

"Yes, Tish."

His mouth moved close to hers, hovered over it. She looked into his eyes and dared him to make contact. "...that I've had absolutely *all* the respect I can stand!"

His mouth smothered her words, promising her she'd have everything she'd ever really wanted for the rest of her life. As he molded her against his body, she felt the thrust of his desire merging with hers and reveled in it, seeking his hot kiss, his enveloping embrace, his power to give her untold, unimagined pleasure.

Until he surprised her by saying, "I'm afraid I can't give in on that point." He murmured the words into her forehead. "I insist on treating you with respect. And what I respect most about you..." A soft laugh rippled his muscles as he threaded his fingers through her hair. "...is the way you make me want to..." He tilted her head back as though he wanted to drink in the sight of her. "...throw you over my shoulder and carry you straight off to my bed. Come on, Tish, let's go home."

She saw the light, the heat in his dark, wonderful eyes. As their mouths met and clung and their bodies melded, Tish knew what she'd been born for.

Love. But like anything else, it was going to take experience. And practice. Lots and lots of practice. Her lips curved against Zeke's. They'd have to practice until she could do it in the dark with her eyes closed.

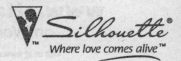

HARLEQUIN®
Duets™

#35

THE DEPUTY'S BRIDE by Liz Ireland
Lone Star Lawmen: Book 2

Trouble with a capital *T*... That stands for Ruby Treadwell!
Heartbreak Ridge's wildest woman has deputy sheriff Cody Tucker
ready to throw in his badge. First she finagles a few free nights in his
jail, then she proposes marriage to the blushing lawman. Cody insists
that Ruby leave town before he falls prey to her tempting charms...
even if the only way is to whisk her off on a honeymoon!

SITTING PRETTY by Cheryl Anne Porter
It Could Happen to You...

Jayde Green is in one heck of a fix. After landing a job house-sitting
for tycoon Bradford Hale, she should've been sitting pretty. She'd
finally be able to help her parents out financially. Only, she never
expected to have to lie in order to get them to take the money. And
she definitely hadn't intended to fall for her gorgeous employer! It
couldn't get any worse—until her family showed up to meet Brad,
their new son-in-law...?

#36

FIT TO BE TIED by Carol Finch

Devlin Callahan is ready to read the riot act to his neighbor—the
fruitcake female who turned her forty-acre ranch into a blasted zoo!
Jessica Porter's exotic animals are scaring his cattle and sheep and
sending them stampeding everywhere. But when Devlin confronts
Jess, the gorgeous warmhearted blonde leaves him tongue-tied. Does
Devlin really want to run her out of town when she's got him all tied
up in knots?

THE LYON'S DEN by Selina Sinclair

Lyon Mackenzie couldn't afford to lose Miss Hammond. But his
seemingly robotic assistant was resigning—to get married, of all
things! When Liv realized her beastly boss was in a bind, she agreed
to stay on temporarily. Only, she hadn't counted on playing mommy to
her godson for that week, or on playing wife to Lyon when their
biggest client caught them in a compromising position!